A Game of Wits

Rachel Gripp

By Rachel Gripp

COPYRIGHT AND ACKNOWLEDGEMENT

ISBN NUMBER - 9780985939656
BOOK COVER – Austin Tsosie, artist
COPYRIGHT 2015 Rachel Gripp

ISBN: 0985939656

dedication

This novel is dedicated to my wonderful grand-daughters, Cassandra Lynn Gripp and Miranda Angelia Gripp, who have brought so much love and joy into my life.

TABLE OF CONTENTS

Prologue

He came to the house with a sheaf of papers Robert took upstairs, giving him the opportunity to approach the emaciated figure lying under a coverlet on the living room sofa.

"I hate seeing you like this." His eyes began to water.

"I know," she said, her labored voice hardly a whisper.

"You must know how I feel."

"I've always known." She gave a long sigh, her eyes half-closed.

"You never...," he stopped. "I had to tell you before...," he paused, knowing the necessity of the moment; his last and only one. "Why couldn't he take better care...look after you?" he blurted suddenly, fighting back his tears.

"No ripples on the water...please." He heard her forced and whispered plea.

"I'm not that forgiving." He turned toward the door and, recognizing the small item caught under his shoe, slipped it into his pocket and left the house.

***

A short time later, Robert returned downstairs to sit with her, but found it no longer necessary.

Chapter 1
Florence

He stood at the window of Pensione Maria, watching the tourists scurry along Via del Calzaiuoli, anxious to reach their targeted destinations before closing time. It was May, the shoulder season for visiting Italy, when rates were cheaper, and tourists raced with their list of places to see in Florence, a directive from some hack writer, who probably never ventured there but needed pin money for writing a travel piece.

Why was he being so critical? He was doing the same thing, but only from a different perspective. Had he not traveled thousands of miles on a pilgrimage of his own making, one to recapture the most memorable part of his life? Was that not the purpose of the whole trip? Yes, he answered his own question and his thoughts centered on his dead wife, Emily.

Was he being foolish trying to recapture a time in his life when he was happiest? Or was he trying to relive those precious memories before his lucid recollection of her faded completely? Three years had passed already and her face was no longer clearly defined. It was at this juncture that Robert Blake determined to visit Italy again, hoping to renew some segment of a happier time. He chose Florence because it was Emily's favorite city. And while he selected the third week of May to duplicate their four day visit, he did not travel from Rome as they had nineteen years earlier. Instead, he flew to Florence from his resident city, Pittsburgh, Pennsylvania via the transatlantic flight from New York.

When they traveled, he always handled the airline or train schedules while Emily made room reservations. Those duties were defined; however, each city selected for touring was a joint decision. They traveled on the cheap like two backpackers seeing the sights on an itinerary of their own making.

She chose this particular pensione for its unique location. Up the street, only buildings away, stood three of the most famous landmarks in the city: the Cathedral of Santa Maria de Fiore, also known as the Duomo, the Baptistry and the Bell Tower. The Galleria dell' Accademia with its famous statue of David was just a few blocks away. Down the street sat the Piazza della Signoria, the Palazzo Vecchio and the Uffizi Gallery of fine paintings. Other galleries and museums were also close by and within walking distance. They made every day an exciting adventure, seeing and doing different things, except of course, when it came to Piazza della Signoria. Every afternoon, at some unspecified time, they would stop for a glass of wine and watch some bird or pigeon knock down the empty glasses before the waiters could retrieve them. Aside from the avian contest, they enjoyed the unique setting of statues bathed in mythology surrounding them. It was a treat having Hercules watch over them as they enjoyed their afternoon respite.

The huge clamoring from the Bell Tower pulled his attention away from the street momentarily. He turned automatically to face the room, an involuntary reaction to the loud clanging clatter that engulfed him, mesmerizing and sweeping him to and fro, with each swing of the huge balls that swayed inside the enormous bells. It was all too real; and yet, even those precious memories were beginning to fade.

"Signore Blake," a woman called, knocking on the door of his room.

"Avanti." The tall dark-haired man responded in Italian.

"HO portato il bucato pulito," She placed the small bag of clean clothes on an upholstered chair. "Sono ripiegati."

He reached into his pocket and tipped her for folding them.

"Sono ancora che serva la prima colazione," she offered, eyeing the sanitized room.

Although neat and orderly, the room was small by American standards. Too small in fact, and she wondered why he requested that particular one, when others, ones completely renovated and much larger, seemed much more suitable for the rich-looking American. She knew they were available when he made the reservation, but learned later he declined the offer of a larger room and cited personal reasons as a factor.

"Non ho molta fame, ma vorrei una tazza di caffe." he replied quickly to her breakfast reminder, wanting only a cup of coffee.

"Vai ora prima di chiudere," she warned of the kitchen closing if he didn't hurry, but then dropped all conversation when he answered, "Ti seguo." and followed her out of the room and down the hall to a passage intersection.

***

The breakfast room held no surprises when he entered it. Everything seemed the same. Although it was the second day of his trip, his arrival the previous day was much too late for the morning offering, but early enough to have his clothes laundered from an airport spillage. And yet, after a long sojourn, the bright and airy breakfast room held the same look as it had back then: a wallpaper of small colorful flowers sporadically blooming above a white wainscoting that ran halfway up the wall. Although the small white tables looked the same, he felt certain some had been replaced. The new carpeting that lined the hallway definitely was. Yet even with the renovations, and he felt sure there were many, Robert had the feeling of sameness, an aura of non-change, when life seemed simpler and happier. Yes. The pensione felt exactly the same to him as it did, almost a score ago.

"Would Emily have thought so too?" Robert pondered that question as he walked toward a table that had been set-up for service.

"Volete caffe?" A large, heavy woman holding a coffee pot caught his nod. As she poured the coffee, she pointed to the sugar and creamer on the table, then said, "IL Panini dolci sono molto buoni."

Something about his blank expression made the woman think there was a miscommunication of language, and she directed his attention to a counter of sweet rolls. As he continued to sit glued to his seat, the woman rushed to the counter in exasperation, placed a sweet roll on a plate and took it to his table.

"Mangiare! Hai bisogno di un grasso le tue ossa come me," she shouted before walking away in disgust.

Outwardly, Robert Blake's impassive face expressed nothing; however, inwardly, his thoughts were whirling. Pretending ignorance in the breakfast room, an area so public, was part of an important directive he had learned early in life, and he chastised himself inwardly for speaking Italian to the chamber maid minutes earlier. "Eat," the woman had said. "You need some fat on your bones like me."

Of course, she was right on both counts; he was quite thin for his height and she was heavy for hers. However, when she walked away in disgust, he knew the woman felt frustrated with his not attempting to communicate with her. From her point of view, he could have said something, even if his effort sounded like some sort of broken Italian. Instead of answering her, he stared at the sweet roll she placed before him and remained silent.

Once she walked away, he broke the roll in half and watched the flakes of icing cascade on his plate. As he began to eat, his eyes swept the room. Aside from the woman serving him breakfast, he and another woman, one who sat much farther away from his table and pondered an unfolded map, were the only ones in the room. He felt certain she had heard the entire one-sided conversation between the man who could not speak Italian and his server.

Almost regretting the game he just played, Robert finished his breakfast in record time, placed a tip on the table and nodded a thank you to the woman who served him.

A broad smile crossed her face, exposing a gap between her front teeth, as she walked to his table when he left the room. Maybe the silent American wasn't so bad after all, she thought pocketing the generous amount he left on the table. Maybe he'd come back tomorrow. Then another thought crossed her mind. His coming back made little difference to her. She had taken the week off.

As he walked down the hall Robert thought about the first directive he had learned many years earlier. And the lingering thought ran through his mind, one that concerned his mother's instructions, shortly after the death of his father. He was just a young child then, and lacking the necessary funds to survive, they were forced to live with his widowed grandmother who only spoke Italian. It was then that his mother took him aside and cautioned, "Listen to our conversations and learn the language, but don't speak it publicly. You will come to learn what people are saying and if they are talking about you. This will be our secret."

That cohesive glue bonded them together that day and the Italian lessons began at an early age. He soon found their importance when someone, conversationally engaged, referenced Robert with some snide comment, thinking him ignorant of the language. Although nothing was said in rebuttal, that misplaced ignorance only fortified the young man's resolve during those formative years and prepared him for the harsher realities of life. But in order to fully prepare himself, he was determined to learn another skill; one that went hand-in-hand with the language lessons and could mask his true feelings in any given situation. And although those skills required years of practice, Robert Blake became a proficient in acclimating his facial expression to any given situation. However, after years of practice before the bathroom mirror, he learned the one facial expression that superseded all others: the one he called practiced calm. He began to picture people speaking Italian freely in his presence because they knew the man had no grasp of the language. His blank facial expression told them that. The man merely stood there with them. Robert smiled inwardly at the notion and his thoughts turned to another directive from his mother.

One day when they were reminiscing about the past, his mother related the story of his first meeting with Nonna, Anna Scaliezzi, when he was only days old.

"Roberto, mi par di capire. Che diavolo di nome e Kilbruth?"

The grandmother understood naming him after her husband, Roberto, but questioned the middle name, Kilbruth. What kind of name was that? How could her daughter allow that to happen? It was not an Italian name. That it was part of the baby's ancestry made no difference. If a child was named after his maternal grandfather who happened to be Italian, then the middle name should also be Italian. That Blake was Robert's last name held no sway in her thinking equation, and his grandmother went around the house grousing about it for days. Then one day she stopped mumbling. His mother told him later that Nonna had an epiphany and renamed him. In her mind his name was Roberto Guiseppi Scaliezzi, the name of her dead husband. Blake was just an afterthought. Occasionally, however, a few words did slip out of her mouth but the only one he recognized was Kilbruth.

"Nonna mentioned Kilbruth again, but with a word that sounded like chooch," he said one day, asking his mother for an explanation.

"She's just wondering what kind of asshole would name his own kid, Kilbruth. That kind of question cleanses her thoughts and justifies renaming you. Don't tell her it's not legal."

"What's that supposed to mean?" he demanded.

"Sometimes what's right is not always legal," she said. "You'll learn that axiom quick enough as you go through life."

As years went by, Robert Kilbruth's mind became more and more embedded with Catherine Scaliezzi's lifelong directive. Then he remembered his mother repeating it again. That was the day she caught him overhearing her argument with Nonna.

"Che lo cacara nella neve e scoperto in primavera!" Nonna shouted in the midst of her tirade.

"Non-fare una mostra!" his mother thundered back, the echoes of her screams bouncing off the walls in every given direction. He remembered his mother's body shaking and seething with rage.

"What was that about?" he asked later…when things began to settle.

"Nonna just goes on and on sometimes. You've heard the saying, 'what goes around, comes around.' She's on that kick," his mother explained and then stopped speaking. "Why are you looking at me like that?"

"I don't think that's what I heard." He studied her in disbelief.

"Nonna was using an old Italian expression: 'He who shits in the snow is discovered in spring.' I just cleaned it up a little," she explained.

Robert accepted the explanation but still did not understand how her favorite axiom, "right sometimes trumps legal," fit into the argument. Nevertheless, he took it as another directive he would encounter in life and put it in his own memory bank for future reference.

***

Only minutes passed before Robert was sitting on the bed of his room and reading from an old faded list he had packed in his suitcase. Slipping out of his shoes, he held the paper gently in his hand, leaned against the fluffy bed pillows and began to reminisce about the life he shared with the woman he adored...his Emily, his elusive Elise.

He was her Mario; and she, his Elise, the romantic reality of names each selected for the other. They always had long conversations about life, love, and everything else while lying in bed. It was on one of those occasions that each christened the other.

Beethoven's "Fur Elise" was perfect for the name he gave her. From the first to the last, the pattern of high note repetition mesmerized him, drew him in as she had, making him prisoner to her sweet music. And he equated the haunting melody, each repetitive high note, to the fragility of a precious crystal, a rarity one feels fearful of breaking.

Was that how he remembered his Elise…fragile and beautiful like a delicate china doll cradled in satin?

She was perfection and he pictured her standing near the bed…a small thin figure whose porcelain skin contrasted her coal-black hair and clear dark eyes.

She was fragile, but even more so toward her cancerous end… when all was lost.

"Why, Elise?" she asked initially. "Some say Beethoven wrote it as "Fur Therese," but Therese Malfatti turned down his marriage proposal. I didn't refuse yours."

"True, but the proposal came later. He expressed his love the best way he could…through his music. It was about wanting to spend the rest of his life with the person he cherished. Refusal or not, by proposing, he wanted to make a commitment to the person he loved. And that, my dearest Elise, is how I feel about you."

"So what's your story," he asked in response to her query. "Why name me Mario?"

"After we saw Tosca, Mario seemed to be perfect. Tall, handsome, black curly hair…you."

"A mongrel high-cheek boned Italian," he interrupted.

"Mongrel, schmongrel. Tosca couldn't keep her hands off Mario and neither can I," she squealed hugging him as they lay on the bed in conversation.

He remembered how he'd bounce on the bed and yell, "Jump!" Then they'd burst with laughter, as they remembered attending the Pittsburgh Opera's lecture series before a Sunday afternoon performance.

On one particular Sunday the story of Tosca and incidents related to it were told. The hostess presenting the lecture was a soprano with one of the touring opera companies. Now, retired, she gave the audience insight into the story of Tosca, and also some of the trials and tribulations she faced traveling from one city to another to perform that particular opera. Knowing she had everyone's attention the former opera singer began her story.

"Anyone familiar with the opera knows Tosca flings herself off a parapet when she realizes Scarpia, the chief of police, double crossed her. Instead of being saved from execution, Mario, the man she loves, has been killed. Now Tosca is being pursued for killing Scarpia. As his men and the soldiers rush on stage to arrest her, she jumps to her death," the opera hostess explained in great detail. "However audiences don't know how the production group back stage protects Tosca when she jumps."

The woman grinned as she continued. "In one case, when I played Tosca, they piled mattresses on the floor so I wouldn't hurt myself. However, after I jumped, the mattresses held their spring, and there I was bouncing up and down on the stage, while in the foreground, the men were singing the finishing number. It was both embarrassing and hilarious."

After that afternoon his Elise would go around the house singing like Tosca, "Mario! Mario!"

A slight laugh escaped his lips. He remembered telling her the only reason she named him Mario was because she wanted to bounce on a mattress with him.

He adjusted his pillow to continue his reverie, but the scenario changed from their playful time together to the reality of his visit to Florence.

He loved her. It was that simple. He couldn't escape the depth of that love, and after her death, knew their life together was over. Robert was left behind, left to grow old, wither and die alone.

Robert Blake knew there would be no other, no replacement of the life they once shared. To revitalize that memory he made a reservation at the same pensione and requested the small room they once had overlooking Via Calzaiuoli's busy thoroughfare. But he didn't come to mourn her passing; he wanted to remember and celebrate the gift she had given him in life, the enrichment that comes with unconditional love for your mate.

That he would grow old alone made him think of his mother and how lonely she must have felt after the death of his father. He was very young when it happened, and had no real recollection of the man or the tears his mother must have shed when she found him sitting in his easy chair. A heart attack the doctor determined after examining him in the living room of their home. Within days, his father's death and burial were over. Yet he couldn't remember a life with just his parents: the recollection of his youth was a small bedroom at the home of his grandmother.

His mother and Nonna were the only real family he knew. Uncle Steve, or Stefano as Nonna called her son, and Aunt Dorothy, his wife, would usually drop by on holidays, but he never felt close to them. However, Uncle Steve visited much more regularly since he only lived a few miles away. He liked coming without his wife because

Uncle Steve could talk openly. Not that he had anything to hide. There were times when the man felt Aunt Dorothy was just a pain in the ass, always interrupting his conversation. Nonna agreed with her son somehow, which was confusing to him as a child. Aunt Dorothy was, after all, Italian and did not have a middle name like Kilbruth.

Now, time had reduced his immediate family to his mother and of course, the beautiful Mackenzie, his daughter. And although Uncle Steve was now considered family, he was not privy to Robert's private matters. Any information the man gleaned came from his sister.

His thoughts shifted to an earlier time.

He could still visualize Emily Scott leaning against the wall of the college coffee shop, waiting in line for a hot drink. The instant their eyes met, his solitary life was over: he had met his soul mate. He asked for the location of "Casey's Deli" and they both laughed, knowing there was no such place. Within two months they were married and their daughter, Mackenzie was born within a year.

He remembered facing objections from his mother and grandmother when they announced their intentions. The Scott family was none too happy with the news either. However, both families acted in a civil manner, even when the second bombshell dropped. No big wedding. They wanted airfare to Europe and money for backpacking on their honeymoon.

In Italy they concentrated on the big three: Rome, Florence and Venice, and visited Sorrento and Pisa as side trips. But in France, they lingered in Paris for almost five days, before crossing the channel to Dover and then, London.

He remembered Emily's mounting excitement in Italy as they traveled from city to city, each one offering something rare and unique. She bubbled with glee at finding stands of fresh vegetables in Rome, and the small cubbyhole eatery in Florence, whose patrons sat benched together near a ceiling of hanging sausages. Then across the Rialto in Venice, Emily raced around the fish market examining the different creatures caught in the Adriatic.

As Robert Blake reminisced about his life and travels with his wife, the paper fell slowly from his hand.

Chapter 2
Catherine

Thousands of miles away from Florence, a man sat in the kitchen of a small one story house in Monroeville, Pennsylvania, sipping a cup of coffee with his sister.

Aside from the man's stocky build, a stranger looking at the two of them would know immediately that they were related. Both had black curly hair, dark brown eyes and the same type of Roman nose. However, it was the high cheekbones and somewhat gaunt facial features that cinched their genetic markers. And although Catherine Scaliezzi Blake was quite thin, those moribund features, so blatantly obvious, made the wisp of a woman somewhat attractive in a macabre sort of way.

I don't get it." Steve told his sister, while continuing to sip the coffee that was much too hot for drinking. "Why go to Italy? What's the point? It won't bring her back. He's spending all that money and can't even speak the language. He should have gone to Vegas. At least he would have seen some good shows."

"It's not about money; it's about closure. It's been three years since Emily died and Robbie's never moved on. I worry. He's too young to be alone."

"He's what, forty?"

"Thirty-nine."

"He's got time."

"That's easy for you to say. You've got Dorothy."

"Exactly. If Robbie waits, he can marry someone for her social security," he said, his manner smug.

"Or it can go the other way around and she marries him now for his money," Catherine corrected, hating that possibility.

"Fat chance. Didn't you say Mackenzie gets the company? You said he signed papers to that effect. Wouldn't she get the house too, as part of the trust?"

"Robbie turned everything over to her when Emily died, but I still get half the insurance. What am I gonna do with half a mil?"

"You'll think of something, but the kid will be sitting pretty if something does happen to him. One thing's for sure. She'll sell the house."

"Why do you say that?" His sister demanded, puzzled by the remark.

"Those five homes up there may be worth a million each, but what nineteen year old wants to live up on the escarpment? You've got a beautiful view along with a death wish."

"You're goofy. His home is gorgeous."

"I'm not talking about the house. I've driven that road too many times in winter for plumbing jobs. It's too narrow. One slip on the ice means certain death on that rocky ravine. Mackenzie's better off in a condo where it's safer and she can connect with people her own age. Where is she now?"

"Studying for finals. She's at her apartment or the library."

"No. I stopped by earlier. The girl across the hall hasn't seen her since last night. But she did mention the library."

"That could explain her being so snarky. I called to see if she could sub for me at the office and she was so snotty. Mackenzie said that I didn't understand the pressure she was under for finals. That ticked me off. Who the hell did she think was around when her father went to Pitt?"

"Something's going on with her. That's definite. Maybe she's flunking a course and doesn't want to tell us."

"I know she's been spending a lot of time at the college library. She said that it's quieter. The girl across the hall plays loud music and parties a lot."

"Did you mention it to Robbie?"

"No. I didn't want to worry him when he was leaving for Italy. I told him we'd look after Mackenzie. As far as the business is concerned, John's quite capable of handling any security problems while Robbie's away. And nothing gets by me at the office."

"Harris. John Harris?"

"Who did you think I meant?"

"I don't keep track of his employees. I know he hired more guys when Blake Enterprises started taking off."

"But they're not like Harris. John's been his assistant for a long time and has a full knowledge of security systems. Robbie depends on him. He's always around, whether it's bringing papers to the house or going to their parties. They've been friends for years.

"Does he know?"

"No. I don't think Robbie would mention it."

"Harris would be so pissed if he thought losing his job was a possibility. From what you've told me, he's always wanted to run the company himself. He'd probably like to own it, but I heard he split everything in half with the divorce."

"True, but that was five years ago. He bought the condo with his share of the money and she bought something near her parents in Chicago. The son's with her. He must be in college or graduated by now. I don't really know. John doesn't talk about either of them. I was never told anything about the divorce, but I think cheating was involved. She wanted it, so maybe there was someone in the wings he didn't know about." Catherine touched the cheating aspect of the divorce lightly, knowing Steve's thoughts on the way she handled her own husband's indiscretions. "But I think he would be angry if he knew or even suspected Robbie might be selling the company and didn't tell him. He's always had his eye on the business."

"What about Mackenzie? Did he tell her about the inquiry?"

"No. He wouldn't do that." She shook her head, and then almost spoke to herself. "Could he possibly be that stupid?"

"Face it, she's his world now."

"I know," Catherine answered sadly.

"Then he better look at her another way," he said, catching his sister's questioned expression. "When my kids start lying to me,

I know damn well there's something in the wind. Mackenzie's gone from a sweet young freshman to a smart-ass sophomore whose been treating her family like dirt."

"I think you're exaggerating," she said and paused thinking about her granddaughter's recent behavior. "She has been sassy lately. Mackenzie does seems different, but I still think she loves us."

"You keep thinking that, sis, but I'll tell you one thing: she was not at the college library. I checked."

It was at that very moment Stefano Scaliezzi caught his sister's outward look of shock. Was she was surprised by her granddaughter's absence, or did his sister resent his intrusion into the girl's privacy? Either way, it made little difference to him.

"Number one," he explained, "I am a father who's been through the mill with my kids. I know what they're planning, because I've been there, done that, long before them. They can't sucker me. And number two," he emphasized, "if I am going to be responsible for my niece, then Mackenzie better be at the place she reported going to. In this case, the library, and she wasn't there."

"Please don't tell Robbie," Catherine begged. "If her grades are bad, he'll find out soon enough."

"Catherine, you're missing my point. Why is she lying? What's happening in her life that's making her grades go down? Is flunking a course really the problem?"

"You don't think so, do you?"

"No. The lying pattern's too familiar."

"For God sake, Steve, don't leave me hanging. What are you suggesting? If Mackenzie's lying about going to the library, where does she go and what is she doing?"

"We know she hangs out with the kids from school and there's no special boyfriend. So it has to be drugs. That's the only thing that makes sense."

"You think she's hooked or selling?"

"If the girl across the hall parties, it could be both. I just hope the hell she doesn't end-up with an overdose or dead."

"Now, I am worried."

"That's a waste of time," he said, grabbing his tool bag off the floor. "We'll know soon enough." He walked to the sink, opened the base cabinet doors and checked a button on the disposal before using a tool. As he started running the water, he asked. "Does this sucker chew up everything you throw down there?"

"Sounds like it will now."

"You look worried." He caught the frown crossing her face.

"No. The disposal works."

"I'm talking about Mackenzie."

"I am worried. She's changed so radically. I don't think Robbie's even aware of it. He calls and asks her to drop by, but her visits are less frequent now. He chocked it up to her studies."

"Let's leave it that way."

"What are you going to do?"

"You were blessed with Robbie. He never gave you trouble. So raising him was different in your house. My two were always hell on wheels. I had to be a step ahead of them. I'll find out what's going on with Mackenzie. I don't want you to worry. We aren't going to tell Robbie anything when he gets back."

"You will tell me, Steve. Stefano…," she echoed his name. "I have to know."

"I know you do," he said, gathering his tools. "I'll drop by when I have some news. Call me if you need something else fixed." His eyes fell on a small bottle resting on the sink. "Are you sick?" He pointed to the vial.

"Harris gave it to me for sleep. It's a concoction from one of his South American vacations. Sometimes he talks about his boat trips along the Amazon. So maybe this stuff's from some of the locals there, you know, their own medical bromide," she sighed loudly. "I heard him tell one of our workers that he has a greenhouse window filled with plants and herbs."

"Like you almost need his crap. You still have some Mulvah left?"

Although his question was simply stated, their eyes met knowingly, neither verbalizing what he always suspected and she continually ignored.

"I gave a lot of it to Robbie." She disregarded the intensity of his stare. "He was going through a bad time after Emily's death and had a hard time sleeping."

"Taking too much means dreamland forever." He bit his tongue after making the remark, knowing his sister would read more into it than he intended.

"No. He knows exactly how much to use." She acknowledged his inference sarcastically.

"Well, I wouldn't trust taking that." He pointed to the bottle again. "You don't know what's in it." He kissed his sister's cheek, indicating her importance to him, his love for her and an apology for his ignorant use of words.

"That's why it's near the trash can." She flailed the bottle off the counter.

Stefano heard the vial hit the side of the garbage container when he turned to leave the house.

As Catherine watched her brother drive away, a growing dread gnawed her thoughts. Was Mackenzie becoming a drug addict? How could she possibly help her granddaughter? Her son would be so devastated with the news. Steve was right. It was better to keep their thoughts hidden until there was evidence Mackenzie was using drugs. But how would they know? Steve led her to believe he would learn the cause of her lies. He thought of drugs immediately. Was it because his kids experimented with them or was it because he knew college kids smoked pot? Robbie never did. At least, she didn't think so. "You really don't know," her thoughts questioned. "No. when it comes right down to it, I don't. But I'm not going to ask, either." Yet she wondered if Mackenzie was really doing drugs or lying about something else. Right now, lying about flunking a course didn't seem too bad. But Steve raised a bigger question. If she were flunking a course, what was the reason for it? Was Mackenzie not studying or was she doing something else instead of?

She thought of the little girl who would visit her grandmother weekly and wished those years were back again. Now, she was fearful of what the future would bring.

Chapter 3
Raine

Robert Blake walked slowly down Calzaiuoli, trying to reconstruct some past landmarks and turned the corner at Piazza della Signoria. Somewhere in the area, on some insignificant street, was a small deli-type market that offered an excellent lunch, one that he shared with Emily so long ago. He remembered her wild excitement when they found that unique treasure nineteen years earlier. He crossed the square centered by a giant statue of Hercules and turned down a small narrow street that resembled an alley. Three doors from the corner, a small incongruous sign over an open doorway read Alessandro Sacchi Market.

A deep satisfying smile crossed Robert's face as he entered the narrow passageway. Assorted casings of Italian ham, salami, cappacola and sausage hung suspended from the ceiling, covering the aisle and deli cases that displayed food offerings for purchase or consumption. He passed under the casings and walked toward the back section of the market where three people sat at one of the two picnic tables used for food service.

"Il cibo e buona." An older man pointed to his plate of spaghetti and meatballs as Robert sat down on the picnic bench beside him. His comment was followed by the two women in his party, who while agreeing with the man's assessment, were savoring plates of ravioli along with crusty bread from a centered basket and sipping water glasses of red wine.

As Robert eyed the food plates hungrily, a large woman wearing a butcher's apron approached him with the daily menu of three items: spaghetti, ravioli and lasagna. She waited for his order.

As he pointed to the man's dish of spaghetti, she whisked the menu out of his hands and began walking away.

"Gratsie." Robert erred deliberately, not trilling his r.

"He speaks Italian!" The older man said, speaking in his native dialect at Robert's feeble attempt with the language.

"And he eats Italian." One of the women answered, meaning the man couldn't be too bad.

As they talked about Robert Blake, the waitress appeared with his food and he repeated the man's "Buona" with each forkful of spaghetti. The waitress reappeared with a bottle of red wine and a water glass. She pointed to the bottle and catching his nod, filled the glass.

"Refill ours while you are here." The older man told her in a dialect she understood.

"Take care of the American," she answered refilling their wine glasses. "He looks like he needs help. God knows how he found this place. I think he's lost."

***

After lunch, Robert thought about his mother as he retraced his steps back to Piazza Signoria. He was satisfied with his meal and the three companions who spoke with him in sign language, Italian and broken English. His mother was right on target about his silence. They took the waitress' advice and enjoyed communicating with the dumb American who spoke no Italian. The waitress was also right, of course. He did need help. Not one of them could understand how he found Allesandro's. It was off the main tourist drag and it was an eatery frequented mainly by locals. However, the market was no longer on his mind.

Instead of turning at Signoria, he angled around Palazzo Vecchio for the Ponte Vecchio Bridge. The Golden Bridge, he corrected his thoughts. It made little difference what he called it. He was interested in buying a gift in one of the small, almost miniscule, jewelry shops that lined it. Emily loved browsing the cubby-hole shops for the gold ring he bought her. Now he would take his time to find the perfect gift for Mackenzie. Since the shops were known for the quality of their gold jewelry, he thought of buying a bracelet for her birthday. It would cost a bundle, but she was worth every penny.

She would make something of herself someday. Mackenzie had the drive and she used her time wisely at school. Each time he called she was going to the college library or already there. Yes. He was a proud father who couldn't ask more from his daughter. She definitely deserved an expensive gift.

As Robert walked along the bridge checking each shop, he spied the exact bracelet he had in mind in one of the store windows. In less than five minutes he haggled over price and walked away six hundred dollars poorer. It was much more than he wanted to pay but he had envisioned the shiny gold bangle on Mackenzie's wrist. All in all, it was perfect. In addition to his purchase, the owner gave him a building miniature of Palazzo Vecchio, which he slipped into his pocket.

He retraced his steps back to Piazza della Signoria, and sat down to enjoy a glass of wine while watching the birds knock over the empty ones.

***

An hour later Robert Blake was sitting on the bed in his room reading the paper he had scanned hours earlier. He felt satisfied that he had accomplished three things: lunch at the deli, a Golden Bridge gift for Mackenzie and a glass of wine at Piazza Signoria. Somehow, it made him feel closer to Emily. It was almost like sharing those activities with her. She would have enjoyed the outing. How he wished she could have been there with him. He missed her excitement with each new discovery, her laughter at betting which bird would knock over a glass first, and the empty blue water bottle they took back to the States. As he reflected their years together, a sadness swirled his thoughts as he remembered those treasured moments. He felt a loneliness growing within him, a longing to have Emily in his arms again. He wanted to tell her how much he loved her, how much she fulfilled his life and how empty it had become without her. A tear fell on the paper he held, causing him to grasp the nearest pillow and give sway.

***

Robert wasn't really hungry when he awakened; nor did he feel like touring churches and museums, although there was a full hour left to visit the Duomo and Baptistry, so very close by. Instead, he decided to get an early start the next morning.

He checked the paper that had left his hand when he fell asleep and began mapping a time-saving strategy. Tomorrow, he would start walking up Calzaiuoli toward the Accademia. There he would see Michelangelo's marble statue of David, and then retrace his steps back down again to visit the famous three: the Duomo, Baptistry and Bell Tower. Afterward he would visit the Duomo Museum to view the dark wooden statue of an emaciated and penitent Mary Magdalene that had left him standing in awe years earlier. Then he would continue his tour to the Uffitzi Gallery and Palazzo Vecchio, which was almost a straight shot. But he did not want to miss the Bargello Museum, also nearby, but in a different direction. Two statues of David, featured there, were done by Donatello, but the one that interested him most was done in bronze.

***

Within minutes Robert Blake was on his way to Piazza della Repubblica, a large shopping and entertainment square around the corner from his pensione, to a little restaurant that had served very good food many years earlier and offered water in a blue bottle, the same kind of glass container that sat in the china closet of his dining room. He smiled remembering the incident. After they drained the blue bottle into their water glasses, Emily put it in the canvas sack she used as a purse and no one seemed to mind.

Those were the days when they were young and frivolous. And even with little money to spend, they were extremely happy. Robert and Emily knew inwardly and implicitly that they would make something of themselves. They would have money: they would be successful; but even more important, they would be together.

Later, after a succulent fish dinner, as Robert walked back toward the pensione, he passed a group of tourists watching the street entertainment of acrobats. He heard gasps and cheers from the satisfied throng, but was not interested in watching the evening's spontaneous event or tossing coins into a can nearby in appreciation of the performance. Instead, he went back to the pensione to get a good night's sleep.

***

The next morning, Robert joined the throng of tourists appreciating the very large statue of David standing on a pedestal behind a railing at the Accademia. As Robert viewed the marble figure, he moved closer to the husband of an English couple who was telling his wife about the twenty-six year old Michelangelo sculpting the statue when other artists refused.

"Why would someone refuse?" she questioned. "Most people are familiar with the battle between David and Goliath in the valley of Elah."

"The sling shot and five stones, yes."

"Book one of Samuel."

"No. It was the marble imperfections."

"But he looks perfect to me," Robert blurted, shocked that what he heard was his own voice infringing on a private conversation. "I am so sorry for interrupting you," he apologized. "Can you explain what happened?"

The older man turned to Robert and began with the statue's history. "The group in charge of commissioning the sculpture wanted a David for the Duomo. They offered it to other artists but no one would accept because of the marble imperfections. The marble sat in a courtyard for quite some time I believe until Michelangelo came along and agreed to the sculpture of David."

"But it's not in the Duomo." Robert questioned further.

"No. It was too large for the high altar, I think. It was moved to the Piazza Signoria to front Palazzo Vecchio. Weather took its toll and years later, it was moved here."

"How do you know so much about this?"

"I read about it somewhere, but don't quote me, I am not an authority."

"Don't let him fool you," his wife interjected. "He's on the mark 99% of the time."

"I'm sorry I interrupted, but thanks for the information."

"You're from the States, aren't you?" the man asked, cognizant of the inquisitor's speech pattern.

"Yes." Robert nodded. "Pennsylvania."

"We live outside London," the woman offered as they walked away.

When Robert turned away from the couple, his eyes met the stare of a woman who had been listening to their conversation. Although she looked somewhat familiar to him, he could not remember where he had seen her, but something told him their paths had crossed earlier.

He moved away from the statue of David to Giambolonga's, Rape of the Sabines, and felt the woman's eyes still studying him. He walked quickly to the exit hall but stopped suddenly to view Michelangelo's Prisoner grouping, the four unfinished sculptures that seemed to erupt from slabs of marble.

"You do know what these famous sculptures are," the Englishman said, passing by.

"They're called the Prisoners or Slaves."

"Study each one: The Awakening Slave; The Young Slave; The Bearded Slave, and Atlas or The Bound Slave."

"They represent the eternal struggle of man."

"To free himself," the Englishman said, "from material trappings. At least that's one of the floating theories."

Before Robert could ask another question, the man's wife took her husband's arm and led him out of the building. She was done sharing him with some dumb Yankee who was so ignorant of the arts.

***

Retracing his steps once again, Robert spent the major portion of the day at the Baptistry, Duomo and the Bell Tower, stopping only to patronize a street vendor who was selling a healthy supply of Italian sausages on fresh rolls. Other tourists in the long queue shared his same lunch idea but the wait was worth every bite.

Sometime later in the Duomo Museum, Robert stood in awe at the wooden figure of a haggard-looking Mary Magdalene. He wanted to touch her, make her understand that he, too, felt absorbed with the sadness of losing one so loved and adored. It was important she understood the suffering that comes to all of us: that we share that same burden of love, grief and death. But, of course, that was impossible. She was cordoned off by the metal railing surrounding her raised figure, allowing all visitors to appreciate Donatello's work from afar.

Leaving the wooden statue, he searched for the Florence version of Michelangelo's "The Pieta," his world famous sculpture that sits in Saint Peter's Basilica in Rome. He remembered how he and Emily were so swept with emotion at the sight of Virgin Mary holding the dead body of her son.

The Deposition or Florence version of "The Pieta" depicted four figures: the dead body of Jesus Christ, newly taken down from the Cross, Nicodemus, Virgin Mary and Mary Magdalene.

If Robert remembered correctly, the hooded and bearded Nicodemus was thought to be a portrait sculpture of Michelangelo and was to be placed on his tomb in Rome. However, at some point, the artist smashed the sculpture and gave it to his servant who later sold it. The buyer, obviously, commissioned some artist to repair the damaged section; otherwise, it would not have been on display.

Robert checked his watch. It was late afternoon and he felt tired. He thought of having a glass of wine as he walked toward Piazza della Signoria. It was time to relax from the day's activities. He was sure Emily would have agreed with that decision. As soon as he sat down to order, a bird knocked over one of the glasses nearby. The act made him smile. He felt Emily's presence there with him…Emily, with the laughing eyes. How much he wished she were there with him again.

"Would you mind if I joined you?" He heard a well-modulated voice ask. "I heard your conversation at the Accademia. I'm from Pennsylvania too."

Robert turned to face the woman who had met his stare earlier that day, when he spoke to the Englishman about the statue of David.

Seeing her up close shook him instantly. She was breathtaking. A bank of dark hair fell carelessly across the shoulders of the dark-eyed, thin-figured young woman and directly contrasted her ivory skin and ruby-red lips. Her beauty reminded him of a children's book he often read to Mackenzie in her younger days, "Snow White."

"Where in Pennsylvania?" he asked, her scent enveloping him as he offered a chair to accommodate her.

"You wouldn't know it," she confessed. "It's a small suburb of Pittsburgh, Penn Hills."

"Small world." His eyes widened. "I'm only miles away from you in the outskirts of Murrysville."

"I'm not familiar with the area," she said laughingly. "I shouldn't say that since I'm a realtor. But I've gone to Monroeville on occasion to show a house, but never Murrysville." She reached into her purse for a small silver case and pulled out a card that listed her name, business address and several phone numbers, including her cell. "I work Penn Hills mainly and Oakmont, if at all possible."

"Then you're taking advantage of the shoulder season in Florence," he said, avoiding a personal response as he slid her card into his wallet.

"Pretty much. My friend was supposed to come with me but she fell and broke her ankle. So here I am."

"Let me get you some wine," he interrupted, catching the waiter's attention just as the woman's cell phone rang. As the waiter approached, Robert heard her say "fatto" before terminating the call.

"Your husband?"

"No. That was Valerie from my office. She's checking to see what she's missed," she answered laughingly. "I told her I was getting fat eating all this Italian food. And no, I am not married, but you are. I noticed your ring."

Although a part of her remark seemed implausible, he let it pass and dwelled on it later.

"My wife died three years ago from cancer."

"Family?"

"I have a daughter in college."

"That's why you're alone. She's in school."

"That covers it pretty much. What about you?"

"No one really. I have a father and stepmother on the west coast. I don't get along with her, so there is virtually no communication. My mother died years ago. I came east for a relationship that didn't work out and just stayed."

"So why Florence? Why not Rome, if you're doing Italy."

"I am going to Rome," she replied. "Flying to Florence was cheaper when I booked. So I'll take a train to Rome, spend four days touring the sights and fly to Pittsburgh from there. I only wish I could have followed the English couple around the city. I learned so much listening to your conversation."

"What have you seen so far?"

"The Duomo, Baptistry and Bell Tower. What about you?"

"The same," he said, neglecting to mention the Duomo museum. "But I plan to see the two Davids tomorrow."

"Where?" she asked, nodding to thank the waiter who arrived with their wine.

"The Bargello." He raised his wine glass to touch hers. "As your Pittsburgh neighbor, Robert Blake salutes you."

"Raine Shaw salutes you back." She tinged his glass.

"Rain? Were you born on a stormy day?" The thought set him laughing.

"No. No. No." She joined his laughter. "It's R-a-i-n-e." She spelled her name. "Actually, it's short for Lorraine."

"I like it." He nodded agreeably. "It's different."

"I'm glad because I have a favor to ask. Will you take me with you to see both Davids tomorrow?" She caught his smile.

"Have you been to the Uffitzi?"

"Not yet, but I want to see the paintings."

"You'll want to see Michelangelo's "Holy Family."

"Obviously, I need a guide. You seem to know your way around. Have you been here before?"

"A long time ago with my wife." He caught her surprise with the directness of his answer. "The hotels get renovated and the stores change but the masterpieces stay the same. Should we meet here tomorrow?"

"It would be easier if we met in the breakfast room of the pensione since we're both staying there. I'll even do sign language for you with the waitress." She laughed, referring to his miscommunication with the woman a day earlier.

"Was that you on the far side of the room?" he asked, surprised she noticed him.

"It was," she said, laughing again. "You were a hoot."

"I didn't recognize you. Your head was down. I think you were reading a map, so I didn't pay much attention," he answered catching the waiter's eye.

"Another?" he referred to their empty wine glasses.

"Please."

"I didn't ask before. I just assumed you wanted red."

"Your assumption was correct. I want to buy you dinner tonight," she said witnessing the dark-eyed man's shock.

"Why?"

"I always tip my guide."

"Tomorrow's tour may not be worth the money."

"Then I should get a second day free," she cajoled, sipping slowly from the newly arrived wine.

"Then you're out of luck. Tomorrow's my last day." Her face seemed to fall with the news of his departure, and suddenly he regretted not meeting her sooner. "I guess I'll have to do a good job keeping you informed and entertained."

"Can I hold you to that?"

"We'll meet at 9:30 in the breakfast room and go from there."

"Then I'll leave it up to you to show me around."

"That's the plan."

"Where shall we go for dinner? I'm buying."

"In that case I'll select a very expensive restaurant." He smiled and paused for a moment. "I know. We'll go to a restaurant that has beautiful frescos on the walls and ceiling alcoves. The ambiance is absolutely breathtaking and the food, wonderful."

"I'm so excited! Do I have time to shower and change into something more suitable than traveling clothes?" Her face glowed with pleasure. "It sounds so wonderful."

"You'll love it," he said, catching the waiter's attention for payment. Within minutes, they were on their way to Pensione Maria with the promise of a special dinner.

***

It was sometime during their dinner of veal Marsala and several cocktails, that they relaxed and spoke freely of themselves.

"You came here with your wife?" she questioned.

"Yes. I wanted to have dinner at this restaurant again, but it is much nicer having someone to share it with."

"Then I'm glad we came."

"Why aren't you with someone?"

"I was a long time ago, but it didn't work out. I guess it wasn't meant to be."

"That surprises me. You are a beautiful woman."

"And you are a handsome man."

"Cut the compliments. I'm holding you to your promise of buying dinner."

"I'll share the secret of my credit card: it never gets rusty."

"Then I'll have to see about keeping it polished."

"I hope you have a good plan."

"You'll have to wait and see."

***

After dinner, Robert led Raine to a narrow street off Piazza Repubblica, where long ago he shared a fire-eating street performer with Emily. However, while the street was totally deserted upon their arrival, they heard loud music coming from the Piazza nearby.

They walked along the outskirts of a crowd watching a troupe of acrobats who had performed the previous night and returned again after a profitable evening. Edging their way into the throng, Robert and Raine watched the performance until there was a brief intermission and a bucket passed for tips. Robert tossed a few coins into the container and led Raine to another location, one he remembered well.

"I thought we could go for an after-dinner drink."

"I'd like that," she said, unaware his thoughts were elsewhere.

He remembered walking toward one corner of the Piazza, where loud music from a nightclub permeated the square. He and Emily gravitated toward the music and laughed when they had to stop suddenly. A chain-link fence separated the nightclub from the crowd of onlookers who stood watching the animated musicians perform while their paid patrons danced. Watching through the fence mattered little to them that evening. However, the next night, he and Emily joined a crowd dancing in the piazza, while the non-dancers sat on stone benches that curved around a statue in the square center, and watched the couples glide by. The memory soon faded upon entering the nightclub.

They sat at a small table farther away from the musicians but found it hard to carry on a conversation.

"Ok, Raine," he shouted and stood up. "Indulge me." He took her in his arms. "We might as well dance. Talking is out."

Her body, so close to his, felt soft and warm as they circled the dance floor. He found the suppleness of her moves surrendering to his so like Emily's. Raine's hip movement and the way her hand held his shoulder were so reminiscent of his past life with the woman he loved. In fact, she was so much like her, the evening passed by quickly.

When they reached the pensione, they learned that both of them had rooms on the third floor.

"Where is your room?" Raine asked as they walked down the hall.

"In the alcove, at the end of the corridor. I thought I'd walk you home." He laughed as they strolled the corridor.

"You're in the old section."

"It's what I remembered."

The man must be reliving his past, Raine thought to herself. It would be in her best interest not to question his reasoning. He was taking her on a tour the next morning and she did not want to spoil their wonderful evening with a bunch of useless questions. He would tell her if capturing a memory of the past was his intention: if he wanted her to have that knowledge. For now, she would dwell on their time together. She stopped at room 316, slid her entry card into the slot and turned the knob.

"I had a wonderful evening, Robert." She inched her body closer to his. "I hate to see it end," she whispered, circling her arms around his shoulders, their lips meeting.

"I do too," he responded feeling the warmth of her body pressed against his.

"It doesn't have to end." Her invitation was explicit.

"Yes, it does. We have a full day tomorrow," he said, using their planned tour as an excuse for his refusal. "I'll meet you at 9:30 in the breakfast room."

***

Back in his room, Robert Blake suffered mixed emotions. He felt a sense of guilt and betrayal, yet he had done nothing wrong or inappropriate. He had stayed the course with his pilgrimage to Emily, revisiting those places they had shared together so many years earlier. And although Robert felt her presence with him that day, he could not run from the inescapable truth of that night. He was attracted to Raine. They were attracted to each other, both mentally and physically. They seemed to enjoy the same things. And they were close geographically. Feeling that way tormented him. How could he justify these feelings?

He had come to Florence to refresh the vision of his life with Emily, his love he could no longer hold in his arms. But the reality was there. She was gone, never to return. Would she want him to lead a solitary life or find a measure of happiness with someone who had her capacity for loving him? He had met someone who made him feel whole again, made him recapture a zest for living. Would Emily understand that? Or would she think of Raine as a replacement? That could never be. There could only be one Emily. Perfection came sparse and solely. He had met only one. With Raine, it would be a love given when all hope had been previously lost.

His thoughts continued to swirl as he lay in the darkness of the room, thinking first of Emily, and then, of Raine. After tomorrow, perhaps he should avoid seeing her. Meeting her could lead him to fall in love again, to be deliriously happy until another tragedy struck. Was he being pessimistic, or was he afraid of taking another plunge at happiness for however long it would last? What would Emily think? Knowing Emily as he did, she would tell him fate may have brought them together. Maybe it was meant to be. Emily had a depth of sharing her love. She would want him to be happy with someone else, but he did not really believe that…deep in his heart.

He thought of the meeting at Piazza Signoria, when Raine spoke on the phone to her friend at work, Valerie. She was the woman who broke her ankle and had to cancel the trip to Florence. But in conversation with her, Raine said, "Fatto instead of fat." Why was he questioning that? She also said, "When I booked a flight, not we." Was being suspicious also part of his Italian heritage?

Within a few short moments, Robert fell asleep.

***

The following day was filled with excitement. Raine enjoyed visiting the Bargello with the two Davids and savoring a vendor's offering when they became hungry. It was later, after their visit to the Uffitzi, that Robert suggested having wine at Piazza Signoria.

"Are we calling it a day after this?" Raine questioned, taking the chair opposite him.

"I thought we should relax with some wine and discuss plans for dinner."

"Are you going to let me treat you tonight?"

"Meaning?"

"I was supposed to pay for dinner last night, remember?"

"I couldn't let you do that."

"No. That's not who you are," she replied softly, totally aware of his generous nature.

"Where can I take you tonight? It has to be an early evening. I leave at dawn tomorrow."

"Could we…," she questioned.

"I'd like that." He completed her thought about a repeat.

"I loved the restaurant. You were right about the ambiance and food."

***

Later that evening when Robert walked Raine to her room, she unlocked the door slowly and turned to face him.

"I don't want to say goodbye."

"I have an early morning flight."

"I know." She circled her arms around him and brought him close to her. "I can't believe we just met." Her tongue circled the outline of his lips as she pressed against him. "Robert, please, I don't want this to end."

"It won't, Raine. I promise," he said, his lips still brushing hers. "Now go inside." He watched her close the door slowly, then turned and walked down the corridor to his room.

Chapter 4
At Home

It was early Thursday evening when Robert arrived at his Murrysville home. He was tired and in no mood to hear about the latest development at work. That would come soon enough. He had spoken with his mother during a flight layover, telling her of his plans to retire early. He left a similar message for Mackenzie, since she was not available to receive his call. He wanted no company from anyone that evening. He just wanted to sprawl-out in bed, watch a little TV and fall asleep. He was too weary for receiving family; not that they were company, but he was not in a conversational mood.

Upon entering the house he hit the alarm code, dropped his luggage in the front hall and turned on a bank of lights as he walked into the kitchen for a glass of water. On his way to the sink, he noticed the blinking light of the landline answering machine and hit the button.

"Just wanted to wish you a happy landing," John Harris' cheerful voice rang out. "I have a surprise waiting when you get in. Rest-up old buddy." With those words, the message ended.

"Whatever it is, I really don't care," Robert said aloud.

But, of course, he did care, particularly if it concerned his business. But if something had gone wrong his mother would have mentioned it when they spoke earlier. Not true. She would have waited until he returned, not wanting to worry him. Still, if something had happened, she would have told him to call when he got in. That would be more like her. Since that was not the case, the message had nothing to do with work. So whatever surprise John had waiting in the wings, it had to be of a personal nature.

Robert thought about John Harris on a personal level as he mounted the stairs, his suitcase in hand. Turning on the lights of his bedroom, he thought of the things they discussed outside of business and only one thought came to mind. The man had bought his dream car: a Mercedes. If that were the case, Robert had no intention of spoiling his surprise. Was John's dream sedan white or black? Even that would not be much of a surprise: it was a given. Nevertheless, he would go along with the revelation, expressing just the right amount of shock. Robert was an expert at facial expressions. The man had years of practice.

He thought about John and his new Mercedes. The two men were close in age. John was three years younger, somewhat taller, and had very expressive brown eyes, a shade that seemed to match the color of his hair. By all accounts, he would be considered a very handsome man with an outgoing personality. The man seemed to remember something of a personal nature about each of their customers and they gravitated to him like a sewn patch on his conversational quilt.

Still, there was something about him that didn't fit. It was almost like there were two of them: one that people related to, and the very secretive man whose private world could not be punctured. And Robert had been trying to pierce it for seven years, when he first came aboard his expanding company. To this day, he still did not know the real mind of John Harris.

The man never spoke of his divorce, ex-wife or son. Anyone meeting him would think he carried no baggage of a past life: his family never existed. Scuttlebutt had it that the wife had been unfaithful, but no one knew the truth. John admitted to nothing. No one saw it coming. It happened so gradually. Sheila had always attended the company parties; and then one day, John came alone, explaining his wife and son went to Chicago to help an ailing parent. At another function, months later, John told him of the divorce, saying it was at her request when Robert pressed him further.

The other thing that seemed strange was the man's annual vacation trip to places off the beaten path, usually somewhere in the Amazon or Far East. He would return with several concoctions for coughs, colds and whatever else his acquaintances conjured up for him. Some company workers attributed it to his being a health nut; however, according to Robert's observation, the only healthy thing

John ingested was bottled water. The man was a devout eater of fried chicken.

His thoughts returned to the Mercedes. If John did buy a new car, Robert would be in for a ribbing about his four-year-old Cadillac. But the men in the office knew his philosophy: 'If it runs and hums, stay with it.' Why buy something for show? That's not who he was. God knows, he had years to prove it. It was tough when he started the security business almost two decades earlier, but Emily and his mother stuck by him and they worked to help it grow. They went everywhere, making new friends and acquaintances to stir up business. It wasn't easy, and often, they had little money. If Catherine Scaliezzi hadn't been there for them, the outcome could have been very different.

With those thoughts in mind, Robert Blake was soon in bed and fast asleep. He saw no television that night.

***

It was almost six o'clock when the phone rang.

"You up?" Catherine Scaliezzi asked. "You might want to sleep-in this morning but I think we should talk. Shower and come by for coffee. Use your key, in case I'm in the bathroom."

"You didn't," he said thinking she added his time to another charity.

"I wouldn't do that and you know it, but this is not for office discussion."

"Put on the coffee. I'll see you in thirty." He ended the call.

***

"What benefit am I doing now?" Robert addressed his mother as she poured coffee for both of them.

"It's not about some charity." Catherine brushed his question aside. "We have bigger fish to fry."

"What's up?"

"Henry Price at Global called."

"And you think he's feeling us out."

"I think someone mentioned Parks Limited and he's trawling for a bidding war."

"I never said I was selling."

"That's been said before. If the offer's good enough an owner might change his mind about selling. Your selling would lessen Henry's competition. He didn't leave a message, but that had to be the reason for his call. I told him you were out of town."

"Was anyone around when he phoned?"

"No. I was alone." She shook her head. "Did you tell anyone about Bruce Parks?"

"No. He mentioned several possibilities after a round of golf. It was just a casual conversation, but I could read the significance of it."

"You're not answering my question."

"Why would I even mention it? There's nothing to tell."

"What about Mackenzie?"

"What about her?" He resented the implication.

"Did you tell her?"

"No, but she heard my end of the conversation when Bruce called to play again."

"So she knows," Catherine insisted.

"No. I told her it was a running joke between us and that he didn't have a pot to piss in, let alone buy me out."

"Did she believe you?"

"It doesn't matter. I'm not selling the company."

"Maybe so, but something doesn't add up. Why would Henry call?"

"I am a sub in his golf league," he answered quickly. "That could be it."

"Who do you think you're talking to?"

"What do you mean?"

"You don't believe the happy horseshit you're feeding me, so put down the spoon and start thinking. Where did Global get the information about Parks Limited?"

"I don't know. Maybe John heard me on the phone, but I don't believe it."

"How long ago was that?"

"I don't remember. A couple weeks before I left. John was standing in the outer office when Bruce phoned. He wanted to play nine holes and brought it up again. I made some smart remark. Harris could have heard my side of the conversation, but I think he was too far away."

"You don't buy that for one minute?"

"No. But I can't see how he got that information, if your thinking is right about Henry…with selling, I mean."

"Robbie, I may not be as educated as you," his mother mused, "but I read people well and learned the lessons of the streets years ago. So don't tell me I'm reading into something that isn't."

Catherine's remarks had a silencing effect on her son. He sipped his coffee slowly, his eyes studying hers. Throughout the years, in business and in marriage, she was there to guide him when he needed her. She was like a steady rock, immovable and unyielding to the threats he may have encountered without her counsel. She was there for him and Emily when they needed her; otherwise, his mother left them alone. She explained it to them once. A good relationship can be sustained by giving counsel sparingly when asked, and keeping mute and distant the rest of the time.

"Alright. Just what are you thinking?" He emphasized the word are.

"Who would benefit by a sale to Global rather than Parks Limited?"

"You have someone in mind, don't you?"

"John. It's logical. He's your assistant. You sell and Harris becomes the head man at Global."

"The same thing could happen with Parks Limited."

"No. You said Bruce talked about a split; two under one banner, if I recall our conversation two weeks ago."

"He did mention something like that when I told him I wasn't selling."

"No one knows about this other idea, so the possibility of selling your company is the only thing surfacing right now."

"And you think John Harris is talking to Henry at Global."

"I'd bet my dentures."

"You don't have false teeth."

"But that's what I think about Harris, false loyalty. He's looking to feather his own nest."

"I can't blame the guy for wanting to get ahead. That's today's reality."

"John could have come to you about a rumor he heard. The man's been with you a long time. You're supposed to be friends, although he's changed since Sheila left. You would have set him straight. Now you have to contend with Global."

"I won't have a problem with Henry. I'll squash the whole thing and they'll know I'm not selling."

"Still, I don't trust John Harris."

"He left a message on my machine about some surprise."

"It's white."

"I'll act surprised."

"That shouldn't be hard. Christ knows you've had enough practice." She got up from the table, took her coffee cup to the sink and turned to face him. "Now get out of here. I have to get ready for work. My boss is coming back today," Catherine said jokingly.

"In a minute." Robert followed his mother's path to the sink, coffee cup in hand. "What does the word, "fatto," mean in the literal sense?"

"Finished. Done. Why?"

"I met someone in Florence."

"She's Italian and said something you don't understand."

"No. She lives here in the area and went to Florence alone because her friend broke her ankle and had to cancel."

"I don't understand."

"Maybe I'm too suspicious about the phone call she received when we met. She told her friend, Valerie, "fat," explaining she was eating too much, but I'm sure I heard, "fatto." I was having a glass of wine at Piazza Signoria. It was late afternoon and she asked to join me. It was like magic, mom. What I feel for Lorraine Shaw is the way I felt about Emily. But I'm scared of making a mistake."

"It might be an omen of things to come. If you care for her, Robbie, go slow and take it from there."

"You think this "fatto" thing is in my head, don't you?"

"No. I think something's gnawing your thoughts. You'll have to deal with it because it will always be in the back of your mind."

"At some point, I want you to meet her."

"Before that happens, straighten things out with Henry."

"I'll report later." Robert kissed her his mother's forehead and left the house.

Catherine heard the roar of his car as she watched him drive away, and thought of a subject she had not discussed with him. Mackenzie. Suddenly, another thought crossed her mind about Robbie's meeting in Florence. He never mentioned what Lorraine Shaw did for a living, but she must have very wealthy friends to be calling her in Italy. Was the woman just joking about getting fat? Sometimes Robbie was too suspicious. Maybe this was one of those times.

Chapter 5
Sweet Pea

After Robert left his mother's house, he headed to the escarpment perched high above the town below. He had a task of his own to perform and it had to be done privately. As he drove up the steep climb and took the sharp curve upward, he thought of the wooded area encompassing the five homes situated there and the dense foliage that shielded them from the noisy bustle of everyday living. He could think of no other place so beautiful. But his thoughts turned to other things when he pulled into the driveway of his home.

Before turning to the task at hand, Robert sat in his home office and punched-in Mackenzie's cell number from the contact list on his phone. Getting no response from the telephone call, he left a text message: "Contact me: Sunday brunch here." His thoughts turned to those wonderful Sundays together, the days when he'd make her favorite breakfast: pancakes, sausage and grilled pecan rolls. Mackenzie's job was to pour the orange juice and coffee. The tradition started years earlier, when Emily was still alive. It continued until Mackenzie went to college and moved to Shadyside, a thriving area of the city inhabited by a large portion of students. Robert knew at some point she would make contact with him.

Now, his thoughts turned to the real problem on his mind. Robert could have obtained the information through his own business channels but knew that would not be wise. He encrypted a computer message to an old government friend and asked a favor. It was imperative that his name not be traced to the information requested: nothing could be connected to him. He knew Elias would not refuse. He had helped the man on more than one occasion. And although they lived in different cities, the coasts were never that far apart when they needed each other. Such was the case when college roommates bonded for life.

The information was standard in a sense: name, identification, marital status, police record and work history. He couldn't ask about a relationship that soured after a move to the Pittsburgh area, but that would not matter if everything else gelled in Lorraine Shaw's history.

He requested paper. Robert would read the report and burn it, leaving nothing behind for a third party to discover. There was no need to ask for urgency. Elias was a devoted slave to the shadowed world he inhabited, and he knew all the dark and murky corners of intense investigations and the tools that were used.

Within seconds, he received a text from Elias. "I heard Will Dooley died two days ago. I'll check it out."

The response made Robert laugh. Will Dooley was a classmate of theirs. Whether his death was true or not, Elias' message was clear. Within two days, the requested information would be in his hands.

He took Lorraine Shaw's card from his wallet and studied it. "Sooner or later, I'm going to learn the truth about fat versus fatto," he said aloud. "I might be suspicious, but am I right?"

***

When Robert entered his office that same morning, his mother and John Harris rushed to greet him.

"Safe trip and rested," John chortled. "Business is still humming if you want the day off."

"He needs to get back to work," Catherine scolded. "I've got papers that need his signature."

"That can wait," John groused pulling Robert to a nearby window. "Look at my new beauty."

"The white Mercedes? That's yours? It is a beauty. Can we go down and give it a good look?"

"I thought you'd never ask." John began to laugh as they walked out of the office toward the Mercedes. "I needed a new car. My Chevy was on its last legs. I mean that literally. It died in the parking lot. The motor was shot."

"This is a beauty," Robert Blake repeated when John opened the car door for a check of the interior. "I love that new car smell, don't you?"

"Yeah. It goes away too soon, though."

"True, but enjoy it while you have it."

"I am. I never had so many bells and whistles on a car before. I even got a Steelers' decal for the window," he said, following Robert back to the office where a tall bearded man, wearing a hat and long coat, stood waiting to talk with him.

"We haven't met, but I have need of your services," the man said, following Robert into his office. He immediately put a finger to his nose when the door closed.

"My name is Juniper Tweed and I need some work to be done. I would appreciate your accompanying me or perhaps we could meet this morning at the address listed."

Robert glanced at his own address and immediately pocketed the slip of paper for future burning. He checked his watch before making a firm commitment. "Let's plan on meeting at ten o'clock."

"Thank you," the man said quietly and left the office.

"Who was that?" Catherine demanded.

"A referral, I think," he replied, "but I'm not really sure. I'm meeting him tomorrow," he lied.

"Here?"

"Springdale. I'll give you the information if it gels." The intended remark hit home with Catherine. They were totally aware that John Harris stood in the doorway of his office listening to every word of their conversation.

"Did you pick it up yet?"

"Not yet. If you don't mind…"

"Just go. You were never delinquent."

At her request Robert gathered his jacket and left the office.

"Where's he off to?" John asked, still framing the doorway of his office.

"The post office for his undelivered mail," she replied, frustrated by his constant questions. "I'm sure he has a stack of bills to pay."

Satisfied with the information, the man turned into his own office and ran through a work schedule.

***

"Juniper Tweed," Robert welcomed Elias Juniper who greeted him from the living room of his house when he entered. There was no need to ask him about the alarm code. Elias could disarm anything or anybody as he sat cross-legged on the couch swirling a solitary ice cube in his glass of scotch. "You sly dog! Your prints were all over the contract." He eyed his dark-haired friend. "What are you doing here and why the beard?"

"The beard is an identity change. Don't ask. I'm here on a case. I didn't know you were back from Florence or I would have called."

"Got back last night but needed this information ASAP."

"You met her in Florence and learned she's from the area. Quite a coincidence, don't you think?"

"That plus "fatto." He went on to explain.

"My advice," he said in a measured voice. "Go slow on this one. This is not an Emily you just met in college."

"I have real feelings for Raine, but I'm scared. This could be a huge mistake."

"Raine, for Lorraine," Elias caught his nod. "Raine Shaw or Lorraine Shaw, I'll check both identities. You'll have the information by Sunday."

"Maybe I'm getting old, but the way we met makes me suspicious."

"Better to be suspicious than divorced…too damn expensive and a real pain in the ass."

"I thought things were better."

"They are. She remarried. Unfortunately, we live in the same city and I run into her occasionally. Carolyn eyes all my dates with glowing hatred because they are so much younger."

"You can't expect her to be generous with some young thing on your arm."

"I didn't ask for the divorce, she did."

"You were never home."

"She knew that before we traded 'I do's.' It was later when the 'I don'ts' set in. But I never gave her cause." Their eyes met. "I guess it was too much. She had the burden of family. When I refused to give up the job, that's when it all went south. But that's not a history worth repeating. The twins are in college and doing well. I don't think either of the boys will follow my footsteps, but that's ok. We're on good terms and that's all I care about."

"I haven't seen Mackenzie. She's either in finals or just over them. I asked for a Sunday brunch."

"Reliving old times?"

"Pretty much."

"Let me see about creating some new ones." Elias referenced the task at hand. "You'll have the report in two days. By the way, I found nine," he said.

"You missed three," he referred to the security cameras that were hidden.

"Don't tell me you have 'Sweet Pea' in the house already." An astonished look crossed his face.

"Bedroom, bathroom and here." Robert pointed to the living room. "I'm just as shocked as you are, considering I don't have a contract for the job."

"How? It's not possible." The surprised look never left Elias' face. "He's not wasting any time on this."

"You mean Claude?" Robert seem puzzled. "When we first met, he told me 'Sweet Pea' had to be done privately, totally separate from the rest of the building contract. I know you people have your own cyber group and I wondered why I was chosen. He gave me a preliminary of his requirements, which I agreed to. This is not the way I do business but it's a lucrative contract. Anyhow, you're looking at the test monkey." He directed the man's eyes to the ornate molding between the ceiling and upper wall. "It's a new concept."

"The technology of a voice activated camera isn't new. I've seen the operation before, but I want to see your test." Elias followed Robert upstairs to the master bedroom and watched him take a small computer from his nightstand and open an encrypted page of letters, numbers and symbols.

"The technology may not be new but 'Sweet Pea' certainly is," Robert answered. "Think of it, a voice activated camera the size of a tiny pea with a protective shield. Not even a sweeper can find it. Think concealment, as you watch the computer," he directed, tapping in a complex code. Immediately, a picture of them appeared on screen. "Where's the camera?" he heard his own voice ask, and then began to express his thoughts. "Although 'Sweet pea's' in my house, I do have questions concerning the operation. How is Claude monitoring me? I know he is. But from where? Satellite? Sound waves? What?" He tapped a code to blank the screen before returning the computer to the nightstand. "I can't wait until this is over and I have some privacy."

"You're installing 'Sweet Pea' yourself?"

"Don't be naïve. Claude and I will have one or two Sundays together when the new building's empty." Robert paused before continuing the original thread of his narrative. "When we met again, he gave me three things: a computer, a complex code and a cylinder of three 'peas' to install in my house. They had to be in some innocuous place: one that captured the room, the conversation and the protected surface passed by a sweeper." Robert studied his friend. "I don't know when he checked the installation, but he did break into my house. He left a coded message on my counter saying I passed. I think I have you to thank for recommending me; however, I don't think Claude's his real name."

"What makes you think that?"

"Instinct and a monogrammed briefcase sitting under a table with the initials PM. Of course, he may have wanted to confuse me further, thinking I would notice it."

"Which of course, you did."

"It doesn't matter really. After my crew finishes installing the security system, Claude and I will connect 'Sweet Pea' while the building's empty, and then, he can format a code of his own. We'll be done. That's how it was left. No need for further contact. Now, smart guy, where is 'Sweet Pea?'"

Elias continued to swirl the scotch in his glass as he scoured the room for some overlooked detail that would fit 'Sweet Pea's' parameters...a camera, the size of a pea, one that was voice activated and embedded somewhere so obscure and so shielded that no sweeper could find it.

"I give up," he said. "That's why you got the contract."

"Just how dumb do you think I am?" Robert groused.

"Meaning?"

"You've got your own cyber group, along with a bunch of sophisticated hackers. So why hire me privately? We both know the answer."

"Don't even think it."

"I don't care about distrusting each other. I want something in writing."

"You will get it. Now show me."

Once again, Robert pointed to the ornate crown molding and showed him a specific area that captured the entire view of the room. "Look up."

"I don't see anything," Elias said, his eyes fixed on the molding.

"You're not supposed to. That's the beauty of it."

"It's in the bathroom too?"

"Different spot, but yes, a total view." Robert began to laugh. "Claude may catch me in the shower but I use the pot in the other bathroom. I guess I'll have to make love in the dark, if that ever happens again."

The remark caused Elias to snicker. "You're always thinking. That's why you get the big bucks." Then eyeing a particular spot in the bedroom, added, "My plant looks great in the alcove. I'm surprised you still have it."

"Why would I ever get rid of something so thorny and horny?"

Elias never answered his friend. Instead, he walked down the stairs quietly and out of the house, taking his glass of scotch with him, a signature routine. Elias Juniper was not one to leave fingerprints behind. This habit was never discussed. Robert just bought scotch glasses by the dozen.

Robert never heard the start of Elias' car as he watched a burning scrap of paper turn to ash. His thoughts were elsewhere…on something Claude once mentioned in passing…a dot the size of a pore with far range portability…a project not talked about openly, but with endless possibilities. Then his thoughts took another turn. There would be no contract… nothing written…no trace. Was 'Sweet Pea' Robert's test for what was to come, if anything?

Chapter 6
Pancake Breakfast

The following Sunday Robert Blake raced around the kitchen preparing a special pancake breakfast for his daughter. They had connected shortly after he returned from Italy, and he could not contain his excitement over spending several hours with Mackenzie, now that her finals were over.

As he gathered dishes and napkins for the table, he thought of his mother's teaching of fork and knife placement. "Pretend you're cutting a steak," she would remind him. As he followed her placement instructions he thought of their conversation when he showed her the bracelet.

"Mackenzie will be surprised," she said. "I think she's expecting money."

"I'll give her an envelope when we celebrate the actual day."

"Has she picked the restaurant?"

"Not yet. At least she hasn't told me, if she has. I thought I'd give her the bracelet now, so she could wear it, and the money on her birthday. I'm giving her this, too." He reached into his pocket for the plastic miniature of Palazzo Vecchio.

"This looks familiar." She examined it. "Emily had one of those."

"True. She got one on the Golden Bridge when I bought her a ring. I remember scratching her initials on the back of it. This one's a darker brown, I think." He took the miniature from his mother's outstretched hand.

"You scratched Mackenzie's," she said. "Why?"

"When I tell her our story, I want her to be a part of it."

"Where is Emily's?"

"The miniature?" He caught her nod. "I have no idea. I never looked for it."

"After all these years who knows where it landed." Catherine said with an air of finality. "I remember seeing it when she was sick."

His thoughts were brought up short when he heard the front door close.

"Hey," he heard Mackenzie's voice echo the front hall as she walked toward the kitchen. "Need some help?"

"You bet." He gave her a bowl and wooden spoon. "You can beat the batter while I get the fry pan ready."

***

After breakfast when the food had been eaten and dishes cleared, Robert sat with his daughter on the living room couch and held a small box in his hand.

"An early birthday gift," he said passing the box to her.

"It's so beautiful," she cooed. "I love it." She placed the bracelet on her wrist and eyed the golden bangle that glistened in the sunlight flooding the room.

He reached into his pocket and pulled out the miniature of Palazzo Vecchio. "This came with it. I scratched your initials on the back, just like I did with your mother's"

"Where is it?"

"What"

"The souvenir you gave mother."

"I have no idea what happened to it. That was three years ago."

"I know she carried it in a little cosmetic bag with her lipstick."

"She must have lost it," he shrugged. "I didn't find it when…"

"I'm sorry, dad." An expression of sadness crossed her face. "I didn't mean..."

"I know," he interrupted, "but this is our day together and I want us to be happy."

"I am happy." Mackenzie placed the box and miniature in her handbag. "I think I aced my finals and plan to attend the summer session. Not the whole nine weeks, just the main one in July and August."

"So you won't be helping in the office this summer"

"I didn't know you needed me."

"It's just that you always helped-out when school was over."

"That was high school."

"And your freshman year…last year. What's changed?"

"Nothing's changed," she bristled suddenly, her attitude becoming surly. "Why are you always questioning me? Why can't I have a life of my own?"

"I'm not trying to interfere or pry into your life," he snapped back. "But if I'm paying the bills, I have a right to know what's going on."

"Nothing's going on!" she vented loudly. "Get a life of your own and leave me alone, dammit. I'm tired of being questioned."

"Mackenzie, please," Robert begged. "I just want the best for you, as any parent would. As for getting a life, I wanted to talk to you about that. I met someone in Florence. I haven't called her yet, but if things work out, I want you to meet her."

"You went to Florence to remember my mother and you shacked-up with some trollop!" she shrieked suddenly, angered by the thought. "I'm sure mother would be thrilled to know that," she bristled again and stood to leave.

"Mackenzie, please. It wasn't like that."

"Like what? You go out of town on some pretense of loneliness and have someone else fill the gap? Nice try but it won't work. Are you planning to kill-off this one too?"

"What are you saying?"

"I don't have to spell it out. You could have done more. You could have saved my mother, but you didn't even try. You wanted her to die."

"That is not true!" He shouted, enraged by her outburst. "I loved your mother. I was heartbroken when we learned she was stage four. There was nothing the doctors could do for her." With all his years of facial practice, Robert found it hard to refrain from crying as he tried to explain.

"You could have taken her to Memorial Sloan Kettering," she challenged. "Instead you waited for her to die. Now that a respectable time has passed, you take a trip on some stupid pretense so you can screw around with impunity."

"I don't know where you're getting all this," he screamed, his years of practiced calm broken, "That is not true. I went to Italy because Emily loved Florence. It was her favorite city."

"And that's where the hunt began," she groused. "I know what really happened. I lived through it, remember? You really didn't care. You were more interested in the business, like you always are. You weren't concerned with her welfare as long as you were in the black. It was much more convenient if she were to die."

Shaken by her remarks, he said in defense, "You can't really believe that."

"You have no idea what I believe. You never cared to find out. You never made time for me or my mother. Well, you got your wish, but as far as I'm concerned, the wrong one went first." She grabbed her handbag and raced toward the front door, leaving her father to watch her exit in silence.

As Robert Blake sat glued to the sofa, the streaks of bright sunshine piercing the windowed room, directly contrasted the sad tears of a man whose heart had just been broken. How could the day have started with such a good account of Raine, a woman he cared for, and end with such hatred from Mackenzie? He had burned the report from Elias that morning. If only he could burn and bury those words his daughter had just spewed.

***

Hours later, a continuous ringing jarred his cramped body from the living room couch to his cell phone lying on the kitchen counter.

"Hello," he answered, hoping it was Mackenzie with an apology for her outburst, but heard his mother's voice instead.

"Robert? What's wrong? You sound strange."

"I must have dozed off. Has something happened?"

"I just wondered how it went with Mackenzie today. Did she like the bracelet?"

"She loved it."

"I'm glad you got a chance to talk."

"She's going to summer school."

"So, she won't be helping me," Catherine mused aloud. "Did she say why?"

"No, she didn't, but I think she wants a lighter course load next semester. Her courses will be harder this fall."

"I don't understand."

"Mackenzie thinks she aced her finals, so it's not a question of grades. She's thinking ahead."

"Well, it sounds like you had a good conversation."

"We certainly cleared a lot of things," he said not wanting to share the misery he felt.

"I'll see you tomorrow." Catherine ended their conversation.

Robert retraced his steps back to the couch and began recalling their conversation. He was telling his mother the truth about clearing the air on a lot of things. Only the clearing came from Mackenzie who made it abundantly clear on two levels: he could have done more to save her mother in spite of the prognosis; and, he was not there for them as a husband or father. Could this have been true? Did he not take care of his family? His thoughts shifted to an earlier time.

He remembered the picnics, the Christmas and birthday parties, the beach vacations and Mackenzie's school activities from kindergarten through high school graduation. They were always together until Emily's death, which left him alone to care for his daughter. His thoughts were never solely on his company; his mother took care of that. Catherine Scaliezzi not only had a head for business, she had street smarts. Little went by her. That fact relieved him from the office worries and gave him time for his family. If truth be told his mother encouraged him to attend those school and family functions. So where was Mackenzie getting this from? Had he said something to trigger her emotions, things she really felt, deep down in her heart? But considering the things and activities they shared over the years, how could she arrive at such a conclusion? She made her father out to be a pariah, a man of no consequence in his role of husband and father. No matter how hurting Mackenzie's words were, they were in fact, untrue. In this instance facts did not matter: it was what Mackenzie believed. In her mind, the words she uttered in rage were his shortcomings and failures. And he realized then, that regardless of any healing that would take place, if any, these were the true feelings of his daughter. This is what she believed. He was a failure to her and her mother. Nothing could ever erase that.

"I know where I stand," he said aloud. "I just don't know why my rating dropped to a sudden low."

Robert walked slowly up the stairs and down the hall to his bedroom. He was badly shaken by the conversation with Mackenzie and had to lie down. But he knew sleep would not come easily.

***

Miles away, Catherine had her own thoughts about the conversation she had with her son.

She had made it a directive never to interfere with Robert and Emily when the woman was alive and she did the same with Mackenzie after her mother's death. The best thing she could do for all of them was be available when needed and invisible, when not. So with that directive, Catherine now found herself in a pickle.

Robbie told her to take care of Mackenzie when he left for Italy. Since she was busy with his security company and all the shenanigans that went on, Catherine asked her brother for help with Mackenzie. She never thought he would actually check on her. Yet, she was glad he did. Since Mackenzie was not at the library studying, and she had not been in her apartment, according to the girl across the hall, where had she been? Where did she spend her days and were these omissions, ones of many? Catherine was worried. She couldn't tell her son about his daughter's philandering. Maybe a psychiatrist would think it was the right thing to do. But what if it amounted to nothing? What if she wasn't partying or using drugs. Maybe she spent the afternoons with some classmate studying for an exam. Robbie said Mackenzie thought she aced the finals. Why would her granddaughter make that statement if it wasn't true? Grades could be checked too easily. Something was going on, but what? She would know soon enough. Stefano was not one to let anything drop. Her bloodhound brother had picked up a scent of lies and nothing could deter him from learning the truth of Mackenzie's deceit.

Still, Catherine worried about her son. If this thing with Mackenzie were cleared, she would feel a lot better about Robbie meeting Lorraine Shaw. He needed someone in his life, someone important, without having to worry about a lying daughter.

Her thoughts continued to churn as she made her way to the bedroom. Sleep wouldn't come easy that night. There were too many questions with no plausible answers.

Chapter 7
Expansion

"You look awful," Catherine greeted him the next morning.

"I need a haircut," he answered, using his appearance as an excuse to avoid the daily update. "I'll get one after work," he said walking into his office.

Catherine watched her son and knew immediately something was terribly wrong. But she also knew to hold her tongue. This was not the time to question him. Whatever was wrong had to concern Mackenzie or Lorraine Shaw because security requests were increasing at a steady pace, and there were times they had more business than they could handle. She wasn't aware of anything else in her son's life, but then, he didn't share much with her these days. He only revealed things she needed to know. Of that she was certain. However, her thoughts were suddenly interrupted by John Harris' voice.

"Did I just hear Robert come in? I thought he might be up for a round of golf this weekend."

Catherine nodded, acknowledging his question, and watched him enter her son's office. Now alone in the outer room, she took advantage of the opportunity and made a phone call.

"Stop by after work." She left a message.

***

"You still having problems with the disposal?" Steve greeted his sister later that day.

"My problem's with Robbie. Something's wrong. I can feel it." With that statement, Catherine proceeded to tell him of Robbie's suspicions about meeting Lorraine Shaw in Florence and his pancake breakfast with Mackenzie.

"Let me get this straight. A lady named Valerie became injured and couldn't make the trip with her co-worker, Lorraine Shaw. Then on the phone with Valerie, Lorraine said that she was getting fat. That was probably a reference to the food she was eating."

"No. Robbie insists he heard "fatto." He also questions the proximity. She lives in Penn Hills."

"He's either getting too old to risk a date or been in security too long."

"You think he should call her."

"Doesn't matter what we think. He'll do what he wants. It's none of our business."

"What about Mackenzie?"

"That spoiled brat is something else. After our last conversation, I went back to her apartment. The girl across the hall refused to talk to me at first. I guess she and Mackenzie exchanged a few words. I told her I was the uncle and wanted to take Mackenzie to lunch for her upcoming birthday. Naturally, I apologized first."

"What did you learn? What did she tell you?" Catherine became excited. She was finally going to get the goods on her granddaughter.

"She didn't say much really. Mackenzie was always armed with books when she went to class. But she made it clear her world didn't revolve around Mackenzie's schedule. The girl wasn't sure about visitors. She works nights at some watering hole in Shadyside."

"We're back where we started."

"No. We are not," he corrected her. "Robbie's back. She's his responsibility now, not ours."

"True, but I'm still worried."

"Worry about it when she flunks out of school."

"She told Robbie she aced her finals."

"Then she must be doing drugs."

"That's not very comforting."

"Would you rather I lie?"

"I just wish it was something we overlooked."

"We'll know soon enough." He kissed his sister's forehead and left the house.

Catherine watched her brother edge his truck out of the driveway, then turn and disappear. What had their meeting accomplished? Absolutely nothing. No. A voice corrected her thoughts. Now, Steve knows the history of Robbie's meeting Lorraine Shaw and his suspicions about it. As for Mackenzie, her brother was right. If something was going on, the family would know soon enough.

While Catherine thought about the conversation that had just taken place, Steve reflected a few ideas of his own. If his nephew was afraid of taking a chance by dating this woman, he could be making a real mistake. If the relationship didn't work out, so what? If it did, he wouldn't be alone anymore. At long last, there would be someone in his life; someone important to him, someone who loved him. It was time he faced the facts of life. He certainly couldn't rely on being with Mackenzie forever. Whatever was going on in her life now was fleeting. At some point, she would meet someone with marriage in mind and make a life of her own. Where would Robert be then? It would be better if he took the plunge now and called the woman for a date. It was time he moved on. Emily was dead. He should take advantage of the chance meeting as an opportunity for a possible relationship.

Steve pulled into the garage of his house and sat still for a moment. Dorothy would start talking the minute he entered and continue chatting until he turned away from her in bed. An imaginary picture of his wife flooded his thoughts.

Maybe Robbie had it right after all.

***

The ringing sound of the doorbell shook Catherine out of her reverie.

"Hello." Robert greeted his mother. "I thought you'd expect me when I left work early."

"I wasn't sure."

"Sure, you were. You haven't cooked anything."

"Steve just left," she said casually, never alluding to the fact that it was at her invitation he stop by.

"Something wrong?"

"He wanted to check the disposal again. He had to repair it when you were away."

Satisfied with her explanation, he asked, "You hungry?"

"Starved. Where are we eating?"

"I thought McManns." It was a restaurant they both liked.

"That works. By the way, I like the haircut. Andy did a nice job."

"Hope Raine likes it. I'm seeing her Saturday night. She'll be home by then." Robert began to laugh. "Must be ESP. She called me from Italy."

"You sly dog!" Catherine laughed and locked the front door of her house.

Robert chuckled at the comment as he walked her to the car. "I want to discuss something more important than a date that might not work out. You heard John mention golf this weekend, didn't you?"

"So?" Catherine said, confused by his concern as she entered the car. They had often golfed together.

"He asked Henry Price to join us." He started the car quickly, drove down the street, and then turned onto a boulevard toward the restaurant.

"And you think the purpose of the outing is to see if you're selling, or thinking about it."

"It's not gonna happen." He pulled into a parking space behind the restaurant. "I asked Bruce to join us."

"From Parks Limited?"

"He's the one who started all this and now I'm going to end it."

"What will you tell them? It has to be believable."

"It will be. I plan to expand the company."

"Oh, my God." She sat in shock. "You got the contract."

"We keep this to ourselves, until I get a firm start date. As you know, it's been in progress for months and has a six figure payout. No more questions."

"You aren't telling them about this."

"No. Just you. I'm telling them I'm hiring more people. Isn't that called expanding?"

"Hiring more people is going to make John nervous."

"That's not my intention."

"Really? So this whole display of strategy is just being done to impress me?" she groused. "I don't think so. This is your way of letting them know you're in for the long haul. That's what this is."

"I don't want to talk about this inside," he cautioned.

"I think we can come up with something safer to talk about." She watched him walk to the passenger's side of the car and thought once again about Lorraine Shaw.

How did she get her son's phone number? Did her coworker, Valerie, check it for her? Robbie never mentioned giving it to her. Had that thought occurred to him or was he too far gone with the woman? There were a lot of things he neglected to mention these days and it was better not to raise any questions. Catherine kept these thoughts to herself as she walked into the restaurant with her son.

Chapter 8
Snow Job

As Robert Blake dressed for his date with Raine Shaw Saturday evening, a number of thoughts crossed his mind.

Neither John Harris nor Henry Price from Global expressed shock when Bruce from Parks Limited appeared at the golf course with him that morning. The gathering looked like a scheduled meeting of companies discussing a merger. But, of course, that assumption was false. His sole intention was to clear the air of rumors, not join hands with one of the other companies. He wanted to make it abundantly clear that Blake Enterprises was not for sale or even considering a merger.

The game ran smoothly on all eighteen holes. The four men were totally competitive, although all missed one shot or another. But it wasn't until later when they sat in the café that the conversation took a turn. As predicted, John steered the dialogue in his roundabout way to glean information. He used the opportunity for a quasi-inquisition. Of course, no one, other than Robert, knew his skilled way of dropping comments so questions would follow.

"I was glad we could get out today," John started. "It's been so busy at work, I needed a few hours of relaxation."

"I think we all feel that way," Henry Price replied in agreement, catching a nod from Bruce Parks. "What about you? How do you feel about needing to relax?" Henry directed the question to him.

"I just got back from vacation so I feel well rested," Robert answered casually. "But I am thinking of making a change."

"What change?" Henry's ears perked, hoping for the response he wanted to hear.

"John already told you how busy we are. I'm thinking of taking on more personnel rather than open a branch for our services."

"Good for you," Bruce chimed in. "You mentioned something like that on the way here." His statement, of course, was a lie.

Although the announcement had a quieting effect momentarily, it changed the direction of the conversation and they parted shortly afterward. Robert laughed aloud. Bruce was so funny on the way home.

He said, "You played them like a fine-tuned guitar. I should thank you for it. I didn't know Henry wanted your company, but then I didn't know about John either."

"What's wrong with Harris?" He remembered asking.

"The two of them are glued to the hip. He could go with Henry if you're not careful. There could be an offer in the making."

"You mean leave my company?"

"Doesn't that bother you? He's your right-hand man. He's been with you for years."

"I can't fault him for wanting to better himself. It happens all the time."

"That would piss me off. You've been good to him," Bruce said thinking of the support John was given during his divorce and throughout his career with Robert's company. When they drove into the driveway of his home, he added, "You are one strange duck."

Robert remembered sliding down the window with an even stranger reply. "It's a matter of whom you quack with that counts."

At that point Bruce threw-up his arms and shook his head as he walked into his house.

Bruce would never understand the meaning of Robert's comment. Nor would he understand the real object behind the golf game façade. The café conversation reminded him of a chess game, where one tries to outwit the other to determine the opponent's next move. To Bruce, it was a matter of putting a rumor to rest. So when the prospect of selling his business came up, he felt Robert quieted those wagging tongues completely. However, there was more to the meeting that was not obvious to Bruce…a veiled friendship hiding betrayal: one that was not warranted nor understood.

Outwardly the whole idea of the golf outing was to determine Robert's intention. He thought he had made it clear to everyone. His business was not for sale. Nor was he interested in a merger. So why couldn't he shake-off the undercurrent that permeated their conversation? He knew the answer but found it hard to accept.

"They think I'm lying. But why would they think that?"

He looked in the mirror at his face of practiced calm, and said aloud, "One reason only. They think there's another player in the bidding war…thanks to the observation of my right hand man and veiled friend."

The remark caused him to laugh when he thought of the strange looking man who visited his office recently. As he recalled John was standing in his office doorway when Robert ushered the visitor into his office. Who would have thought Elias Juniper would pose such a threat? Robert began to laugh again when his eyes inadvertently fell on a framed picture of Mackenzie.

He grasped the photograph sitting on his dresser and thought of their estranged relationship. For years, they had been so close, done so many things together. Why the sudden change? Had it been coming and he failed to see it? Where had he gone wrong? Robert didn't know her anymore. His daughter no longer loved him. That was obvious. Mackenzie wanted him dead, and it didn't take an interpreter to understand her message when she said, "The wrong one went first."

Her angry outburst brought tears to his eyes and he could feel the growing tightness in his throat. He closed his eyes, swallowed hard, and then took a few deep breaths to regain his composure. This was not the right time to think about his daughter. Whatever changed her opinion of him would be uncovered soon enough. He would use every resource available and all the tools of his trade to determine her sudden change in attitude. He might not be able to re-establish the relationship they once had, but he sure as hell was going to find out why it happened.

He checked his appearance in the closet door mirror, then sailed down the stairs and out to his car on the driveway. He pulled the directions Raine had given him from his pocket and read them over again. They were as specific as MapQuest from his computer.

He drove down a highway filled with stop and go traffic and within twenty-five minutes turned behind a small plaza onto a private road that led to three tall apartment buildings. He drove toward the last of the three and, passing the large lot reserved for that particular building, parked in a small solitary area near a back door. Almost immediately, Raine stood facing him in the open doorway.

"I see you made it."

"Your directions were great." He studied the beautiful woman greeting him, and then followed her into an elevator and down the hall to apartment 216. "Am I mistaken or did you have room 316 in Florence?" he asked, and then noticing the decor of the unit, added, "This is quite nice."

Although familiar with the floor plan, Robert felt the apartment as a whole, particularly the fire-placed living room, was quite large and roomy. And he chalked it up to the age of the building. Years of apartment living reminded him of that. Older apartment buildings usually offered bigger units. Of course, the amenities were more dated, but that mattered little to tenants looking for more space.

"How many bedrooms do you have?"

"It's listed as two but the second is miniscule. I use it as my office." She led him down a short hall. "That's the lav." She pointed to a closed door. "This is what I mean."

"You're right. It is small." He scanned the second bedroom before moving on. "Wow!" He commented on the size and decor of her bedroom. "This is a surprise."

"I'm glad you like it."

"Actually, it's a great apartment," he said and then checked his watch. "We should go."

"You never told me where we were going for dinner." She followed him out of the apartment to his car.

"That's because I wanted to surprise you." He closed the passenger door.

Robert drove away from the apartment complex onto the same busy highway but turned in a different direction. Within minutes he exited the highway onto a long winding road that circled the side of a mountain. Within a few miles, he turned onto a narrow private lane that became level at the top. There before them sat a pillared structure with a long overhead canopy that protected waiting diners from the elements.

A valet greeted them immediately, opening the passenger door for Raine after taking Robert's car keys.

"This looks nice," she said as Robert ushered her inside.

Within minutes they were seated near a bank of windows overlooking Allegheny valley.

"This is beautiful." She studied the view. "Why didn't I know about this place?"

"If you were a food critic, you probably would have." He laughed at the remark, causing her to join him.

"So you're saying the food is good."

"It's wonderful." He took the menu one waiter offered, watched another fill their water glasses and then disappear. "I've never had a bad meal. Everything is good here."

After placing their dinner orders, Robert broached the subject foremost on his mind. Elias Juniper's report may have found the woman completely innocent and credible, but he couldn't get her use of "fatto" out of his thoughts.

"I know you told me you went to Florence alone because your friend broke her ankle. That I understand. But you never told me what made you stay in Pittsburgh after your relationship ended. How long ago was that?"

When her eyes met his, Robert knew from her facial expression that he had hit an explosive button. "I really don't want to talk about it." She dismissed the question abruptly. "I'm on track now and that's more important."

"But why did you stay here?" He continued to press. "Why not go back home?"

"I became a successful realtor and made a comfortable living. I may not be wealthy, but I do fine. Living here is a lot cheaper than Los Angeles," she offered before switching to another thought. "I think I mentioned not being close to my father's second wife."

"You did. I forgot," he lied. It was important her second rehash matched their first conversation.

"What about you?" She turned on him quickly.

"I run a small business installing security systems. I think I told you my wife died three years ago and that I have a daughter in college." He wanted to steer the conversation away from his company. This was not the time to talk about business. He wanted to know more about her on a personal level.

"You mentioned that in Florence but never told me if you were seeing someone," she blurted suddenly. "I'm sorry I said that," she quickly apologized. "It's none of my business."

"Are you?"

"No."

"Do you like theater?"

"Very much."

"Maybe we can do something about that."

***

Later that evening as he stood at the door of her apartment, he reminded her of their next date to the theater and leaned down to kiss her goodnight.

"I had a wonderful time." A broad smile crossed his face.

"Let's make it perfect." She brushed his lips and slowly drew him into the apartment.

Chapter 9
Birthday Party

Robert Blake had never been happier in the weeks that followed. Raine had changed his life completely. She brought him the love and tenderness he so sorely missed after Emily's demise. And in those quiet moments, when he recalled their conversations before her impending death, he knew she would approve of his finding another soul mate. Emily had made that abundantly clear as she lay dying. She did not want him to spend his life alone. In her wisdom, Emily reminded him of the rule of life. Mackenzie would leave him one day to make a life for herself, alone or with another.

Had that time come to pass already? Had Mackenzie found someone else? She gave no indication of that during their Sunday breakfast. What she gave instead was a complete venting of her true feelings. There had been no communication between them since. No phone calls or texts. Of course, that would come to an end. Their meeting was inevitable. She had selected a restaurant for her birthday dinner according to his mother, and Robert decided to have Raine accompany him to meet the entire family.

He was certain his Uncle Steve and Aunt Dorothy would have a lot to say afterward. His mother, on the other hand, would offer nothing, unless asked. Even then, his mother would say little that really mattered. She had refused to interfere in his marital relationship with Emily and she would extend this same philosophy with Raine. The woman was smart. She knew his feelings for Raine ran deep. He wouldn't be taking her to meet the family if they weren't.

These thoughts crossed his mind as he drove to work that Monday morning.

"Before asking if there are any calls, Mackenzie wants you to phone her this morning." Catherine told him as soon as he entered the office. "She probably wants to talk about Saturday's dinner."

"No message?"

"She didn't leave one. Is there a problem?" she asked unaware of the estrangement between them.

"No. She probably needs a check for school," he said casually before closing the door of his office.

Within minutes he spoke slowly and carefully to a daughter who hated her father and wanted him dead.

"I'm sorry, dad," she began. "I've been thinking about our pancake breakfast and I was out of line, saying all those mean things."

"It hurt. Your words…"

"I know and I'm sorry," she interrupted. "I was thinking of mother, I guess. But you do need someone in your life. You're still young. Nonna said that you're bringing someone to my birthday party on Saturday."

"I want the family to meet her and thought the party would be a good time."

"I'm glad. I think you should. I'll see you at seven then."

He listened to her end the conversation and wondered what caused such an epiphany. He wasn't certain he believed his daughter. This was not like her; this was not the temperament of the girl he knew during her formative years. She was never a light bulb of feelings: one she would turn on or off. No. Mackenzie was an unforgiving person. She always had been. Resentment ran deep within her, like the scar over a wound that never healed.

When it came right down to the conversation between them, Robert felt Mackenzie was not forthright about Raine coming to her party. Although her words expressed happiness for him, he felt her disapproval in the tenor of her voice. She was not happy about it but could not exclude her father's date. That thought prompted something else he gleaned from talking with her.

He remembered Mackenzie spewing her hatred of him when he first mentioned meeting someone in Florence. That brought on the venting about his lack of care for Emily. Should he have told his daughter the truth?

When Emily fell ill, Robert did take her to Memorial Sloan Kettering, after many consultations with their family doctor, but they hid the trip as a New York vacation to see Broadway shows. That no one was to know its real importance was Emily's wish, particularly when nothing more could be done. She was given a life sentence in weeks, not months or years. Since the holidays were fast approaching, she wanted a last celebration with the family before surrendering to the fast ravages of pancreatic cancer. It was then that Emily extracted his promise to marry again, if he found another soul mate, one who was loving and true to him.

Tears clouded his eyes as he remembered their last moments together. They knew the end was near as she lay on the living room sofa crouched beneath a coverlet.

"Remember your promise," she whispered. Her breathing was so labored; her voice, so weak.

"I remember." He recalled sitting on a nearby chair, holding her hand when he answered.

He had been gone only a few minutes…those precious few minutes…but it was too late.

For years he lived this memory with regret: he was too late to say those precious words to the woman he cherished. Words that should have been said years earlier…many times over.

Maybe Mackenzie was right: maybe the wrong one did die after all.

Robert wiped the tears from his eyes and abruptly left the office, leaving his mother to wonder where her son was going.

***

Where he was going was nobody's damn business. Only he and the park bench at Boyce Park knew the history of his sorrows.

***

The dinner on Saturday went better than Robert expected. The introductions went smoothly, the conversation flowed evenly and the meal seemed to please everyone. Toward the end of the evening, however, his uncle Steve made a comment that embarrassed both of them.

"You told us how you met in Florence but never said how grateful you were to your friend for not showing up."

"What do you mean?" Raine turned abruptly sounding somewhat cross.

"Only that you and Robbie may not have met if she were with you."

"Oh." Raine laughed, catching his meaning. "That's probably very true."

"But that's life," Steve answered. Although his eyes met hers directly, his peripheral vision watched the waiter take Robbie's money for the meal. "Things have a habit of working out. Shall we go?"

After exchanging pleasantries, Mackenzie cornered her father about his generous birthday check and her glowing approval of Raine.

"She obviously cares about you," she said. "You can see it in her eyes…the way she looks at you."

"So what do you think?"

"She's a keeper." With that response Mackenzie kissed her father's cheek, approached the rest of the group with a few more niceties and went to her car.

After a few more brief exchanges, Steve ushered Dorothy and Catherine out of the restaurant.

"Your Aunt Dorothy talks a lot, doesn't she?" Raine questioned as they approached Robert's car.

"You have no idea, but we're used to it." He saw her safely inside the vehicle.

"They make a good pair."

"Think so?"

"Definitely. She babbles; he questions."

Robert remained silent but thought her comment rather cruel. Yes. His Aunt Dorothy did talk a lot. In fact, there were times she would drone on and on. There was no stopping her, short of leaving the room. But that was Aunt Dorothy and the family accepted her like a faucet of running water. But the comment about his Uncle seemed unfounded. To his recollection, Uncle Steve never asked one question the entire evening. So what part of his conversation was so unnerving to her? Was it the comment about Valerie and their meeting?

"Where are we going?" She watched him turn in the opposite direction of her apartment.

"You met my family tonight, so I thought you should meet my house."

"You're taking me to your place?"

"That's the plan."

"What else do you have planned?" she asked slyly, glancing at him.

"The plan is very open-ended."

"I like having you as my architect." She slid her hand up his thigh.

"Any higher, and I'm going to hard pencil you on the back seat of this car." He moved her hand away and continued driving in silence.

"Within minutes, Robert pulled into the driveway of his house and, taking Raine inside, began kissing her delicate, soft skin as he led her to the bedroom and slowly removed all of her clothing and jewelry...in the dark. However, he pocketed her one ring...the one Raine thought she lost.

***

When Robert walked into the office Monday morning, he found his mother taking a telephone message.

"We need to talk," he said when the phone conversation ended.

"At the house?"

"I'll be over around seven. Don't make dinner."

"I have left-over spaghetti."

"That sounds good," he answered taking the morning mail from her desk. She watched him close the door of his office, realizing then and there, that her son was in the process of making a decision that would change the course of their lives, his and hers.

Something strange began growing deep inside her, a foreboding of sorts. Catherine sensed she was going to be reliving a past that ended badly. Why would she think that? She didn't know what Robbie was thinking. That's not true, she re-thought the statement. Whatever it was, it had to do with Raine. She felt sure of this. He wanted her approval.

Still, how could she approve of someone she had met just two days earlier? And why the rush? Suddenly she sat frozen in her chair. A frightening thought came over her. Robbie was repeating his life with Emily all over again. The hasty marriage, their struggles and life together. They were young and in love. They couldn't wait. But repeating this all over again left a bad taste in her mouth. She didn't dislike Raine: she didn't know her well enough to have feelings one way or the other. Yet somehow, she felt a sense of distrust but could not explain why. Maybe she was too beautiful, too perfect and too elegant to suit her. Still, didn't Robbie deserve someone attractive and glamorous? Yes, he did. But not her. She didn't fit in.

If Robbie wanted to talk about marrying this woman there was nothing she could do. Catherine would listen and offer little. Otherwise, she'd sound like some jealous harridan that refused to allow her son to re-cut the apron string. And Catherine couldn't say, "Something's not right." She had no justification for that, no ammunition. It was all in her head…her mind was working overtime. No. It was best she sit patiently and listen to him verbalize his thoughts.

***

"Something smells good." Robbie kissed his mother's cheek.

"Garlic bread?" He watched her butter thick slices of French bread with her own private mixture of butter, oil and garlic.

"Goes good with spaghetti." He watched her pop the tray into the oven and immediately questioned her when she turned toward him.

"Why don't you like her?" His demanding tone surprised her.

"Where did you get that idea? I don't know Raine well enough to have feelings one way or the other. She's very beautiful. I'll give her that." She took the tray from oven and began setting the table with serving dishes of spaghetti, garlic bread and a toss salad that rested on another counter.

"You didn't go out of your way to speak with her at the restaurant," he said, sitting across from her at the kitchen table.

"Either you're being funny or you lost your marbles." She met his stare. "No one gets the floor when Aunt Dorothy's around. Are you that far gone not to remember how our family works? I couldn't speak to my granddaughter let alone converse with a stranger. What's the matter with you?"

"So that's why Raine made the statement."

"What statement?" Catherine demanded.

"She said that Aunt Dorothy talks a lot."

"Well, amen to that. At least she picked–up on something we're all accustomed to. Nobody in the family questions it. When Aunt Dorothy's around, nobody even bothers to have a conversation. We just sit and listen, whether we're interested or not."

"Then you like her?"

"I don't know her, Robbie. Raine made a wonderful impression and she's beautiful. What more do you want? Why is my opinion so important?"

"I was hoping you talked to the family over the weekend."

"No. I haven't spoken with Steve since Saturday night." Catherine sopped the remaining sauce in her plate with a remnant of garlic bread. She watched Robbie follow suit and smiled inwardly. Raine, miss petite fingers, would probably look at his actions with disgust.

"But you think he likes her?"

"Ok. Enough of this happy horseshit. What's going on? Are you getting serious?"

"Enough to marry her."

Catherine had steeled herself for this particular moment and remained composed. "And you want our blessing." Although she smiled as she spoke, her body churned inside with disdain and suspicion.

"I want you to be happy for me…for us."

"Have you asked her to marry you?"

"Not yet. We're almost into July, and since our project starts in August, I thought September would be a good month for the wedding. We could get away for a honeymoon. What do you think?"

"It works on the calendar. What are you planning?" she asked but soon realized her question could not be answered.

"That would be up to Raine. I don't think she wants something big. I don't know why I said that," he spoke aloud. "She's never been married and may want a big affair."

He studied his mother and remained silent momentarily. Something was wrong. He could see it in the coldness of her eyes and the vapid expression on her face. He knew her too well. He could see what others did not. The lessons he mastered from her teachings now caused him to read her like a book. He knew her feelings about the woman he hoped to marry, but couldn't determine her reason for them. Until his mother revealed her true feelings about Raine and why she felt such disdain, their conversation could go nowhere.

"Mom, be happy for me. I love this woman." He pleaded with her.

"I've always wanted the best for you. If this is the woman you cherish, I would never stand in your way. It just seems so fast."

"It is fast. I wanted to talk with you first, before I tell Mackenzie."

"How about Raine? How do you know she wants to get married?"

"She loves me. Of that I am sure."

"And the fall wedding?"

"Oh. That's the other thing." His thoughts changed direction. "I met someone interested in a job. He's single and free to travel if necessary. I'll have John interview him before we make a decision to hire."

"Is this part of your expansion plan?" She caught his nod. "I like it, particularly if he's willing to travel. How far along are you with the new contract?"

"I'll have all the particulars next week." He stood up from the table and began taking the dishes to the sink.

"Leave it. There's not much here."

After he kissed her goodbye, Catherine heard the sound of his car edging out of her driveway. Going through the motions of clean-up exacerbated her thoughts of Robbie with Raine. Why did she have these feelings about the woman? Was it because she would no longer have Robbie to herself, particularly after Emily died? No. That was not true. Although she loved Emily, a woman of total perfection, Catherine never considered taking her place. After her mother's death, Mackenzie stepped in and went everywhere with her father. They would celebrate the holidays with the family, but for the most part, Catherine usually saw Robbie at work.

Still, she knew in her heart this marriage was not right, but didn't know why.

Chapter 10
Elias

When Robert returned home, he was joined by his old friend, Elias Juniper shortly afterward.

"How long have you been waiting?" He asked his friend.

"About twenty minutes. I didn't want to sit in the living room, just in case you came home with company." He walked to the bar and poured several fingers of scotch in two glasses.

"You mean Raine?" Robert clinked Elias' glass which also held a solitary ice cube.

"Or Mackenzie. I assume she still has a key to the house."

"She does," he nodded, "although she seldom visits anymore."

"That sounds ominous since you two were glued to the hip after Emily…"

"That's changed since last year. She's taking some tough courses and stays in the city. An apartment in Shadyside," he reminded his friend.

"And you believe the bullshit she's feeding you?"

"What do you mean?" He defended his daughter, his tone somewhat harsh.

"We've both been there, done that. Mackenzie could pop in for an hour on any Sunday if she wanted to. No. She's young and into other things. Face it. You're not as exciting as her peer group. Remember our college days?"

"That's probably true. This is the best time of her life."

"Let it alone. After a few battle scars, they all come home eventually. You'll be a hero."

"I just had her meet Raine over the weekend...her birthday dinner Saturday night. I think Mackenzie liked her but I'm a little worried."

"Because you're thinking of marrying this woman."

"I need to talk with her about it. I'm waiting for her to get back to me. I left a message."

"And when are the nuptials taking place?"

"I'm hoping September."

"Hoping?"

"I haven't asked Raine yet. I wanted to talk with Mackenzie first," he repeated before catching his friend's outburst of laughter.

"You'll never change. The kid's going off on her own someday, so you better realize that. You'll be all alone, unless you do something about it. That's how it is." Elias ended his sermon on life to ask the determining question. "So if Mackenzie disapproves, are you going to end your relationship with the woman?"

"No. But I won't get married."

"That may work out better. It sure as hell would be cheaper."

"I don't want that. I love this woman. I want to grow old with her."

"Then you'll have to work it out with Mackenzie. If they seemed to like each other when they met, she'll probably give her blessing."

"That's what I'm hoping," he said, then changed the subject. "Why are you here?"

"Just learned I'm going to be around for a while and wanted you to have my new phone number. Contact me the same way."

"What else? That's not the real reason you're here." He watched his friend refill their glasses.

"Here's to you." He clinked their glasses. "The contract will be in your hands on Friday."

"And the money?"

"In thirds. Take it and don't fuss. There may be something else in the wind. Probably next year, if everything works out."

"How do you know all this?"

"I'm not married, remember? But I am good at listening to pil-low-talk."

"I'm so relieved," he sighed. "I wish there were something I could do for you."

"There is. Don't invite me to the wedding. I'd like our relationship to remain between us." He said, swirling his glass of scotch. "Address yourself as Nix when you call and hang up."

"If that happens, it'll be a matter of life or death," he replied ignoring the bearded man's life of intrigue. "But you're in trouble. I can see it in your eyes." He studied the gaunt face of his friend and became silent, knowing he would never be privy to the man's activities. "I'm here, old tree," he said quietly, a reference to Elias Juniper in college that meant, 'You can count on me.'"

"I haven't listed your name anywhere. It's better that way in case my phone gets lost."

"I don't buy that."

"Like I really care." He patted Robert's shoulder and left the house, scotch glass in hand.

Robert remained seated on the couch and listened quietly for the start of Elias' car, but it never came. Where had the man parked? This was the second time Robert waited for a sound that never came. Then again, why should he care? Elias Juniper was like a wind that controlled its own whistle. He was: then, he wasn't.

***

Robert checked his watch and then his cell phone. Mackenzie would not be calling that evening. It was too late. She was either in bed or, if Elias was right, out partying with her friends. He would wait another day before calling her again. Maybe he would text her instead. He could do both. Call first, then text.

"You sound like a nervous father who is fearful of making a mistake," he said aloud. "No. I am only fearful of hurting a daughter who hates me," Robert corrected.

Knowing there was very little that could be done that night, he emptied his glass of scotch, took the stairs to his room and undressed for bed. His thoughts began churning in a different direction. It mattered little what Elias said about his assignment. The fact that he was in town for a while meant only one thing: something big was coming down. How did it affect Robert? It didn't really. Elias wanted him to have the information. But why? Then he began to smile, thinking how unnecessary it was to mention their college code. Elias knew he could always crash at Robert's house if necessary. He was just alerting Robert beforehand...but in his uniquely coded way. Was that the reason Elias questioned the month of the wedding? So he could crash before it took place, if necessary? He was so casual with his conversational questions. So disarming and charming. But that's who he was…a seasoned spook who could disarm and charm.

***

The next morning Robert called John Harris into his office for a short meeting.

"I looked over the stats," he addressed his handsome assistant. "You've done a great job placing the men and equipment servicing our contracts."

"Is something big coming in right now?" he asked, a puzzled look crossing his face. "I'm assuming there is."

"Why do you say that?" Robert asked openly, fearing a possible leak of information.

"When we played golf you mentioned expanding."

"So, I did." He took an envelope from his desk. "I met this man in line at Best Coffee and we started talking. He's looking for a job and gave me his list of credentials."

"And you want me to interview him." He took the envelope.

"That's the plan."

"What if he doesn't fit?"

"Don't hire him," Robert replied to the ringing of his cell phone. "Hi," he answered, lifting his finger to John, meaning to stand by while he terminated the call. "I'm in a meeting. Can I call you back in a few minutes?" He nodded to the caller's response and pressed the end button.

"I'm sorry. That was Mackenzie."

"No trouble, I hope."

"No. Just a family matter. She's always busy with school or friends," he said thinking of his conversation with Elias. "Now she'll need a check for summer school and that means no time for old dad."

"Be glad she's interested," John pressed. "If Mackenzie takes her required courses in summer school she'll graduate sooner."

"I guess there's merit in that."

"I'll let you know what happens." He waved the envelope and left the office.

Robert smiled as he thought "mission accomplished." Would Jim Ashton, the man he just recommended, start working for his company or would John have Global hire him first? It didn't really matter. Robert had several other men on the hook, ones with real experience. Catherine kept a current list.

Within the next few minutes he was talking on the phone with Mackenzie. "It's important we talk," he said trying to sound casual, "and I want to discuss something in person." A sudden response to his request shattered his thoughts completely. "I haven't," he started but was interrupted by a ranting staccato of rage coming from his daughter.

"Was I supposed to be surprised with the news after you brought her to my birthday dinner? Just let me know the date so I can plan ahead." Mackenzie stormed loudly, her heated fumes strong enough to melt the phone. "I'm sure she'll say, 'Yes,' when you get around to asking her."

"Are you OK with that…my getting married?"

"You have my blessing, dad. Isn't that what this is all about?" The sarcasm continued.

"I just want you to be comfortable with the idea."

"Since when? That's a new twist on old history." Her verbal knife dug in deeper. "I gotta go." She pressed the end button, leaving her father in a state of confusion. Why had Mackenzie played 'nice' at her birthday dinner and changed to a vicious bitch just now with her father?

Something was going on in his daughter's life. Of that he was more certain than ever now. At their pancake breakfast, Mackenzie made it abundantly clear that she blamed him for her mother's death. The fact that he couldn't save Emily was his fault. And it was his fault because he didn't care enough to see the changes that occurred: her loss of weight, her growing fatigue and finally the skeleton she became. Of course, the promise to Emily of their trip to Memorial Sloan Kettering remained just that, a hidden promise of three years.

Then there was Mackenzie's outburst of his meeting Raine in Florence, a trollop he supposedly bedded; one who could possibly replace her mother. Those assumptions did not sit well with his daughter. Her mounting anger that afternoon clarified her feelings and was all inclusive: the wrong one died.

Then suddenly she had a change of heart. Mackenzie was a completely different person. She could not have been kinder or more accepting of Raine at her birthday dinner. Granted, Aunt Dorothy did monopolize the conversation, but he did see an exchange between them, a warm friendly one that seemed sincere.

Three days later, everything changed. Why? What was going on? Would he have to use his own equipment to spy on his daughter?

He already knew the answer.

Chapter 11
Mackenzie

During the next few nights, Robert monitored his daughter's activities, only to find Elias's was right after all. In fact, after three nights and two days, he found nothing of consequence. Her routine was boring. Almost nightly, she frequented bars and dance clubs with her group of friends. And with classes over, Mackenzie spent most of her days shopping or having lunch at some chic restaurant with the same female crowd. As boring as it was to him, Robert was relieved Mackenzie showed some restraint during these gatherings. She was usually home before midnight and in some cases by eleven. Although this discipline made him happy, it did not solve the problem of her change in attitude. He would have to find another avenue. The thought of bugging her apartment bothered him. He would give her another week before going that route.

Of course, when spying was no longer a concerted effort, and the long hours of sitting in his car proved fruitless, Robert missed the visitor Mackenzie had on the fourth night. That he missed the person who caused the real change in her attitude would have displeased him greatly.

***

She sat quietly on the living room sofa propped-up against the pillows watching television when she heard the tumble of the door lock. A flood of emotion swept over her as she watched her handsome suitor enter the apartment. Tightening the belt of her loosened robe, she rose to greet him but stepped back to turn off the television.

"Hi." He pulled her to him and kissed her passionately.

Her arms circled his neck. "I hate this schedule."

"We have to be careful. You know that. If your uncle broke in on us, your father would have you home in a minute and I'd never get to see you."

"You're talking about my neighbor." She sat down on the sofa with him.

"You're lucky she keeps you informed. Most people don't want to get involved."

"I just hate the hours. It'll be worse when classes start."

"We'll make it work." He kissed her again and studied her face. "You're so beautiful, so beautiful," he sighed, fingering the length of her hair and the texture of her smooth skin.

"I want you to think I'm beautiful. My grandmother thinks I look just like my mother when she was young. She was so pretty."

"And so are you," he said, suddenly dropping the subject. "So besides getting ready for summer school, what else have you been doing?"

"Pissing off my father, mostly," she chortled, causing a frown to cross his face.

"What did you do?" he asked, obviously annoyed by her antics. "What is wrong with you?"

"Aside from hating him, nothing's wrong with me," she snapped back. "He's responsible for my mother's early death and now he wants to replace her."

"I understand where you're coming from. Believe me when I say that. But you don't want to do anything to jeopardize our relationship."

"That's not going to happen."

"It will if he gets suspicious."

"So I should be happy he's replacing my mother, the woman he let die. You always felt he could have done more."

"I can't change my feelings, never could," he said softly, his thoughts so distant from the woman sitting beside him. "But we have to plan." He brought himself to present time.

"I don't understand."

"What did your father tell you?"

"He asked for a meeting. He wanted to tell me personally about getting married, but I didn't give him a chance. I told him I knew what he wanted and gave him my blessing."

"Were you nasty?" He continued to be annoyed.

"Very." She emphasized the word.

"You better get over that attitude or we're done."

She captured the full meaning of his words but was surprised by the anger of his harsh ultimatum. "You said you loved me. How can you end a relationship with an 'or else?'"

"An 'or else' offers direction. You haven't given one thought to us."

"That's not true," she groused. "I've done everything to please you, told you everything, including the fights with my father. You agreed then, that I was right."

"This is a different matter entirely." He took her hand, making certain she understood the full meaning of his words. His eyes fixed on hers as he asked in a quiet, almost mesmerizing tone. "Do you love me? Really love me?"

"Yes," she answered, her voice filled with emotion.

"Do you love me enough to follow my instructions?" He continued his hypnotic hold.

"What is it you want?" She breathed deeply, her expectations high.

"A relationship usually ends with a breakup or continues with marriage. I think we can agree on that."

"Are you proposing or are we breaking up?" She asked flatly, unhappy with the sudden turn in their conversation.

"You really are a piece of work." He brushed her lips. "Now answer my question."

"You want me to apologize."

"That's the only thing that makes sense. But you have to do it carefully. Make a date for lunch or something, tell him you behaved badly and wish him well. You need a face to face exchange."

"Why is it so important? I don't particularly like the woman I met this weekend...Lorraine Shaw or Raine as she likes to be called."

"So?" He wanted her to continue.

"She's beautiful, has a gorgeous figure and a great deal of charm. So what does she see in my father? He's not bad looking, I admit, but he's no barrel of laughs. I think she's after his money. She'll be hanging out to dry when I get the house and company."

"You already told me about the trust fund," he said, eager to drop the line of information already known to him. "Let's talk about the marriage."

"Dad wanted my blessing before asking her to marry him," she offered. "I gave it, end of story."

"No. It was how you gave your blessing. It was wrong and you are going to correct that, if you're smart. And I happen to think you are a very smart young lady."

"Give me one good reason why I should grovel with an apology."

"Because it leaves the field wide open for us. He gets married, lives happily ever after with his new bride and won't object when we decide to tie the knot. You must admit, it makes sense. There will no longer be a void in his life. He will have a companion of his own."

"I never thought of it that way." She broke into a wide grin.

"That's why we need to keep a low profile."

"You think of everything."

"I try," he said silencing her with his lips.

***

It was after two when he drove home, feeling smug and satisfied with the outcome of the evening. She was so beautiful, so very beautiful…a living replica of the woman he loved and would always love. He had taken great care in molding the younger version, right down to the hairstyle.

It had taken some effort and cajoling, but in the end he accomplished everything he set out to do. Things were moving along nicely, just as he planned. He could almost hear wedding bells in his thoughts.

But then, his thoughts shifted to an earlier time: to those few precious moments…when he told the woman he loved, as she lay dying, "I am not that forgiving."

Suddenly, a wide smile crossed his face and his thoughts lingered. A man stripped of what he values most makes revenge so much sweeter. So very much sweeter. Yes. Everything was falling into place as planned. In six months or less, he would have it all.

***

Several days later, Robert called Raine for a date that weekend. He planned to take her somewhere quiet…a place they could talk without interruption. He thought of two well-known inns that offered seclusion but they were already booked when he called for reservations. His second option was better. He would take her to an elegant restaurant for dinner, perhaps in Mount Washington overlooking the city, and then to his home. They could spend the entire weekend making plans for the wedding once he proposed. If the job contract came through that Friday, as Elias said it would, he could more readily explain the need of a fall wedding. A large contract would require further meetings, a great deal of effort and perhaps some travel. Even more important he wanted his secret meetings with Claude behind him. These he could never discuss openly with anyone, other than Elias who knew every detail of the Sweet Pea project but used the veil of ignorance to cross examine Robert's own experiment. He did not want to start his marriage during that window. Once his assignment was completed, he could concentrate on their nuptials and take Raine on an extended honeymoon. That's what he really wanted…a time together…away from work and the strain of family.

A multiple task person would find his reasoning stupid. Perhaps it was. But Robert always operated this way and built his business by giving concentrated and personal service to every customer. That's why his referral business was so large and his competitors, so envious.

Many years earlier, when Robert first had the idea of starting a security firm, building the business became a joint effort with Emily. When their business began to grow, his mother came to help them as a bookkeeper and became known as Catherine Scaliezzi, dropping the surname, Blake, for business purposes. She worked the office while Emily manned the phones. Robert was out installing security systems and later offered computer services to his customers. Over the years, the company became even more family oriented. Mackenzie joined them on holidays and summers helping around the office.

A good feeling came over him when he thought about the past few days. He was surprised but very pleased when Mackenzie invited him to lunch. He knew she felt uncomfortable at first, but that soon changed when he spotted the birthday bracelet on her arm. It gave him a chance to talk about the Golden Bridge where he purchased the gift and his accidental meeting with Raine at Piazza della Signoria. He felt good about seeing his daughter. Mackenzie apologized in her own unique way, saying she was out of line venting the way she did. Then she added something that really surprised him. She did not want him to spend the rest of his life alone. If her father found someone who made him happy, he should go for it. She wished him well.

Her thoughts and wishes made him happy. Mackenzie was echoing her mother's words. Emily wanted him to find another mate, one true and loyal. Those two words always stuck with him. Now, Mackenzie added the same sentiment, but in a different way. His daughter wanted him to be happy. She almost dripped with sincerity trying to convince him she spoke from the heart. Yes. He was doing the right thing by asking Raine to marry him.

Still, with all of her apologies, Robert remembered her pancake breakfast vent and nasty attitude days earlier on the telephone. Why would his daughter suddenly have another epiphany? Deep down where it really counted, he felt much of the conversation was superficial. His daughter still believed the wrong parent died. But what she believed mattered little now. Mackenzie had given her blessing overtly and now he planned to marry the woman he loved.

Chapter 12
Proposal

As part of his plan, Robert took Raine to a gourmet restaurant overlooking the Pittsburgh Triangle and then to his home in Murrysville. When they entered, he directed her to the living room couch, filled two wine glasses and sat down beside her.

"I don't know how you managed a window table. The view of the city was spectacular," she offered, taking a sip of wine before placing the glass on the coffee table.

"Luck of the draw," Robert lied, thinking of the money he slipped the head waiter. "Although the view was breathtaking, I enjoyed the quiet atmosphere. We could actually have a conversation."

"You're right. I never thought about it," she agreed. "We were able to talk without any background noise disturbing us."

'That's why I thought it would be a good place for dinner."

His remark caused her to laugh. "Good place? The food was fabulous."

"You know what I mean," Robert said fixing his eyes on her. He set his glass on the coffee table and took her hand. "This is not what I had planned," he faltered. "I wanted to reserve a weekend escape in the Highlands but they were booked." As he continued talking she remained silent, her face an expressionless mask. "I know this seems fast, but I've fallen in love with you, Raine. You are so beautiful and I don't know what you see in an average Joe like me. But I know we're good together and I will do everything to make you happy."

"Are you asking me to marry you?" She expressed no surprise at the proposal.

"Yes," he faltered again. "But I'm doing this badly. I want to spend the rest of my life with you. I hope you feel the same way." Reaching into his pocket he pulled out a small box containing an engagement ring with a huge center diamond and slid it on her finger.

"I do." She clasped her arms around him, pushed his body down on the couch and kissed him passionately. Robert felt the rustle and quick shift of clothing before he heard her whisper, "Maybe we should go upstairs."

"You have great ideas."

"And you found the ring I lost! Now I know why my ring fits so perfectly."

***

"Want some coffee?" He greeted Raine the following morning when she entered the kitchen.

"How long have you been up?" She took the cup he offered.

"Long enough to read the paper." He sat on a stool beside her.

"I haven't slept that well since…last weekend," she laughed.

"I'm glad you like the bed. We'll make good use of it."

Although his implication caused her to laugh again, she suddenly grew serious. "After," she started, "upstairs when we talked, were you serious?"

"About September?"

"You want a fall wedding?"

"It will work out better for both of us. You'll have time to make plans for a reception."

"And you?"

"A good time to concentrate on my bride," he said without adding anything further. He neglected to mention the large contract he had just received or the huge amount of money involved. Something gnawing his thoughts told him to remain silent on that issue until the start of the project. Maybe a respective silence was something he learned at an early age.

"Instead of a reception, I'd like a cocktail party with a group of our friends. Is that ok with you?"

"Just as long as it's not here at the house." He tapped his finger on the counter.

"I can think of several hotels right now but I need a fixed date."

"The second Saturday in September," he answered quickly, setting the date. Her strange look in response caused him to explain. "Labor Day falls on the first weekend and I don't want to travel then. We can get married the following Saturday and leave Sunday for a honeymoon."

"Where are you taking me?"

"If it were up to me I'd rent a hotel room for a week and order room service."

"We could do that here," she said provocatively.

"No. We couldn't," he countered. "Something would occur. A client would need help or you would be showing houses."

"You want some suggestions?"

"Of course."

"How long? One or two weeks?" She caught his glimmer of agreement. "I'd like to go to the Caribbean or Hawaii. Could we do that?"

"Paradise Island would be a fabulous honeymoon but so would Maui."

"What about the other islands?"

"I'll arrange a two week stay," he agreed. "You might enjoy seeing your counterpart."

"My counterpart?" She looked puzzled.

"The active volcano on the Big Island."

"How the hell can you equate me to an active volcano?" she groused.

"Because you were so full of hot lava last night." He grinned, refilling her cup. "Face it, you were ready...you wanted me."

Without a word of warning, she thrust her hand across the stool, reached the front of his fly and said, "Right! Who's ready now?"

***

Several weeks later while Robert waited in line at Best Coffee, a tap on his shoulder caused him to turn and face an acquaintance he had met a month or so earlier.

"Hi." Robert greeted the red-haired portly man.

"I wasn't sure you'd remember me." Jim Ashton returned the acknowledgement.

"I gave your letter of credentials to John Harris. Has he contacted you yet? I asked him to talk with you."

"No. No." He brushed Robert's question aside. "He was very generous. We talked at length, but he thought I'd be a better fit somewhere else since I'm more interested in computers. He recommended another company and got me a job at Global."

"Are you working there now?" Robert asked, embarrassed at not being told of the interview or its outcome. A further embarrassment was not remembering the burly man's basketball height as he tilted his face upward to speak.

"Been there two weeks." He reached for a coffee cup when his number was called.

"You like it?" Robert asked hurriedly, wanting some response.

"It's exactly what I wanted," he answered and turned to leave.

Robert watched the man step outside and suddenly disappear around the corner. His thinking had been right on target. He had predicted the whole scenario weeks earlier. John Harris would interview Jim Ashton first. If he found the man to be a good candidate, John would send him to Henry Price at Global. The whole idea stemmed on one thing and one thing only: John would head some large operation at Global. He would be in charge. Still, if Robert didn't sell his company to Global, how could they expand? Was Henry Price talking to another company? Where was his money coming from? Contracts were hard to land, unless you had political contacts or moneyed people in your corner.

Still, something didn't seem right. Jim Ashton found John Harris to be a generous man. That was an adjective Robert would not have used in describing him. The man was self-driven and ambitious...ambitious enough to protect himself from any competition that could threaten his standing or advancement in Robert's or Henry's company. His ego matched his arrogance. But perhaps, in this instance, Jim Ashton posed no threat during the interview. John must have checked his credentials and staffed the man at Global in preparation for his next move.

Still, regardless of ambition, his assistant was good at his job and also with Robert's family. John showed so much compassion during those last stressful weeks when Emily became so frail and still. He would deliver stacks of papers to his home and leave quietly, never disturbing Emily as she lay dying on the living room couch.

Everyone said he was lucky to have a man like John Harris assisting him. He coordinated all the assignments and knew each man's location on any given work day. He assessed their skills and expertise with each new incoming contract and was observant of their job performance by requesting merit raises for outstanding work. His outgoing personality and unharnessed wit made him likeable by everyone in the company. That was the side of John Harris he allowed everyone to see.

It was the manipulative side, the side badgering him on the golf course for Henry Price's benefit that very few people, if any, saw through his facade of deception. That side he kept well-hidden. Of course, Robert was prepared that day and the answers he gave caused an unexpected jaw dropping.

If truth be told, he wanted John as his assistant but not as a friend. The man had a closet full of secrets. Of that he was certain. The man never spoke of his divorce, his private life or where he actually vacationed in South America. He mentioned the Amazon once, but that was only when he brought a worker some cold medicine. Then he thought of the man's license plate, 'Amazon 1.'

As his thoughts came to present time, he saw a woman staring at him from across the counter. She held a cup in her hand. "Do you have number 93?" she asked him directly.

Robert checked his ticket and nodded.

"Thank God. I've called this number twice already and thought I'd have to toss this sucker." He took the cup sheepishly and ambled around the other customers to the front door.

***

Robert sat in his car thinking more and more about his encounter with Jim Ashton. Why was the man's move to Global bothering him so much? He had lost other job candidates before. No. It wasn't the loss of a potential employee, he reminded himself. It was the fact that his scenario came to fruition. That bothered him. He thought it would happen and it did. Now Robert had a problem. Were other job candidates placed at Global when interviewed? Would there be any way of learning the truth? John knew Robert wanted to hire new people, so why would he deliberately sabotage his effort so openly? Did he think Robert was that stupid? Yes. He answered his own question. However, he did have an avenue to pursue. There was one person who would know if there were other job applicants: his mother.

Had John Harris always been this way? His recollection of the man wasn't like that at all. Years earlier, he was happy, friendly and a 'go to guy' for anything. It all seemed to change after his divorce. He became progressively silent and secretive on all personal matters. In fact, Robert had no idea if the man even had a social life. He never spoke of anyone important to him. Yet if he had someone, it could not have been serious. The man was always too available to have something going on in his private life. So what changed an outgoing man, so interested in the company and its employees, to a secretive individual bent on destroying Robert's business? The man had to feel secure in his job, particularly when Robert announced an expansion of his work force. That alone should convince any employee that Robert was not interested in selling his company. But then a further thought crossed his mind. What made John Harris think he was selling in the first place? Why would he think that? Was he listening to his phone conversation with Bruce Parks? There was no other way he could have known Bruce's interest. That had to be it. In the future, he would have to be more careful with his telephone calls.

After finishing his coffee, Robert drove to the office to greet his mother with a terse directive. "Seven, your house."

She caught her son's message, just as John Harris opened his office door.

"I thought I heard you come in," he said. "Henry Price just called and wanted to play a round of golf. You interested?"

"Now?"

"This afternoon, around three."

"Let me check my schedule." He walked into his office, followed by Catherine who held a document for his signature.

Chapter 13
Coffee Shop

"Whatever you're cooking smells good." Robert greeted his mother who was stirring a batch of onions and tomato pieces in a skillet.

"Sit." Catherine pointed to a chair at the kitchen table before topping the mixture with four beaten eggs. "I didn't have a chance to shop, so were having a frittata, Italian style." She cut the fluffy omelet down the middle and placed half servings on two dinner plates. "I made the salad as soon as I got in." She repositioned two bowls of mixed greens, placed the dinner plates on the table and sat down.

"Looks good." He nodded with approval.

"What's up? I know you didn't come here to eat." Catherine came right to the point for his visit. She studied the blank expression on his face and smiled inwardly. Robbie had learned his lessons well. He sat facing her, totally calm, unruffled by anything she said.

"I ran into Jim Ashton this morning at a coffee shop," he started.

"Am I supposed to know him?" she asked, somewhat confused by the statement.

"I told John to interview him because I thought he'd be a good fit with the company. Today I learned he's working for Henry."

"And you think John's screwing you by padding Global for his next move."

"It makes sense. If I don't have the work force, I can't solicit more business. So he diminishes my expansion on two fronts. It's too bad," he sighed. "Jim Ashton had glowing credentials. I could have used him."

"The name doesn't register."

"I wonder where John interviewed him."

"Makes no difference. You can't ask if you run into him again. He'll think you have no pulse on the people you employ."

"That's probably true." He agreed with her theory.

"That's not the point, is it? You want something else."

"I want numbers."

"As in…" He caught her frown.

"There must be some record of people seeking employment with us."

"I've nothing current. I give every inquiry to you or Harris." She heard him sigh again. "I never thought of keeping a running record."

"I'm cooked. I have no way of knowing if he's directing our good prospects to Global."

"Not so fast," she interrupted. "If memory serves, in the sent box of my emails, I have a copy of a letter requesting more information from someone John interviewed recently."

"Can we?"

"After dinner." She took another bite of her frittata, which was a firm warning not to press the issue. "So what's new with the wedding?"

Robert looked at his mother incredulously. He was up to his eyeballs with worry and his mother wanted to talk about something else.

"We've set the date… Saturday, September tenth, the weekend after Labor Day, but that's as far as we've gone."

"What's the holdup?"

"I'm not sure there is one. Raine wants a ceremony and cocktail party, then we're off to Hawaii. Next day, of course. We'll spend the night at some hotel near the airport."

"No reception?" she questioned, puzzled by the plan.

"No. She wants to invite a lot of people and have cocktails and hors d oeuvres within a three-hour window."

"Sounds like she's either hiding or in a rush."

"It's not that at all," he disagreed. "She dislikes attention. Raine wants to get married and start our life together without a big hoopla. What's wrong with that?"

"Maybe you should get married in Hawaii and be done with it."

"We'd still need some sort of celebration on our return." He caught his mother's disdain, but was unable to understand her look of discontent.

"I guess you don't have a choice."

"I told her to check the hotels and country clubs without me."

"You don't care about cost?"

"Not really. She can select whatever she wants. I just want Raine to be happy. It's her wedding day," he emphasized the word, 'her.' "I just want to show-up."

"You are one lovesick puppy." His mother said in disgust. "You may regret giving her free reign."

"I think you're mistaken."

"I hope I am for your sake. Sometimes giving too much freedom comes to be the expected norm. When it backfires, you'll find yourself in an impossible situation."

The distant look in her eyes spoke volumes. He knew instantly she was talking about herself. What was the reference? Was it about his father? He remembered an Italian remark his grandmother once made about 'stocking-off certain body parts.' Was Nonna referring to his father? There was so much family history behind him: things he couldn't remember or was purposely shielded from, an ugly truth of sorts. What he did remember were the lessons his mother gave after his father's death. Her one directive flashed boldly in his mind. *'Sometimes what's right is not always legal.'* Those thoughts continued to spin until his mother's voice brought him out of his reverie.

"I think we should check the computer now," she reminded, clearing the table. Robert took his plates to the sink before trailing her to a small bedroom that had been turned into an office.

It took Catherine only minutes to scroll through the sent email. "This is the one. See? John wanted more information." She pointed to the text, and then scrawled the name Cameron Trox on a tablet adjacent her computer. "Here." She ripped off the sheet. "I don't want to know the how, just the status."

"I'll know within three days." He caught the meaning of his mother's scowl. "Don't worry. Nothing will be traced back to me, no matter how good the hackers are," he reassured her. "But I have to know if I am being consistently screwed." He folded the paper and slid it into his jacket pocket. "Thanks for dinner and this." He patted the pocket and kissed his mother's forehead before leaving the house.

As Catherine watched him leave without a thread of further conversation, a flood of anxiety swept over her. Something didn't feel right. Now, Robbie had problems on two fronts. The one with John would be resolved. Of that she was certain. Once Robbie established the man's treachery, the cat and mouse game would end with the man being fired. But John Harris was not her son's main worry; Raine was. Catherine felt it in her bones, although she couldn't put her finger on those feelings. Maybe the woman was too beautiful, too overtly perfect. Or maybe Raine dripped with too much sweetness at the birthday dinner for Mackenzie. Whatever it was, Catherine knew something about the woman was not right. If Robbie would only open his eyes, take some time and not be led by his passion for her. He was caught in a web of love and desire but was unaware of the black widow enveloping him. Catherine continued with these thoughts as she rinsed off the dinner plates, but was soon brought out of her worries when the telephone rang.

"Hey," a familiar voice greeted her. "How's the disposal working?"

"Where are you?" She asked her brother. "Should I put a fresh pot on?"

"You must have some coffee left over from dinner," Steve interrupted quickly.

"How do you know?"

"I'm parked on your driveway right now. I didn't want to run into Robbie so I parked down the street and waited until he left."

"That makes no sense."

"You can bitch about it when I'm inside," Steve barked getting out of his car.

"You could have come in when Robbie was here." She led him to the kitchen.

"No. He had something on his mind; something he wanted to discuss."

"And you know this, how?" She watched him take a chair at the kitchen table facing her.

"When someone parks in the grass, a clear two feet off the driveway, his thoughts are not on driving."

"He did want to talk to me. He thinks John is padding Global with our job prospects." She placed a carafe and two coffee cups on the table.

"Pretty clever," he chuckled. "Nothing like going to a new company with your own work force."

"Cute." Her sarcasm could have soured the coffee creamer on the table.

"Hey!" he growled back. "If it's true, best face it and fire his ass."

"Why are you here?" She changed the subject.

"When I told Dorothy I had a late job tonight, she invited some hens over for cards."

"So you came here."

"You have me until nine," he smirked. "I thought we could talk about Raine. I don't know how you feel but I don't trust the bitch. I'm not romantic enough to believe in coincidences…like their meeting in Florence, particularly when she lives within ten or twenty miles of him.

"Amen to that." Catherine agreed. She rose from the table suddenly, took two small glasses from the cupboard and filled them with Nocello. "I need something to smooth my pipes before talking about the witch who's taking my son to the cleaners." She clinked his glass. "How good are you with the malocchio?" She thought of casting a spell on the evil woman. All Italians talked about this at some time or another.

"It wouldn't work on her. She's probably wearing the cornetto horn in her asshole."

"You really are in a mood," she said thinking of the horn orna-ment used to dispel the 'evil eye.'

"And you are blind."

"Meaning what?"

"Did you take a good look at your granddaughter Saturday night?"

"No. I was too busy listening to Dorothy drone on and on," she spat back sarcastically. "So what are you trying to tell me?"

"She looks like Emily, right down to the new hairstyle."

Steve's remark left Catherine somewhat confused. "She always did resemble her mother."

"Yeah, well now, Mackenzie's the spitting image."

"I guess I didn't notice."

"That's because you were too busy concentrating on the woman who is screwing your son in every given direction. We both know she's after his money."

"You'll never convince him of that."

"I'm not planning to. He'll learn soon enough," Steve answered flatly. "Being in love doesn't mean he's stupid."

"He'll be married and it'll be too late."

"Providence and death can go hand in hand," he groused, knowing she caught the implication. When a silent second passed between them with no glimmer of rebuttal, Steve drained his small glass of liqueur and kissed her cheek before departing.

Catherine watched her brother leave, feeling more depressed than ever. Earlier that evening, she was concerned about her son, his company and the coming marriage. Now, after Steve's visit, she had an additional concern; her granddaughter, Mackenzie. Why should Catherine feel that way? Steve offered no real infor-mation about his niece. He just mentioned her resemblance to Emily and the change of hairstyle. But if nothing new was going on, why mention her at all? Thinking about all of this was giving her a headache.

Within minutes, Catherine Scaliezzi took two aspirins and was in bed for the night.

***

It was after eleven when Elias Juniper arrived. "You said it was urgent," he said walking to the bar for two fingers of scotch and an ice cube.

"I think I'm being screwed."

"I told you staying single was not a bad thing."

"It's not Raine. I think John Harris is padding Global with our job applicants. They come to us for employment and he sends them to Henry. The man's in the process of building a compatible group, knowing they will be eternally grateful when he makes the move."

"You have names?"

"Jim Ashton was one. I ran into him this morning and learned he went to Global after John interviewed him. Cameron Trox is the only other name I have."

Elias listened to his friend rant on, laughing inwardly at the ridiculous situation, but then became serious and issued a firm directive.

"Forget about John's hiring methods. I want you to continue as usual."

"I can't do that." Robert rejected the idea. "I need new hires to service my regulars so the more experienced ones can work the new contract. The powers that be want state of the art technology installed and I don't have to tell you how tricky surveillance equipment can be. And I am not referring to 'Sweet Pea' with Claude."

"Then advertise or go to an agency for help. Have applicants contact you directly. Just tell John time is of the essence and you are conducting the interviews yourself. Harris can't fight you on that. He knows about the new contract, right?"

"He does now that the contract's confirmed. It just gives him more impetus to screw me."

"Don't worry about that. It will all work out."

"What aren't you telling me?"

"You need more scotch." He grinned, exposing a dentist's dream of even white teeth. "I'm here for you. Remember that." Drink in hand, he was gone without saying another word.

Saying anything more was unnecessary. Essentially, Elias told him to ignore John's hiring efforts for Global. Did that mean Henry's company was being investigated? Was Elias working the case? The more Robert thought about it, the more confused he became. No. His friend's meaning was clear. If he were to go on as usual, then forgetting about Jim Ashton or Cameron Trox could only mean one thing. The two men were planted at Global deliberately to further an investigation, one in the computer section, and the other, in security or surveillance. But why? Was there some evidence of illegality? But even more important, how did Elias know John Harris was sending job candidates to Global? Were Henry's offices being bugged? Then a second thought hit him. What about the offices in his own building? Would Elias bug them too? Although he had been protective of him, of their years together, Elias Juniper was by far his sneakiest friend. He'd bug a mortuary if he thought the dead had something to tell.

***

In another part of the city, a congratulatory moment was taking place.

"I am so proud of you."

"It was your suggestion." Mackenzie offered, recalling the lunch with her father.

"But you pulled it off."

"You said that it was the right thing to do."

"It was." He drew her closer, feeling her silk-like skin pressed against his. "You are so beautiful. I knew it would be like this the moment I saw you as a blossomed woman," he whispered, "and it keeps getting better every time we're together."

"Will it always be this wonderful?" she sighed, thinking of their repeated assignations; a quick lunch at his place, a prolonged evening at hers, or both on those days when he needed her most.

"Always." he said softly, blending his body with hers.

Love was in the making: the one side, expressing his intense love for an imagined and older version of Mackenzie; the other, the first love of a young thing who had been brainwashed into doing his every bidding.

Chapter 14
Bruce

━━━━━━━━━━━━━━━━━━━━━━━━━━━━━━━━

The next morning Robert sat in his office scrolling the computer for employment agencies, when his cell phone rang.

"What's up? Do you want to meet for lunch?" He greeted Bruce Parks, only to have his expressionless face freeze as the conversation progressed. "I'll meet you in ten." Robert ended the call.

"Where are you off to?" Catherine watched her son whiz by.

"I forgot something at the house," he said, a code meaning something important came up; I'll tell you later, and in the meantime, cover me.

"Being forgetful comes with age," she yelled, watching him exit the office.

"Where's he going?" John Harris asked on his way in. "I reminded him of our meeting when we passed each other in the hall."

"He'll be back long before that." Her statement quieted his curiosity. "He went home for something he forgot. Probably for the meeting." She turned to her computer and listened for the click of his office door. Looking up briefly, Catherine whispered, "Creep." Yet she was thankful he left the office more frequently these days. Catherine never questioned those absences, even with his two hour lunches.

***

Robert slid into a booth at Spoons' Eatery, and sat directly across from Bruce Parks whose ashen face had the haggard look of someone deep with worry. "Tell me," he said quietly.

"I don't know where to start or what to do. Jenna would kill me if she knew I was telling you her diagnosis."

"Cancer?" Robert questioned, unaware there had been a problem.

"She got the results four days ago. You've been through all this. I don't know how you managed to survive."

"What did the doctor tell her? His exact words."

"She has tumors on her lung. He's certain it's cancer."

"What did he suggest?"

"He's recommended an oncologist. Jenna has an appointment tomorrow. I don't want to lose my wife, Robert." His eyes filled with tears. "I can't eat. I can't sleep. My company's going down the tubes and all I can think about is Jenna."

"First things first," Robert said quietly. "Go with her tomorrow, but don't make a commitment for surgery or anything else. Call your doctor afterward and tell him you want a second opinion. Then make arrangements at Memorial Sloan Kettering in New York. Take Jenna there. You'll want to see Dr. Andrew Haig. I'm sure he's still there. Check the computer," he said to the shocked man facing him.

"That's where you took Emily. You never said. No one ever knew." Bruce expected an acknowledgement of sorts, but Robert's expressionless mask told him nothing else would be forthcoming. "And you think he can help Jenna."

"I didn't say that. He will tell you the prognosis and suggest options, if there are any. He will also offer his own opinion, if asked, and how he would approach the case. If Jenna has any possible chance, I would go with him. He's tops in the field."

"How can I tell her about this doctor? She'll be pissed knowing I told you anything."

"Better to have her pissed and possibly saved, than mum and regretful."

"You have a strange way of putting things."

"You don't want to lie to Jenna, not at this critical time in her life. Tell her the truth. You are an absolute wreck with worry and you reached out for my support, knowing my history with Emily. Put your arms around her and tell her what you told me, 'You don't want to lose her.'"

Bruce listened to Robert and a strange thought ran through his mind. They had been friends for years, but this was his first real glimpse of the man's depth. Friendly as he was with everyone on an impersonal level, Robert was difficult to really know. He had always kept an imperceptible distance when discussing personal things. It was almost like the man had built an impenetrable wall shielding his private world from the one he allowed people to share. However, at that very moment, Bruce felt Robert had come to help his friend on a very personal level, one that mattered greatly.

"Thank God my brother can take over when we go." His elbow rested on the table, his hand held the side of his face as he spoke.

Although his reference had little meaning to those who knew nothing of Bruce's family, Robert remembered the handicapped man well. Teddy would fill in for Bruce on occasion and knew the daily mechanics of the business. But being on disability, he would take no money for his hours of work. Just being able to help his brother made him feel more independent. Still, as Robert recalled, Bruce compensated him in other ways: a 54 inch TV in the family room, house repairs by Bruce and a complement of his hired friends, and the forever BOGO items which Jenna supplied. Whether the sale was real or not made little difference. Jenna was a supermarket shopper, a dealer in coupons. That was the story and most of it was true. Jenna did shop at the local supermarket and there were times when she exchanged coupons with her friends.

"I think you should concern yourself with going to Memorial Sloan Kettering as soon as possible for Jenna's sake."

"Why does everything have to happen all at once?" Bruce lamented. "I don't want 'a time to live and a time to die scenario, or a time to make money and a time to downsize.'"

"A little English would be helpful here." Robert eyed the gaunt-faced man. In all his years of knowing Bruce Parks, this was the first time he noticed the man's rather pointed chin. Dark hair, dark eyes, yes, but never the pointed chin. His triangular face just seemed to end there...at his pointed chin.

"I lied to you about buying the company. I really wanted to merge because I'm losing business. I have to furlough two of my guys or use them part time. I went through this two years ago, thanks to Henry expanding his computer services. But now, with Jenna, I can't go out and hustle new business." He paused momentarily and with a great deal of resignation added, "I just lost a service contract, which I think Henry got."

"I already knew your business was in trouble. I checked when you first approached me. But maybe we can do each other a favor," Robert mused, thinking of his friend's last statement. "I could use two more men to service my regulars until the new contract is completed. You could subcontract them during the interim and help us both out. What do you think?"

"You got a new contract?"

"The Federal office building that's going up in the Warehouse District. Took eight months of negotiation."

"You got it!" He expressed shock. "Scuttlebutt had Global the prize winner."

"Where did you hear that?"

"One of my men overheard a conversation between Henry and some loud mouth at Pitts'Charity Play. He was hunting his golf ball in the brush when he heard a man's raspy voice say two companies were left in the running: Global and Blake Enterprises, and that he was voting for Henry. He thought the man was a politician but didn't recognize him," Bruce added. "Is that important? You got the contract."

"I didn't know Henry was in the running."

"We all were. I received a cut letter early so I was out of the game."

"The bids may have been open, but it must be nice to have someone with clout in your back pocket."

"The man must have dug deep inside Henry's," Bruce chided quickly, causing Robert to laugh. "Henry's gotta be pissed."

"That's the thing about Henry. He'll let it fester inside and never let-on how really pissed he is." After making the statement Robert found it amusing. Was he not the one who also stayed calm when angered? So if Henry concealed his feelings over losing the contract, why should Robert fault him for doing the same thing? Everything was so much crap. Why even bother with the thought? Henry was never in Robert's league when it came to masking emotional display.

"That's true up to a point."

"What do you mean?"

"Sometime, down the road, he'll explode with not getting the contract and eventually it'll get around. He's a sore loser. I know. I went through it when one of his men came to work for me. Alex Tree. Strange name but a good worker. Too bad he moved away."

"How long did he work for you?" Robert asked casually but his thoughts were ticking like a time bomb. What the hell was going on?

"Maybe three months tops. He knew his way around though. Why do you ask?"

"No reason, really," he lied. "I was just thinking of Henry. If losing an employee could upset him that much, what would losing a contract do to him emotionally?"

"Well, he's lost them before and survived; so he'll blow his cork and move on."

"Of course, you're right," Robert agreed.

"Now tell me what's going on with you, now that you're rested from the trip to Italy."

"I'm getting married in September."

Robert's statement came as a shock. A coming marriage was the last thing he expected from his friend. Bruce had no idea the man was even dating. "That is a surprise. Do I know her?"

"Doubt it. I met her in Florence but she lives in Penn Hills."

"Is she as beautiful as Emily?" he sighed. "She was always so warm, so engaging." Fearful of saying anything more, he reflected in silence.

"Raine's a gorgeous woman but she's far more distant than Emily. There will never be a duplicate. At times, I hurt so much because I want her with me. She's like a wound, deep inside, one that will never heal until I lay beside her. I know that now, but I don't want to be alone. I don't want to grow old and be that lonely old man people feel sorry for."

Surprised by the confidence expressed, Bruce said, "Life's a bitch, but I'm happy for you." Then changing the subject, added, "When do you want the men?"

"They should come over this month. They can go with my men to learn our service schedules."

"Their wages will still be the same. Just so we're clear."

"I wouldn't have it any other way. They're your men. I'm just hiring them temporarily. Make certain they understand the necessity of our working together. It beats being laid off."

"Robbie," His eyes became misty as he used the man's familiar name. "I feel so lost…my Jenna. I can't lose her."

"We've been friends for a long time." Robert's voice rang with sincerity. "The only comfort I can give you is that she will be in the best hands at Memorial Sloan Kettering."

***

On his way back to the office, Robert's thoughts continued to tick like the minutes of a clock with a sweeping second hand. "Alex Tree, my ass. What the hell are you up to Elias? What are you looking for? Did you check Bruce's outfit after Henry's to see if there was some connection? Have you investigated mine too for something illegal? We need to talk."

His thoughts moved from Elias Juniper to Jenna Price, the real reason for meeting Bruce. Had his advice been helpful? "Only if Jenna has a chance of survival," he answered aloud. Would Bruce blame him if the doctor told them otherwise? Robert thought not. He had made it clear that Dr. Haig would give them Jenna's prognosis, a suggestive procedure and nothing more? Any further decision would be left to them.

In their own case, they put all their legal things in order, those necessary to prepare for death, and then took time off…until it stopped for Emily.

Robert parked in the lot of his office building and thought of the agony he suffered with Emily's death or more clearly, her dying. Now,

Bruce was experiencing the same thing. He felt sorry for his friend. Yet, there was nothing more he could do. His memories were being relived by the meeting: an emaciated Emily, the vomiting, the tears and the waiting for death.

"Oh, Christ, Emily. Why couldn't it be me?" Tears welled in his eyes. "I miss you so much."

He slid out of the car and walked around his vehicle twice to compose himself before entering the building.

"What were you doing out there? I saw you walking around your car. Is something wrong?" John Harris asked.

"I don't know. My tire pressure looks low," he lied, knowing the answer would satisfy his assistant.

"You ready for our meeting?"

"Let's talk about where we stand without the new contract and where our men are being utilized." John wondered what Robert meant by the remark but knew an explanation would come be forthcoming.

Chapter 15
A Kindness

The next afternoon, Robert received a phone call from Bruce with an update on his wife's medical condition.

"The oncologist thinks the tumors are cancerous. He recommends surgery."

"How did you leave it?"

"I called our doctor and requested Haig for a second opinion. He wasn't too pleased because my insurance might not cover. I told him I didn't care."

"How's Jenna taking it?"

"She's taking advantage of every option available. I thought she'd be angry when I confessed telling you, but she broke down and cried. Jenna and Emily were close.

"So she's ok with Memorial Sloan Kettering?"

"She was on the computer checking everything out after I mentioned your recommendations. I think Jenna feels better emotionally. It's like she's been given a chance to beat it. I think that's what's going through her mind."

"When are you leaving?"

"As soon as Haig can take us."

"Call me," Robert said, ready to end the call.

"Wait," Bruce yelled. "I cleared two of my crew for you."

Between Jenna's medical condition and Bruce's loss of business, Robert felt the emotional agony of his friend. The only support he could offer now concerned the man's work force.

"Send them over Monday morning. We start at eight."

"I knew you'd understand."

"Let me know about Jenna." He cradled the phone, wanting to ignore the grateful exchange that would follow.

Although Robert needed workers, Bruce knew his friend hired the men earlier than scheduled to help him financially. It fit Robert's persona. Rumors had persisted for years about him. It was said that Robert's financial hand had helped many families over the years. He never talked about it, nor did any of the people involved. And although those good deeds came back tenfold, no one could accuse him of acting like the very rich man he was. Of course, no one knew the real ticking of the man's mind or his own set of troubles. Those, he shared with no one. Instead, he masked his own private world from the piercing eyes of the public.

To Robert, however, the grateful implication took a different stance. In helping Bruce, he was bypassing John Harris completely. There would be no search for applicants, no interviews and no filling an employee void for Henry Price. Robert was simply being cost effective by hiring a few subs on a temporary basis while complying with the new contract. Then too, an early hiring would give more time for training the two men in the mechanics and routine of the company. John could not object, but he would not like losing control.

Robert smiled inwardly when he asked John into his office. He knew the man would be unhappy with the news.

"You're getting two new men on Monday," he started.

"That was quick. What changed since yesterday's meeting?"

"We're subcontracting two men from Bruce. It was a hard sell but I talked him into it," he lied. "It will be cheaper than hiring permanent or part time help. They're experienced in security technology so no training's involved. Get them established with our routine until I pull my crew."

A shocked expression never left John's face. "I don't understand what's going on here."

Robert pulled a folded sheet from a briefcase that sat on the floor near his chair. He unfolded it slowly and spread it on his desk. "I'll have more details but this is where we stand so far."

"You're to supervise the new installations?" John studied the sheet that gave very little information. "There's nothing here to indicate placement."

"That's why I'm relying on you." He took another sheet of paper that contained a list of names from his desk drawer. "After we met yesterday, I've picked these four men to install the security needed for the new building. You'll be servicing our regular customers with less men, but the two subs should help."

"That should be no problem. What about the new equipment? Did you order it? Nothing came across my desk."

"I'm in the dark on that score. When I submitted the bid, I had to list the equipment needed for the job or what I thought was needed. They interviewed me later on supplies and cost. I must have been in contention of getting the contract, but there was no indication of it at the time."

"I don't understand."

"Neither do I. Everything I recommended will be shipped directly to the building. They ordered it. Our job is to install it."

"I've never heard of such a thing. Even building there is crazy. The Warehouse District is primarily used for shopping and dining?"

"There are office buildings at the far end," Robert pointed out.

"The whole operation still sounds strange. We've never had a customer buy his own installation equipment."

"We've never had a government contract like this before. I present it and they make changes. Maybe it's the new norm. As long as they get the right equipment, I don't care where it's shipped." Robert could not discuss anything further. How could he? The contract that was presented was not the one being installed, at least not all of it.

"Maybe they thought we'd sabotage the equipment to spy on them."

"You've been watching too many spy movies."

"Maybe. But it makes a good story," John said taking the list.

Robert gave no response to the comment but changed the subject completely. "I'd like to meet with the men tomorrow morning. I have an announcement."

"They already know about the new contract. I told them when the letter came through Friday."

"This is personal."

"Well?" he demanded. "If something's going on, shouldn't I know about it first?"

"I'm getting married in September," he said, noting John's strange expression. "I wanted to tell the men before the news got out."

"Who is the lucky lady? Do we know her?"

"I doubt it. Although she's from Penn Hills, we met in Florence. It was strange, our meeting like that. We seem to have so much in common. We hit it off immediately."

John shook Robert's hand. "I'm happy for you. I really am. To find someone after…Emily. That's rare."

"I think you'll like Raine when you meet her."

"Raine?"

"It's short for Lorraine," he said just as his phone rang.

"I'll keep your secret." John tiptoed out of his office but left the door partially open.

"You mean now?" John heard him ask. "It will take me an hour with all the traffic."

"This contract is killing me." He stormed out of his office to exit the building.

"Do you know where he's going?" John was quick to question.

"How the hell should I know? I just work here." Catherine answered dryly. She would know the answer later…when he dropped by the house and she grilled him.

***

"What am I doing here?" A tinge of fresh paint filled his nostrils, as he followed the short stocky man named Claude to the fifth floor of the empty building. At the far end of a hall, the older man led Robert to a room within-a-room that was completely filled with equipment.

"We have to take inventory. I want to know if something's missing." He held a clipboard listing the materials that Robert submitted in his bid. "This is just for the building, not our Sunday meetings."

Robert caught the 'Sweet Pea' reference immediately but stuck to the man's subject at hand. "How do you know something's not missing now? You have no door on the room, no locks, nothing. Some workman could have taken a piece of equipment already."

"No box has been opened. I can assure you."

"Don't be naïve. The whole box would have been wheeled out. If you're so concerned about someone stealing information, have you thought about stealing the machine used for that purpose? Hackers love new computers."

The gray-haired man began to smile. "I was told you would not be an easy push. What do you suggest? I want your men to begin work on Monday," he said expecting a negative response.

"Claude or whatever your real name is, I'll have my men start taking inventory tomorrow morning. As for Monday, if the inventory's wrong, we might not be able to start until the right equipment comes in, so let's take care of that first." He turned away leaving Claude to trail him to the elevator.

"Robert," he said when they reached the first floor, "You are a piece of work."

"People always know when they're cut from the same cloth," Robert answered. "Tomorrow at nine."

As he watched Robert walk to his parked car the older spook was very happy with the chosen bid. This man, Robert Blake, had both intellect and common sense. They would work well together. Maybe not. 'Sweet Pea' could become problematic. Time would tell. There were always steps to be taken if he didn't work out. Still, if he read the man well, and Claude was very good at profiling, Robert Blake was a very private man who kept his world just that...private. And concerning 'Sweet Pea,' he would reveal nothing about floor six to anyone. The thought made him smile. Why even think of 'Sweet Pea' on six when their concerted effort was on five right now? After the installation was completed and operational, their Sunday meetings would begin.

After leaving Claude, Robert received a text message from Raine saying she was busy that evening with appointments, and one from his mother asking him to stop by.

***

"What's up?" he greeted her at the door.

"I overheard John on the phone with Henry Price. He mentioned the contract and subcontracting two of Bruce's men. When did you make that decision?"

"Sit down. I have something to share with you."

Catherine Scaliezzi listened to her son tell his story of Emily's sickness, their trip to Memorial Sloan Kettering and his promise of silence; a promise now broken, and how it related to Jenna Parks and Bruce's loss of business."

"That's why you're using his men. When did you arrange this?"

"Today. He called about the doctor's prognosis. It's not good. Bruce talked with two of his men who were willing to subcontract. I took them early to lessen his payroll. It really is more cost effective. I don't have to hire anyone and they leave when the job's finished."

"I'm glad you told me, Robbie. You did the right thing, the honorable thing for your friend. But what about John and Henry?"

"You mean with the contract?"

"Why is John blabbing all this to Henry? He can't do anything about it?"

"Henry's probably interested in learning our involvement. They will be surprised though."

"What do you mean?" His comment left Catherine confused.

"Nothing will ever get out. The men will be expected to sign a disclosure to that effect. In other words, the type of surveillance installed and the location of all equipment will remain within the government's domain. My men will not be able to discuss any of the surveillance used. They face a fine or prison if they do."

"Do the men know this?"

"I'm keeping it as a surprise."

"You're sick. They won't like it."

"The four I picked will ignore John's questions, if that's what you're asking. They're loyal to me." he said, thinking of the help he gave when they needed it. "Besides, I plan to give each of them a healthy bonus."

"So what's the announcement about tomorrow morning? John told the group you had something to tell them."

"My marriage. It will be a short. I'm taking my crew to the building."

"There can't be a problem at this late date."

"No, but I'm expected to supervise right to the end. We're dealing with a bureaucracy, remember? They're known for having meetings." As he spoke his stomach began to rumble. "Did you have dinner?"

"No, but I am hungry."

He took his mother's arm as they walked toward the door.

"McMann's?" she asked.

"Right on."

Chapter 16
Claude

The next morning, an important phone call took place.

"He made the announcement today."

"So, it's public now. Everybody knows my father's getting married," Mackenzie said in disgust.

"Well, not everybody. Just the men who work for him but I'm sure the word will spread."

"She'll make sure of that."

"You don't sound too happy."

"I'm not. I still think she's after his money."

"If I came by later, would that make you happy?" His soothing voice oozed with charm…and implication.

"I'd like that."

"I'll be there in an hour," he said knowing all his workers were out on jobs and Robert and his men were on their way to the new building.

He pressed the end button on his cell phone, a smile crossing his face. It was all falling into place. Robert would be married soon and he would be free to make his next move. He thought of Raine. Then he thought of Mackenzie. They certainly had a lot in common.

***

The men were waiting at the front door when Claude appeared from inside the building allowing them to enter.

"Good timing." Robert applauded his promptness as they gathered in the elevator to the fifth floor. He made first name introductions and said, "If the inventory's correct, we start Monday."

To Claude's surprise, when they entered the outer room, Robert gave each of the four men stapled sheets of paper which contained the entire list of surveillance equipment on Robert's bid.

"I don't care how you divide the inventory. We need to get it done ASAP. If something's missing we'll get it ordered and shipped while we work some other area." Still holding their attention, Robert added, "Since this is a federal building, you are not permitted by law to discuss the surveillance equipment, the locations or all other concerns of this building. I was told during the negotiation, we are required to sign a disclosure."

"Like we almost care," piped Josh Kwell, an older man who had been with Robert the longest. "We've signed so many for the banks, what's one more?"

His statement garnered a group nod from the four men as they began pulling boxes out of the inner room and dividing them into several groupings along sections of the fifth floor. Claude watched the men silently, as they moved like programmed robots, totally unaware of Robert's arm moving him out of their way.

Later, after the men finished grouping the equipment, they worked in two man teams itemizing and crossing-off the numbered inventory on their given sheets.

"What would you like me to do?" Claude asked.

"I think we should go for coffee." Robert said quickly. "When we return, you can take me to the sixth floor and show me your secrets."

"What makes you think I'm hiding something?" He defended himself. That Robert had an inkling of some clandestine activity unnerved him. He began to wonder if he made some slip during a conversation with him. However, that thought was soon put to rest with Robert's reply.

"My bid covered five floors. Either I fell short of your request or you people think I'm stupid."

"Just what are you driving at?" His eyes fixed on him.

"Take me to the sixth floor and I'll tell you." His request never wavered.

"It would be a waste of time."

"No," Robert challenged. "We would be utilizing it while my men do the inventory."

"What did you have in mind?"

"We could start talking about 'Sweet Pea.' I know you want it hidden, secreted and shielded from inspection, so to speak. Taking me there would give me an idea of placement. It would save time for both of us."

"Tell the men we're leaving." Claude began walking toward the elevator.

***

Instead of going for coffee, Claude took Robert to the sixth floor thinking the man would be surprised when the elevator doors opened. Instead, the man's expression never changed as he stepped into a huge reception area that greeted him. Facing him, but farther away, was a large reception desk fronting an enormous wall with a mural design of cascading colors. Behind the wall that separated reception from the rest of the floor were two large conference rooms, two smaller ones, several private offices and three end rooms, one of which seemed different from the rest.

Robert looked at Claude as he lingered in the last of the three smaller rooms. "You've kept it well hidden. Who would have thought?" He referenced a hidden room within a room.

"You know?"

"I've done enough surveillance work to know what encrypted rooms look like. You're coupling with offices on the lower floors is a nice touch, particularly in this location. But you have bigger plans, more optics and it's not here. The main operation, I mean. Washington, maybe, for Big Brother and satellite intervention. We'll all be swept in eventually, if not already."

Claude dismissed the comment. "That's total speculation on your part," he said realizing that Robert, having seen an important part of their operation, had guessed even more.

"Whether it's now or later doesn't matter. I would have known the purpose of this floor. What we should do right now is determine the placement of 'Sweet Pea.' Take notes on your clipboard. I don't want a copy in my possession. You're the supplier. I'll merely install with you."

Claude wrote furiously as they toured the entire floor. There was little disagreement between them, as they went room to room, each making suggestions on 'Sweet Pea's' placement. What surprised Claude most was Robert's insistence on a rich crown molding in the conference rooms. He suggested a dark brown hardwood carved with a very ornate design, a color that matched the room's carpeting. Then 'Sweet Pea' would be so well hidden when the bigwigs met, leaving Claude privy to their conversations.

"What exactly are you suggesting?" he asked trailing Robert back to one of the large conference rooms.

"I think the crown molding should go around the room with 'Sweet Pea' in the mitered corner. Remember, I said brown and very ornate. By that I mean heavily carved." He pointed to a particular corner that encompassed much of the entire area. "That would work unless you want two in the large conference rooms. I don't think that's necessary."

Claude agreed with Robert's assessment but was puzzled. "Where would I go for something like that?" It was obvious that Claude wanted to buy the molding privately and without govern- ment intervention.

Robert took the man's pen and wrote down the name and address of a supplier.

"Someone you worked with?" The implication was clear.

"Don't be ridiculous. He supplied the molding for my house. Just don't mention my name." Claude caught Robert's meaning immediately.

"So how are we leaving this?"

"I can't do anything until…" Robert never finished the sentence.

"I'll call you."

"You don't have my cell."

"Now who's being ridiculous?"

***

Things progressed rapidly in the following weeks. The men had finished installing the surveillance equipment and now Robert waited to hear from Claude. However, during that interim, he was able to devote more time to Raine's plans for their wedding.

"You said you found a perfect place after the ceremony." Robert commented one evening over dinner at one of their favorite restaurants. He was very surprised by her enthusiastic reply.

"You will love it. I went to all of the local hotels and talked with so many people. In the end I liked the Macroft. The hotel has a beautiful room for our cocktail party and I loved the different hors oeuvres listed on the banquet menu."

"The Macroft on Longmeadow?"

"It's the one high on the hill overlooking the valley. The location was something to consider too. Everyone knows the place and there's loads of parking."

Robert was less enthused with her choice but remained silent. He had eaten there some time ago and found the food less than appetizing. Perhaps they hired a new chef. He allowed Raine to ramble on in her excitement. After all, it was her day or would be in approximately seven weeks.

"Did you reserve it?"

"Tentatively. I have to let them know by Monday. I went back for a second look on Thursday. I told the caterer I needed to check with you before making a decision. What do you think?"

"I've been there for weddings. They just move the partitions to make the room larger for big receptions. It's quite nice," he said. Inwardly, he thought of the terrible food and felt grateful that it was only a cocktail party they had to contend with.

"Don't you want to see it?"

"I will, if you think it's necessary."

"I want you to be satisfied."

He captured the insistence in her tone and acquiesced. "On Monday morning, we'll go the clerk's office first, apply for the license, and then make a fixed reservation at the hotel. But you're in charge of the menu. Just tell the caterer I want the food and drinks to flow freely. Cost is not a factor."

After making the statement, he wondered if he were giving Raine too much Carte Blanche. His mother had made some sort of statement to that effect. Still, he wanted the day of their marriage to be a happy and memorable one. Spending money never bothered him, but someone taking advantage would. He could never put Raine in that category. They were two people who loved each other and wanted their friends around them to celebrate their special day. To make it memorable, it would have to be costly. That thought seemed to satisfy any suspicions that could have arisen.

"You make me so happy." Raine glowed with excitement. "I never thought I would ever meet someone like you, Robert. You are so good, so generous. I don't know what I have done to deserve you."

"This is just the beginning of a life we can make together. I want you to be happy." He patted her hand.

"I just wish there was something I could do for you." She gazed at him sitting across the table from her. "Maybe there is." She winked.

Chapter 17
Sunday

On one early Tuesday morning, during the second week of August, Robert received a phone call from Claude. "I haven't heard from you in weeks, and now you're up with the birds." He greeted the spook.

"If you'd stop with the sleepovers, we might be able to get something done," he groused in reply. "Everything's ready: carpeting, furniture, molding and borders. What's missing is your final contribution, so let's get on the stick."

"You're saying the building is now completed and you need me for a 'walk through,'" he said, careful not to reveal the true purpose of Claude's call.

"Exactly." Claude caught his meaning.

"I know this may be inconvenient, but Sunday is the only day I have available. I'm getting married in a few weeks."

"Congratulations," Claude replied, continuing the game. "I'll try not to detain you. Shall we say nine o'clock?"

"Perfect." Robert ended the call and thought of their meeting that coming Sunday.

Claude must have taken his suggestions and ordered everything immediately. Of course, the man had nothing to do with the carpeting and furniture. Those things were already selected when his men installed the surveillance equipment. Robert had talked with Claude about that earlier. The molding was merely an add-on when they toured the sixth floor. If Claude had the right material necessary for 'Sweet Pea,' they could get the whole operation done that Sunday…that is, if it went as planned. His mind took another turn at that moment.

Would Raine question his working on Sunday? What would he tell her? What excuse could he use? They had been spending all their weekends together lately. Obviously, Claude was aware of their activities or he would not have brought it to Robert's attention. Had he been trying to contact him? No. He thought not. But Claude had been watching him through 'Sweet Pea' or his own surveillance equipment, making Robert question the man's motives for doing so. Perhaps he wanted to determine Robert's trustworthiness, although he never gave the man pause for any kind of betrayal. Still, it seemed outrageous to have a stranger know the ins-and-outs of his own personal life, particularly when his security company operated the same way on marital cases. He did not like being monitored. But once again, his thoughts turned to Raine.

He would be honest with her. That was the best policy. The people in charge of a project that was completed by his company wanted a final inspection before releasing their money. If they saw a problem, this was the time to correct it. For the most part, that scenario was true. There was to be an inspection. If something was not quite right, his fixing the problem would save time and the money would come in quicker. Raine would buy that explanation. There was definitely a ring of truth to it. While Robert was considering this explanation, Claude had a few thoughts of his own.

The more he talked with Robert Blake, the more he liked the man. Not once did he refer to 'Sweet Pea' during the conversation. Nor did he refer to anything other than his schedule for a 'walk through' on a Sunday, the only day he had available. This, of course, was the day of the week they had talked about many weeks earlier. Someone listening to their conversation would think it was about a man accommodating someone for a final inspection. That thought made Claude smile. Robert might have made a good spook himself: quick on his feet, a blank sheet on his face.

***

Later that day when Robert phoned Raine, he was in for an unexpected surprise. "You mean this Sunday?" she asked when he explained the need for a final inspection. "That would work perfectly. Valerie decided to sublet my apartment and take over the lease. She would appreciate my helping her clear-out the clutter. Her friend is holding a garage sale next weekend."

"What about dinner Friday night?"

"How about a nightcap at my place later."

"I'll hold that thought. See you at seven." Robert pressed the end button, his mind going in a different direction.

He wondered if people thought their relationship was a bit strange. There they were, two adults engaged to be married and living apart. He and Raine had discussed this much earlier. Both decided in favor of the arrangement until they were married. Robert preferred the idea of living separately to satisfy outward appearances in general and Mackenzie, in particular. Not that she offered an opinion. She did not. His daughter had a key to the house and was more than welcome to drop in at any given time. That she would visit late Saturday night or early Sunday morning was not even a consideration. His daughter was either too damn busy or too lazy to care…he didn't bother to pick which one.

Raine's situation was different. She came and went at all hours, making appointments, showing houses. This was her busy time with referrals coming in and clients making housing changes before the start of their children's school year. This was not the right time for change; real estate would slow down soon enough.

Shortly after Robert's call, Raine phoned Valerie with her offer of help.

***

Later that same night Mackenzie had an unexpected visitor.

"I wanted to surprise you." The man slid a key into his trouser pocket. Then pulling her to him, kissed her hard on the mouth with a full burst of passion. He led her into the bedroom and began slowly undressing her, kissing her body with each piece of removed clothing. He studied the nude body before him, completely satisfied that she was solely his. "You are so beautiful."

As he spoke he placed one hand on the small of her back, while the other ran down the center of her loins. She yielded immediately to his touch, wanting him to continue, but knew it would not to happen. "Now, me," he whispered, "the way I taught you."

He watched her kiss his body with each article of removed clothing and yielded as her hand inched along the lower lines of his nude body to acknowledge his readiness. "I want you." She pressed against him, her message unequivocally clear…as he placed her body gently on the bed.

"It will always be like this." He looked down at her face, her body moving in rhythm with his. "You're mine. You always will be," he whispered to the woman whose soft rapturous moans justified his possession of her.

"I can't get enough of you." She rolled into his arms after they made love. "I wait for the weekends, hoping you'll stay longer." Her eyes held expectation.

"Then you're in for a surprise. I'm taking you to dinner Friday night."

"Can you stay over?" The question was almost a plea.

"No, but I can stay longer." He brushed a lock of hair away from her face and, brushing her lips, said, "I plan to remove your clothes slowly and kiss every inch of your body before we make love. You belong with me. I want no one standing between us…ever."

"I love you." She cuddled closer to him.

"I'll always want you."

"Do you really love me?" Mackenzie asked. "I wonder sometimes. You don't say it very often."

"Of course, I love you. I wouldn't mention marriage otherwise." He nuzzled her neck. "But I have to leave now." Mackenzie watched him dress and marveled that a man this handsome could love her. Upon leaving he reminded her about Friday. "I'll be by at seven."

She closed the door behind him and while locking it, wondered how he got a key to her apartment and why he visited her unexpectedly. Did he not trust her? Did he think there was someone else of interest? Perhaps, he missed having her in his arms. Yet, that seemed unlikely after making love at lunchtime in his condo. Maybe he needed more of her. Still, he always called before coming to the apartment. It was safer that way. So what changed? Had he learned something new about her father…something that could hasten their marriage? No. If something new had occurred, her grandmother would have called. There was no point in speculating. It would get her nowhere. She turned off the lamp switch and made her way to the bedroom.

While lying in bed a sudden thought occurred to her. Had he been checking her apartment when she was out with her friends? Although she had nothing to hide Mackenzie did not appreciate a home invasion.

***

After leaving Mackenzie, he placed her spare key under the doormat and went to his car. He would remember to tell her to find another hiding spot. The mat was not a safe place for hiding a key.

He felt good. Her body was so supple, so yielding with his. She was the younger version of his love, the small, youthful one…the goddess who ached with longing for his touch. He had trained her well.

These thoughts brought a smile to his face. Things were coming together. Her father would be married in a few weeks, leaving him more time to court his daughter. The thought made him laugh. The father would be living high on the escarpment with his new wife, while he was fornicating with the man's daughter in the valley.

***

"You've come prepared." Claude greeted Robert at the door of the building. "Are those papers or tools?" He pointed to a case Robert held.

"We both know what's inside. If I missed something, we're in trouble." He alluded to the stain kit and tools as he followed Claude to the elevator.

"That's what I thought."

Robert followed him behind the wall on the sixth floor to one of the large conference rooms.

"Wow!" The ornate brown molding captured his attention immediately. "This is perfect. It goes with the carpeting and furniture." He referred to the large conference table and upholstered chairs sitting on a plush carpet that embellished the room's highlights.

Within minutes, Claude brought in a ladder and all the materials necessary for installing 'Sweet Pea.'

"Where's the computer?" He caught Claude's hesitation. "I'm not prying into your business but we have to know if it works. You have an office somewhere with a hidden bank of computers just for 'Sweet Pea.' So let's get on with it. I really don't give a shit about your agenda, but I do take pride in my work."

He followed Claude to an office at the end of a long hall. From inside, the office looked normal. Behind a large desk facing the entryway stood a walled bookcase. Two chairs fronting the desk, a filing cabinet and a stand holding a potted plant seemed to fill the nondescript room entirely. Within minutes that vision changed. Claude pressed a corner frame of the bookcase causing a portion of it to slide and allow entry into a windowless room. A bank of computers lined one wall. Below them sat an equal amount of desk space and only two chairs. Robert noticed the writing materials resting there and remained silent throughout Claude's tour.

"Now you see why I am skeptical."

"No. I don't see that at all. You seem to know my schedule pretty well, so you know I'm not a threat to you or your security. As we install, we'll check the computer. If the placement seems wrong, we'll correct it. You ok with that?"

"Maybe I'll have you killed when we're finished."

"Do it before the second Saturday in September. I left everything in trust to my daughter, Mackenzie. The estate would be too messy once I'm married."

"You are one strange man, Robert Blake," Claude said walking back to the conference room.

Chapter 18
Steve

On Saturday morning, the week before Robert wedding, Steve Scaliezzi was kneeling under his sister's kitchen sink, repairing her garbage disposal once again.

"I'm not sure this disposal is big enough. What are you throwing down here? Not egg shells, I hope." He stood up to check his work.

"Coffee grinds, soft stuff, mostly," she said, setting the table with cups and plates. A carafe of freshly brewed coffee and a small platter of biscotti toasts centered the table.

He ran some tap water down the drain to hear the disposal purr. "It's fixed, for now," he said. "If you have any more problems, I'm getting you a new one." He began washing his hands.

"I made fresh coffee." Catherine pointed to the carafe.

"I can smell it." He poured coffee into his cup, took a biscotti and sat down.

"So, it's all happening next week." He shook his head. "Too fast for me. How the hell can you really know someone in four months? You tell me that."

"Four months? Is that what it is?" Catherine paused. "Mid-May. That's when he met her."

"If you take half of May and half of September, it totals four months. It's no mathematical equation."

"What are you saying?"

"Robbie's a dumb ass for rushing into marriage. What do we really know about Raine, other than she's young, beautiful and smart. Nothing." He answered his own question. "If it's sex, that'll soon fade. Nothing ever stays the way you think it will."

"You sound like you have a problem."

"No. It's the same old shit, different day. Dorothy wants to remodel our kitchen. I didn't marry a woman: I married a project. She goes from one thing to another."

"Are you going to?"

"Not now. I just bought the truck. The old one was falling apart. You knew that. If I don't have reliable transportation, I'm out of business."

"So she's upset."

"No. I have her busy with brochures." Her brother began to laugh. "She got a new dress for the wedding. Now Dorothy's looking for shoes."

"She's not alone. I bought something a month ago but damned if I know why."

"You're the mother of the groom. You should have something new."

"For a cocktail party?"

"I don't think I understand." He looked thoroughly confused.

"It's not going to be a big affair. Raine wants a small ceremony with just the family and a cocktail party that evening. No dinner. No reception."

"She may think that's the way to go, since Robbie was married before."

"I don't buy it. Every woman dreams of a church wedding and reception. It doesn't have to be big; it just has to take place."

"You don't like the idea."

"Her big ceremony will take place over his coffin…when she comes into his money."

"You really don't like her." He met his sister's stare. "I never realized you felt this way. I mean to that degree."

"I don't trust her. I don't know why, but I don't. When Emily looked at Robbie, you could see the love in her eyes. This cornache, this witch, lacks the look of a woman in love."

"And you never told Robbie your true feelings?"

"I couldn't. He's so damn lovesick, I want to throw-up. He even took the car to have it serviced and detailed for his princess. When was the last time he had it detailed? Years, that's when." Her rage continued. "Maybe, it's me. I kept hearing that screeching brake sound, but the man at the garage said he still had wear on them. I guess this marriage is making me crazy."

"I wonder how Mackenzie's taking it. There's what? An eight or nine year age difference. That's got to rub her the wrong way."

"From what I heard, she gave him her blessing months ago, when they met for lunch."

"She's another piece of work that needs checking, but I am not going down that road. Let him contend with it."

"Apparently she came out with a high average according to Robbie. So she must have been studying when we thought otherwise," Catherine informed him.

"It's the "otherwise" that still bothers me, but we covered that history when he was in Italy."

"Speaking of Italy, Raine sublet her apartment to Valerie. She was the friend who had an accident and missed the trip. After Robbie left Florence, Raine took a train to Rome. At least that was my understanding."

"I can't blame her for going. After spending all that money on airfare and hotel reservations, she had to go by herself. I would have done the same thing. It's that or lose a bundle. It's good she took in Rome too."

"I'm not faulting her. I just wish she had gone a week earlier or later."

"She wouldn't have met Robbie."

"Exactly."

"Bite your tongue Sis," he cautioned. "She'll turn you into an enemy and ruin the relationship you already have with him."

"I just feel like the family's going to hell." Her eyes began to glisten. "It's all changing and not for the better. Why couldn't he have found someone who was real? Someone who truly loved him? I know he could never replace Emily, but Raine? She doesn't even come close."

"I agree, but you have to accept her or lose Robbie."

"I am going to die knowing my son made a tragic mistake."

"You are not going to die, and if she becomes more of a bitch, he can always divorce her or…"

They stared at each other and began laughing hysterically.

"I'm glad you came."

"Anytime, Sis." He gathered his tools and walked toward the front door with Catherine following him. "Wonder what Chatty Cathie has going for me when I get home."

"Dorothy should only know how you talk about her."

"She's a good lady. Really she is. It's just sometimes, a little duct tape would come in handy."

Catherine watched her brother leave and wondered how a family could be so screwed up. Were all families like that? If she had to guess, the answer would be yes.

***

"Tomorrow's the day," he reminded Raine during a phone conversation. "You getting nervous?"

"No. I can't wait. I'm ready."

"I'm wondering if we should stay near the airport after the cocktail party."

"I thought we were staying at the Macroft Saturday night. I took my luggage to the room they gave us."

"I'm not cancelling it," he reassured her. "We need the room to freshen-up for the cocktail party. I asked my uncle to take our wedding clothes back to the house on Sunday. I don't want to leave them in the car at the airport. He can collect them when the party's over."

"If we are keeping the room, why should we go to a hotel near the airport? Why not sleep at the Macroft?"

Before Raine could ask another question, Robert interrupted their conversation. "We had a flight change. The airline called last night. We leave thirty minutes earlier than scheduled and staying near the airport seemed to make more sense. I really don't want to be driving to Pittsburgh International at three in the morning."

"Whatever you decide is fine by me," she said unruffled by the news. "The caterer called with a question about serving but we're still set for seven. Everything seems to be falling in place. I even picked-up my bouquet for tomorrow."

"I'll see you in the chapel at four." He referred to a small stone chapel which was adjacent the Church of God on Blackstone Road and a mere ten minutes away from the Macroft hotel.

"My limousine comes at three-thirty."

"Fine. Look for me. I'll be the one in the tux."

"You are so funny." She ended their conversation.

***

Later that afternoon Raine had her hair done at a salon she used regularly. Knowing that her wedding was the following day, her stylist suggested a softer look, something that would complement the white ankle-length dress she described. The end result was perfect. The hair style suited her face.

"If you need a comb-out tomorrow, come by. I'll take you immediately." The stylist reassured her.

Seeing her stylist, if needed, would present no problem. She would still have her car. In fact the vehicle would be sitting in the parking lot of her old apartment until she returned from Hawaii.

Raine left the shop feeling beautiful and very hungry. She checked her watch. It was after five. Not wanting to eat alone, she wondered if Valerie would be interested in meeting her and placed a call.

Chapter 19

Wedding

As planned, the family gathered inside the stone chapel on Blackstone Road at four o'clock to witness the marriage between Lorraine Shaw and Robert Blake. To an outsider, the gathering would have seemed strange indeed, for those in attendance were on the groom's side of the family. No one came for the bride…not parents, nor relatives or friends. However, the glaring vacuum did not dampen the spirits of the two people standing before the minister.

"They look so happy." The remark came from Dorothy who was so taken with the couple at the altar that she failed to notice the exchange of ugly looks between her husband and his sister. "She's so beautiful." Dorothy wiped her eyes with a tissue Mackenzie gave her. "Your father is so handsome," she whispered to her niece.

Mackenzie studied her aunt for a moment, wishing the woman would stop blabbering, and then turned to watch the ceremony. When the rings were being exchanged Raine signaled Mackenzie to hold her flowered bouquet of lilies until the ceremony was over.

As soon as the minister pronounced their union, the family rushed to the couple, kissing, cheering and congratulating them.

"We're so happy for you," Dorothy screeched joyfully, her high-pitched voice hitting the chapel rafters.

Catherine kissed her son and hugged her daughter-in-law quickly, noticing Mackenzie standing behind her.

Last in line, Steve joined the chorus of well-wishers with a hug for Robbie and a cheek kiss for Raine.

"Ok." Robert sought their attention. "I want to thank the family for sharing our special day." He beamed at his new wife, his arm wrapped around her. "Raine and I will meet you at the Macroft for dinner, just as soon as we finish here. They reserved a special room for us."

The group took "finish" as an indication of the minister's payment.

***

The Macroft Hotel held the reputation for having a beautifully appointed ballroom. Along three walls and strategically placed were carved wooden pillars that framed festoon-draped windows and lighted wall sconces. However, it was the domed frescoed ceiling that commanded praise by those who attended functions there. The highly polished hardwood floor, walnut brown in color, acted as a mirror that brought the room together as a whole. Double wooden doors, matching the carved pillars, served as the main entrance to the magnificent room.

Aside from its beauty, Raine found the room large enough to accommodate a hundred guests for her lavish cocktail party. White-clothed tables, carefully placed, held several varieties of hors d'oeurves. In the center of each one sat a small candelabra whose flickering flames added additional ambiance to the dimly-lit room. A bar at the far end held a full display of liquor and wine bottles on shelves behind it. On one side of the bar counter sat a pyramid of different-sized glasses. Beneath it were containers of ice. Waiters in black uniforms added an exclusive touch to the expensive affair and knew a large tip depended on the quality of service they provided. The caterer had already researched Mr. Blake's wealth.

***

It was shortly before seven o'clock when the family greeted the caterer who was walking around the room inspecting the tables of assorted hors d'oeurves.

"What do you think?" she asked, directing her question to Raine.

"Everything looks so beautiful." Raine glowed with pride. Her plans had come to fruition.

"I'm having a waiter place a small table in the corner, just in case someone brings a gift." She pointed to a specific area.

We requested no gifts on the invitations," Raine sighed, "but that might be a good idea. I'll have Mackenzie keep an eye on it."

"You never know." The caterer stopped speaking suddenly, her eyes focused on the doorway. "You have guests coming." She watched the couple walk away to greet their friends and left the room hurriedly.

***

Somewhere around eight o'clock, when the cocktail party was in full swing Steve left his wife with a cluster of chatty women and signaled his sister to keep her occupied. Catherine assumed he wanted to get away to give his ears a rest. But instead, she watched him study the group of realtors Raine introduced to her husband and walk toward the hors d'oeurves table of their choosing.

"Do you know what those triangles are? The stuff on top?" he asked the short, squat woman standing next to him. Her red hair, the color of pimento, was a vivid contrast to the white suit she wore. And for some reason, Steve pictured her as a woman with a hot temper and knew he would have to tread carefully.

"I think that's tuna. Try the bread toasts. They are really good."

Steve took her suggestion and approved the selection. "Cheese toasts. They are good." He took another one and followed her lead by moving away from the table so others in line could make their selections.

"They make a nice looking couple," he said, glancing across the room at Raine and Robbie."

"Who would have thought she'd have her own cash cow?" the woman groused. "Raine is such a loner. Nobody really knows her socially."

"I heard they met in Rome." He ignored her sarcasm.

"No. They met in Florence." She corrected him immediately.

"Wasn't there something about her friend having an accident and couldn't take the trip with her?"

"What do you mean?" She challenged him, somewhat confused by his remark.

"Her friend, Valerie. They work together, I think."

"We don't have a Valerie in the office. In fact, there's no one named Valerie with our company. I should know. I'm the secretary, Gracie Lacey," she said, her snippy tone derisive. "And don't say one word about my name. I'm sick of people mocking it."

"Stephen Scally." He introduced himself. "I apologize," he added humbly. His thoughts, however, were whirling with mistrust for the bride. "I am so bad with names. I've always been cursed with forgetting some-one's name. Now I'm even mixed-up with first meetings. I'm terribly sorry."

"That happens." She understood, totally softened by this pathetic man's apology. "But she went alone to Florence. I schedule office time so I have to know the availability of our sales people." She became quiet for a moment. "If someone were to accompany her privately, I wouldn't be privy to that."

"Still, it was a wonderful opportunity to see all the historic land-marks of Florence, Rome and Venice."

"You really are a confused man. She never went to Rome or Ven-ice. That's what's so surprising. She was gone for six days. Four, really, if you count two days travel. It was a total waste of money, if you ask me. But then she came back with a man, money and marriage. You can't beat that."

"But they did meet in Florence?" His face took on a crazed expres-sion purposely when he asked the question. Steve needed to look like a forgetful man bordering senility.

"Yes, they did."

"I am so glad. I love happy endings." Following his statement, he continued the façade with her. "Have you been there yet?" He pointed to the table they had just left. "I want to check it out."

"I think you should." She dismissed him and walked away in disgust. Why was she left to converse with a senile old man who didn't remember names, places or where he had his last hors d'oeurves? She would keep their conversation secret. The office would mock her otherwise.

***

When Steve returned to his wife and sister, Dorothy was still talking with the same group. He signaled his sister and moved away to speak with her privately.

Before we go home, I have to go to Robbie's room for their wedding clothes. They don't want to leave them in the car while they're in Hawaii. You and Dorothy can wait in the hotel lounge."

"Is that why you signaled me?" she sighed. Catherine could not understand his need for a private conversation when he only spoke of clothing.

"We have to talk," he said, an urgency in his voice. "The clothes are my excuse to leave Dorothy tomorrow morning."

"You learned something." Catherine stiffened. "It's about that witch he just married."

"Lower your voice," Steve cautioned. "We'll have time to talk tomorrow. You still have a key to his place, don't you?"

"I do. Is it bad?" she pressed, "the information you learned? I'm not going to sleep tonight. I knew she was trouble."

"Too late now. They're married…but maybe there is something we can do."

"I am not going down that road." Catherine shook her head in response.

"I wasn't thinking of continuing the family tradition."

"If you have an alternative, I'd like to hear it."

"Coffee and biscotti, tomorrow, he said, walking toward Dorothy's group.

Catherine watched her brother and wondered what crazy plan was going through his head. She hoped this one would work. He never did find the answer to Mackenzie's scheduled absences. Yet, somehow she felt this was a much more serious matter.

***

"How did you get away so early?" Catherine greeted her brother as she climbed into the passenger side of his car.

"I told her the truth. Dorothy saw the clothes last night when I put them in the trunk, so she knows I'm going to Robbie's. It all worked out," he added. "She's going to church with one of the neighbors and I'm off-the-hook for a while. Did you remember to bring the key?"

"It's here," Catherine patted her pocket. "I think we should lay their wedding outfits on the living room couch. Raine may not appreciate our going into their bedroom."

"Like I really care what she thinks!"

He was angry. Catherine knew it but refused to press him further. He would reveal its source when he was ready and focused. That meant he would reveal the problem and correct it with a solution. They drove in silence for several minutes before he spoke again.

"I hate this steep grade. Why the hell people want to live on the escarpment escapes me. I always said this place was meant for goats. One of these days someone's going to get killed. Mark my words."

"Did you see that?" Catherine tapped her brother's arm when he turned onto her son's street. "Someone just left Robbie's house."

"I didn't see anything."

"Someone was there. I saw him."

"A man?" he asked, pulling into the driveway. "Let's have a look. You do know the code for his alarm system, don't you?"

"Of course." Catherine scolded as she punched in the numbers to disarm it.

Catherine watched her brother lay the wedding clothes on the living room couch before inspecting every room of the house.

"Everything's fine." He reassured her. "We should go."

"Stefano, I saw a man come out of this house."

"Well, he isn't here now. We should leave." He ushered his sister out of the house and into his car.

***

When they arrived at Catherine's house, Steve watched her pour coffee into two cups from a carafe centering the table.

"The coffee's fresh. I made it before you came. We weren't gone that long so I know it's still hot." She placed a biscotti on his plate from a platter adjacent the carafe and then sat down. She sipped her coffee slowly and remained silent.

"You saw me talking to the woman at the hors d'oeurves table last night."

"The witch with the flaming red hair and white suit? I thought she needed a trident to complete her costume."

Her brother ignored her sarcasm and repeated his conversation with the woman. "She's the secretary at Raine's real estate office. She had a funny name like "Henny Penny." No. It was more like "Goosey Loosey." That's not it. It's Gracie Lacey."

"Are you telling me the sky is falling?"

"It already fell. There is no Valerie in her office or within the entire company. Raine went to Florence alone."

"Then Valerie must be a friend. Otherwise, Raine wouldn't have sublet the apartment to her. Maybe she did have an accident. The secretary wouldn't have that information."

"That could be true," he conceded, "but why lie about going to Rome? I even added Venice to the itinerary. According to the office schedule Raine was gone for six days. She spent two traveling and four in Florence. Why lie to Robbie about the other city? Then Gracie Lacey called Robbie, Raine's 'cash cow.'"

"Meaning she married him for his money. He was right about "fatto." The phone call meant, "Done." The whole thing was a set up."

"Exactly."

"Did the woman know that you're Robbie's uncle? She may say something to Raine."

"No, but it won't come back. I used a factitious name, close enough to be misconstrued, if necessary, and acted senile toward the end of our conversation. She was dying to get away from me. The woman was embarrassed. She's not going to share our conversation with anyone."

"What do you mean misconstrued?"

"I doubt that she'll ever see a picture of me, but if she does, nothing will happen. Gracie Lacey will think she misunderstood the introduction or that I was so far gone, I couldn't remember my own name."

Catherine snickered at the explanation. "You are a piece of work."

"Now that we have the information, what do we do with it?"

"We can't tell Robbie," Catherine mused. "He's so in love with her, he'll hate us."

"We can't let it go on," Steve argued. "He's been taken."

"But if she makes him happy, there's nothing we can do about it. It's his money."

"You still don't get it!" He became even more upset with her. "What part of this situation don't you understand? How did Raine, a complete stranger, know Robbie would be in Florence the third week of May? And don't tell me they could have met by chance. This was a carefully planned trap to lure your son. Who knew he would be away then?"

"All his friends, workers, business people. Robbie had to tell them he'd be gone for a week. He might have told them he was going to Florence but he wouldn't tell them his reason for the trip."

"That's no help at all. Someone planning this with Raine would have been at the cocktail party. We wouldn't know her contact because she played the whole starry-eyed scene so well. Raine stuck to Robbie like glue." Steve sat still, a puzzled expression crossing his face. "There has to be a benefit. What benefit?" His question lingered. "How would Raine's partner benefit by her marriage to Robbie?"

"We'd have to discover the name of her partner first," Catherine said. "Once we have that information, we can track their deception."

"And how do you propose we do that?"

"I don't know. I can sniff around the office but where we go after that…?" Her voice trailed off.

"I am so sick of this family!" he exploded. "First, it was Mackenzie. I got nowhere with that. Now, it's Robbie and it is serious. Using his money on herself is one thing, but suppose this is a plan to affect his company. Bring it down somehow. Then what?"

"You're making me nervous. What should we do?"

"We should tell him. I'd rather have him pissed and knowledge-able instead of dumb and happy." His insistence bothered her.

"Couldn't we wait until they're home for a while?"

"A while means one week or until we see an opening for a private conversation. You invite him to come here alone. I want to talk with him. He should know about Gracie Lacey's conversation." He stood up, kissed his sister's cheek and left the house.

Catherine watched her brother drive away, so many questions crossing her mind. How would they ever discover who was in this scheme with Raine? Was it the man she saw coming out of Robbie's house? She felt so helpless. In fact, she felt this same way when Emily lay dying. Was this situation a precursor of bad things to come? Catherine already knew the answer.

Chapter 20
An Addition

"What are you doing here?" Catherine demanded. "When you called last night I thought you weren't coming in today." The woman was very surprised to see him, since he had just returned from his honeymoon.

"I have a lot to catch-up on and so does Raine," Robert explained.

"I stacked some personal mail on your desk: wedding congratulations, that kind of thing. But I think you should call Bruce. He's called twice this week."

"Probably about Jenna," he mused. "I didn't expect them at the cocktail party." Robert left her with that thought as he walked into his office.

"Hello bridegroom," Bruce answered when Robert's name appeared on his caller ID. "When did you get back?"

"Last night."

"And you couldn't stay in bed for the rest of the day?"

"Raine had to go to the office and things are piling up here. You know how that goes, but enough of that. How is Jenna?"

"It's slow, but she's improving. I knew you'd understand our situation. I mean about the cocktail party."

"I'd never let a cocktail party split our friendship. Your priority is Jenna. How is she really? I mean after the surgery?"

"Breathing is difficult with a third of her lung gone. She tires so easily. But we were fortunate, Jenna doesn't need chemo."

"Who's handling the case?"

"Our family doctor. We're done with Haig unless there's a problem."

"Were you satisfied with him?"

"His methodical approach made Jenna trust him immediately. She didn't feel like a statistic. He spent a lot of time with us, and that gave Jenna the kind of medical support she needed."

"I am so glad it worked out."

"I'm sorry I couldn't call you before. With everything going on, Memorial Sloan Kettering and the surgery, I was an emotional mess. I knew you'd understand, having gone through it yourself."

"That's why I didn't bother you. I knew the hell you were going through. When life is in the balance, you focus on the best outcome possible."

"Still, I'll never be able to thank you enough...for Jenna and my two men. I didn't expect you to carry them an extra month."

"They helped us with our vacation schedule."

"Someone threw away your mold a long time ago." He ended the call.

When Robert began reading the cards congratulating him on his wedding, he found one that captured his complete attention. It had no stamp or return address and sat mixed in the stack as a deliberate effort for concealment. How did he get into his office? That was his first thought. What a stupid question. Robert revised his thinking. The man was like an apparition: he could materialize anywhere he wanted. Now Robert had two. He found that thought disconcerting.

He reread the typed but plain card again. "Three's not good enough. You need two pair."

Robert folded the card and slid it into his pocket. If his thoughts were correct, Robert had to get home before Raine returned. Now, he needed an excuse to leave the office, one that would make sense and not arouse suspicion.

As soon as he approached the outer office, John Harris greeted him as he stood near Catherine's desk. "Congratulations." John shook his hand. "Catherine said you got in last night. How was Hawaii?"

"Really beautiful. The weather was perfect, but I must have picked-up a bug in Maui."

"You don't look sick," he said, surprised by the news. "You don't sound sick either."

"I agree with John," Catherine offered. "What's the matter?"

"Nothing, really. I just feel tired."

"You just got back from a long trip, maybe you should go home," his mother advised.

"I can't." He caught John's puzzled look. "Someone sent a wedding gift and I forgot to have my mail delivered."

"Are you coming back to the office?"

"That's the plan," he replied, knowing John would be on the phone updating Henry as soon as Robert left the building.

"By the way, you throw one helleva cocktail party."

"That was all Raine's doing."

"Well, tell your beautiful wife I enjoyed it."

"You can tell her yourself when we have the group over for steaks."

"Great!" He watched him leave the office and turned to Catherine. "Do you know where he's going?"

"The post office for a package," she said, knowing his tricks.

With that response, John walked away. Although it was a quiet exit, Catherine heard his door close. She knew immediately he would be phoning Henry Price at Global; however, she was comforted by the thought that Robbie knew it too.

***

After leaving the office, Robert drove directly to his home. Questions ran through his mind as he took the steep grade to the escarpment. He already knew what made the second pair. But why was it necessary? Where would it be? The last thing he needed was a treasure hunt. He felt so tired.

Robert was glad to find the driveway empty when he pulled in. That meant Raine was still at the office and he had time to explore and inspect the house. He took a flashlight from the glove compartment of his car, disarmed the alarm and, before beginning a detailed inspection of his home, ran to his bedroom and checked the computer inside his nightstand. He was not surprised by the note lying on top of the keyboard. Only one word was written in capital letters: DUNCE. He captured the meaning and smiled. He was not to check the computer for the location of 'Sweet Pea.' He had to find it on his own. These were the rules of the game: find first, recheck later. He slid the note into his pocket.

Robert examined the molding in the master bedroom and bathroom. 'Sweet Pea' was in place. A flashlight examination of the hall and three other bedrooms revealed no installation. "Damn you," he swore on his way down to the first floor. Finding the living room intact with 'Sweet Pea,' he went to his private office or den when Emily was alive, the family room and formal dining room. The last room he examined was the kitchen. In a mitered corner of the molding sat 'Sweet Pea,' the most miniature surveillance system he had ever worked on.

Now, he understood. It wasn't a matter of two pairs. At least he didn't think so. This was a confirmation of having two pairs. When Robert was tentatively awarded the contract, he agreed to a trial installation of 'Sweet Pea' in his home. This was with the understanding that someone would inspect his work before the contract was finalized. However, no one ever came and he was still awarded the contract. At some point someone must have inspected, but without his knowledge. So this was Claude's way of imparting that information. Still, Robert remained confused.

Did Claude actually think he needed a fourth 'Sweet Pea?' When did he install it? Was it when Robert was away on his honeymoon? Was he being watched? Neither Claude nor Elias would have had trouble getting into his house. Both were experts at home invasion. The only difference between them was Elias' affinity for Robert's scotch…and his drinking glasses. No. This was Claude's handiwork. There was no doubt whatsoever in his mind. But the question of its need remained. Why would Claude think Robert needed a fourth 'Sweet Pea?' He also wondered if his friend, Elias, knew Claude. He knew the answer but would never ask.

Robert reached into his pocket and, pulling out the card and note, watched them burn to ash in a deep dish he took from the cupboard. He rinsed the dish quickly, dried it with a paper towel and returned it to the cupboard shelf. Within seconds he ran upstairs to check the computer. After placing it on his lap, Robert tapped-in the very complex code to scan all four rooms. Satisfied that the system was totally operable, he closed the small computer and returned it to his nightstand. He had completed the rules of the game. Would there ever be a time he would use this very sophisticated surveillance system in his home? Robert didn't think so.

Would he ever see Claude again? That question remained in his thoughts. There would be little point in asking Elias. He would lie and say he didn't know the man. No. Any meeting would have to be initiated by Claude. Robert had no way of getting in touch with him. If he recalled correctly, Claude had his cell number. With Claude, it was always one way…his.

Robert felt tired. He needed to lie down.

***

In another part of town, a pointed conversation was taking place.
"I'm surprised at your call. How was it?"
"Couldn't have been better."
"Did you follow my instructions?"
"Of course."
"Any problems?"
"None." There was a slight pause. "When can we meet?"
"It's too dangerous."
"I miss you."
"I'll work something out." The call ended.

Chapter 21
Gracie Lacey

"Hello!" Raine shouted as she walked into the living room, expecting to see her husband. She peaked inside his office then wandered into the kitchen. Robert must be upstairs asleep she thought. She remembered how tired he was that morning. Raine took the stairs quietly to her bedroom where she found Robert under the covers and fast asleep. She removed her clothing and slid under the covers with him.

"I love the way you greet me," he said, awakened by the nearness of her body.

"My motives are pure." She pressed against him.

"I love you so much." He moved to her welcoming arms.

**

Later, Robert and Raine lay in bed giggling and laughing over silly things.

"Know what I'd really like to do this weekend?" Robert queried.

"With your mind, I can't possibly imagine."

"We seal this place, stay in bed, talk and play. Just lounge around in pajamas the whole time. I would like that."

"You're on for Saturday, but I have an open house Sunday. The homeowners on Stoller requested it."

"I thought real estate was slowing down now."

"October is still a good month for sales. Mine die in November and December, unless an out-of-towner takes a new job in Pittsburgh and needs a house."

Robert began to laugh. "I look forward to coming home and finding you barefoot and ready."

"That would become boring. I mean finding me in bed every day."

"I'm sure I could think of something to make it more interesting." He pulled her to him and pressed his lips with hers.

***

Later that evening when Raine was on the phone with one of her clients, Robert received a phone call from his mother.

"I just wanted to know if you were alright. When you didn't return to the office, I thought you might have gone home to rest."

"I did take a nap."

"How do you feel?"

"Rested," he said. "I'll be in tomorrow." Before ending the call, he added, "I may drop by for lunch on Sunday. Raine has an open house."

"Plan on it. I'll make shells."

"With meatballs?"

"Of course."

"You're on." He ended the call, feeling very satisfied with his mother's menu.

***

"What's up?" Steve asked when his sister phoned.

"Robbie's coming for lunch on Sunday. I cinched it by offering shells."

"What's the catch?"

"What do you mean?"

"Is he coming alone? You didn't mention the bitch he married, or is she coming too?"

"She has an open house."

"This is our opportunity to tell him. What time should I come?"

"My guess would be one o'clock, but I'll ask him tomorrow at the office. What are you going to tell Dorothy?"

"Same old. You have a problem with your disposal again." Steve pressed the end button when Catherine heard Dorothy's voice calling him.

At long last they would have Robbie to themselves. How would Steve approach her son with the information he received from Gracie Lacey? Her brother was not exactly diplomatic when discussing difficult matters. She was fearful he would come-on like a Mack Truck and anger Robbie. Nevertheless, Steve had his own way of doing things. The information he would impart would be direct and pointed. She hoped he wouldn't interject his own opinion of Robbie's new wife. That alone could estrange their relationship.

***

"You said one o'clock," Steve walked into his sister's kitchen, the smell of sauce permeating the house. "I came a little early hoping I could help." He eyed the three place settings. "What can I do?"

"Everything's under control," she offered. "I'll put the meatballs and shells on the table when he comes." Catherine watched her brother sit down.

"You're nervous. I can tell."

"I just don't want to anger him."

"I don't really care if he gets pissed. Robbie should know she lied to him. If there's more to this, he should be aware of it," he added.

"Promise me you won't argue with him."

"That was never my plan. I just want him to have the information I received at the cocktail party." He stopped speaking suddenly. "I heard a car. I think Robbie's here."

***

"Hey, Uncle Steve." Robert shook his hand and then hugged his mother. "Can I do anything?"

"Sit down," Catherine said filling platters from the pots on the stove. She placed the platters on the table and sat down. "How do you feel?"

"A lot better now."

"Were you ill?" His uncle expressed concern.

"I picked-up something in Maui."

"What happened?" Steve continued to ask.

"I almost collapsed and spent the day in bed. Raine went to the beach alone."

"That had to be a hardship." The sarcastic remark slipped from Steve's mouth unintentionally, causing him to apologize.

"Ok. What's going on?" His eyes slid from his mother to his uncle. "I come for lunch with my mother and find my uncle. The table's set for three people and my mother cooked a humongous amount of food. This is a family meeting. That's the only thing I can think of."

Before Steve started speaking, Catherine took the opportunity to fill everyone's plate.

"I met the secretary of Raine's company at your cocktail party and learned a few things that bothered me. Things you should know." Steve went on to reveal his whole conversation with Gracie Lacey."

"You're saying there is no Valerie at the company."

"That's what she said. Maybe you were right about 'fatto.'"

"What do you mean?" Robbie couldn't understand Steve's change in direction.

"He's translating idiomatically about the phone conversation you overheard," Catherine explained. "It's done…fatto. That word could have signaled Raine's meeting you."

"I find that hard to believe. Raine loves me."

"If she loves you so much, why did she lie about going to Rome? Why was that necessary? Was it to make her trip more plausible?" Steve questioned, seeking a response.

"There has to be an explanation."

"I'm sure there is, but satisfy me for a minute. Let's just say that you were lured into a honey trap. Who would benefit?"

"Where are you going with this?" Robert found his premise unbelievable.

"Suppose your meeting Raine was part of a larger plan to ruin you."

"You've been watching too much television."

"It wasn't television when I saw a man leave your house!" Catherine interrupted loudly. "We were returning the wedding clothes when I saw him."

"When was this?" He broke a meatball with his fork.

"The Sunday after your wedding," Steve interjected.

Robert remained silent during that portion of the conversation and continued eating. Now he knew when Claude installed 'Sweet Pea.'

"Your food is getting cold," Catherine scolded her brother.

"No. It's not." He took a bite of a large stuffed shell. "These are so good. I wish Dorothy could cook like this."

"Aunt Dorothy didn't have Nonna as a teacher. She was a fabulous cook," Robert interjected.

"She really was. Does Raine cook?" The question came from Catherine.

"She's pretty good in the kitchen, but not like you."

"Where is she today?"

"She has an open house. Stoller Road I think."

"You sure?" Steve dropped the question and continued eating.

***

After dinner, Robert stayed long enough to clear the table and engage in a short conversation. Although his thoughts were running rampant, the calmness he portrayed would never have suggested the rage running through him. He had to get away, but it had to be done in an appreciative manner.

"This was a wonderful meal." He kissed his mother's cheek and shook hands with his Uncle.

"I'm glad we had this conversation." He addressed his Uncle before leaving the house. "I appreciate your having my back."

Catherine and her brother sat at the table, facing each other in silence, each wondering if the conversation had the intended impact.

"Did it make a difference?"

"Doesn't matter," Steve answered.

"That makes no sense whatsoever."

"Regardless of what he thinks right now, at this very moment, there will come a time when he'll wonder if someone really did set a trap for him. It may not be tomorrow, but it will happen. I pity the bastard when it does because Robbie won't have any mercy in destroying him."

"What make you so damn sure?" she demanded.

"I know people. Deep down inside, everyone has a destructive vein. Most people just rationalize, hoping things will get better. Robbie's another story. You never know his thoughts. He's a calm piece of work. That's what makes him so deadly."

"He took your conversation with Gracie Lacey pretty well."

"You keep thinking that, Sis." He kissed her cheek, ready to leave.

"You think I'm wrong."

"I'm saying we've given him food for thought."

Chapter 22
Lies

Robert drove away quickly from his mother's house, his thoughts on Raine. He had to think through the information imparted. Were those things his Uncle mentioned true? Had Raine lied about Valerie's accident as an excuse for traveling alone? Was that the pretext for one solo traveler meeting another? Of course, being from the same city was just supposed to be a coincidence, nothing more. What about "fatto?" Was that Raine's signal for accomplishment? It was done: they had met and now she would let his hormones take over. That thought led to another.

Why did Raine lie about Valerie being a co-worker when the secretary told his Uncle otherwise? Why not just acknowledge the friendship? Raine sublet her apartment to the woman, so an element of trust had to exist between them. Still, why hadn't he met her? He would have, had she not been on a scheduled cruise the week of their wedding. She did, however, send a beautiful wedding gift, a Waterford crystal bowl. Then another thought occurred to him.

If Raine lied about Valerie to cement their meeting, why lie about going to Rome? He already knew the answer. It gave credence to her trip. She couldn't just go to Florence for a few days. Who travels to Italy without seeing Rome? Usually, tourists see the big three: Rome, Florence and Venice. He could trap her on that lie without much effort.

Robert checked his watch. It was almost three-thirty. Her open house ended at four. He knew the location was Stoller Road but lacked the address. His best bet was to go home and check the Sunday paper. The address would be listed, if Raine really had an open house. There were still a few more Sundays in October and he would become an avid reader of the real estate section: open houses in general, hers in particular.

As he drove down his street, Robert was surprised to see Raine's car parked in the driveway. Why was she home so early?

"Raine," he called as he walked from the living room to the kitchen. Thinking something was wrong, he took the stairs to the bedroom and found her coming out of the shower.

"Are you ok? You had me worried." He deliberately expressed concern.

"No. Just bored. I closed early. It was a long afternoon with just one walk through." She brushed his lips, pressing her nude body against him.

"You smell good."

"Got any ideas?"

"Maybe." He lifted her suddenly, placed her on their bed, and began to undress hurriedly

"I like your surprises."

"I have a few more in mind." As his tongue inched between her lips, he could feel the tenseness of her body in anticipation.

Sex was something he would take: revenge was a given.

***

"What would you like for dinner?" he asked as she lay cuddled in his arms.

"I thought we had dinner." She laughed but her smugness did not resonate with Robert's placid expression.

"Do you want to go out to eat?" He wanted a serious answer.

"Can't we just have something here, sandwiches, bacon and eggs?"

"You're on." Robert climbed out of bed, got dressed and sailed downstairs to the kitchen.

"You must be hungry." She trailed behind him.

"I am," he lied. But Robert was not hungry. He was anxious to check the newspaper for an address. Cross examining her on Italy was another matter. "How about bacon and eggs?"

"Good. I'll make toast."

They sat on the kitchen stools deep in conversation when Robert mentioned his travels.

"I always regretted not going back to Rome and Venice. Even the island of Capri with its "Blue Grotto" was memorable. You would hear the men who guided the boats singing in the caves. It was a wonderful experience. I would like to take you there."

"Sounds beautiful."

"Maybe we could go there next year and also tour Rome and Venice. I know you just visited Rome, but would you mind?"

"Not at all. It would be fun seeing those cities together."

"What did you like best about Rome? The Spanish Steps?"

"I didn't get to that section of the city."

"Remember the huge square with all the fountains? I can't remember its name."

"I can't either." She scratched her head.

"Did you get to Piazza Navona?"

"It was too far away from the main attractions on my list."

"That makes me feel so much better. We'll put it on our own list of places to see. Want some more toast?" He gave her a plate and went on to a different subject, his expression giving no hint of the rage growing within him. The cross examination was complete. His wife was a liar…

When dinner was over, Robert turned on the living room TV, grabbed the Sunday paper and settled on the couch.

"What are you watching?" Raine entered the room.

"The news. Put something else on. I want to read the paper."

***

Raine was still at home when Robert left for work the next day. He didn't go to his office. Instead, Robert drove to a nearby park and sat on a bench, his bench, the one that captured his tears when Emily passed away. That memory always stayed with him. He sat in solitude for hours, weeping for his dead wife and wishing he had one more moment with her.

Now his weeping bench witnessed another emotion, one of rage for his new bride's deception. Raine had lied about their meeting and she lied about visiting Rome and the two main attractions he used to trap her. In the tourist area of Rome, throngs of people would sit on the Spanish Steps, just to watch the parade of people passing by, coming or going to other landmarks merely blocks away. Everyone sat on the famous Spanish Steps, so framed with fresh flowers, if only for five minutes. Then too, and within walking distance, Raine lied about Piazza Navona, the huge square with Bernini's famous Fountain of Four Rivers, a main attraction everyone visited. Robert particularly like the church of St. Agnes in Agone facing the Piazza. It had an austere, yet hauntingly beautiful aura about it. He remembered seeing her skull and lighting candles for dead relatives. Whoever schooled Raine did not know Rome.

Maybe his Uncle had a point. No one would go to Europe for the purpose of meeting a particular stranger unless it was part of an elaborate plan. Was someone really behind Raine's façade of love and marriage? Someone out to ruin him? He found it hard to believe since his wife played the "loving" part so well. Throughout their entire relationship he felt her love for him was real. While she may not have been verbal, her actions proved otherwise. If she really cared, why not tell him the truth?

Then Robert considered something else. Was Raine being coerced or blackmailed to some degree? Who would want to ruin him? John Harris? Henry Price? Neither man would use a woman to ruin his business. Henry would use cost as a competitive edge. John would ruin him from within. His hiring methods proved that. Still John had plans with Henry. So who was left? Bruce Parks was not even a consideration.

Within minutes, Robert left the park and was on the way to an address on Stoller Road in Penn Hills. He parked on the street fronting the two-story Colonial and walked up the driveway looking like a prospective buyer. To his surprise, the house was vacant.

He walked around the home, peeking in windows and noting the few items of furniture that remained. As Robert approached his car, he noticed a woman walking her dog.

"Can you tell me how long this house has been vacant?"

"I don't know. Maybe a couple of months."

"Looks like a nice house."

"You should have been here yesterday. I think it was open but I'm not sure. I live one street over," she yelled, walking away.

Robert climbed into his car, satisfied that Raine had been honest about her open house. That had to be a first...

With that in mind, he drove to his office.

Chapter 23
Illness

During the following week Robert watched Raine's real estate activities more closely. He drove down Stoller the following Sunday, saw her car parked in the driveway and felt satisfied she was telling the truth. However, when Raine came home, she gave him a quick kiss and hurried upstairs to shower. That curious activity made Robert suspicious. Why would she shower after an open house? Two Sundays in a row. Only one thing came to mind.

"How was the open house?" He questioned casually, when she entered the kitchen. "Coffee? I just made it."

"Please." She nodded before answering his question. "It was boring and dusty. I hate sitting on that crappy couch in the living room."

"No other furniture?"

"The house is vacant. I thought I told you that," she insisted questioning his puzzled expression.

"You might have. I just forgot," he said absent mindedly, knowing full well that particular fact was never mentioned. "Maybe, I'll visit you next week with a pizza."

"That would be a treat, but I don't think the boss would like my socializing during an open house."

"Well think of it this way, you have only a few more weeks and October will be over."

"And my business will go with it."

He purposely avoided her comment. "Maybe we can go somewhere for a few days."

"Let's go south, where it's warm. It usually starts to snow in November."

***

Two days later, a loud, constant ringing awakened him. Realizing it was the house phone, Robert tried sitting on the side of the bed to grab the receiver but knocked the telephone off his nightstand instead. He heard his mother's voice calling him. "Wait," he yelled. It took every ounce of strength to gather the telephone parts on the floor, and he could not remember feeling so weak or sweating so much. "Hello."

"What's the matter? It's two o'clock. When you didn't come in, I thought you might have had an appointment. But then you didn't call. You usually report at some point. What's wrong?"

"I think it's the bug I caught in Maui. Just tell everybody I took the day off."

"You should see a doctor."

"I will, but not now."

"You sure you're ok?"

"Absolutely." He ended the call. The last thing Robert wanted was his mother stopping by. He needed to be alone...he needed time to think.

Robert felt sweaty and the need of a shower. But first, his thoughts centered on Raine. Where was she? Was he alone in the house? Why didn't she awaken him? He slipped into his robe and shuffled through the house. On the kitchen counter he found a note.

Robert,
You took the day off and wanted to sleep.
Love,
Raine

Robert sat on a kitchen stool contemplating the reoccurrence of his illness. It was "Deja vu" all over again: the sleeping, the sweating and the weakness he felt.

His mind wandered back to their honeymoon in Maui. On the second night of their stay in Kaanapali, they enjoyed a glass of wine in their hotel room after attending a luau and hula show. The following day, he felt the same symptoms he was now experiencing. The same symptoms, his thoughts repeated, and the same format. Raine brought two glasses of wine to their bedroom on both occasions, offering wine first and then, nectar. Wasn't she the sweet little bitch? He felt certain she had doctored his wine the previous night. That was the only conclusion he could draw. That two could play the game was his first thought.

He still had some Mulvah left, the herb he took for sleep when Emily passed away. The small leather pouch from his mother was still tucked away in the corner floor safe of his walk-in closet, along with stacks of money and papers. Robert had always been very careful to tack down the carpet after using it. Someone checking his closet would completely bypass it with the array of shoes lining the floor. The last time he checked the safe was right before his September wedding. The thought that 'Sweet Pea' couldn't see it made him smile. That Raine couldn't find it was even more satisfying.

After they married, Robert showed Raine the bedroom wall safe that was securely tucked behind a landscape painting, when he placed their legal documents there and gave her the combination. Of course, she noticed the banded sums of money and other personal items there and felt she had complete access to his innermost secrets. However, she missed the point completely, which was exactly his intention. If a thief found a wall safe, he would not be looking for a second one. Yet, if given enough thought, was it not a ridiculous place for an owner of a security firm to hide a safe…behind a wall painting? Although Robert thought so, that idea escaped Raine completely. He, of course, went along with the ruse. Suddenly, his thoughts shifted. All this was well and good but Mulvah would not solve the real problem. He had to determine why she doctored his wine and who else was behind it. Raine could not have thought of drugging him on her own.

The more Robert thought about the situation, the more determined he became. He had to define a course of action. To protect himself, he had to know the contents of the wine. What was in it? Was it some sort of sleeping powder or was she slowly poisoning him? Whatever it was, he had to find the container. It had to be hidden somewhere in the house. Robert inspected the kitchen shelves first. Finding nothing, he moved to their bedroom and checked the contents of Raine's dresser and closet. Again, he found nothing. Totally frustrated, he realized he had one alternative and one only. He had to be prepared for the next scenario. He didn't know when it would happen, only that it would.

Robert raced back down to the kitchen. On the lower shelf of the base cabinet, he found a sealed jar of olives. Its size would easily hold five ounces of wine, and the diameter was small enough to be elusive when hidden. He opened the jar, threw the olives into the disposal, then washed and dried the container. He sealed the jar thoroughly before sailing upstairs to his bedroom. Robert looked carefully around the room for a hiding place. Between the leg of the bed and the room wall he noticed a space that fit the jar perfectly. Someone looking under the bed would miss it completely. The container was so well hidden.

He checked his watch. It was after four. Raine would be home soon. He wanted to shower but reconsidered. It would be much more beneficial if he stayed in bed, pretended to be weak and listened to Raine's tall tale of his day off.

***

"Robert." Raine shook him awake. "You must have really been tired." She watched him slowly open his eyes.

"What time is it?" He hated playing the game. She was so beautiful, looking down at him with her dark luminous eyes.

"Time to get up," she answered. "You've been sleeping all day."

"Why didn't I go to work?" His voice was almost a whisper.

"You took the day off," she said, pretending to be annoyed. "I wish you would have told me. I could have stayed home with you. It would have been nice to cuddle all day."

Inwardly, Robert smiled. She was so convincing. So caring. What a bitch. "I should take a shower but I feel so weak." He climbed out of bed slowly and ambled toward the master bathroom. "I'm not sure I can make it downstairs. Maybe I should see a doctor."

"I'll make poached eggs and bring them to you on a tray." She ignored his last remark.

"I'd like that," he said. Actually, Robert did feel weak; he also felt damp from perspiration. Whatever Raine gave him was playing havoc with his body.

Robert listened to her take the stairs to the first floor and quickly returned to the bedroom. He pulled the small computer from the nightstand drawer to turn on 'Sweet Pea.' Without a minute to lose, Robert entered the digits of the complex code, and switched images from the living room to the kitchen, but he was too late. Her message must have been very short. He watched Raine return the cell phone to her purse. He would try again, but at a faster pace. Robert turned off 'Sweet Pea' using an end code and placed the small computer back into his nightstand. Somehow, some way…he had to get his hands on Raine's cell phone.

***

Late that evening, in another part of town, Mackenzie had a surprised visit.

"I didn't expect you until the weekend." She flipped off the television set, but continued sitting on the couch, thinking they could talk before he took her to the bedroom and removed her shorty nightgown. Removing her clothing had become his ritual before making love. It was almost an art form, his touching her body with each article he removed.

"I couldn't wait." His strong arms pulled her small body up to him. As he carried her to the bedroom, his lips kept pressing hers. "I need you. This waiting is killing me." He removed her nightgown and ran his hands along the curves of her body in adoration before placing her on the bed. "You are so beautiful. I want you so much." He tossed his clothes on a nearby chair.

"We want each other." Mackenzie gazed up at him, moving slowly to his rhythm. He was such a wonderful lover. She wanted to make it last.

***

Later, as she lay cuddled in his arms, Mackenzie raised the question of marriage.

"We have to wait until the time is right. Your father's been married, what, a month? Let the marriage cement a while. When he and Raine become bonded, he will agree to our marriage much more easily. Keeping him happy with his new wife. That's our key to getting married."

"How will we know?"

"Functions, parties, observations." He shrugged-off her question. "We'll know. Until that time we must keep our relationship secret." Suddenly, he started to laugh. "By the way, I loved your performance at the cocktail party. I meant to tell you that."

"That was four weeks ago." She emphasized the word, weeks.

"You were brilliant. No one suspected…not your father or his new wife."

"I was pretty good, wasn't I?"

"I wanted to rip-off your clothes. You looked so breath taking… you always do." He ran his fingers down her smooth tight body. "Your skin's like silk."

"You've always want to rip-off my clothes."

"When I saw you last fall, I knew it then. Immediately. I had to have you."

"Seeing you at Korky's surprised me. It's usually the college crowd that drinks there. I didn't know you cruised the bars."

"A fluke, believe me. I had business in Southside and stopped by for a nightcap."

"So much for that. You took me home and later," she giggled. "Here we are nine months later and still…"

"And you thought I was too old for you."

"I'm sure my dad would. You never gave me a second look years ago."

"But you have my attention now. You are a beautiful woman."

"Some people think I look like my mother."

"Come to me." His arms opened wide. He pressed her body with his and felt her taut breasts against his chest. Running his tongue along her lips, he whispered, "You must understand how badly I want you. How I long for us to be together."

"Can you stay with me tonight?"

"I can't. Maybe sometime this weekend." He climbed out of bed to dress, knowing Mackenzie was watching his every move as she slipped into her nightgown hurriedly. He brought her to him and kissed her passionately. "You have to bolt the door." He gave her the apartment key. "This is not safe under the mat. We'll have to think of another place."

It was then that Mackenzie realized where he got the key to her apartment. "Keep it. I'll get another one."

***

As he drove away from her apartment a smile crossed his face. It was coming together faster than he anticipated. There were no hitches or glitches so far; nor did he expect any. As long as Mackenzie kept their relationship secret, his plan would materialize. And deep down, his psyche told him she would never reveal their secret to anyone. Mackenzie loved him. He thought of her young, taut body, and fantasized it with the woman he adored. The replica becoming the original was even more than he had bargained for.

Yes. It was all coming together. He would have it all…very, very soon.

Chapter 24
Recognition

"You didn't come today," she spoke angrily on her cell phone, referring to the third open house on Stoller Road. "When can I see you?"

"It's too dangerous. We can't afford to mess it up now."

"That's easy for you to say," she fumed. "I have the day to day."

"Yes, but you will also be a very wealthy woman."

"You mean, we will be wealthy," she corrected. "Afterward."

"True, but that has to be our secret for a while."

"When can I see you?" she asked again.

"Our place, Tuesday night."

"Should I do a repeat?"

"Of course." The conversation ended.

***

Things were going smoothly, too smoothly to satisfy Robert. This thought churned in his mind as he sat in his office. Raine couldn't have been kinder, sweeter or more giving. The "more giving" bothered him. He felt like the master of a house whose dog brought him the morning paper, his slippers and a possible pipe, if he smoked. With all this service, Robert was certain a glass of wine was in his immediate future.

Suddenly, a thought jolted him. How could he have been so stupid? It was something he had not considered. When Raine brought them wine, he had an excuse ready, one that would have her leave the room for a short while. However, Robert had not considered a replacement. What could he use to replace the wine that he transferred to the olive jar? He had missed that step completely. He thought of the small wine bottles carried by the local liquor store.

Then what? He already had the answer. Elias' plant. He could lift the basket innards and hide the small bottle inside.

So it was no surprise when Raine, dressed in a shimmering night-gown, brought a silver tray with two glasses of red wine into their bedroom two days later. She placed the tray on a small table that sat between two boudoir chairs. With such a romantic performance, Robert assumed she had plans for that particular evening or the following morning. Neither really mattered since the prime object was to have him drugged or poisoned.

"I thought we could have an early night together." She stood near the table, ready to offer him a glass.

Robert pulled her to him then turned away abruptly.

"What's wrong?"

"I don't know," he sniffed. "You should take a shower."

Raine glared at him almost fixed with distraught. She was upset by the glitch in her plans, yet glad that he noticed a problem. "I can take care of that," she said somewhat embarrassed before leaving the room.

As soon as Robert heard the water running, he took the glass of wine she offered him, emptied its contents into the olive jar and wiped the glass clean with the cocktail napkin it rested on. After stashing the olive jar, he filled his glass with the wine hidden in Elias' plant and returned the empty bottle to the basket innards. Still hearing the water running, Robert grabbed Raine's cell phone from her purse on the dresser and began scrolling her contacts. He recognized no name other than Valerie's. On a wild hunch, he tapped the woman's name and felt an immediate rage surging through his body. The number displayed was one he knew so well.

His first impulse was to pull the woman he married out of the shower and beat her to death with his fists. Instead, he returned the phone to her purse and sat on one of the bedroom chairs, his facial expression one of practiced calm. Inwardly, however, his thoughts roiled for retaliation.

When Raine entered the bedroom she sauntered over to him and leaned down. "Any better?"

Robert looked up at his wife from his sitting position. Although he sniffed her neck, he really wanted to bite her jugular and let the blood flow. Unfortunately, that act was reserved for vampires.

"Incredible." He found that description quite apt.

She crossed behind him to the boudoir chair directly across from his and reached for her wine glass. "I thought we could have a quiet evening together," she repeated again, tinging his glass. "We are still newlyweds."

The last thing Robert wanted was a pretense at love. He could not forgive her or her actions against him. Who in his right mind would want to make love with someone who wanted you drugged or dead? But Robert clearly understood his situation. He had to act the part of a husband who was helplessly in love with his wife, no matter how he felt inwardly.

"Why are you looking at me like that?" Raine studied him, puzzled by his expression. Was he becoming suspicious? The thought worried her.

"Why wouldn't I? You are so beautiful, so wonderful," Robert oozed with compliments. "Things are going so well for us and I'm in good health according to the doctor. The tests results were normal." He lied about seeing a physician.

Raine sat positively speechless. "You saw a doctor?" Her eyes widened.

"That was the good part. I may have to leave you, if only for a few days." He continued to lie.

"What?" She placed her wine glass back on the tray. "When?"

"I don't like talking about business, but I'll know by Thursday or Friday if I'm in the running for another project. It will be substantial."

"Where is it?" Her pointed question made him smile inwardly.

"I can't talk about it. I'm sorry." He became apologetic. "I'll have to leave Sunday morning if it comes through. But between the two of us, I have a good feeling about resolving all the issues involved."

"Then we shouldn't waste time," she clinked his glass again and watched him finish his wine.

***

Hours later, Raine checked Robert's sleeping stupor and found his condition perfect for her plans. With the amount of Quala used in his wine, he would not awaken until the following afternoon.

She rushed to the bathroom to cleanse her body then tiptoed back to the bedroom for jeans and a shirt. With clothing in hand, Raine took another look at the immobile body lying in bed. She felt safe. Dressing quickly, Raine took the stairs gingerly then fled to her car.

As soon as he heard her car drive away, Robert checked the clock. It was after eleven. Raine would probably be gone for two hours, perhaps a little longer. He dialed Elias' number as he dressed, knowing a return call was a distinct possibility. However, much to his surprise, Elias answered almost immediately.

"This better be important." A voice greeted him.

"Matter of life or death."

"What life, whose death?"

"Mine, in both cases."

"Excuse me, darlin." He heard Elias' voice talking to another party. His friend was entertaining some young thing, while Robert was being victimized by his wife's nefarious plan. Where was the justice in that?

"I had to move to another room," Elias explained. "What's going on?"

"I want you to check some wine for me. I think I'm being drugged or poisoned." Then Robert detailed his wife's activities beginning with his honeymoon and ending with the hidden olive bottle of wine.

"I warned you about marriage, but you wanted to grow old together! So much for that. Where is she now?"

"Out with her planner. I think I know where to look."

"You check on her and I'll come by tomorrow. Don't worry, I'll make certain the house's empty."

"Bring your own scotch. Nothing's safe here."

"Damn. You really did marry a bitch." He ended the call.

***

Robert grabbed his car keys, climbed into his car and drove directly toward a main highway in Plum Township. Within twenty minutes he arrived at a complex of four large condominiums that formed a quadrangle surrounding a center pool. He searched the parking lot of one particular building but could not find Raine's car. She was not there. Raine would not have parked in one of the other three lots, so much farther away from the building in question.

His second location of choice offered a better outcome. It was really their best meeting place. He would have realized this earlier if his brain had been functioning on all synapses.

As he drove away it seemed like second nature to be going to Raine's old apartment. This would be a defining moment for him. At last, he would know the true identity of Valerie. Although he recognized the phone number, all too well, Robert wanted a confirmation. And he wanted it now.

He turned into Penn Center and drove directly behind the plaza to the three apartment complex. He passed the first two buildings quickly before circling the third parking lot. There in a space near the back door sat Raine's car. Beside it, sat a white Mercedes: John Harris' white Mercedes. The phone number and car matched. John Harris was Valerie, the same Valerie that called Raine in Florence. Her "fatto" meant, "It was done." Raine had completed her assignment to meet Robert. Left to blossom between them were unbridled hormones.

He looked up to the second floor of Raine's end apartment. That it looked dark did not surprise him. They were in the bedroom making love and developing further plans for his demise.

Robert was filled with mixed emotions. He ached with unbelievable pain. How could the woman he loved so much betray him like this? He believed her…believed she loved him. He thought her emotions were real. They felt real when she kissed him, made love to him. How could she have done this? How could she go from him to John Harris in the same night? One to the other? Obviously, the relationship had been going on for some time. How long had she known him, and even more important, how long was their plan in the making? Six months? A year? They obviously knew of his trip to Florence. Robert's entire group knew he would be on vacation.

As Robert drove to his home on the escarpment, other thoughts churned his mind. He had to get over this emotional crutch. That was paramount to a solution. Yes. It was painful. And yes, he thought it was true love. But he was wrong. Marriage drove Raine, not love for Robert. She had to benefit from it in some way. What was it? Money? There had to be more involved than money, particularly with John Harris calling the shots. No. They were into something with much higher stakes. But What?

He pulled into his driveway, entered the house and went to bed. However, Robert did not fall asleep. He waited for his faithless wife to return.

Chapter 25
Assignation

While Robert's thoughts were confirming Raine's betrayal and his possible demise, a heated conversation was taking place in her old apartment at Penn Center.

"I can't help my feelings." Raine embraced him.

"Are you're sure it's safe?"

"I gave him the usual dose. He'll be out until late tomorrow." She led him to the bedroom and began undressing.

"Wait." He stopped her. "I need some reassurance. This will be his third time. People have to believe he's really sick now."

"They will." She climbed on the bed waiting for him to join her. "But I'm running low. Can you get more Quala?"

"You should have more than enough to finish the job," he answered. John still had a small amount of the powder but kept that fact to himself. He was saving it as a precaution. "How will they know?" He returned to their initial conversation.

"That's all we talk about anymore: Robert this and Robert that. Where's "us" in this conversation? After I did the Florence bit, you said, 'We'd be together.'"

She was getting angry and he had to appease her somehow, make her understand how dangerous their union was at this time. He tore off his clothes hurriedly, joined her in bed and, pulling her to him, felt her surrender.

Later, as they lay cuddled, Raine told him of Robert's trip to the doctor and his plans to leave town.

"The doctor, when?"

"After he got sick again. I guess he got scared. But it's ok. The doctor didn't find anything," she said, her manner convincing.

"He wouldn't. In the end it will look like a heart attack." He agreed with her thinking. "But I'm more interested in the contract. Did he give any names?"

"He refused to talk about it. He leaves Sunday morning if he's in the running. That's how he phrased it."

"And you don't know anything more about it?"

"I know it's my last open house. We can come here instead of using the couch. He mentioned our taking a trip somewhere if he gets the contract. That's when I should finalize the dose and end it."

"We'll co-ordinate that when the time comes."

"I hope no one discovers his condition."

"Can't happen. The powder of ground herbs comes from a very small village. The place isn't even on the map." He caught her worried expression. "You will become a very wealthy woman when it's over."

"You keep saying that." She eyed him closely. "When can we be together?"

"Depends on what happens."

"We should keep the apartment."

"That's a given," he agreed, "but I think we should leave now."

"I hate being away from you." Raine watched him dress and followed his lead. "I can't believe it's been two years for us. It's gone by so fast," she reminisced.

"You got a bad rap when you left Los Angeles." He switched off the dim nightlight.

"We were in love, so I thought. How did I know he was married? He played me for years. Thank God, I found you."

At the apartment door, John embraced Raine and kissed her. "We found each other. Never forget that."

They walked to the building exit, eyed each other over their respective cars, and drove away in opposite directions. They did not schedule another rendezvous. It was totally unnecessary with Robert leaving town on business. If that changed Raine would make contact.

***

As Raine drove toward the escarpment, she was not worried that her husband would awaken in her absence. She had duplicated the amounts given him on Maui and at home both times, amounts John had prescribed. If she used a miniscule amount for a glass of wine, what would be needed for his final deep sleep? She would ask that question the next time they met.

For the first time, in such a very long time, Raine felt closer to their goal. The end was in sight. Her husband would be dead by Thanksgiving or Christmas, the latest. She hoped he would be gone before the New Year. The last thing she wanted was to ring in the New Year with a dead man. The thought made her smile. The New Year. It would be a new year for her. She would be with John. Then another thought occurred to her, a very important one she had not considered. Perhaps, she should wait.

Robert had always been very generous to her. Raine already had access to his cash in the wall safe, but what if she could get more? He would shower her with presents at Christmas, expensive ones. That was a given. But what about the house or the company? Would those assets be left to Mackenzie? Where was her share in all of that? What would she inherit? No. She would not be a wealthy woman. John was wrong. It didn't matter what John thought. Raine would not go along with anything further unless it benefited her financially. Until that was settled, Raine would remain the loving and caring wife Robert married.

Most women would have been happy with Robert. He was a sweet and considerate husband. The man was also boring and very structured. He was no fun. His idea of a night out was dinner and a play. No spontaneity…no nothing. There were countless evenings of television and bed. No getting in the car and just driving somewhere exciting. No need for packing, no planned reservations…just go on a whim, buying things along the way. She longed for an element of excitement. That was John. With him, the unexpected was the norm. Was that the reason she loved him so much? No. There was so much more to him. That's why he had so many friends. People were drawn to this man who had a great personality and a wonderful sense of humor.

While Raine was lost in thought, John Harris had a few concerns of his own. Was his partner becoming uncontrollable or was she just scared? Seeing each other was dangerous, particularly now, when they were so close to their goal. Couldn't she see that? It would be over in a month, two at most. Robert would be dead. So what was her problem? He already knew the answer. Raine was unsure of him, of his love. John sensed it, although he tried everything to make her feel he still cared. He had handled the physical aspect during her open houses and tonight, but it was getting to be a chore. He had ideas and wants of his own, ones he certainly couldn't share with her. His thoughts went back to their first meeting.

He was looking to buy a condo after the divorce. As he recalled Raine was the listing agent who accompanied the realtor to a showing in Penn Hills. John was not aware of her situation at the time. However, he later learned she had come east five years earlier with a man whom she loved; but upon discovering his marital status and his intention to stay with his wife, she refused to become his mistress. Having nothing left in California, other than a father and step mother whom she hated, Raine settled in Pittsburgh and became a successful realtor. However, he did purchase his condo in Plum from the realtor who introduced them. Raine never let him forget that.

Fluke that it was, he recognized her when they ran into each other at a department store in the city and stopped for coffee. When they bonded over mutual friends and interests, he found her company enjoyable and continued seeing her. That was two years ago. Two long years. Then something strange happened to change everything. *The angel he always loved fell out of the sky and into his world.*

No longer would he have to adore her from afar, nor wait for a stolen glance, a touch of her hand. He would bring her to him, pressing her with his love, molding them into one. She knew…Emily always knew his true feelings but wouldn't succumb. Instead she allowed herself to be neglected.

He had never forgiven Robert for not taking better care of his sick wife, when saving her life mattered. Nor had he forgotten his last moment with an emaciated Emily, the angel who knew the depth of his love, although one from a distance. Then, on one fortuitous night John was given a chance to right that wrong. In doing so, his revenge was further sweetened by a young goddess whose delicious nectar he continually sampled. And his thoughts went back to meeting Mackenzie by chance, who by then, had blossomed into a fully curvaceous young woman.

It was early evening when he stopped for a drink after a dinner meeting. He saw a beautiful, dark-haired woman standing across the room with a group of people and immediately recognized her. She was the image of her mother, the love of his life. John knew at that exact moment, he had to have the young woman. He had to make this goddess of his dreams love him. He had to possess her in every way possible and mold her into his reality: she would blame her father for her mother's death.

That night was John's only chance to get her alone, without family or her father. John also knew a relationship between them would never have been allowed to go forward, although Mackenzie was of age legally. So, it was a now or never situation…and John decided to win his goddess, regardless of cost…to anyone.

John sauntered over to the group, made small conversation and knowingly captured her interest. That night changed his life. The woman whose porcelain skin and luminous dark eyes had melted his heart completely. However, from past experience, John knew he had to sway the small young woman emotionally before he could begin to mold her into the goddess he adored. When he accompanied her home that evening, he began a slow steady foreplay of words to gain her interest and trust. Several dates later, as they became more involved, he made her first experience so memorable his goddess cried for an encore. They had consummated their love and she no longer felt an age difference. His angel had fallen in love. His goddess needed him. Mackenzie wanted permanency.

He had succeeded in molding his goddess: his thoughts were hers; his every request, granted…hairstyle, clothing and scanty underwear of his choosing. In shaping the goddess of his dreams, although a younger and more delicious version, John's love never altered. His feelings were the same as they had been years earlier. If nothing else, his hunger for her increased. However, as much as she loved him, Mackenzie was still very close to her father at the time.

To insure their relationship, John developed a plan, laid it out carefully and set in motion at the right time.

First, he made an outward attempt at wanting to move on… to another company and have more responsibility. He continued the facade at a golf course outing and with potential employees. Making Robert think John was going elsewhere was completely necessary. It hid his real agenda, that of making Mackenzie his wife and inheriting the company.

His second obstacle had been separating Mackenzie from her father. It took time but fracturing their relationship was necessary. He had Raine participate in the plan but he did it through deception.

His plan dealt with love and death: Raine's love, and Robert's death. It was really a very simple plan. Raine needed more convincing at the time, but in the end, succumbed to his wishes. That would bring them together sooner and with a lot of money. Although she loved John deeply, Raine wanted all the money her marriage could bring. Although everyone knew of Robert Blake's wealth, the man never flaunted it. So a meeting had to be arranged, an accidental one in a most unexpected way.

In planning the costly encounter, John had learned the date and hotel of Robert's stay in Florence. The rest was left to Raine. The woman knew how to flirt and get a man's attention. All John had to do was check her progress. She couldn't say "Geronimo" when contact was made, so they coined the word, "fatto" instead. The ultimate goal was marriage first, then death. Poor Robert never suspected. He never spoke or understood Italian.

All went better than expected with the Florence meeting and subsequent marriage. Now, everything was going as planned, including Robert's first dose of Quala in Maui. He had "picked-up" a bug on the trip. That information passed from his group of workers to his friends and then business associates. John kept everyone informed.

"Wasn't that sad?" People would say, "And on his honeymoon."

Then, after Robert had a second repeat of the illness, more tongues wagged. "He should see a doctor."

And tonight, Robert would be suffering a third time.

Soon everyone would become even more concerned with his health. However, John felt secure knowing Quala could never be traced once the system flushed out. If Robert died later of the same symptoms he suffered months earlier, no autopsy would be needed. At least, he didn't think so. It made little difference. Given a larger dose, Robert's death would have the same symptoms as a massive heart attack. That, of course, was the plan.

What to do with Raine was another story. That would be no problem in the end, he thought to himself. After Robert's death, he would marry Mackenzie, have her inheritance and run the company. What could Raine possibly do other than feel like a used woman? She could either be a quiet co-conspirator or a dead one. She knew his capabilities. For now, however, he had to play the role of her lover. Apparently, he was good at it. Raine never suspected he was also making love to someone else; the woman he really loved, or her molded image.

John arrived at his condo feeling very satisfied and unconcerned.

Chapter 26
Olive Jar

Raine felt safe when she returned home from her rendezvous with John. Robert had not moved from his earlier position. He was still lying on his side, facing the nightstand and bedroom window. Poor Robert. He had no idea what was in store for him. She undressed hurriedly, climbed into bed and, turning away from his immobile body, fell fast asleep.

As soon as he heard her soft snores, Robert's eyes blinked open to check the clock on his nightstand. It was after two. Their assignation had taken approximately three hours and he was certain they had discussed further plans for him. He lay in bed, thoughts roiling through his mind. What would be his best course of action? The two of them wanted him dead. Robert was certain of that, now that he pieced together the first part of their plan: his meeting Raine accidentally in Florence and their subsequent marriage. Yet, something made him believe money was not the only motivating factor.

Killing him so they could be together and share his money was too simple. Granted, there many cases of people being murdered for money, but this was not one of them. Most of his money was tied to his business and his wife was well aware of that. And since Raine would only get the few thousand from the wall safe, murdering him for that sum of money would have been ridiculous. There had to be much more involved; things he had not considered but were pertinent to his investigation. He had to probe deeper. It was his life in the cross hairs for extinction. But he had to have a plan. He had already told Raine about the trip for a possible new contract. He was certain she gave that information to John during their tryst. Tomorrow, John would tell Henry Price about it. Then that information would cause Henry to start an investigation of his own. He would be busy on the phone questioning his contacts, all of them. Robert had set the perfect stage for leaving town and Raine cemented his departure over "pillow talk." It was a good start.

He began to smile inwardly. Raine would be so pissed if she ever discovered the treasure chest in his closet floor or more precisely, its contents. The money stashed there would not be considered "chump change." Robert had hidden the funds for emergency purposes. In fact, he remembered so many occasions when he used some of the money to help both workers and friends. People often turned to him when financial problems suddenly arose. Robert had their trust: they knew he would keep silent. No one would ever know their financial difficulties. Of course, he always replenished the amounts taken, sometimes from the money repaid. Often, however, in cases of sickness, when a household budget was tight, Robert refused repayment and considered his help, a gift. He would replenish the given amount himself, knowing in his heart it was the right thing to do. Now, he would use a portion of the money for the fight of his life and a plan began to take shape in his mind.

Every transaction would have to be done in cash. It was important that nothing could be traced back to him. He would take his wallet of credit cards and everything else one takes on a trip, not to arouse suspicion. Robert knew Raine would search the entire house in his absence, particularly his personal things, to determine if anything she discovered would be to her financial benefit. His thoughts then shifted to present time.

He thought about Raine's schedule. She would leave him in bed the following morning, thinking him drugged and asleep, then awaken him ever so gently that afternoon. It would be a repeat of his drugged stupor weeks earlier. So she thought. Of course, Raine was not totally correct on that score but he would neglect to mention it.

His mother phoned when he lapsed into his second stupor and checked his absence from the office with great concern. That was several weeks earlier. Yet, somehow, everyone learned of this lingering illness…from the bug he caught in Maui to his present condition, one that continually worsened. This whispered gossip passed from workers to friends and then business associates. Although John had planned it well, he underestimated the power of Robert's mother.

"What's going on?" She cornered him after his second stupor. "Don't tell me nothing. I wasn't born yesterday." Robert knew she was angry.

"I just felt sick." He refused to say anything further. Robert did not want to worry her with his new found knowledge.

"That's what people are saying, but you would have called. You always have before," she insisted. Catherine fixed her eyes on Robert and studied his facial expression to get more insight to the problem facing him. "It's something else."

As he lay in bed his mind went back to her initial phone call. At that time Robert had no idea Raine had drugged or even poisoned him. It was the constant ringing of the phone that jarred him awake. It was late afternoon and Robert had not called the office for messages or to update his mother on his absence.

"I don't know what's wrong with me." He told her at the time. "Maybe I'll see a doctor on the QT. No matter what happens, just cover my ass for the time being. I don't want anybody thinking I'm terminal."

"Rest up for a few days. I'll handle it here."

"I have to. I'm too weak to come in."

From that day on, Catherine was quick to challenge anyone on Robert's debilitating sickness, insisting instead, that it was more of an allergy due to some form of ragweed. Inwardly, however, she knew something bad was happening to her son. There was no point in pressing him. Robert wouldn't tell her until he was ready or thought she should have that information. In fact, Catherine might never know the cause of his problem, but it wouldn't surprise her if Raine was at the root of it.

However, it was shortly after that call, when Robert was alone, that he began to review the history of his weakened condition. In both cases, the common denominators were Raine and red wine. In Maui, Raine had doctored his glass of wine when they toasted in their room after the luau. The trial run had to start on their honeymoon. Who would suspect a new bride of wanting "to off" her husband so soon? Then too, contracting some bug, one that made him ill, seemed more plausible, particularly in a warm climate.

Even more credible was his continued, and perhaps, worsening illness, particularly when it occurred a few weeks later at his home. Robert had no clue of a coming reoccurrence. Once again, Raine had dosed his glass of wine with something that knocked him out and left him feeling very, very weak. It was only after his mother's call that the wheels began churning in his mind; Raine and red wine. Her note of his wanting the day off was just so much claptrap intended for him solely. His lingering illness had been slowly circulated throughout the community, but Robert had not been privy to it until the conversation with his mother.

However, learning that John and Raine had hatched the plan together gave him the insight he needed to retaliate. He had to devise a plan, a devious one. Then he remembered. Elias was coming by after Raine left for the office. Robert knew he would be facing a mountain of questions from his very bright friend and perhaps it was a good thing. Although he could use another point of view, what Robert really needed was a course of action.

***

Raine had been gone less than thirty minutes, before Elias walked through the front door, raced up the stairs to the master bedroom and greeted his friend who was sitting on a lounge chair.

"Not dressing today?" Elias eyed his friend, whose dark robe covered a pair of dark blue pajamas. "I forgot. You have to play the part of a drugged husband."

"Soon to be a dead one," he corrected. "I'm sure of it after last night." Then Robert revealed Valerie's real identity, the use of the apartment and the coded name on Raine's cell phone.

"I don't get it. Were they together before your marriage?"

"I don't really know." Robert arose from his chair and kneeled to the bed leg hiding the olive jar of wine. "This stuff knocked me out for almost two days in Maui and here at the house a few weeks ago. That I do know." He gave Elias the olive jar. "I searched the house for a container of powder but found nothing."

"Maybe they're after your money." Elias spoke aloud, thinking of a reason for his demise. "What does she inherit on your death?"

"A little money. I was going to set-up something for her. The business and house go to Mackenzie. That's tied in my trust."

"We have to think of something to delay your demise."

"I told her if I were in the running for the huge contract, I would be leaving Sunday. That would give me time to check the closeness of their relationship. I want to know if money is the only motivating factor. I just feel I'm missing something."

"Well, whatever you're thinking, you'll need to watch Raine's activity here at the house. Telling her you're leaving town is only a temporary fix. Let me think about it," he mused but had another thought. "Where are you staying?"

"I thought I'd take my car to the airport and rent something innocuous from a rental agency. I plan to follow each of them. I didn't make a hotel reservation deliberately. I was going to ask you where I should stay." He began to laugh. "You're the spook, not me."

"I don't like your plan," Elias groused. "Here." He gave Robert a slip of paper with an address. "There's a car in the garage and the house is fully furnished."

Robert read the slip of paper. "Turtle Creek? Are you serious?"

"Would anyone look for you there?"

"No. It's absolutely perfect! I can come and go unnoticed."

"You have a friend who is looking out for you, besides me." He grew serious. "Just remember to pack the computer. Your friend has a global connection for 'Sweet Pea.' I'll see you sometime on Sunday. In the meantime, don't eat anything your wife offers you."

Elias sailed out of the house, olive jar in hand. It was a different kind of feeling for him. He usually carried-off a scotch glass.

Chapter 27
The Search

After Elias left the house, Robert continued to sit on the bedroom chair deep in thought. He had to come up with a concrete plan, one of retaliation or revenge while away from Raine. Not true. He did not want retaliation or revenge. Robert wanted to expose them. He wanted them to know he was aware of their scheme…the meeting, the marriage and the drugs. But even more important, he wanted to expose them for attempted murder. The law would step-in from there. He would see to it.

Then something occurred to him that he hadn't thought of. Why was the dosage given him in Maui and several weeks later different from the one last night? "You dope," he told himself. "You didn't drink the wine Raine gave you." At that moment, Robert realized he wasn't thinking straight. The walls were closing in on him. He was an emotional wreck. The woman he loved wanted him dead. How was he supposed to react? He couldn't turn off his outpouring of love like a spigot of water. But could he turn it into a faucet of anger? Stop with the spouts, he chastised himself, and come up with a plan.

Robert walked to his closet and quickly removed a large sum of money from the floor safe. After restoring the carpeting, he returned two pairs of shoes back to their original position on the closet floor, pulled a suitcase off an upper shelf and stashed the money in a false bottom. He placed the suitcase back among the others lined there, knowing it looked normal. Within minutes, he was checking the basket innards of Elias' plant for the small, but empty wine bottle. Robert could not chance leaving it there knowing Raine's search would be extensive. He doubted she would check the plant but what if she accidently knocked it over? Finding a wine bottle there would make her suspicious.

He took the wine bottle downstairs, wrapped it in two plastic bags and pushed it underneath a pile of garbage in the trash can outside. He was certain Raine would not discover it. He couldn't see her searching through garbage for something that might benefit her. And since his house was the last on the street, Robert had only one home of peering neighbors next to his. Fortunately, they were away visiting family, making his trip to the garbage can a safe and private one. He could have thrown the bottle into the woods on the other side of his house, but that would have been ridiculous. He always hated litter.

He returned to the house for another search of powder or granules that Raine used to drug him. Once again, he inspected every wall and base cabinet in the kitchen. Finding nothing, he moved upstairs to the master bedroom and began searching Raine's dresser and closet one more time. To his surprise, he found a ten thousand dollar Certificate of Deposit held by a local bank his company monitored. At another bank, Raine had a money market of eight thousand. Robert had no idea Raine had that kind of money available. Why had she not told him? "Don't be silly." He spoke to himself. "She wanted his money. Sharing hers was not part of their nuptial contract."

He assumed Raine carried a checkbook in her handbag, since it was not with her finances in the corner of her drawer. He looked for a box of blank checks, but couldn't find one. There was only one other place it could be. But why would she keep it at her old apartment? She must have kept the smaller bedroom as her office and left the box of blank checks there for convenience. Still, it made no sense. Why leave the blank checks there and the bulk of her money at the house? Did she feel the money was safer here or was there another reason? She didn't tell Robert about the money and he wondered if she told John. It made no sense, unless she didn't trust him either.

After finding nothing other than bank transactions, Robert started to inspect Raine's closet, when the phone rang. He heard Catherine's voice beginning to leave a message as he raced to the telephone on his nightstand.

"Don't talk," Robert demanded when he answered the phone. "Just listen. When people ask about me, say I told you during a conversation we had yesterday, I would be tied-up in meetings for a possible new contract and will be in the office at the end of the week. Emphasize the yesterday. Say you forgot, are getting senile or post-menopausal. Yes, I'll explain when we're alone, but not now. Say, 'Yes, I'll give him the message,' just in case someone is listening."

Catherine repeated the last line of their conversation and ended the call.

Robert knew the conversation worried her, but it was necessary that she follow his instructions. It gave more credence to the illusory contract he was pursuing while away from home. Robert knew he could count on his mother for help when asked. Otherwise, she would never interfere, regardless of her true feelings. And she would never voice her opinion unless asked for it directly. That's how it was with his marriage to Emily, although Catherine really adored her, and that's how it started with Raine. Catherine was not impressed with his new wife. She never told him that. He just felt her lack of love for the woman. Well, Catherine had read her correctly, but never issued any kind of opinion. Now, Robert wished she would have.

Something else also occurred to him. Robert told her he would be in the office at the end of the week. Today was Wednesday which meant he should still be too weak to go to the office tomorrow. The drug given him required a two-day convalescent period on both prior occasions. Or at least one and a half days he corrected, thinking back to his second episode when the ringing phone jarred him awake. He would have to continue the charade and go to the office on Friday. Then sometime during that morning, Robert would receive a fabricated phone call about a make-believe contract and leave town the coming Sunday. That would work out well with his planned departure.

Somewhere in the middle of this hoax, his mother would demand an explanation. Robert did not want to lie, but felt telling her the truth might be dangerous. She could easily slip unintentionally…a word here, a sentence there. John was crafty. He would nose around Catherine to glean any information about the new contract Robert was bidding on. John had not been privy to it and would feel snubbed. Aside from being ticked, John had Henry Price to contend with, and many questions he couldn't answer.

There was only one way he could protect his mother. Robert would fabricate the same story saying, he could not divulge the names or company requesting the meeting. His company was in the running. That's all he could say. Of course, his mother would ask if the contract looked promising. Robert would tell her the same thing he had been saying for years. "I don't know." Those words always silenced her. She would feel his uncertainty by not pressing the issue. She could tell he was worried.

Of course, after Robert's departure, John would try to confuse her somehow, thinking he could get more information. The man was a master of extracting information; however, he would soon find his questions a waste of time. The woman knew nothing. And Robert would make certain of it. As he thought over this idea, his face took on his usual look of practiced calm. He was beginning to like the idea of exposing their plans. The fact that they wanted him dead began to grow on him as more ideas fomented his thoughts.

Robert returned to the dresser he had just searched. Bank books, lingerie, jeans, sweaters…all clothing but no container with drugs. He checked her jewelry box and found nothing there. Where would Raine keep the stuff she was feeding him? Feeding? He checked his watch. It was after twelve and he felt hungry. Could he chance eating something now? Raine could just as easily come home for lunch, using it as an excuse to check on him.

Robert walked to the window facing the street. There was no sign of life or activity on the street. He rushed down the stairs for something to eat. After checking the refrigerator, Robert realized his wife would become suspicious if the lunch meat, somehow, disappeared when he was supposed to be so sick in bed. He turned to the base cabinet and settled on a few crackers. He felt certain she wouldn't miss three of them. Yet, he was very careful about folding the cracker sleeve exactly how he found it before sliding it back into the box.

After returning to the master bedroom, Robert felt at odds with himself. He propped his pillow against the headboard and slid under the covers. His thoughts continued to linger. Something was missing…something he had overlooked. And he began to review the situation from the very beginning.

John and Raine hatched a plan for a meeting, a very expensive one. They spent a great deal of money for the trip to Florence so Raine could meet Robert accidentally.

"But why?"

"Marriage was their goal," he answered his own question.

"If marriage was their goal, why drug him?"

"His only conclusion was money," Robert told himself, "but that didn't make sense. He had not set up an inheritance for her."

Then his thoughts shifted. Maybe Raine was counting on that. Get him sick, spread the word about his deteriorating health, and then buy an insurance policy big enough to warrant killing him.

Robert could understand her reasoning, but that still seemed illogical to him. A life insurance policy would be a mere pittance of his wealth. Mackenzie stood to inherit the bulk of his estate, unless they planned on killing her too. Robert had never thought that far ahead: that she, too, could be a victim of their scheme. He would have to warn her, but at that particular moment Robert had to concentrate on finding the drug they used on him. If he found Raine's cache, he could expose both of them and Mackenzie would be safe.

Robert's thoughts returned to the money angle. If money were the motivating factor in all of this, what was the benefit to John? Granted, they were lovers, obviously, but would money from an insurance policy warrant this kind of planning…sending Raine to Europe just to meet him? That made no sense. There had to be more. Robert knew John Harris too well. His devious assistant wouldn't settle for a split of money or perhaps marriage. Robert was missing a piece of the puzzle. But what? Was the man thinking of killing Raine too? Almost instantly that question brought his thoughts back to Mackenzie.

If Robert were dead, Mackenzie would inherit the house and business. Then Raine could file a claim legally if Mackenzie died sometime later. She could live in the house, John would run the business and they would live happily ever after on Robert's money.

That was the plan. Robert was sure of it now. But before warning Mackenzie, he had to find the drug to expose them. If it wasn't in the house, it had to be at the apartment. Since he couldn't run the risk of searching the unit himself, perhaps Elias would do it for him. His friend had a knack of getting in and out of places so easily. Alarm systems to Elias were merely annoyances he had to contend with. Robert's own security system, a complex scheme he designed himself, was just another touch-pad toy to his friend. It was no surprise to find Elias sitting on Robert's couch, drinking scotch in the man's living room. Cracking a security system brought Claude into his thoughts.

This was another man who by-passed his security system and installed the fourth 'Sweet Pea' in his house. These two men were like shadows in the night: appear and disappear. No sound and no appearance of a car anywhere. How could that be? Why did Claude install 'Sweet Pea?' What did he know? It was much too strange for a wedding gift. He wanted Robert to have access to the kitchen. But why?

Suddenly, Robert understood: that's where Raine prepared the wine. Although Claude didn't know about the wine in Maui, he must have seen Raine doctor Robert's wine at home. How often had he been watching them through 'Sweet Pea?' What else did Claude know? Robert would never get an explanation since he had no way of contacting the man.

Then he thought about the house in Turtle Creek. The offer came from Claude according to Elias. Was it a rental or a safe house he used? Why offer it to Robert? What did Claude know about his situation? He would ask Elias these questions when they met again on Sunday.

He heard a door close downstairs and immediately turned on his side.

Chapter 28
Conversations

Before leaving the real estate office Wednesday afternoon, Raine gave her co-workers an update of her husband's deteriorating condition. She went to great lengths recalling the story of his illness in Maui, saying the bug he caught on their honeymoon seemed to have had lasting effects. With her anxiety over his illness and the frustration of an unsold listing, they even understood her reason for holding an open house on Stoller Road that weekend. Since the property was vacant, she could close the house immediately should the need arise.

Of course, Raine neglected to mention the possibility of her husband's leaving town that coming Sunday. She had been very careful in setting the stage for Robert's impending demise. However, during her journey home, Raine's mind was on an entirely different matter.

Raine knew the drug would affect Robert for approximately two days. He would be weak today and somewhat stronger tomorrow. Perhaps, Thursday would be the ideal time to approach him. She could stay home, cater to his needs while expressing a few of her own. With his reoccurring illness, it would follow logically that she would be concerned about the future. Raine would pretend the deepest regret should something ever happen to him. How could she go on? She would pose that question. Raine would continue her narrative by asking him for guidance. She would ask how he wanted things done spiritually and financially. Perhaps they should have an exchange of ideas and have financial concerns done legally.

To avert suspicion, she would begin with matters that concerned her. Raine had decided years earlier that she preferred to be cremated upon death. That would be a good starting point. Then Raine could end the discussion by saying he would inherit all of her possessions and what little money she had. Perhaps she would suggest a will.

Suddenly, a thought occurred to her, one she had not previously considered...her two financial documents. She had to remove the Certificate of Deposit hidden in the dresser drawer under her lingerie. The other bank book would remain as a theatrical prop. It would reinforce his inheriting her money. Yes. Tomorrow would be a good time to talk about finances.

Raine thought more about it as she approached the steep escarpment to the house. "I will sell this sucker, when it comes my way," she said aloud. "This place should be a home for mountain goats."

As she pulled into the driveway, Raine parked in her usual spot and smiled. She knew exactly how to handle her husband with the inheritance problem. Then she thought about John. He would be furious with her for pursing this angle. Robert's death was supposed to happen without further trappings. "What does he know about my financial needs?" she groused aloud. "I'm not in this as a trophy wife."

***

"Robert." Raine tapped the shoulder of the sleeping man. Her husband was still lying on his side. He had never moved from his morning position. "Robert," she called again.

His eye opened slowly then closed again.

"Robert." Raine shook him. "Wake up."

Her husband opened his left eye again. "I feel so weak," he whispered. "Maybe I should go to the hospital. The doctor didn't help me."

"You said your tests came out fine." She resisted his suggestion. "It's that bug again. I'll make some soup and bring it up." Raine stroked his dark hair lovingly with her fingers. "You'll feel better once you eat something."

Robert heard her race downstairs and smiled at her resistance to his need for medical attention. What a wonderfully caring wife. What a bitch. Yes. Raine wanted him dead, but somehow, Robert knew money played a big part of her scheme. The woman wouldn't try anything lethal until she was fixed financially. He doubted she would doctor the soup. He had another day for healing. Then too, Robert was leaving town, pending some news, the kind that could be rewarding to her. He would toss out a few financial crumbs, knowing how greedily she would devour them. Perhaps he should mention the doctor again to draw her in. Would that bother her?

***

"I don't know what's wrong with me." His voice was hushed and low, when Raine entered the bedroom holding a tray. "I should go back to the doctor when I'm up to it. Maybe Friday."

Aren't you getting a phone call about a possible contract?" She spooned soup into his mouth.

"I forgot," he lied and looked at her directly. "This tastes good but I feel tired. You shouldn't sleep with me tonight."

Raine took the soup bowl, placed it back on the tray and left the room.

Robert heard her take the stairs and knew she was not happy. Raine wanted to fawn all over her sick husband; she was so concerned with his health. No doctor, of course. His wife had a plan in mind, something that dealt with money. Care for him now and discuss the future tomorrow, when he felt stronger. Was that her plan or was it John's? One thing was certain: both of them were in it together.

"Robert." Raine entered the room again and began adjusting his pillow to make him more comfortable.

"I love you so much," he said, his voice a whisper. "I will take care of you, if something happens to me."

"You rest." She brushed his lips. "We'll talk tomorrow."

His eyes followed the woman leaving the room. He had to admit it. She was a piece of work, although a very beautiful one.

***

"Now what?" Steve sat across the table from his sister and sipped a cup of hot coffee. "You told me to stop on the way home from work. You made it sound urgent."

"I don't know what's going on, but something's wrong with Robbie. It's not good when my son tells me to say, 'He's at a meeting or taking the day off,' especially when Robbie's too sick to see a doctor."

"I don't understand what you're telling me." It was obvious by his expression, Steve had no idea what message his sister was trying to convey.

"You remember when he got sick in Maui?" Catherine was insistent her brother know the whole story and retold it from the beginning.

"I remember hearing about it. He was laid up for a day or two."

"He had a second relapse, weeks later. I don't remember when exactly."

"I think I heard about that."

"Everybody has. That piece of news circulated everywhere except the daily paper."

"And you don't think he's sick. It's just a rumor," her brother interrupted.

"You're missing my point. The second time he got sick, I called his house. I wanted to know why Robbie hadn't phoned the office for messages. He could hardly talk. Robbie was sick and maybe still is."

"If he is, there's nothing you can do about it. He's a grown man."

"I know that," Catherine smarted sarcastically. "But there's more to it. He told me to cover his ass if people start to question his absence. Then Robbie tells me he's going away to quote a possible new contract and gives me no information about it."

"That's good, isn't it? Getting a new contract, I mean."

"What kind of Italian are you?" She questioned his intellect. "There is no contract. I would know if something was coming in and there is nothing to indicate that."

"That is strange," Steve agreed.

"Then, he tells me to pretend I'm bordering senility. I'm to say I had forgotten he wouldn't be in until Friday. That's what I told the group. Of course, I apologized and reprimanded myself. So what does that tell you?"

"You first." Their eyes met. "You must have some kind of theory that's worrying you."

"That's just it," Catherine insisted. "Nothing makes sense."

"It must to Robbie." He countered. "Think about it. Why would he go away if there's no contract?"

"He's suspicious. That's the only thing I can think of. John's sabotaging the company. He's sending our prospective employees to Henry Price. I know that for a fact."

"I don't buy his going away for that," Steve disagreed. "That's small stuff."

"What about Robbie being sick?"

"Now that's a possibility. Suppose he's sick and has to leave town for tests or even surgery. Robbie wouldn't want anyone to know about it. Certainly, not you."

"Did he say anything to you?"

"No. He didn't. I don't think he would tell Mackenzie either." Steve offered an opinion he thought accurate.

"Would he tell his wife?"

"Raine's another story. They seem so lovey-dovey together, he may not want to worry her. We'll all know if something's wrong medically. He'll have to tell us at some point."

"Robbie did say he would tell me later." Catherine added to her brother's premise.

"That's the real story behind all this. He's going on a medical trip and doesn't want anyone to know about it."

"So what should I do?"

"Do what he says. Cover his ass." Steve finished his coffee and left the house.

Catherine watched her brother as he left the kitchen. She continued to sit at the table, her thoughts filled with mixed emotions. Maybe Steve was right and it was a medical problem with Robbie. Still, something deep inside her disagreed with her brother's thinking. Somewhere, somehow, she felt her daughter-in-law's hand all over this ruse. Whether she was or she wasn't, Catherine still hated the woman.

***

Robert stood hidden by the curtained window of his bedroom and watched Raine enter her car. He insisted she go to the office that Thursday afternoon. There was nothing more she could do for him by staying home. They had already finished their conversation about death and money.

She started so easily. In fact, her narrative unfolded like the rehearsed lines of a play. Raine was so skilled explaining death and inheritance requests. Of course, Robert agreed with her wishes, explaining he, too, would be taking steps for her welfare upon his demise. After Robert threw a few numerical figures in the air, Raine's face lit-up like a lottery winner. She got what she wanted: to be a wealthy widow.

A wide grin creased his face. Raine wouldn't be wealthy. Nor would she be a widow. She would, however, be in prison.

He walked to her dresser, checked her lingerie drawer for her bank books and began to laugh. The Certificate of Deposit document was gone. Only the money market valued at eight thousand remained. Raine took the other one with her when she left. His wife was a real piece of work, a greedy one at that.

Chapter 29
A Pretense

Each of Robert's men stopped by to greet him on his return to the office Friday morning. Even Bruce Parks called to check on the health of his friend. Robert sluffed-off every inquiry, saying he never felt better. Obviously, the bug he caught in Maui was getting wide berth among his friends and business associates. Robert knew John started those rumors but could not reveal the truth until he had proof of the man's murderous plan. Until that happened the office routine had to function normally.

Sometime during that same morning, Robert pretended to receive a phone call about a possible contract. Shortly afterward, Robert told Catherine he was leaving that weekend for a city he refused to name. As he spoke, Catherine gave more and more credence to her brother's explanation. Robbie was leaving town for medical reasons.

"Where will you be staying?" she asked, continuing their conversation, knowing John Harris would be sneaking around the outer office, his ear at Robert's closed door.

"I can't answer that. Someone, who prefers anonymity, will be meeting me with room arrangements." He answered directly.

"When will you be back?" Catherine's head bobbed toward his door, raising the question of being overheard.

"I'll have to leave that open. I don't know."

"But you will call to check in," she insisted, "in case something comes up."

"That's no problem. I'll call every morning, if possible."

"We're good." Catherine sailed out of his office, just in time to watch John's office door close.

She knew he would be around her constantly with questions concerning the new contract, the company involved and Robert's location. In her mind, the whole thing was crazy. Why didn't Robert just tell her the truth? Was he afraid of worrying her? There was no incoming contract, but she had to go along with his story. Robbie was her son and his welfare was all that mattered.

***

That Friday afternoon, Raine called her husband with an inquiry. "Do we have any plans for Saturday?" she asked. "A man being transferred to Pittsburgh wants to look at houses. His wife flew in this weekend, which means they are serious about buying."

"Go for it. We'll find a restaurant for dinner afterwards."

"You sure?"

"Do it. I have work to do. I'm leaving Sunday morning."

"So, you are leaving Sunday."

"Raine, I want you to make your appointments." She could tell by the sound of his voice, he was getting annoyed with the conversation.

"Love you." She ended the call, leaving him to wonder if the out of town client with the imaginary spouse was Valerie. Couldn't she wait one more day without seeing him? One more day until he left? His thoughts continued to churn.

Maybe she did have someone coming in from another city, but Robert didn't believe that possibility. If he wasn't mistaken, Raine had an open house Sunday. She would probably spend the night in her old apartment with John. Robert would drive around the end parking lot to check. His thoughts however, were interrupted by a knock on his office door.

"Hey," he addressed his assistant. "Good timing. We need to talk. I'm leaving you in charge while I'm away to discuss a possible contract. Whatever comes up, you handle it."

"What's with a new contract? You never talked about it."

"I didn't know we were in the running until I got the phone call this morning. It's connected and quiet. I can't talk about it because I don't really know what's involved or the sponsorship. I can only do an approximate cost based on need. When I get back, we will price everything to the penny. That is…if we're being considered."

"Who's the competition?" John's question was an attempt for more information but Robert refused to be drawn in.

"If I don't know what's involved or the people really requesting this meeting, I sure as hell wouldn't know the competition. My gut tells me this could be big and bring us a lot of money. That is, if we get the contract. You would like your share, I'm sure."

"What does that mean, exactly?"

"A big bonus. You would be in charge of the entire project. I plan to take Raine on an extended vacation to the Mediterranean."

"Does she know?"

"It's a surprise. I'm thinking a month to six weeks."

"That is a shocker." He had not expected that kind of news.

"We've always taken care of our own, haven't we?"

"Yeah, I guess we have," his assistant said still shocked by the news.

"I'll keep you informed as we go." Robert ended their meeting.

Robert watched him leave the office in high spirits. The man would be in charge of a ghost contract and get a huge bonus with Monopoly money. How much sweeter could it get? He pictured John making two phone calls: one to Henry Price; the other, to Raine.

The call to Henry Price would not be informative. Robert gave him no information to pass on. Instead, John would ask Henry if he received an inquiry for future project. If not, another possibility existed. If Robert lost the bid, Henry could be another option. Once satisfied with that conversation, John would phone Raine with the news of a grand and glorious trip…one she would never take.

He had other plans for the woman. Yet, he wanted his wife to toy with the idea of an extended trip. He could see her planning a new wardrobe for a Mediterranean vacation. Of course, she would also need new coordinating luggage.

"True," he whispered and kept the rest of his thoughts silent. While Raine would be concentrating on travel, John's thoughts would be elsewhere. He would plan to dispatch Robert as soon as the company received the ghost contract. John would fulfill their requests and be the man in charge. This "being the man in charge" was something Robert had not considered, should something really happen to him. His status under Mackenzie would be one of an employee until she, too, was dispatched. Then he would own the company.

All of this was true. Mackenzie had to name someone to handle his company if he were to die. His assistant was the logical choice. If only Robert had proof to show his daughter. It would explain Raine's betrayal and her relationship with John. But would his daughter realize the depth of their undertaking? Would she understand they wanted him dead? How could he tell Mackenzie they were killers when she felt that same way about him? She still believed he wanted her mother to die.

Somehow, Robert needed a way to convince her of the truth. It came down to the same thing over and over again. He needed proof and there was only one way to get it. It was the same thought he had earlier. Elias had to break into Raine's old apartment, search for the container of poison and take a sample. Robert also wanted him to find the Certificate of Deposit for confirmation purposes only. Once Robert had proof, Mackenzie would be convinced of their lethal intentions. There could be no other explanation.

Robert sat back in his chair, satisfied with the planned scenario. It was going to be an interesting few days. He would start shadowing Raine on Sunday afternoon to determine her itinerary. Then he would follow John. Somewhere in the mix, Robert would visit Mackenzie. She had to be aware of the situation. He was fearful harm could come to her too. Without question, he had to warn his daughter and it had to be done soon. He would ask Elias to act quickly as a favor to him.

***

Two events occurred the following night, each quite separate from the other, although a common thread ran between them. And despite the show of interest or love, deceit comes in all forms, and is after all, just plain deceit.

***

Raine surprised her husband by asking the out of town clients to join them for dinner. The invitation was not unexpected on her part. Since they were thinking of buying the house on Stoller Road, she wanted to cement that thought with a purchase offer before the wife left town. She explained her thinking to Robert hoping he would understand. Not only did her husband understand, the man was grateful he did not have to spend the evening listening to her lies. She could concentrate on her clients and deceive them with all her chatter about the dud she continually held open. It was so refreshing to be an observer instead of a victim. He found it intriguing, watching her draw them in. It reminded him of Florence.

***

In a different section of town, a second event was unfolding.

"You're full of surprises tonight." Mackenzie took the gift box offered her as he unlocked the apartment door. "I was so happy we went to Maribel's. It's my favorite restaurant in Southside. The food is always so good." She snapped on the light switch.

"He took the box from her hand, turned-off the light switch and drew her to him. "I couldn't wait for this tonight." He kissed her passionately, her firm, young body tight against his. He knew she felt his readiness as his hands pressed her lower back even tighter against him. He felt her yielding and led her to the bedroom, taking the box with him. "Open it." He turned on the bedroom lamp.

Mackenzie opened the box to unfold a very sheer sky-blue mini-gown centered with a dark blue tie that held the opened front together. Inside the box were three nightlights. "What are these?"

"You'll see soon enough." He took the three nightlights. "Go into the bathroom and slip on the gown. Don't come out until I call you."

Within minutes, he spaced the nightlights around the room to give it a soft, romantic glow. Satisfied with the ambiance, he turned-off the bed lamp to further darken the room, removed his clothes quickly and sat on an armless side chair. "You can come to me now," he said quietly.

When Mackenzie stepped slowly into the room's soft glow, her eyes fixed on his nude body. She realized something different was about to happen, something she had never experienced before. She faced him directly and felt a hunger growing deep within her body.

"You are so beautiful." He studied the small but fully-endowed figure standing before him. She stood veiled in the finest sheer netting, a very short gossamer that revealed the dark nipples of her bosom and the triangular patch of her loins. He had pictured her like this so many times before, the perfect goddess surrendering to her masterful lover.

"Turn," he said softly. As she circled slowly, the sheer, short gown flounced out and upward in coordination with her extended arms and showed him the artistic movement of her loins, gratifying his every expectation of conquest. He felt the need of her immediately as she stood facing him again. "Come to me," he said, his arms open wide. He straddled her on his lap, and feeling her soft silky skin on his, slowly pulled the tie of her gown.

"Will you stay with me?" She felt the tip of his wet tongue circle and re-circle the hollow portion of her throat several times, causing her whole body to ache with want. "Please," she begged.

"Yes," he whispered, his own need increasing. "I'm going to love you in every possible way tonight. You won't want it to end." He positioned her to move with him. "I love you so much," he moaned. "You make my life so real."

"It is real!" she gasped, knowing her moment was near.

Chapter 30
Departure

"I hate to see you go," Raine said, watching her husband enter his car Sunday morning.

"As I said, a few days, a week at most.'"

"Call me. I'll be home later. Pray they make an offer this afternoon."

As Robert started the car, he thought about their conversation the previous evening. Raine told him she would be showing the Stoller Road house again and hoped her clients would make an offer on it. The owner had lowered the price and was anxious to sell. Raine felt it a good buy for her customers. It had met their requirements. Granted, the next door neighbor was a bit of a bitch, always moaning about the lawn, but Raine couldn't help that. Then, too, a marble would roll downhill on the master bedroom floor, but who kept an aggie in his pocket when shopping for a house?

Robert watched his wife wave good-by as he pulled out of the driveway. "Stupid bitch," he mumbled aloud, and then concentrated on the scenario he had outlined for the next few days. He drove down the main highway and turned onto another major road that led down a steep hill to Turtle Creek. He made a right turn at a small business district only to realize that most of the area's retail stores were closed on Sunday. Robert drove six more blocks up another steep hill, turned right and located a street with the house address given him. He passed by the house slowly to get a feeling of the street and then circled the block before pulling into the driveway of his 'home away from home.'

A small white wooden structure sat in the center of a fenced yard, completely separated from its detached garage. The two-story house looked moderately well-kept and blended in with the other homes, giving a passerby no reason to notice, since there was nothing outstanding about it.

Leaving his car, Robert walked around the side fence abutting the driveway to the front gate of the yard. The street seemed particularly quiet with no one around. The possibility of people going to church and gathering for a late weekend breakfast occurred to him as he sauntered up the walkway to the front door. He turned the knob slowly, not knowing what to expect and walked in. Robert had an eerie feeling. There was no one around. The house was empty.

He walked from the living room to the kitchen thinking to check for food supplies but found a note on the counter and a metal ring with two keys: one for the house; the other, a car.

Robert understood his having keys; however, the note baffled him.

'Pursue with caution. It's deeper than you think.'

Who wrote the note and what did it mean? None of it made sense to him. Once again, he thought about the situation with Raine and John. He knew the ultimate plan was to get rid of him, but what was he missing? He had already thought of Mackenzie. They wouldn't do anything to her until he was out of the way. Or so he thought. There must be something else he overlooked, but what?

Did Elias write the note because he couldn't make their meeting today? What did he know that wasn't shared? If he didn't make it by three, Robert would be on his own. He needed proof for his plan to succeed. Then his thoughts suddenly shifted to the house.

The property belonged to Claude. Robert felt sure of it. But why offer it to him? Did Claude know Raine was cheating on him? If the man wafted into his home to install 'Sweet Pea,' he did it for a reason. Claude placed it in his kitchen so Robert would have access to the most used room of the house. No, he retracted the thought. That's where Raine prepared his wine. Did Claude know she was poisoning him or was it something else? Robert's thoughts wandered back to his honeymoon and the time Catherine saw Claude leave his house. That was long before anyone knew about the bug he caught in Maui. What Claude realized but couldn't reveal was the relationship between Raine and John. With the added kitchen installation Robert would have access to Raine's phone conversations and planned activities. It was Claude's way of alerting him to the bitch he had married. But that thinking drew him to another conclusion.

If this house belonged to Claude, and the man installed 'Sweet Pea' in Robert's home to warn him, then he must have also written the note. Robert wished he could have a conversation with him. He knew far more than Robert ever realized. Why was he so protective of him but not more forthcoming? What did Claude mean by '*It's deeper than you think*?' What had Robert overlooked? His thoughts were getting him no closer to the solution of his problem.

Taking the keys from the counter he walked back to the driveway, passed his own car and opened the garage door. Inside, sat a black Chevy sedan. It was small and innocuous, the type of car that receives little attention from drivers on the road or in a parking lot.

Robert drove his car to the front of the house, backed the Chevy out of the driveway into the street and parked his own vehicle inside the garage. He took his luggage out of the trunk, placed it over the side fence and parked the Chevy on the driveway. This was the car he would now use. Robert retraced his steps back to the front yard, grabbed his luggage against the side fence and re-entered the house again. It was time to investigate the rest of the furnished home.

The first floor offered nothing unusual: a living room, kitchen, den and lavatory. The bedrooms on the second floor seemed small compared to other houses of its size, yet the bathroom was quite large. Robert sluffed the bedroom sizes to the age of the house and thought nothing more of it. At this point, he didn't really care. Since he would be occupying the house for only a few days, room sizes didn't matter. Right now, he was more concerned with food and took the stairs to the kitchen.

The refrigerator contents were his biggest surprise. He expected little or next to nothing; however, either Elias or Claude must have considered his situation and realized food would not have been his priority. He noticed the bread, milk, water and juice sitting on the upper shelves, but a further perusal of the meat drawer made his stomach emit groans for sustenance. The supplier had to be Elias. Who else but a roommate, knowing his likes, would buy prosciutto, cappacola, salami and provolone? Robert grabbed all the lunch meat and cheese, along with the bread, and tossed everything on the counter. On the lowest refrigerator shelf he found a head of lettuce and two tomatoes. Elias went all out for him. Maybe this was his way of repaying for all the scotch he consumed, but Robert did not believe that for one minute. Elias was more like the brother who shared mutual fruits with him.

Robert scoured the cupboards for dishes and glasses first, then began making a sandwich, when the door opened and Elias walked into the kitchen.

"Make me one too. I want salami." He leaned against the kitchen counter.

Robert slid the salami down the counter and offered him his plate with two bread slices. "I thought I locked the door." He reached for another plate from the cupboard, placed two open slices of bread on it and began unwrapping the package of prosciutto.

"I have a key. Who do you think filled the refrigerator?"

"Who?"

"Right, this who did." Elias reached into the refrigerator for bottled water. "Smart ass."

"Want lettuce and tomato?"

Elias shook his head. "I'm good."

"Thank you for doing this." Robert grew serious. He stopped speaking for a moment, pausing long enough to collect his thoughts. "I'm in trouble."

"Damn right you are. The mice died."

"What?" Robert did not comprehend Elias' message at first. Somehow his words had not impacted Robert's brain.

"They weren't drunk on wine: they were dead."

"Who was?" Robert's expression was one of listening to a foreign language he could not understand.

"Put down your sandwich and listen. I took the olive jar to a friend at the lab. He tested the wine on two otherwise healthy mice.

They died. He couldn't trace the poison but felt sure a larger dose would be lethal to a human."

"So it's true. Raine is trying to kill me."

Robert held his hands to his face. What he believed about his sickness was no longer theory. The tested wine was proof of her evil undertaking. The realization, that the woman he loved and married wanted him dead, brought within him a raging anger that thumped the synapses of his brain.

Elias studied the frozen look of his friend and knew instantly Robert had a plan in mind. "I don't think she's alone in the endeavor. Where would she get the stuff to poison you?"

"John would be my guess. The man travels a lot. He went to South America last year."

"I remember you telling me about his cough medicines."

"Well, now he's graduated to poison," Robert answered sarcastically. "With me in mind."

"So, what's the plan?"

"I need your help. I want you to search Raine's old apartment at Penn Center for a container of poison. Take samples and pictures. It's apartment 216. I also want to know if she stashed a ten-thousand dollar Certificate of Deposit there. It's probably in her office, the smaller bedroom."

"When?" Elias had no intention of refusing. He wanted to kill the woman himself for using his friend.

"She'll probably sleep there tonight with John. But they both work tomorrow, so that might be a good time to search the place."

"What are you doing in the meantime?"

"I plan to follow her today and tonight, but I am confused about something. I don't understand what 'deeper than you think' means."

"I'm not following you." Elias looked puzzled as he caught the note Robert passed to him. He read it quickly. "I didn't write this."

"Does Claude own this house?"

"This place belongs to him." Elias offered nothing further.

"Then he must have written the note. I would like to talk with him. What does he know? What am I missing that's deeper than I think?"

"I don't know, but I do have something to show you. This is from Claude." Robert followed Elias upstairs to one of the bedrooms and watched him open the door of a small closet before unscrewing a decorative knob on the bed headboard. Then he pressed a button on the exposed base, causing the back wall of the closet to slide open.

"What the hell...?" Robert trailed his friend inside another room that had several computers and a small globe-like top resting on one of the desks.

"It's a pocket door," Elias explained. "Some homes have them, not like this, of course," he said, referring to the button on the headboard base which signaled the door to slide inside another wall and provide an opening. "Now, where is your computer?"

Robert raced downstairs then returned to the inner room holding the small laptop. "Now what?"

"Open it and pull up the antenna. It's on the left in the indented space." Elias arced the thin tall spool upward. "Now watch what I do." Elias snapped the small globe on the tip of the antenna and turned on the computer. "We are at the highest elevation here. That's why Claude bought this particular house. Now put in the codes."

Immediately, Robert saw the bedroom of his house. He watched Elias rotate the globe a quarter turn. His bathroom came into view. "Now, you do it." Robert turned the globe again to see his living room appear. On another turn, he captured an entire view of his kitchen. "Do you understand what Claude has done for you?"

"It's not the elevation." Robert said, studying the computers while smiling inwardly at the superficial globe that disguised the real means of communication. "He's given me something I shouldn't have. It's either satellite or something even more secretive." He paused. "How could Claude have pulled it off?" Robert said aloud but did not explain the meaning of his question. Suddenly, his thoughts turned in another direction. "This will help me learn the real motive for wanting me dead. I'm completely in the dark on that score. Aside from a few thousand in the safe, Raine doesn't get any of my money right now and I don't see a direct benefit for John."

"Unless Mackenzie dies too," Elias corrected.

"But I have to die first."

"I think that's why Claude's helping you." Elias seemed convinced of the statement.

"Why? He doesn't even know me." Robert frowned.

"Maybe not in terms of time spent together, but Claude knows you. That's saying a lot coming from him."

"That surprises me, Elias. It really does."

"You have any questions about this?" He pointed to the computer and caught Robert's negative nod. "Take off the globe and close the computer until you use it again." He led Robert to the outer bedroom. "Press the button again to close the wall-door before screwing on the bed knob."

Robert followed Elias' instructions and trailed him downstairs to the living room where they stood facing each other.

"I have to leave now but I'll see you tomorrow or Tuesday. Do something useful. Buy some good scotch."

After Robert watched his friend sail out of the house, he raced to a front window but never saw Elias or heard the start of a car.

Chapter 31
Martha

<hr>

After Elias left, Robert began to implement a plan. He wanted to check the house on Stoller Road but felt it was a bad idea. Raine had already shown the house by now and possibly persuaded the buyers to bid on the property. He could always swing by her office. If she were drawing up a purchase offer, her car would be in the parking lot. Still, something told him to drive by Stoller Road first. He was all set to leave the house, when the doorbell rang.

Thinking it was Elias returning for something, Robert was ready with a smart remark upon opening the door. Fortunately, he held his tongue and studied the thin, dark-haired woman standing before him, a wide smile on her face. Although she appeared to be rather attractive, his eyes were glued to her white, even teeth. She would have been perfect for a toothpaste commercial.

"I'm sorry to bother you." The small woman continued to smile. "I check Mr. Manchen's house when he's away. Will you be staying long?"

"Only for a few days," Robert replied.

"Oh. That's strange. I thought it would be longer. He told me to give you this." She gave him a sealed envelope. "If you need anything, I live next door. Martha. My name's Martha Buccili." She stood waiting at the front door in silence, their eye level not even close. "Ok, I'll just call you Toby Too. We'll see who comes first, you or the dog." As she turned to leave, Martha heard the tall man beginning to laugh.

"At least I have a sense of humor!" Robert shouted, his eyes following her to the small house next door.

"But you can't do this," Martha shouted back when the dog greeted her at the door. "Jump the fences, Toby." She told her dog.

A German shepherd, the size of a miniature pony, immediately jumped the fences on her command, trotted to the porch and began barking at Robert.

Although taken back, he yelled, "What, jumping fences or barking?"

"Come. Toby," Martha called. "Your namesake's no fun." She watched the dog jump the fences again and, leading him into the house, left his alias to reflect on what just happened.

Robert entered the house again, amused by the incident with Martha and Toby. He eyed the blank envelope in his hand and hoped Claude had some news that would help him. He doubted Manchen was the man's real surname, yet wondered why he kept-up the pretense with Martha. Was it because she cared for the property in his absence? From the little conversation they had Robert got the distinct impression Claude was not at the house very often. But regardless of the man's activities, this Martha was hell on wheels. Not much would get by her pert little nose.

Robert opened Claude's envelope and slid out a sheet of paper that contained a terse note.

'Martha's a big help. Be nice to her.'

"Big whoop," he said out loud and walked to the kitchen counter. Placing the note adjacent Claude's other one, Robert read them again and began searching for an ashtray. Finding none, he took a deep bowl from the cupboard, placed both notes inside and burned them with a match from the pack in his pocket.

"Pocketing a pack," was one of Elias' rules. "Burn the written word so it won't come back to bite you in the ass," he would say. Although Robert destroyed them, he would not forget either note easily.

Granted, he did not understand the first note. Yet, Robert felt certain it meant uncovering something deeply hidden; some fact he was not aware of. The second one was a matter he had not anticipated. Being nice to Martha would not be a problem. Essentially, she was the caretaker of Claude's property and Robert did not want to destroy that relationship. Naturally, Robert would make amends…if he offended her. Yet, thinking back on their conversation he couldn't think of anything he said that could be misconstrued. In the next few days, he'd wave or do something to get into her good graces. Robert would worry about that another time. Right now, Raine was on his mind and it was getting late.

***

Hours much earlier, that same Sunday morning, a couple lay in bed, their arms entwined.

"Will you always wake-me-up this way?" Mackenzie asked.

"It would be the highlight of my day." He brushed his lips along the side of her face. "I long for the day when we're together." He turned and kissed her before climbing out of bed.

"Do you really have to leave?" Her face took on a sad expression.

"Not because I want to. But you do understand why I must," he cautioned. "We cannot be caught together. Not now." He sat on the side of the bed and drew her to him. "I don't want to lose you."

"You really do love me, don't you?" Her eyes fixed on his. "Tell me you love me."

"I adore you." He kissed his young goddess again. "I want to spend the rest of my life making love to you." With that statement, the line between his past and present love was becoming a blur, but he was not fully aware of it.

"Through marriage?" She continued to stare.

"Will you marry me when the time is right?"

"I want it so badly, I ache."

"It will happen," he said walking into the bathroom to shower, leaving Mackenzie with her thoughts on marriage and the running water as background music.

He left Mackenzie pondering their night together, while more sober thoughts ran through his mind. How solid was the marriage between Raine and her husband in terms of public appearance? After something happened to him, would she overtly stand in the way of his happiness?

***

Robert drove by the house on Stoller Road that afternoon but found the property deserted. If was after four o'clock and the Sunday open houses were closed. Passing Raine's office would be a trickier move, although she would never suspect her husband of being in town or driving a small black Chevy. Still, he had to be careful.

Robert took the main highway that led to Raine's office. At the top of a hill, he made a right hand turn and passed her office building. Although he was not driving fast, Robert missed seeing her parked car. He circled the block and passed Raine's office again. Her car was not there. Where was she at that hour? With her buyers? That was not possible. Since his wife was leaving town that afternoon, the woman's husband had to be with her at the airport.

Two possibilities crossed his mind but checking one of them could be a very bad move, if caught. There was no feasible way he could pass his own house, particularly, when he was supposed to be out of town. However, he could check her old apartment at Penn Center.

Robert turned from the main road onto another highway leading to Penn Center. Within fifteen minutes, Robert passed the third parking lot of the complex to the small end section but did not see Raine's parked car. He continued driving and began searching all three lots. Raine's car was nowhere to be found. Where else could she be at that hour? Suddenly, another option occurred to him. The more he thought about the third possibility, the more absurd it became. His wife would never go to John's condo. She could not risk being recognized. Raine was probably at home.

Robert was becoming totally frustrated when a sudden thought hit him! 'Sweet Pea.' He didn't need to pass his house. Using 'Sweet Pea' he could see his wife at home. Robert would know soon enough. He maneuvered the car around and drove straight to Turtle Creek. As Robert approached his driveway, he noticed Toby sitting in the middle of his own fenced yard watching him park. As soon as Robert opened the front gate, Toby bounded over both fences and met him at the front door.

"Hello, Toby," Robert greeted the huge dog, but not knowing what else to say, ignored the animal and unlocked the door. He realized immediately that it was the wrong move. The German shepherd dashed through the opened door and raced directly to the refrigerator where he sat on his haunches and waited.

"I don't believe this." Robert told the shaded brown and black dog eyeing him with disgust for having him linger.

"He likes lunchmeat, particularly salami." Martha leaned against the open doorway, offering him a suggestion. "He won't leave until you feed him. Mr. Manchen always gives him a slice of salami. I think it's called mutual blackmail. Toby guards the property for salami. Have any?"

Robert opened the refrigerator and pulled out the lunchmeat packages. "You sure he wouldn't like a piece of provolone to go with it?"

"Now, you're being sarcastic." She watched her dog devour the salami, and never moving from the doorway, said, "Watch him."

Toby sat up straight and raised a paw.

"Take it. He's thanking you," Martha explained. "Don't screw-it-up for Mr. Manchen."

Robert took the dog's paw and said something like, "You're welcome." After the paw acknowledgement Toby took off like a shot, out of the front door and over both fences.

"Thank you for continuing the tradition, Toby Too." Martha left the doorway and returned to her house.

But before she entered, Robert shouted, "If you come back, I can give you more than salami."

Martha turned abruptly to face him. "Go screw yourself," she bellowed and banged her door closed.

"What the hell is your problem, lady!" he yelled to her closed door. "It must be her time of the month." Robert told himself, locking his own front door. Right now, he had more to worry about than a dog who liked salami and an irate neighbor who didn't like anything.

Robert took the stairs to the second bedroom, unscrewed the bed knob, pressed the base button and entered the inner room to check his house. He turned on his computer, arced the antenna and placed the globe on its tip. After a quarter turn, his bedroom came into view. Raine was not there. Nor was she in the bathroom or living room. However, he did find her sitting on a kitchen stool eating something that looked like spaghetti and reading a paper. As always, she looked like a fashion plate from a magazine. The woman was beautiful. There was no denying it. Yet, Robert felt confused.

When he was home, she drugged him for a chance to meet her lover. Now that Robert was away, Raine sat at home, alone, eating dinner. None of these actions made sense. Why wasn't she at Penn Center with John?

Robert looked at his watch. It was a little before six. Maybe it was too early. They could be meeting at a later time. Her last meeting started somewhere around eleven. Somehow, that did not seem right to him. They would meet tonight, but at an earlier time. Robert felt sure of it. One of them would phone to confirm and he would video Raine's call. Then he would drive to Penn Center, wait for them to show-up and take pictures. But first he should eat something. Then he could sit in front of the computer and wait for an exchange to occur.

***

Somewhere around seven o'clock, Raine made a phone call. "I thought you were going to call me." Robert heard her statement, but could not hear John's response.

"Then you'll be nice and rested to see me," she said. "I'll meet you at the apartment." Robert found the implication quite clear. More than a tryst was in the wind when Raine added more to John's response.

"Around eight. Bring your toothbrush. This is our opportunity to spend the whole night together. It's our safest bet since he just left town today. Who knows when he'll be back," she added. "Ok. Then make it nine," she agreed to his time change.

Robert heard a click from John's side. While waiting the extra minute for something else to occur, he heard Raine swear before pressing her end button. Obviously, she was angry about something. Was John not being attentive enough or was their relationship beginning to sour? If so, it wasn't on Raine's part. She initiated the phone call...and Robert captured it all.

He had until nine o'clock to photograph the two lovers. Actually, he should be parked in the lot, somewhere unseen but with a good view, at a much earlier time. Eight o'clock would be his target time. Raine would arrive early. She was never one to be late for an appointment which meant he would have to photograph them separately. He thought about taking a picture of their parked cars. But for now, he had to wait. Robert dissembled 'Sweet Pea' and headed downstairs. He had just enough time to mend a fractured meeting, but wished it were still daylight.

***

Robert could hear Toby barking as he stood outside Martha's door.

"What is it with you?" Martha greeted him in the doorway, a rendition of barking music in the background.

"I came to apologize for whatever I did...that I don't know about. Can I come in? It's getting cold out here." She reminded him of a silhouette against the lighted background.

"No. You're not staying." Martha was about to close the door when Robert put his foot in the doorway.

"Listen, Martha. I don't know what the hell I've done to you, but I'm trying to be a gentlemen." His mounting frustration now turned to anger.

"That's crap and you know it. A gentlemen doesn't offer something in addition to salami." She spat back.

"Don't you like cappacola or prosciutto?"

"What does lunchmeat have to do with it?" Martha was beginning to think the man was a half-wit.

"That's what I have in the refrigerator. If you didn't like salami, I had other lunchmeat." Although his explanation seemed plausible to him, he could tell Martha was not buying it.

"That's not what you said," she groused. "You had something else to offer if I didn't want salami."

"I don't get it." Robert looked completely puzzled.

"And you won't. So move your foot before I stomp on it."

Robert placed his hand firmly on the door and held it there. "Just what did you think I was talking about? Sex?" He shook his head in amazement. "How could you misconstrue a sandwich for sex?"

"I didn't. It was implied."

"Don't take this the wrong way, but I have no intention of having sex with you. Not that you're unattractive. Someone would find you quite appealing."

"You know what? You should quit while you're ahead."

"Are we ok?"

Martha could tell he was really getting cold. "Go home, Toby Too."

"Is that a number or an also?"

"An also." She closed the door.

***

When Robert returned to Turtle Creek that evening, he felt totally dejected. Capturing photos of Raine and John, although singly, since they arrived within minutes of each other, just made it all the more real to him. His thoughts centered on Raine. He was drawn into her web of deception, thinking she loved him. It wasn't love; it was expediency. It was all concocted with a simple formula: love, marriage and death equaled money and power. Rid yourself of Robert first, then get Mackenzie. His anger increased with each successive thought as he pulled into the driveway of his Turtle Creek hideaway.

The night was colder than Robert expected when he got out of the car, but then again, it was the end of October and before long, it would snow. The first blast usually hit before Veteran's Day, if he recalled correctly. His immediate thoughts centered on the snow blower and driveway for a minute. As he rounded the fence to the front gate, Robert thought he heard a growl. He turned to glance across the side fence to Martha's house but saw nothing. Toby was not in the yard and the house was totally dark. It took a minute but the realization finally sank in. Toby paced behind Martha's front door when he heard Robert's car in the driveway.

"Nothing like having a miniature pony announce the arrival of someone in hiding," he said aloud. "I must be losing it," he added. "I keep talking to myself these days."

Robert continued having this conversation with himself as he entered the front door, took the stairs to the bedroom and after undressing, climbed into bed. Robert's last thought before drifting to sleep was finding a liquor store to buy scotch. It couldn't be just any old scotch. It had to be top quality: an Elias Juniper scotch. Then he had an alarming but connected thought. Robert would also have to shop for glasses…glasses…glasses. He fell asleep.

***

That same Sunday evening, a conversation was taking place at an apartment in Penn Center, the same location Robert and his camera had visited earlier.

"I don't understand. This is a perfect opportunity." Raine was visually upset.

John studied the woman lying beside him in bed. "I'm not so sure."

"He just left today. He won't be back until Tuesday, the earliest." She tried convincing him to stay the night.

"It's not a good idea for either of us," he disagreed. "Suppose a meeting took place and didn't go well. Robert could be coming home tomorrow morning and you wouldn't be there."

"That's not going to happen," she countered angrily. "You just want to go back to your condo."

His first impulse was to slap some sense into the woman. He knew, however, she was on edge. He took her into his arms and caressed her. He brushed her lips and said, "I wouldn't have come if I wanted to be in my condo."

"You think it's too risky…being here."

"No. Risky is staying here," John corrected. "We're playing a game with an unknown. He could be back tomorrow."

"So, you think I should sleep at home tonight."

"Exactly." He climbed out of bed and began to dress.

"When will I see you again?"

"Here, right after work tomorrow. Leave a note saying you have to show a house, just in case he comes back and you're not home."

"Then we'll only be together for an hour or so," she complained.

"But we'll be together." Raine watched him leave the bedroom and heard the apartment door close.

***

John was upset when he left Raine. Her incessant need to be with him was wearing thin. Although he liked the woman, John was not in love with her. They shared a mutual need over the years, but he had never made a commitment to her. Now, she assumed there was one. Although not openly verbalized, John felt it. Raine was becoming more and more demanding of his time, and he didn't like it. John acquiesced to her wishes, fearful she would fall apart and ruin their plan when it was so close to completion. But he didn't like their meeting constantly.

As he drove back to the condo, his thoughts on Raine continued. Would she alter their plan, thinking he would marry her once Robert was dead? That was not their agreement. She would inherit his money; John would run the company and probably own it in time. The last thought made him smile.

"No," he said aloud. "She wants wealth and prestige." Her thoughts of him would vanish, once she had money. Raine was not one to share anything. Yet she wouldn't stand in his way for acquiring the company. The woman knew he wanted it from the very beginning, when they first formulated their plans for snaring and killing Robert. Yes. Raine knew better than to challenge her partner. Another murder would mean little to him…and Raine was smart enough to figure that out.

Chapter 32
Shopping

Robert awakened the next morning thinking of scotch. He searched every cabinet in the kitchen for a bottle of liquor but couldn't find any. Was Claude a teetotaler? A non-drinker? Robert didn't believe that for a minute. Then a strange thought occurred to him. There was something about the house he had completely overlooked. He started a slow search, starting once again in the kitchen. Slowly, it began to dawn on him. The kitchen held non-descript dishes, glasses, and various utensils for cooking and eating, but nothing of real value. Canned food or cereal was nowhere to be found. The only food in the house was in the refrigerator. Elias had put it there. His friend knew the house offered nothing but shelter, which to Robert was a lot. But otherwise, what would the house be used for? A safe house? In Turtle Creek? No. Whatever Claude used it for was off the grid. And whatever the man designed for Robert's surveillance purposes could never be traced. Of that, he was certain.

Robert checked the drawer of the lamp table in the living room but found it empty. He took the stairs to the bedrooms and checked each one. The night stand drawers were empty. Robert checked under the beds. Again, he found nothing. The house was wiped clean. He assumed the only fingerprints in the house were his. Maybe it was a safe house; maybe it wasn't. Whatever its use, he wasn't asking. Robert didn't want to know. He was just glad Claude made it available.

Robert went back downstairs for something to eat. He stood facing the refrigerator contents. Nothing appealed to him. Although he couldn't face eating another sandwich, Robert pulled out the makings for one and devoured it greedily. At that point Robert came to a decision, one out of necessity.

Robert raced upstairs, showered, shaved, dressed and fled the house to the one next door. It was not quite nine o'clock.

"What now?" Martha greeted him as Toby edged her body from the doorway to peak at the man who gave him salami.

"I need a liquor store."

"Isn't it a little early for that?"

"No. I need it for a friend."

"Right," Martha interrupted.

"Can we start over? I have a problem." Robert tried to explain.

"I'll give you the address of an AA."

"I am not a drunk," he argued, "and I'm getting cold."

"Okay."

"You believe me," he said, becoming relieved.

"No, but I can see you're getting cold."

"The hell with it." He turned to retrace his steps back to the house when Toby came bounding over the fences to meet him at the front door.

"Maybe you know where there's a liquor store." He addressed the dog sitting on his haunches waiting for a slice of salami. He was totally unaware of Martha standing in her open doorway.

"Send him back when you finish the paw routine. I'll be by in thirty. I'm driving your car."

***

"Can you tell me what the hell you're wearing?" She greeted him as he climbed into the passenger seat of the Chevy.

"Why am I not surprised you have the keys to the car I'm currently using." Robert ignored her question about his sport coat.

"Look, Toby Too, if we're to get along, you better answer my questions. I don't ask many. Mr. Manchen can attest to that."

"It's all I have with me."

"Jeans, sweaters, jacket…" She began a list as she drove away from the house.

"Not with me. Where are we going?"

"You'll see soon enough."

Martha drove approximately ten miles before parking in a side lot. "I'm assuming you have money." She watched him open his wallet to display several one-hundred dollar bills. "Are you nuts?" She pulled out one of his hundred dollar bills and exchanged it for five twenties from her purse.

"Why are we parked outside a surplus store? Is the liquor store next door?"

"Take off your sport coat and get out of the car." She took the lead into the store. "Get a sweater, jacket and jeans. You might want a hoodie and a cap."

An expression of disgust crossed his face. He was not interested in purchasing clothes, particularly here. Some of it was used. When he made no move to look at any item, Martha tapped his arm. "It's here or Goodwill. The other option is to freeze your ass off and be recognized."

"How do you know I don't want to be recognized?"

"You just told me." She eyed him with disgust. "Mr. Manchen didn't tell me I'd be looking after some numbnuts. Hiding must be something new for you, but I don't want to know the particulars." She stopped at a counter stacked with jeans. "Pick."

Martha led Robert all around the store, having him select items necessary for his warmth and comfort. The hiding problem was not her domain. When they finished shopping, the bill came to over one hundred dollars.

Robert placed the five twenties on the counter and reached into his pocket for more bills, but he was short twenty more dollars.

"I handle the money in the family, but unfortunately, I only have a hundred dollar bill," Martha told the old gentleman at the register.

The man held the bill up to the light. "It's ok. You have an honest face." He took the bill and one of the twenties on the counter, leaving Martha to pocket the rest.

As they left, the man heard Martha say, "Maybe you should wear the jacket. Your mother would never let me hear the end of it, if you catch cold." The statement made him smile.

"You owe me twenty dollars." Martha told him after they left the store. She watched him pull out his wallet for another hundred which he exchanged for the four twenties.

"Where to now?"

"Give me five hundred dollars."

"I only have three left with me." He gave her his money.

"Then you'll owe me a hundred after I add mine," she said, parking in a bank lot. "You stay in the car."

Martha returned a few minutes later, drove away and then parked at a liquor store. She reached into a bag on the back seat and pulled out a cap. "Put it on. They have cameras in there." She approved the look. "I hope you know the kind of scotch you want. This is not the place to linger."

She followed him into the liquor store for his selection and paid for it with a small portion of the bank funds. Once in the car, she returned the rest of his money, all in small bills and the little change from his purchase.

"You can repay me the hundred when we get home. You'll need the small bills to get by." She turned in the direction of Turtle Creek.

"We can't go home…not just yet. I need glasses."

"I didn't know you had problems with your eyes," Martha said, surprised by the news.

"Not those glasses. Ones for scotch."

"What?" She drove into a fast food lot and parked. "What are you telling me?"

"Could we get a hamburger?"

"You are killing me with you drips and dribbles." Martha led him into the fast food restaurant and, after getting their order filled, sat in a booth to continue their conversation. "You need good scotch glasses. Is that what you're saying?"

"In a manner of speaking, yes."

"How about a store like Target?"

"I can make do with that." His response couldn't have been terser. "Is there one nearby?"

"There's something near the surplus store that would work."

"Second hand?" His question had a sarcastic ring.

"Who's going to tell? You?" she asked. "Don't soil your shorts. It's a gift shop." She caught his nod of agreement, wrapped the empty burger paper into a ball and tossed it in the trash can on her way out. Martha didn't have to look back. She knew Toby Too was following her.

"Ok. Knock yourself out," she said as Robert trailed her into the gift shop.

He looked at an array of glassware and immediately selected a set of six bar glasses. He paid the clerk and watched her pull-out sheets of wrapping paper.

"They are beautiful," the salesclerk volunteered, wrapping each separately before bagging them. "They make a nice gift." Robert nodded in agreement but said nothing.

Martha stood by and thought the whole thing ridiculous. Eight dollars for one glass was crazy. But it was his money. And although Mr. Manchen never offered any information about the man, something told Martha the glasses had special meaning, some significance of importance. Was Toby Too trying to impress someone…the special scotch…the glasses? Maybe he was telling the truth about not being a drunk. She just hoped the woman was worth it. It had to be someone special.

"Martha, thank you so much for helping me." Robert offered his gratitude upon leaving the shop.

Martha found his serious tone disconcerting and wanted to keep the conversation on a lighter scale. "Flattery won't cut it. You still owe me a hundred dollars."

"Are we going back now?"

"One more stop, unless you have something else to buy." She caught the shake of his head as they continued walking to a store adjacent the gift shop. The sign read, Doggie Treats and Greets.

"For Toby?"

Martha stared at Robert, wondering about his mentality. "No. I thought a cookie would be good with lunch." The sharp tone of her voice was filled with sarcasm.

"Then I'll buy two and we'll each have one." He shot back, opening the door for her. "Tell me which cookie is your favorite."

Martha began laughing as she walked toward a showcase filled with different kinds of dog treats. "I'd like one of those." She selected a flat cookie.

"And I'd like one of those." Robert pointed to a cookie twist. "Put them in the same bag. We're sharing." He paid the clerk who wondered about the couple who liked dog cookies.

"That was fun." Martha laughed again. "You are quick."

"Good thing they don't know you."

"They don't but Toby likes their cookies."

As they headed back to Turtle Creek, Robert thanked Martha once again for helping him. He was satisfied with his purchases for Elias and the clothing Martha urged him to buy. He felt nice and warm in his new jacket.

Chapter 33
Conversations

After coming back from the shopping trip, Robert raced upstairs to the bedroom, pulled his suitcase from under the bed and pulled a small wad of money from the false bottom. He ran next door to return the amount he owed Martha and greeted her just as she was leaving the house with Toby.

"I'm glad I caught you." He gave her the hundred dollar bill.

The woman had a strange look on her face as she palmed the money into her pocket. She wondered how many more hundred dollar bills the man had in his possession, but verbalized something entirely different. "You are one strange man, Toby Too, but you pay promptly. I like that. I've got to go."

"Where are you going?" he asked, then caught himself. "Thank you for this morning." He turned away.

Martha watched him return to the house before pulling her own car out of the garage. When he disappeared inside, she backed out of the driveway and turned in the opposite direction of her earlier excursion. As she drove away, Martha thought about her phone conversation with Mr. Manchen a few minutes earlier.

"It's going fine," she said. "But we had to go shopping this morning. It's cold like winter and he brought the wrong clothes. The surplus store," she answered when he asked where they shopped. "I didn't know how much money he had," Martha added, but was confused by the man's laughter. Then he gave her a number to call, explaining that an exchange would contact him in case of an emergency.

When the phone call ended Martha began to wonder about the turn of events with the house next door. In all her years as caretaker, she had met only one other visitor: a young man introduced as Paul. Although he no longer came, Martha did notice a resemblance to Toby Too and wondered if they were related. She pushed the thought aside, never questioning it again. It was none of her business. She liked her relationship with Mr. Manchen and did not want it to change. And although he was not around very often, the man had always been very thoughtful of her and the way she cared for his property. He often placed a fat envelope on her kitchen counter when he was in town. The man trusted her completely: with his keys, his car and his house.

She pulled into a plaza parking lot and entered a store whose overhead sign read: Simply Flowers. Martha unlocked the door and turned over the 'closed' sign to 'open.'

"Ok, Toby. Let's get started." She studied two delivery slips.

***

"Hello." Raine sweet voice answered his call from the kitchen of their home. "I was getting worried when you didn't phone." Of course, she had no idea Robert was watching her during their conversation via 'Sweet Pea.'

"After a long meeting yesterday, I was tired and fell asleep." Robert thought his explanation was plausible. "I miss you," he lied.

"I miss you too. When will you be home?"

"Tomorrow or the next day. I'll let you know. You busy?" He asked deliberately bating Raine for her next tryst with John.

"I'm making appointments right now for showings after work. My client wants her husband to look at a few houses she liked."

"Don't work too hard."

"I'll rest-up when you get home." She began laughing. "Love you."

"Me too." He lied again and ended the call, his synapses cracking as he walked to his bedroom to rest.

Wasn't it amazing how they continued to lie to each other? Neither one cared for the other right now. Of course, she never did. Now that Robert realized how serious they were in killing him, he was none too thrilled with her either. How could he have fallen in love with such a ruthless woman? He was so blindsided by the way she played him…slow and deliberate. And very expensive, he thought. She traveled all the way to Florence just to trap him. Who knew? Who would have thought? But John was clever. Robert had to admit. The man had planned everything down to the last detail. And although he credited John's skill, Robert found him a loathsome human being. Robert stretched out on the bed and continued his thoughts.

He hoped Elias would be lucky today at Raine's old apartment. Everything hinged on retrieving the poison. A second thought crossed his mind. Raine's showing houses after work meant one thing: she was meeting John at the apartment. That's what she meant by making appointments when there was really only one. They felt safe seeing each other, never suspecting that Robert was aware of their duplicity or in town to spy on them. He would be there, camera in hand, waiting for a few shots of them together. Since this was not an overnight, they would leave the apartment together.

Robert's thoughts shifted from John and Raine to Elias. Elias would be gone by then, hopefully. Of course, Elias would be gone, he chastised himself. The man was like a whirlwind…a whoosh one minute, the next, nothing. His thoughts faded as he drifted off to asleep.

***

It was almost four o'clock when Robert awakened and checked the time on his watch. He had just enough time to call his office before heading to Penn Center.

"Are you still covering my ass?" he questioned his mother.

"As always, I'll do what Dorothy wants." Catherine said calmly.

"I take it, John's around."

"Yes. I know, Steve, but you can call me later if she decides to come. Love you too." She ended the call.

His mother was a very clever lady. Her message was loud and clear. He was to call her later.

Robert eyed the bag from the surplus store sitting on a bedroom chair. He pulled a pair of jeans and sweater from it, tossed them on the bed and began removing the price tags. Robert slid into the jeans and pullover sweater then opened a closet door for a mirror to check the fit. There was no full-length mirror. The only mirror was the medicine cabinet door in the bathroom.

"Well, they feel good." Robert told himself, transferring all his trouser pocket items to his jeans.

He walked downstairs to the kitchen refrigerator for a sandwich before grabbing his camera, jacket and hat. He had a standing appointment. Actually, it was one of waiting, point and shoot. Would they come together? Robert didn't think so. He was more likely to get shots of the duo leaving the apartment at the same time.

***

"You told me to stop after work." Steve told his sister as she poured coffee into a cup near his usual seat at the table. "What's up?"

"Scuttlebutt has it that Henry Price's in trouble." She sat across from him.

Steve looked at his sister, somewhat puzzled by the news. "And this affects me, how?"

"Don't you get it? Nobody knows what's going on. Some suits were over there today. I don't know why or where they took him and Robbie's out of town. Don't you see what this could mean?"

"If he's arrested, then his business falls apart and Robbie could pick-up more customers."

"Exactly, but he's not available."

"You talked to him, right?" Steve caught her nod. "Then he knows."

"No. I couldn't tell him. John was around sniffing for information. But I did pretend I was talking with you about Dorothy. I told you to call me later, hoping Robbie would take the hint.

"Didn't we think his bidding contract might be a ploy to cover some medical tests?"

"That's true, but remember what I told you before...rumors about him being sick? Today, he asked if I was still covering his ass.

That's all the conversation we had because John was hovering over me."

"Robbie's smart. I'm sure he caught on. You'll get a call here at the house."

"I don't know. When he called, I thought he'd tell me something or maybe the truth." Her eyes started to glisten.

"Did he say anything to Mackenzie before he left?"

"I doubt it. She comes around even less since the fall semester started. It's like she moved to another planet."

"Listen." His voice held a sharp edge. "If Robbie told you to cover his ass, then there is a good chance he'll unload on you when he gets back. Until then, do nothing." He finished his coffee, kissed his sister's cheek and left the house.

Catherine watched her brother leave, saddened that their conversation did not make her feel any better. His insight never changed from their first conversation about Robbie's absence. "Cover his ass and leave well enough alone." If Robbie's absence was medical, Steve was right. Her son would go it alone until he had all the facts. Only then would he tell her the prognosis. That thought saddened her all the more.

She wondered about Mackenzie.

If something happened to her father, how would she cope? Granted, she was an educated woman with a wonderful future. She would inherit the company as part of the trust. But what about emotionally? Other than Catherine and Steve, who did Mackenzie have? Her maternal grandparents had passed away and there was no one else she could turn to. At least, no one Catherine knew about. Surely, if Mackenzie were serious about some young man, she would have brought him to her birthday dinner or the cocktail party after the wedding ceremony. Catherine didn't think her granddaughter had a special person in her life. Unfortunately, Mackenzie couldn't turn to Raine. That piece of work would be busy latching on to someone else. With her looks, she'd remarry within a year, if that long.

There was no love lost with the family either. Since the wedding, there were no family dinners, no togetherness, nothing. Mackenzie would be left out in the cold if she depended on Raine. The woman was in the family for everything she could get out of it. Catherine was convinced of that fact. Her phone calls were cold, her voice was icy and all communication was nil. The woman was a bitch in every sense of the word. How she duped her son was easy. She was the devil incarnate.

Catherine rinsed out the coffee cups thinking Robert would call her later if he deciphered her message. Steve was right. If she wanted to do anything for her son, her best bet was to support him by covering his ass.

***

Sometime after eight, Catherine received a phone call.

"Are you alright?" she asked immediately.

"You sound distressed. Are you ok?"

"I'm worried about you."

"I'm not sick, if that's what you're thinking. I'm working on something really big, that's why I need you to cover for me. I'll explain later."

"I think Henry Price is in trouble. Some men came to his company today. Someone said that they wore suits."

"Probably an income tax glitch," Robert sluffed it off. "His accountants will straighten it out."

"You think so?"

"Absolutely. Tell everyone we talked and I'm tied-up in meetings."

"Wait!" his mother shouted. "I know this isn't the time, but the office really needs painted."

"Get samples. We'll go over them when I get back." He ended the call.

For some reason, Catherine did not feel relieved after talking to him. She wondered what was so big that he couldn't share it with her. He wasn't concerned about her news on Henry Price either. Did he already know about it? No. She didn't think so. Every company had accounting glitches. That's why he was unconcerned. Maybe she was reading too much into Robbie's absence. If he came back with another big contract, Henry Price would be so pissed. John Harris wouldn't be too happy either.

***

Robert sat on the living room couch and felt satisfied with everything he had accomplished so far.

He now had pictures of Raine and John together at Penn Center and several of them in a kissing embrace. Robert thought seeing her arms around John would make him angry. Somehow, he no longer felt that way. His anger had melted to disgust and revenge. What he wanted now was to get even, not by brute force but through the justice system. He wanted them tried for attempted murder, providing he had enough evidence. Robert also wondered about the poison. Did it come from one of John's trips? Was it legal?

His satisfaction mounted when he thought about quelling his mother's fears. At least he had for now. Catherine would spread the word of his meetings and still cover him.

Suddenly, Robert realized he hadn't eaten a real meal in days. Having another sandwich was out of the question. He slipped into his jacket, grabbed his car keys and went next door.

***

"Don't tell me you finished the scotch." Martha greeted him in an old pair of jeans while Toby edged for a spot in the doorway.

"I was wondering if you could take me to dinner."

"What?" Martha was visibly shocked by the man's arrogance.

"No. No. I'll pay for it." He explained hurriedly. "I just can't face another sandwich. Please Martha. You know the area and I don't. Any restaurant would be fine."

She noticed the car keys dangling from his hand. "Wait." She closed the door in his face and returned minutes later wearing a jacket. "You must feel a lot warmer," she said, noticing the clothes from the surplus store. "I'm driving." Martha took the car keys. "You feel like steak?"

"That sounds so good," he sighed appreciatively, climbing into the car.

Before Martha started the ignition, she dialed a number from her cell phone. "I'm bringing a friend by for steak. Yeah, totally secluded," she answered. "Could you throw a candle on the table? He's used to the finer things in life. He owns a sport coat." They could hear the laughter on the other end of the conversation as Martha ended the call.

"We're all set." She told Robert, as she drove away from Turtle Creek toward a highway that looked familiar to him. Within ten minutes, Martha parked behind a steak house and walked into a kitchen filled with activity. She led him to an alcove at the end of the kitchen and sat down at a small table. On it were silverware wrapped in napkins and two menus. She began reading the menu. "Anything look good?"

"Steak, shrimp and chops," he said. "It all looks good." Inwardly, Robert was shocked at the menu prices. Everything offered was so reasonable.

"Anything you order here is good." Martha started talking about the food when a tall, heavy woman approached them with two glasses of water. "Angie," Martha greeted her. "I called Sal before we came."

"I know. He told me," she said, a twinkle in her eye. "He said you were bringing a date."

"No." Martha stammered. "It's just dinner." Her eyes went from Angie to Robert. "This is Toby Too." She introduced him.

"It's nice to meet you," Angie said, her mind filled with questions about him and their need to eat in the kitchen. "Have you decided on dinner?" She caught their nod.

When Angie left them to place their order, they could hear her ask Sal, "What nationality is Tooth? His name is Toby Tooth."

During dinner, the conversation focused on the quality of their steaks and Robert's clothes. And although the conversation flowed evenly, neither one asked anything personal of the other. It didn't matter. Within days or a week at most, Robert would be gone and life would be normal again for Martha.

"So, Toby Tooth," she snickered, "did you enjoy your dinner?"

Robert caught the reference and began laughing. "I can't remember when I've had a better ribeye. It was cooked to perfection." He did a thumbs-up.

"Then put ten dollars on the table."

"Where's the bill?"

"The meal's 'on the house' for us."

"Then I should give Angie twenty."

"Ten dollars shows appreciation; twenty's just pretense…a big spender who doesn't have jack."

Robert placed ten dollars on the table, thanked Angie and Sal for their hospitality, then followed Martha out of the kitchen.

It was not long before they were back in Turtle Creek and parked in Robert's driveway. Before Martha returned his car keys, she took a package sitting on the back seat.

"What's that?"

"Bones for Toby. You didn't think I was going to forget him, did you? Goodnight Toby Tooth," Martha said, as they both climbed out of the car at the same time. After acknowledging her departure, Robert watched Martha walk into her house and heard Toby barking for the treats she carried.

As he headed toward the front gate of Claude's house, Robert thought about the package for Toby. Martha had left the car unlocked purposely, hoping Sal would have bones for her dog. Did this happen on a regular basis? No charge for meals, and treats for Toby? There was no point in asking questions. Martha would say she was helping Mr. Manchen by taking care of his friend that evening for dinner. Anything else was none of his business. Yet, a feeling of satisfaction grew somewhere within him. He was glad he had met Martha. The woman was remarkable in her own way. She was not some polished beauty who demurred at things said in most conversations. No. Martha said what she meant and meant what she said. It was a refreshing change. Robert always knew where he stood with Martha. And although his apology went badly after their first meeting, he was glad he made the effort. In his entire life, no woman ever told him to go screw himself... until Martha. The woman was a piece of work. Robert pitied the poor bastard who crossed her: he'd be wearing his balls on his nose.

Chapter 34
Updates

Around nine the next morning, Robert phoned Raine telling her he had a full day of scheduled meetings and a follow-up dinner that evening, inferring a further absence from home. Of course, he had already set-up 'Sweet Pea' and was watching her antics the entire time.

"So you won't be home." She expressed concern. "I miss you so much." He watched a smile widen across her mouth.

"I know," he lied, "but these meetings are important."

"Is it going well? You couldn't talk about it before." Robert knew she was fishing for information to give John.

"Better than I expected. It's been a real eye-opener." The statement brought a smile to his face.

"When will you be home?"

"Maybe tomorrow or Thursday. It all depends on what we accomplish today." Robert used the "we" thinking of the poison sample Elias was to have taken from her apartment. "I'll call tomorrow if I need another day."

"I love you," Raine said softly, pretending emotion while stirring her coffee.

"I love you too," Robert lied again, as he watched her reach across the counter for the morning paper before ending the call. Nothing could describe his emotions at that point. The woman was such a cold-hearted bitch.

He watched her phone John immediately.

"We have another night," she greeted him, her voice filled with excitement. "Just now." She referred to Robert's call. "He may be home tomorrow or Thursday." Suddenly, her gleeful tone turned sour. "What do you mean it has to be early?" Then, it became obvious from her sudden change in tone again that his response had a calming effect. "Oh, you had me worried. After work, then." Robert watched her end the call.

Something was not right in Raine's garden paradise. Were they not on the same page anymore? She seemed worried about their relationship. Was it getting shaky or becoming stale to John? Was he worried Raine was losing her courage to go through with Robert's murder or had he found greener pastures elsewhere and was losing interest in her? It didn't matter at this point. They were in it together and he wanted them arrested for attempted murder. And since they planned on meeting at the apartment again, Robert would be there to witness it. At this rate, he could fill a picture album.

***

Shortly before noon, Elias greeted Robert with a pizza. "I hope you did the same for me." He placed it on the kitchen counter.

"The scotch and glasses are in the cupboard." He pointed to a particular wall cabinet, causing his friend to check its contents.

"Excellent choice," he said pleased with Robert's purchase. "How did you manage it?" From the expression on Robert's face, it was obvious that he did not understand the full meaning behind his question. Elias eyed his friend and rephrased the question. "How did you find a liquor store so quickly when you don't know the area?" Although Elias' questions were about scotch, his eyes focused on the outfit Robert wore. He had not seen him in jeans since their college days.

"Martha. She lives next door and takes care of the house for Mr. Manchen, which of course is an alias for Claude. She took me to a liquor store out in the boonies yesterday."

"And did she buy you those?" His hand went to the clothing Robert wore. "I've never seen you dress so casual. You look good."

"She took me to a surplus store."

The unexpected remark made Elias shake with laughter, the whole incongruity of it. That this very wealthy man, one who lived in a million dollar house and was accustomed to the finer things in life, was now wearing clothes from a surplus store just seemed insane.

Someone running into Robert would think he was in financial ruin. Not that Robert looked bad in jeans. No, that wasn't it at all. It was the look he always portrayed. Robert usually wore slack pants and a sport jacket. And although this was his normal wear about the office, Robert's clothes were always finely tailored and expensive. At home, his friend always dressed in casual slacks, never jeans. So, this was a first.

"She must think you're some poor bastard who can't afford a wardrobe." Elias continued to laugh.

"Maybe, but I don't believe it. She thinks I'm in hiding and took me places where I wouldn't be recognized. Although she didn't ask a lot of questions, my answers were few and far between."

"What made her think you're in hiding?" He grew serious, thinking an identity problem could arise.

"I told her I didn't want to shop in the area for scotch. She drew the inference but never questioned me." He paused momentarily. "That's not true. She questioned my not having a jacket since it's getting so cold. I guess Martha thought the jeans would complete the look of an area resident. She wears them," Robert said absent-mindedly, thinking of their shopping trip. "I'm not worried. Claude trusts her completely. Anyhow the clothes are really comfortable. I should have bought another pair."

"You'd never make it as a spook." Elias marveled at his trusting friend.

"Speaking of that, I heard Henry Price was taken in for questioning."

"You talked with your mother."

"The plan was to call the office, just to check-in, remember? Did you arrest him?"

"We're not interested in Henry. One of his men was connected to a group under surveillance. "

"Then they must have been hacking or selling security codes… involving what? Banks? Stores? No. It's more serious than that," Robert said, his eyes fixed on Elias. "It involves a government agency, doesn't it? A security threat, maybe." Then his thoughts turned in a different direction. "You planted men at his company, ones that interviewed us. You knew John would send them to Henry. How did you know?" A bell went-off in Robert's head. "You were following him to Global, weren't you?" He continued to push.

"I could say something provocative like, 'If I told you what happened, I'd have to kill you.' But we know that's bullshit. It's been resolved. That's all you need to know. As usual, you ask too many questions."

"I haven't asked about the poison yet. Did you find it?"

"And the Certificate of Deposit. I have pictures of both. After leaving the apartment, I took a sample of the poison to the lab. We should have the results later today or tomorrow, but don't plan on going home until we have more information. We know Raine doctored your wine. We have that evidence. But we need more incriminating proof to bring a case against her for attempted murder." Elias rested his arms on the counter.

"I called Raine this morning," Robert said. "Just to check in. When I told her I wouldn't be home, she called John. They're meeting after work. For some reason, he insisted they meet early."

"You dog! There is some hope for you after all." Elias shouted with surprise. "You actually watched her on 'Sweet Pea' and listened to her conversation! How did she sound when he wanted an early meeting?"

"Pissed at first, but then she seemed to calm down after something he said. I may drive by the apartment to get more pictures." Robert had nothing more to add and wanted to change the subject to something more pleasant. "Want something to drink?"

"It's too early. But I'll drop by around eight or so for a raincheck. That should give you enough time for another run. I know a crappy joint in the area that serves good food and great drinks. Wear what you have on." With that terse statement Elias sailed out of the house.

Robert didn't bother racing to the window. Instead, he opened the pizza box, took out a slice and thought about his friend. Meeting Elias at eight was perfect. Robert needed the company of someone he trusted after seeing his wife in the arms of another man.

***

Hours later, Robert sat on the couch waiting for Elias. Since his friend had a key to the house, Robert expected to find him sitting on the couch with a glass of scotch in hand when he arrived home. However, their eight o'clock meeting had long passed, but Robert was not worried. He had heard nothing to indicate a cancellation. There was no point in wondering if Elias would appear that evening. Chances were, he would show-up, give no excuse for being late, and just go on with their plans. Ten minutes later, Robert's thinking was right on target.

"Good. You're ready," Elias greeted him with the nonchalance of the nobility.

Robert eyed him silently, shrugged into his jacket and followed his friend out of the house. "Do we know where we're going?"

"I told you this afternoon. We're going for ribs and a ride. I'm driving your car."

Robert did not feel that statement was quite accurate; but knowing Elias as he did, it was better to remain silent.

***

When Elias described the restaurant where they planned having dinner as a crappy joint, he overstated the ambiance of the small facility. Nothing in the entire place matched. The tables were odd sizes; the silverware, assorted pieces; and the lighting, dim, yet bright enough to see the several men behind a tall counter cooking their food. A chalkboard posted on a wall of chipped paint gave the patrons the full daily menu. It also included a sentence telling them to keep their silverware throughout the entire meal. If some party got a shaky table, which was often, the waitress would steady it with a matchbook.

They were seated at a wooden table upon entering the restaurant, told once again to keep their silverware and their rib orders taken. The waitress returned with two glasses of water and a basket that included rolls, two small paper plates and a small mound of butter in a minute cup, the kind dentists use for mouth-rinsing purposes. The rib baskets which were also laden with baked beans and coleslaw followed almost immediately. Robert couldn't remember ever being served so quickly. Yet, he and Elias attacked the ribs greedily and savored every last bite, right to the sauce on their fingers.

"Good, isn't it?" Elias grunted.

"The best," Robert agreed, his mouth full of coleslaw. "And no pressure for the table."

"Nah. People will always wait to get in."

When the waitress came by with the bill, Robert stopped her to pay the check with cash. She took the money immediately, thanked him for the tip and watched them leave the restaurant. The woman hoped they'd return soon. It wasn't often she got a hefty tip like that. However, she did find it rather bizarre. The two men didn't seem wealthy. The pathetic one who tipped her looked less fortunate than the other. Maybe he made a mathematical error. Well, too bad for him!

"Did you enjoy the meal?" Elias asked as they climbed into the car. His question seemed strange since he was never concerned with Robert's taste in food before.

"The ribs were delicious. I already told you that. Why are you asking me again?"

"Don't read anything into it? I just won't, that's all." His thoughts turned inward.

"You aren't thinking of taking some sweet young thing there, are you?"

"You know me too well. The food's good and so are the prices. Thanks for treating me, by the way. I thought you would anyhow, seeing how much money you saved on clothes." Elias laughter became contagious.

Robert began laughing and thought of a reply to Elias' first question. "First date, absolutely not, she'd think you were broke. But if you've already dated her, I'd go for it. She would enjoy the food. Recommend it as an adventure in good eating."

"You are so full of shit," Elias said as he drove down a main highway. "An adventure in good eating would be grilling a steak in Yellowstone Park."

"Say what you want, but your rib joint is an adventure in itself. I'm surprised they don't ask you to bring your own silverware. But I'd go back there for the food alone." Robert looked at the passing surroundings. "Where the hell are you taking me?"

Elias remained silent then pulled into an isolated parking lot. "You stay in the car."

Robert watched Elias enter a small one-story brick building. Within five minutes Elias joined him again, holding an envelope.

"I think we should go back to the house," he said, an urgency in his voice. "I thought we could swing by the lab testing the poison but found this envelope waiting for me. I need to check it out."

"Hey, Elias," Robert interrupted. "I understand. You've got priorities. It's your job."

"I know. But I wanted to handle this differently," he sighed, picking up speed.

"The test results were inconclusive. Is that what you mean?" Robert asked, thinking Elias wanted to soften the results with discussion and drinks at the house.

"Oh. No. You're still dead…the mice are. The stuff is a different type of poison. A large amount will kill you. The test results show that." He pulled into Robert's driveway. "We don't know the entire composition. It acts like some form of alkaloid I think, the deep sleep and the feeling sweaty, weak and dizzy. Its breakdown is very lethal. That we do know." After Elias climbed out of the car, Robert followed him into the house, snapping on lights as he trailed him into the kitchen.

Elias unsealed the envelope and read a hastily scrawled note that covered its contents. "This is a message for me," he said, walking away from Robert.

"And you don't know who sent it?"

"No name. But I have a very good idea who did." Elias took the envelope to the living room couch and, after removing the scrawled note, found four photographs inside. He covered his face with his hands after studying the last one. This was something he never anticipated. How could Claude have known?

Now he understood why the man left the envelope for him at the lab. Since Elias was Robert's closest friend, his job was to keep him from doing something stupid after seeing the pictures. The initial shock would be followed by a rage to kill. That act had to be prevented.

Elias knew there were other photographs, more graphic ones of the couple in the fourth picture, but they were not included. Elias knew Claude's work. The man was very thorough. If he found something untoward during an investigation, perhaps even unrelated to it, the man's analytical nature would take hold until he found a relationship. Through surveilling 'Sweet Pea' in Robert's house after installation, Claude must have connected the dots with Raine and John to begin his own investigation. This, of course, led to another surprising relationship. Fortunately for Robert, the man was trying to protect him. However, Robert would not have been happy knowing how fully his house was being monitored.

"When do I get a chance to look at them?" Robert asked, still standing at the counter. "I know they're photographs because you aren't reading anything. They're pictures of Raine and John in bed, aren't they?"

"I want you to promise me something. Before you go bonkers after seeing these, we need to talk," he said, his solemn expression commanding attention. It was important that Elias make his friend understand the seriousness of the situation. "I mean it. This is the evidence you need against Raine and John. I don't want you to unravel the case for attempted murder after seeing the last picture."

"I understand." Robert sat down beside him to study all four pictures. His emotional unconcern for the first three photographs was predictable. He had already witnessed their assignations. However, it was the fourth photograph, the one of a man and woman seated together at a restaurant that turned his facial expression to stone. Robert sat calmly studying the picture…in silence.

Elias had never seen Robert like this before. His friend wasn't being stoic and he didn't seem enraged. Why was Robert so calm after seeing John and Mackenzie together? Did he not believe it?

"Are you alright?" Elias asked. "I know this is a shock seeing them together but we really don't know what the picture means," he lied. "It could be an accidental meeting."

"I don't think so. The plan is either clearer or cloudier. Which is which? I have to find out."

"You're not making sense," Elias insisted.

"Yes. I am. For the first time, it all makes sense. Someone is being used and it's not me. I'm the victim, remember?" Robert shrugged into his jacket as he spoke.

"And where the hell do you think you're going?"

"To play spy. I think I know why John wanted an early meeting with Raine. Now I need to know if I'm right." Robert had to follow a hunch. If Mackenzie was involved with John, his naïve daughter could be in great danger.

"You're going to visit Mackenzie, aren't you? That's not a good idea."

"Spying and visiting are two different things. Of course, I have to know if the bastard's there using her. Nothing will happen until my demise. If I can prevent that, the ballgame's over."

"You going there will only prove John's using both women," Elias said.

"Exactly. Does one know about the other, or is this tryst with Mackenzie part of another plan? If the latter, where does that leave one of them? One woman gets burned."

"How will you know?" Robert's analysis did not surprise Elias.

"I'll know with 'Sweet Pea's' help." Robert grabbed his camera case. "Wanna come?"

Chapter 35
Discovery

"What are we looking for?" Elias questioned his friend who was weaving in and out of parking lots near Mackenzie's apartment.

"Parking's a premium here. Look for a white Mercedes with a Steelers' decal on the back window." He drove slowly around the last lot and stopped suddenly. "Is that a decal or my imagination?"

"It is. Take pictures. We'll verify the plate later."

"I have a tablet and pen in my case," Robert muttered as he scrambled from the car snapping pictures. Then he quickly exited the parking lot while listening to Elias on the phone with one of his confederates. "It is, isn't it?" he asked when his former roommate ended the call.

"The car is registered to one John Harris. Anybody, you know?" Elias snorted on his ability to get the information so easily. Then changing the tone of his voice, he said, "The dirty bastard."

"I don't like it either; but now that I see a plan unfolding, his creating a relationship makes more sense. In fact, it's clever."

"And you don't think Mackenzie's in any danger?" Elias questioned again.

"Physically, no. Not until I'm dead. He's playing with her emotions right now and that scares me." As he spoke, Robert soon realized Elias was not following his logic and went on to explain. "He's riding the hips of two women. One of them is going to get hurt. If they do plan to murder Mackenzie, it will happen after I'm dead so Raine can lay claim to the estate. Right now she gets nothing to satisfy her greedy little hands…just a small token of money. But now, there may be a caveat. And the question I raise begs an answer."

A strange look crossed Elias' face. "I'm not following you."

"Suppose the initial plan, the one to kill me and then Mackenzie, changed direction. Suppose John found a scheme much more to his benefit. Marry a naïve Mackenzie, after killing her father, and get the house, the business and all of the dead man's money. No waiting, no claim, the estate is his. Raine is left out in the cold. What happens to her? Does John kill her too? We know he supplied the poison. Raine can't confess to murdering me and she can't blackmail John since they are in it together. She has two alternatives: live with it or die."

As Robert detailed the plan involving John with the two women, Elias marveled at the calm, clear narrative offered by his friend. He had expected outrage and revenge, a loud reviling of the situation. Instead, his former roommate remained composed outwardly, as if discussing the current events of the day, and the clarity of his thoughts captivated Elias completely.

"You just described two possible scenarios. How would you know which one to follow?"

"That's what I meant back at the house when I compared the fourth picture to the other three. At the time, I said, 'Which is which?' I don't have the answer right now, but I will make it my business to find out."

***

When they returned to the house, Robert joined Elias for a drink and revealed a few thoughts clouding his mind.

"I want to better understand my situation," he started. "The lab results indicated the presence of an alkaloid that's been given to me in very minor doses. However, the lab could not determine its nomenclature or where it's grown. In a larger dose, however, it's lethal. Am I on the right page so far?"

"I think you pretty much nailed it."

Robert set his glass on the coffee table and began walking around the room to hypothesize. "So in his travels, John Harris was able to find this drug, whatever it is, bring it home in powder form and administer it to me through wine supplied by Raine." Robert became quiet as he took another turn around the room. "He must still have an ample supply in his possession."

"What makes you think so?"

"It's the only thing that makes sense. How much did you find in the apartment?"

"Enough to kill a horse. I'd say there's about a tablespoon left in the small vial. Why?"

"Then Raine has just enough for me. John has the rest."

"Maybe, but remember, she doctored your wine three times so he could have given her everything he had."

"No." Robert disagreed. "He's too slippery. John would have kept a supply for himself in case he needed it."

"And you think he's going to use it on Mackenzie or Raine, don't you?"

"It's logical. Two women, one man. One woman too many. One has to go," he sighed. "Something else doesn't fit. When you stopped by the lab, did you know about the envelope?"

"It was as much a shock to me as it was to you," he explained. "I went there expecting test results, but I am gratified by the evidence."

"Claude dropped it off, didn't he?"

"That would be my guess," Elias agreed.

"There are so many things I don't understand. Why was I offered the contract in the first place? I know it had to be handled privately, away from the piercing eyes of his cyber network. He couldn't have his own people spy on themselves. So who developed 'Sweet Pea?' Why was all this needed and why me? Then again, why offer me this house? Why the search for evidence against John and Raine? And most important of all, why is he helping me? I respect the man. He is brilliant. But Claude doesn't know or owe me."

"I don't have an answer. What little I know of him is a history of seclusion. His work takes him everywhere, although few people see him. Claude keeps to himself. That's what I'm told. I hear he has very few friends. I don't know why he selected you." He emphasized the statement. "Maybe, he just took a liking to you and regrets this thing with Mackenzie. Leave it at that until tomorrow." Elias finished his drink and walked out of the house, glass in hand.

***

Within the hour, Robert lay in bed thinking of Claude and the first message left on the counter.

'Pursue with caution, it's deeper than you think.'

Without going into further detail with Elias, Robert knew the full meaning of the message and did not like it one bit. More important, what could he do about it? There was only one way, which of course, was not possible. Eliminating John was beyond the scope of reality. But the more Robert thought about the message, the more perceptive he became about Claude's intervention.

Robert climbed out of bed and snapped on the nightstand lamp. "Damn it, Claude. I never gave it a thought. I should have, but didn't!" he shouted, shrugging into his jeans and sweater.

He raced to the garage for a flashlight in the glove compartment of his car, never thinking of slipping into a pair of shoes, until his bare feet hit the cold concrete driveway. "Shit," he said out loud, hearing Toby's sudden growls next door. Robert ignored the dog and ran back to the house. It wasn't long before he realized his thinking was right on target.

Claude had installed 'Sweet Pea' at the house in Turtle Creek and used an auxiliary feed to connect Robert's private residence. That included Claude's kitchen installation of 'Sweet Pea,' the wedding gift he so graciously planted when Robert was on his honeymoon. Connecting all these together from some unknown command center now made sense. It would explain the man's knowledge of everything that happened. Claude had been watching the newly married couple the entire time. He knew Raine was drugging him and was well aware of her trysts with John. Claude also knew of John and Mackenzie's assignations. The man followed every lead, installed photography equipment into the respective apartments and the rest was history.

So why hadn't Claude included other pictures, more compromising ones with Mackenzie? Did he think Robert would be damaged emotionally seeing her in bed with John? Robert dismissed that thought immediately. No. Claude knew they were unnecessary. The single frame was his way of drawing attention to the man's daughter.

Robert had not been aware of the relationship until the picture surfaced and yet, he knew there were others that followed. It was part of a code. The one picture held a message with a deeper meaning.

Claude dated the compromising pictures of Raine over three different time periods. The one of Mackenzie predated Robert's September marriage by several months, leaving him to draw his own conclusions about his daughter's erratic behavior. Then Claude compounded these thoughts with a terse admonition.

Pursue with caution, it's deeper than you think.

Robert thought about his daughter with John Harris, and the man's parked car in Mackenzie's lot, merely confirming their relationship. It also confirmed John's reason for wanting an earlier tryst with Raine. He had to service both women the same night.

Now as Claude watched Robert's activities with Elias, Martha and Toby, a look of practiced calm inched across his face. Claude chose to help him for some reason and perhaps the compatibility of a solitary nature had brought the two of them together. He thought about their private Sunday meeting. They worked together and were often alone in separate areas, yet the deafening silence of the empty building never bothered either of them. Although conversation was not necessary, great intellectual respect was paid by each on both sides.

Robert was glad Claude installed 'Sweet Pea' in just the kitchen and living room. It was nice to know he had some modicum of privacy. With that thought in mind, Robert opened his camera case to pull-out a tablet and pen. In very large letters he wrote a note and left it on the counter. It read, "GOTCHA."

Since it was now after two, he knew Claude would see it in the morning. The man would not respond, of course, but he certainly would wonder why it took Robert so long to determine 'Sweet Pea's' presence. What could Robert say? He had not expected his "hideaway" to be bugged. But Robert should have known better. He would have not expected less from Claude. The man was protecting his own territory. Robert couldn't fault him for that. The fact he offered the house in the first place was very generous of him.

Robert felt tired but knew sleep wouldn't come as he climbed into bed. There was something he overlooked, something important. Claude's note kept crossing his thoughts and Robert began to review the situation as he saw it. Yes, he would pursue with caution, but how could the situation be deeper than it already was? He knew about his intended murder and was now aware of his daughter's relationship with John and its possible consequences. So what could be deeper than his death?

Robert dwelled on the question for some time before having an epiphany. Now he knew the answer to Claude's conundrum...a single picture showing a seated Makenzie with John Harris. From that one frame, Robert now understood what Claude was trying to convey. He didn't need more pictures to understand the gradual deepening of the relationship. Yet, he found cause to wonder how Mackenzie, naïve as she was, could love someone with such a twisted agenda to destroy her father. Robert thought about the consequences of his death.

Death had certain finality, particularly with the loss of a loved one. A deeper loss, one even much more severe, would be losing a "loved one" among the living. Had Robert lost Mackenzie? Was that John's intent from the beginning...turning his daughter against him? A sordid revenge?

The realization had finally set in. He now knew the meaning of Claude's admonition.

Mackenzie was now gone forever. Robert had lost his daughter. John had taken her physically, emotionally, and most destructive of all, mentally. His daughter had been brainwashed against him and there was no turning back. His practiced calm totally disappeared as tears flooded his pillow. He only wished Emily were there with him. He needed her arms to comfort him in his time of loss.

***

Elias shook Robert awake Wednesday morning, never expecting to find his friend in bed at eleven o'clock.

"Hey." Elias sat at his bedside. "What's the matter? Why am I even asking?" He smacked his forehead. "You couldn't sleep thinking about Mackenzie with John." He looked down at his friend still lingering in a prone position. "Think of it this way, now that you know about the relationship, you can do something about it. Both women would be pissed if they discovered their cowboy was riding both mares." With that statement, Elias grabbed the bedcovers and ripped them off Robert's body. "Now get your stinky ass in the shower. We're going out to eat and I don't have a lot of time."

Robert heard Elias tromping downstairs to the living room, knowing he had to move fast with his morning routine. His closest friend had been overly generous with the time and effort expended on his behalf. Robert trusted no one else to determine his poisonous fate. There was a deep bonding love for the man: they were brothers, regardless of bloodline.

"You must really like the surplus store," Elias greeted him, laughing at his friend dressed in sweater and jeans.

"You're driving." Robert tossed him the car keys from his jacket pocket.

"Of course, I am." He caught the keys then led Robert to the car. "We're headed to a pizza joint in the boonies."

"Should we have brought our own silverware?"

"Shut up. I know you enjoyed the food."

"She will too."

"Who?"

"The sweet young thing who's twisting your shorts. That's why you asked my opinion. You want to take her somewhere "off the rails," a place the two of you can joke about," Robert sighed. "She must be important."

"After we eat, I'm using Raine's powder to poison you myself."

"What's the fun in that?"

Elias pulled into the parking lot of a dilapidated looking restaurant that should have been boarded up and condemned by the Department of Health. A small red sign on an inside wall read, 'Pizza Joint.'"

"I told you," Elias said pointing to it. "You will love this place."

When Elias opened an inner door of the dimly lit restaurant, the aroma of fresh pizza filled Robert's nostrils. However, the freshness soon evaporated and merged with an odor of spilled beer and stale cigarettes.

"People smoke in here?"

"Pick a table and sit down."

Robert moved toward a corner table. "The chair's broken."

"Picky, picky, picky!" Elias grabbed a nearby chair. "What do we want? The chalkboard's on the wall."

"Why do I feel like I've done this before?" Robert's eyes rested on the chalkboard after scanning the portion of the room behind Elias' chair. Posters, dollar bills and artwork plastered the wall, lending credence to a bar filled with locals bent on having a good time.

"I don't know. Maybe I wanted you to feel comfortable," he answered. "We need to talk before you go home today."

"I am?"

Elias nodded. "You can't stay away forever, but I needed to resolve a problem first."

"I don't know what you mean."

"How did Raine transfer the poison from the vial? It's still there. I checked this morning."

"You were there?" Robert caught his nod.

"Now I know how she did it. Since Raine couldn't hide the whole stash at the house, she transferred a tiny amount into a pillbox. I mean, who would look inside a pillbox?"

Robert listened to Elias' narrative before adding to it. "She has two. They're made of a metallic gold and both are square with black enamel tops. One has a picture of a rose on the lid; the other, lilies of the valley. I saw them the first time I broke in."

"I saw the rose pillbox near the vial. Don't worry, I wore gloves," he said as an aside. "Have you seen the other one? I mean lately."

"I can't remember. Once, maybe, in her lingerie drawer, the day I searched the house for poison. I never thought to look inside."

"Well, you will now. I'll continue to check the apartment. When the vial is empty, that means their plan is in full swing."

"Why can't I have them arrested now?"

"On what charge? You'll have to catch Raine in the act of trying to murder you. What about your daughter? Have you given any thought of telling Mackenzie that her lover is also sleeping with your wife?"

"I can't do anything right now."

"On the contrary, keep your eyes and ears open, and most important, don't eat or drink anything Raine fixes for you. Thank God, you have 'Sweet Pea.' Let's order."

Chapter 36
Return

After Elias took him back to Turtle Creek, Robert sat on the living room couch thinking of a strategy for his homecoming. He needed to report the possibility of getting another contract or something of value for the company. What he needed was a valid excuse for his absence from both the business and Raine.

Of course, he had to delay Raine's plan of "offing him" with a lethal dose of poison. Now would be the perfect time, since Robert had been down with the Maui bug three times already. Who would have thought it would be fatal?

As these thoughts churned in his head, Robert walked to the kitchen for bottled water when he noticed a sheet of paper on the counter. On it were three words: *Offer an incentive.*

"Damn it, Claude. A little more clarity would help," he shouted at the crown molding high above the cabinet, knowing the man had slipped into the house while he was out eating pizza with Elias.

"Why am I shouting?" he asked himself. "Claude can't hear me unless he's tuned in right now. I doubt that he is." Robert took a sip of water as he thought about going home. Before leaving, he had to thank Martha. She had been a good neighbor. He should also alert his mother at the office. Robert needed a private conversation with her concerning things he had missed while away. Robert would understand his mother's code if someone were standing by, namely, John Harris.

Robert heard his mother's business greeting when she answered the phone. "I'm taking a poll," he said, knowing she recognized his voice. "Do most people shop after work or do they go straight home?"

"This is a business," she groused. "Get your call list straight!" She slammed-down the phone complaining of solicitors, knowing full well John was listening to the conversation from the open door of his office.

Robert caught his mother's message immediately. They would be meeting at her house 'straight' after work. He knew she would expect a full report covering his absence, but that would not be forthcoming, not for a long while, if ever.

Robert slipped into his jacket before venturing next door. He stood before the entrance and, after ringing the doorbell several times, wondered why Toby was not barking. Obviously, neither Martha nor Toby was home. Robert retraced his steps back to his house, took a tablet and pen from his camera case and wrote a thank you note.

Robert returned to Martha's house, folded the note and stuck it in the fitting between the door and its frame. Martha would see the paper sticking out when she came home. He only hoped Toby wouldn't eat it first. The thought made him smile as he retraced his steps back to the house again.

Robert took the stairs to the bedroom, changed back into his regular attire and packaged the surplus store purchases into its original bag lying on the chair. Other than sundries and dirty underwear he had very little to pack. After making the bed, Robert checked the bathroom. Everything looked uncluttered, except for the solitary used towel on the bathroom rack. He retraced his steps back to the bedroom and, after slipping into his sport coat, took the suitcase and bag downstairs to the living room. Robert would have Elias empty the refrigerator of food, for he could offer no believable reason for carrying half-used groceries home.

When Robert left the house momentarily to switch cars, he felt the wind-chill of not having a jacket. How could he have been so stupid not to pack one? He looked at his watch. That it was after four o'clock did not surprise him, the month, however, was another matter. It was now the start of November and very cold. In fact, it felt cold enough for snow.

Within minutes, Robert was stowing his luggage and camera case in the trunk of his car. After placing his flashlight in the glove compartment, he set the clothing bag on the floor of the passenger's seat, hiding it totally from view. Robert did not want to leave the clothes behind. If nothing else, they reminded him of very caring and helpful friends.

He had one last thing to do before he left. Robert took Claude's note, tore off the written portion and watched it burn in one of the cupboard dishes. He rinsed out the dish and wrote a note with a pen from the inside pocket of his sport coat. It read:

Deeply Grateful

Robert placed the note and the ring of keys on the kitchen counter directly fronting 'Sweet Pea.' After adjusting the lock, he left the house and never looked back. Claude would have wanted it that way. He wanted Robert to move forward and do something about a very bad situation.

***

It was dark when Robert pulled into the driveway behind his mother's car. With daylight savings time, it got dark early, making him very grateful for that. He took the clothing bag from the car and tapped softly on her door.

"I'm so glad you're back." Catherine embraced her son lovingly, before sending him to the kitchen where the table was set for dinner. "I made penne."

Robert set the bag on a nearby chair and sat at the table. "Smells good."

"What's that?" She pointed to the bag.

"Work clothes. I want you to keep them for me in case I need them later," he lied.

"And you don't want to take them home or to the office." Catherine's eyes narrowed as she studied him. Something happened that no one was privy to and she wondered what it could be. Why would he need special clothes? "A secret meeting?" She caught his nod.

"Several." He watched her serve him a plate of penne from a bowl that centered the table.

"I'll put them in your old room," she pushed, "but I want the truth. Were you seeing a doctor? Was that why you went away, telling everyone about a non-existent contract?" she asked, serving herself, "Come on. Eat while it's hot."

"I think we should talk seriously," he said. "I was not seeing a doctor. That is the truth. I was also truthful about the meetings. I just can't go into detail. We will get a contract you think non-existent, but there may be many more meetings before that happens."

"Is Henry Price in the running? One of his men was fired and two others quit. I think John recommended the ones who left the company."

Robert smiled inwardly thinking of his conversation with Elias. His mother would absolutely shit figuratively, if she knew the men were agents. "No. He isn't. But a lot has happened in my absence. Didn't you tell me Henry was arrested?"

"That was a mistake. The suits only asked him questions about his employees. I think the man Henry fired did something illegal. It's been resolved according to John."

"He seems to be in the know about everything. How did he handle the business while I was gone?"

"We didn't have any problems. But I do think the offices are beginning to have a jaded look."

"Did you get paint samples?" he asked, then referring to the penne, said, "This is so good."

"We can go over them tomorrow if you want."

"I plan on coming in, although Raine may not like it. I haven't been home yet."

The remark caught Catherine off-guard. "You haven't seen your wife?" She was shocked by the announcement.

"I wanted to surprise her."

"It wasn't just the clothes," she insisted. "Why come here first?"

"There is something I want you to do for me when the time comes. None of it will make sense and you may want to raise questions. But please, mom, I need your support in this. I really do."

"Are you selling the company?"

"The company has nothing to do with this. I haven't done anything monetarily for Raine and I need to do more for Mackenzie. So when I come up with a plan, I'll need your help, particularly with Mackenzie."

Catherine had seen that sober look once before and it worried her. "Just let me know."

Robert took his dish to the sink, kissed his mother and left the house.

***

Catherine listened to the slight squeal of Robbie's brakes as he backed out of the driveway. She wondered about that. His brakes were checked shortly before he married that miserable bitch. Why were they squealing now? Then her thoughts centered on Raine. The woman never phoned during Robbie's absence. Not once. Catherine guessed Robbie's concern wasn't just about money. It was all about Raine's haughty ass. Was there a problem in their marriage? Already? Her thoughts continued as she cleared the table.

The more Catherine thought of the visit, the more confused she became. Leaving clothes based on future need was ridiculous. She wasn't buying the story he was selling. Maybe he did meet with customers and even install equipment. That would account for the work clothes. But why the secrecy about them? Raine wouldn't care. No. That wasn't right. Robbie left the clothes with her because he didn't want Raine or anyone else to know about them. There had to be some sort of connection; otherwise, Robbie would have taken them home. Maybe the connection was John, and Robbie was covering all bases. He knew there would be no conversational slips if the clothes were left with her, and that particular reasoning met all plausibility.

Aside from the clothes, there was this sudden need to provide for Raine. If he were ill, she could understand his reasoning. But she believed he was telling her the truth about his health. Then too, he mentioned Mackenzie. Why would he even mention the daughter who never bothered to call her own father or grandmother anymore?

What more could he provide the girl who already inherits the bulk of his estate? None of it made sense, but he had already given her that information.

Then what was his real purpose for the visit? All she got from it was a bag of clothes and a request for support; the rest of the conversation was a peripheral jumble of nothing that made sense. Nevertheless, Catherine was worried. Something bad was happening to him and she laid it at the feet of her daughter-in-law, the greedy witch he married.

Catherine wished she could discuss her concerns with Stefano. He would give an honest opinion. But more important, she needed his steady hand to halt her roller-coaster emotions. Talking with him, of course, was not possible, and these thoughts continued as Catherine washed the dishes.

***

When Robert entered his house he found his wife sitting at the kitchen counter having coffee.

"Hi," he greeted her with a long passionate kiss, continuing his pretense of affection.

"Ooh, I like that." Her arms went around him.

"Did you want dinner?"

"Only if you're on the menu." She took his hand and led him upstairs.

Although he went willingly, the image of her with John repelled any romantic thought crossing his mind. Raine was no longer the woman he once loved, but he was forced to play the game. His life depended on it.

***

While Robert was at home with Raine, a phone conversation was taking place in another part of town.

"I noticed the lights weren't on when I came home," Martha explained. "I used my key to unlock the door and found a note of appreciation on the counter." She listened for his reply but never mentioned receiving a note of her own.

"Yes, Mr. Manchen. I went through the house. It's very clean, although he left a bottle of scotch and five glasses. I was with him when he bought six, so one is missing. No," she answered. "It's still half full. Do you think he's coming back?" Martha listened to her neighbor's questions and wondered why he took such an interest in Toby Too.

"He took all of his clothes, even the ones from the surplus store." Martha heard the man begin to laugh and tried to explain the situation from the beginning. "He wanted to buy scotch but not in the area. So I took it to mean he was hiding from someone. He didn't have a jacket and you know how cold it is now."

"No," she answered his question. "I had no idea how much money he had. That's why I took him to a surplus store." Martha was becoming upset with the man's continued laughter. "He had a few hundred dollar bills, but I wasn't impressed." She stopped speaking suddenly. "Why are you laughing? If you were hiding the man, you should have told him small bills command less attention."

Martha listened again to his side of the conversation and interrupted. "No. He didn't tell me. I just assumed that, since he wanted to shop outside the area."

Martha's eyes grew larger the more she listened. "No. It was nice of you to offer help. If there is anything more I can do, just let me know." She ended the call.

Martha looked at Toby lying near her feet. "Well now it becomes clearer. Toby Too has a health issue. He wasn't in hiding. It was more of an escape." She studied the German shepherd. "Do you believe that fairy tale? I don't swallow it for one minute. Then he tells me it wouldn't surprise him if Toby Too wanted another reprieve. Something's going on; something he doesn't want me to know about." She petted Toby and turned on the T.V.

Chapter 37
Paint Samples

On Thursday morning, several employees greeted Robert with questions concerning a possible contract and future expansion. Since there were so many rumors floating the office, they wanted to know which ones were true.

Robert had already prepared himself for the onslaught of questions long before he returned home. He expected them and knew the source of the rumors. It was John's way of gleaning private information. The set-up reminded him of the Saturday golf outing when the sale of his company became the topic of conversation. Now the questions would be of a different nature. John would wait until some meaningful answer slipped out unintentionally then question it vigorously until he was satisfied. That was his method of getting information. However, Robert had given his first day back very serious thought. His answers had to be short and they had to be vague.

"Yes, I attended several meetings," he said, "but I don't have anything definite to report. I don't think we're in competition with another company, but we've been down that road before," Robert added laughingly. "I will keep you posted." He took the morning mail lying on Catherine's desk and walked into his office knowing John was trailing him.

"Is it true? No one else is in the running?" John began his list of questions.

"Not to my knowledge." Robert felt his answers thus far had been truthful. He had met with people, had nothing to report and was not in competition with anyone, unless it was Toby's fight for salami.

"Don't you find that strange?" He asked deliberately, hoping Robert would provide a definitive reply.

"Everything is, but who am I to question the possibility of getting new business?"

"And you won't tell me the name of the company."

"Once the plans become clear, you will be the first to know. I told you that before. You will be in charge of the whole operation," Robert lied.

"That sounds fair."

Robert watched him leave his office, so satisfied with a possible bump in responsibility while humping the women closest to his unknowing boss. Yet, Robert knew it was only a matter of the time before John and Raine would activate the plan they hatched in May. But he would have another surprise in store before that happened. At least, that was his hope.

***

Shortly after lunch Catherine approached Robert with five paint samples clipped to a cardboard. Her idea was to unclip one sample, hold it against the wall and determine a preference after viewing all five that way.

"I got several colors: ivory, antique white, off yellow, mint green and light grey. I thought we'd check every office since the lighting is so different in each one. I didn't bother with the tool and locker rooms. We'll paint everything the color of the main office."

She placed each sample on the main office wall for viewing, then proceeded to Robert's office for another, and finally to John's. When she held a sample against the wall, a paper clip fell and slid under John's desk. As Robert circled the desk to retrieve it, he noticed the top right drawer was partially open. When his eyes inadvertently fell on the contents inside, his face turned to stone. Lying there were two miniature souvenirs of Palazzo Vecchio from Florence. While his mother fussed with the paint samples, Robert turned the icons over quickly searching for scratch marks, then returned them to their original positions. John entered his office just then and found Robert reaching under his desk.

"What's going on?" he groused, feeling the intrusion of unwanted guests.

"Paint samples," Catherine explained. "One of my paper clips fell under your desk and I sure as hell wasn't crawling under there for it."

"Here." Robert gave her the paper clip, his expression one of perfect calm. "Do you like any of these samples?" Robert asked his assistant. "The lighting seems different in all of the offices."

"I like the antique white," Catherine offered.

"I'd go with mint green," John countered.

"You two work it out. I have an errand to run." Robert moved quickly toward the exit door.

"Where's he going?"

"How the hell should I know? I'm not his keeper." Catherine rebutted as they watched him leave the office.

Yet Catherine knew something was wrong. But what could have stressed him so suddenly? They were only looking at paint samples. Nevertheless, she knew something was bothering him. He had left the office without a coat.

***

Robert fled the building and raced to his car. He had to get away... away to hide the deep hurt and mingled anger twisting inside his body. He felt the intense churning of a treachery so deep, that life itself was nothing more than a sham. It mocked a relationship he thought perfect. Lies, all lies, nothing was true between them. He tasted the bitterness of despair, as he drove blindly toward the park nearby in search of his weeping bench, the silent companion who listened to all his past miseries. It was his safe place; a haven he could think through his problems, now that he no longer had the house to himself.

He sped to the park entrance and, putting the car in neutral, opened the car door and vomited. Minutes later, Robert drove deeper into the park in search of his weeping bench, the wooden monument of dirty slats that heard his mournful sorrows when Emily passed away.

As he rounded a curve, Robert spotted the small lane that veered off the main road. It had always reminded him of the letter E's middle line, a small road going nowhere, but ending abruptly in a forest of trees that shaded a solitary bench in summer. Now the place was just an isolated area that no one visited in winter. Robert parked the car nearby and sat on the bench. He was ready to bare his soul again, giving the seat a confession of sorrow, anger and disbelief.

His mouth tasted a bitterness welling deep inside him again, and he recognized the feeling of another coming retch, one that moved in neither direction, leaving him so unsettled for a vomit yet to come.

Never could Robert remember feeling so alone. To learn the love of his life, his lifelong partner, had betrayed and deserted him during their years of marriage stabbed his heart with pain. The unbearable ache would not dissipate. A healing would never come. There was no trust with his women. Each had deceived him. However, Raine's duplicity was no surprise. Once the plan unfolded, the logistics of Raine with John was a forgone conclusion. Robert had been the target from the beginning; Raine was merely the baited nectar to draw him in. The couple cared little on the cost of such an elaborate plan: the end justified the means. Emily, however, was a different story.

Three years earlier, he had shared his memories of Emily on this same bench. He had lost her then to earth's plantings and a higher nature. Yet, he always felt they were together. Nothing could sever their love or devotion for each other. Where one went, the other followed. They were inseparable, not because of need or distrust; they wanted to be together. The two had a history of love and humor between them which no one could ever understand. She was his Elise; and he, her Mario.

"How could she?" He asked the bench, his voice echoing through the barren trees. "Emily belonged with me. She was mine alone." His gut wrenching voice continued, his eyes glistening. "Why? Tell me why! I loved her. I thought she loved me...me and no one else."

Robert began to weep, the image of Emily's scratched souvenir etched in his brain. His token of love was now one of infidelity. His agony would not subside: stabbing his heart would have been less painful. It would have been over. Now, he had to live with that memory. He began thinking of Mackenzie. His daughter's own perfidy merely proved an irreversible disloyalty and belligerence he now understood. But Emily? Why was this happening? When did it begin? How could he not know? The icons were just left there in a partially opened drawer…left for everyone to see. Was that the purpose… the partially opened drawer? Was Robert supposed to discover them accidentally and realize that Emily, too, had been duplicitous?

The man, so sadly absorbed with his thoughts, was totally unaware of the snowflakes falling around him.

Robert drew his hands to his face and tried to wipe-away the tears as his sad thoughts mounted. First, with his wife, and then, John sweetened his own revenge with Robert's daughter. He inflicted pain where it hurt most: through his family. Was that the plan from the beginning? No. The poison was very real. The infidelity was just an added perk. Yet, it didn't make sense. Emily died three years earlier, why wait until now to murder him? Perhaps Robert was approaching it the wrong way. Maybe he should explore another avenue.

Robert drew his arms around his chest unconsciously. As his staccato-like thoughts dissected his planned death, he never felt the icy hand of winter's chill. Instead his thoughts took a different turn.

What if something unexpected changed the direction of the murderous plan? Suppose the picture of Mackenzie with John seated at a table was the beginning of a true relationship? Would Mackenzie have given him the Florence souvenir of Palazzo Vecchio if it were not meaningful? Robert thought not. John must have made overtures and they had to be real. Something happened between them that changed his once loving daughter into a brainwashed brat intent on crucifying her father. Would a love between them be that far-fetched?

But why would a young, beautiful Mackenzie, just now in her bloom, seek a man much older than she, someone with so much baggage? The young woman had so much to offer while he had nothing to his credit but a conversational line to draw people in. The man had a divorced wife, another female lover, a questionable reputation and no money. Anything John Harris sought would always be to his benefit alone. Could Mackenzie understand that or was she too far in love with the scoundrel? Regardless of her feelings, Robert had to protect his daughter. Emily would have wanted that. His thoughts returned to his first wife. Somehow, one way or another, Robert was not totally convinced of her infidelity. She was too loving, too caring of him. To her, Robert was the most important person in the world. He came first, even before Mackenzie. That love could not be disguised. No. She loved him. Him, only.

Robert came out of his reverie and soon realized he was shaking with cold. He ran to his car, turned on the heater and prayed for a quick thawing out. There was so much to do, so much to think of. He had to come up with a plan, one that would entice the greedy Raine and slow John's murderous plan. The one thing both had in common was money. Of course, John wanted Robert's company, but he would get that anyway if Mackenzie married him. Now twenty, she certainly was of age to do what she wanted. Mackenzie no longer needed his consent. That thought gave him an idea worth exploring.

He needed an investment to promote, some major asset involving a large sum of money for both women. But what? Stocks? Bonds? Life insurance? Would something of this nature hasten his demise? Of course, it would, but Robert could control the timeline. Mackenzie would report her father's intended gift in a conversation with John. The news of another windfall would cause him to postpone Robert's death temporarily. And Raine wouldn't make a move against him until the documents were signed and officially classified as legal. Then he would watch Raine poison his wine through 'Sweet Pea' and have her arrested. Elias would be standing by.

Robert studied the snowflakes that fell through the leafless trees around him. The oncoming winter seemed to come as a surprise. Yet it mattered little to him. He was trying to outwit the people who wanted him dead. Still, he felt the icy cold as he sat in his parked car. Robert thought about returning to the office, but headed instead for his home on the escarpment.

He thought of Raine. How would she feel learning John had another lover while servicing her, one he intended to keep? Would Raine become fearful? She had nowhere to go, no one to tell of the planned murder without implicating herself. Of course, there was always the possibility that she too, could be dispensed with. It all fit, except for Emily.

As soon as Robert entered the house, he headed straight for bathroom. He needed a shower to thaw his frozen body and warm, dry clothes for comfort. He thought of the clothes at his mother's house and sighed. It wasn't the clothes bothering him. Robert wished he could see Toby again. The time with Martha felt very real. He shook off the thought and stepped into the shower.

Turtle Creek was a necessary step to make certain he was moving in the right direction. He had evidence of the poison used and pictures of the lovers during their assignations. Now he had to think of a plan that would bring it all together.

His chest felt tight, his head stuffed and he chastised himself for going out in the cold weather without a jacket. Had he not done the same thing recently? It reminded him of going to the surplus store with Martha for a jacket. Robert shrugged-off the thought. That was past. Today was a new story.

He knew exactly what to do. Robert dialed Mackenzie's number and, to his surprise, found her at home. She seemed warm and enthusiastic to hear from him, yet Robert felt an estrangement between them...one of John's making. Although certain the man was responsible for separating him from his daughter, Robert stated his reason for calling and ended the conversation in a warm friendly manner. There was no need to be ugly. When Mackenzie learned of John's other lover and their intention to kill him, her mind would take a very different turn.

When Raine came home from work, Robert greeted her from their bed and, pretending to be ill, imparted the same information he gave Mackenzie. He watched her take the stairs to the kitchen and call John before returning to him. He felt fortunate for being able to stow 'Sweet Pea' before Raine entered the bedroom.

It was only when Raine showered that Robert remembered to call his mother.

Chapter 38
Instructions

Across town that same night, Mackenzie had a visitor.

"Hi." John took her in his arms and kissed her. "I'm glad you missed me."

"I always miss you," Mackenzie said, "but we need to talk." She led him to the couch and sat down.

"Has something happened? You look serious."

"My father called this afternoon. He is taking-out another life insurance policy naming me beneficiary. He's talking $500,000 dollars. Why would he do that? He wants to see me tomorrow night. There are papers I have to sign. Is he ill?"

Inwardly, John was thinking of the new windfall. Not only would he get the company and Robert's other assets, a half million would now be added to the estate.

"Do you know?" She jogged his mind, bringing his thoughts to answer her question.

"I think he's protecting you." He reassured her. "He probably talked with his lawyer or CPA for advice. In some instances insurance policies are used to cover the inheritance tax of an estate. I wouldn't read anything into it."

"You think that's what happened?"

"I'm sure of it. Your father doesn't want to worry you. It's just part of doing business. He probably was told to get more coverage for taxes."

"You are so smart. If something does happen to him, I'll need you to run his operation."

"We'll be married. Did you think I'd let you down?"

"No. I didn't mean it that way. I'd want it done legally, so you would be in charge of signing contracts and all that legal stuff."

"Let's not worry about that right now."

"After I sign the papers tomorrow night, I'd like you to read them. We can have a sandwich while you explain the process of claiming my inheritance. I really think he's sick but wants to be stoic about it."

"Call me before you go." He stood up and took her hand. "I'll use my key."

"Where are you taking me?" She mocked, as he walked her to the bedroom.

"To the land of enchantment, dear Princess Mackenzie."

***

When John left Mackenzie, he could not determine her father's rationale.

Raine had called him much earlier that evening with the same news. Robert was also taking-out a life insurance policy with her as beneficiary. The $500,000 thousand dollar amount was just the same. However, the difference was in the explanation.

Apparently, his boss believed he was ill and wanted to protect his wife in the event something happened to him. That he had caught a very bad cold only compounded his belief. And along with the insurance policy, Robert had also set aside a tidy sum of cash for her, but Raine failed to disclose the amount. Non-disclosure of funds was the norm for Raine. The only thing the greedy little bitch thought about was money. Well, now at least, she would be somewhat fixed after Robert's demise. Raine planned on much more after Mackenzie's death, but John had other plans, ones beneficial to him alone.

When he thought about it, there was nothing Raine could really do after his marriage to Mackenzie. John would not publicize it beforehand. They would marry quickly and leave town for a honeymoon. If Mackenzie wanted a huge affair afterward, that was her prerogative. He would be agreeable. However, getting away after the ceremony occupied his immediate thoughts. It would be easy if he planned it carefully.

His office would think he was traveling to South America or the Far East on his annual vacation. And if Mackenzie's relatives didn't see her now, why would leaving town be a problem? The path seemed clear for both of them and it mattered little where they went. His young goddess would follow him anywhere.

Yes. He was pleased his plans were progressing. It would be over very, very soon. As soon as the ink dried, Raine would spring into action with Quala, cry over Robert's grave and reap his insurance money. John would take Mackenzie to bed, give much needed comfort, and then take her for the marriage license. It was all falling into place…then his thoughts took a contemptuous turn.

How could Robert have been such a dolt? He didn't deserve Emily. The woman knew John's feelings for her. She acknowledged it in the end…when he could do nothing for her as she lay dying. Later, however, John was given a gift, the opportunity of loving Emily again, although a younger version he molded in her image. He gave her all the love and affection she deserved. He cared for her like no other lover could. Now, his young Emily craved his touch, his tenderness and his undying love. The joy of loving her burned deep within his body, and John could not remember when he was happier. The line between his past and present love had now fully merged into one.

***

Earlier that same evening Raine was not the only one to receive unexpected news. Catherine also got a phone call full of surprises.

"Remember our conversation at the house?" Robert asked quickly. He had to get his message across before Raine stepped out of the shower.

"When you asked for my support, is that what you mean?" Now Catherine was puzzled. Robert was up to something, but what?

"That's the one. I won't be in the office tomorrow, but come to the house with Mackenzie about six o'clock tomorrow night. I'll want you to notarize some papers."

"Is that why you are not coming in?"

"If you must know, I have a cold that's moving to my chest. I might have bronchitis. I'm going to the doctor tomorrow and then bed where I plan to stay."

Robert felt his statement wasn't a lie. He would drop by the doctor's office for something to ease an oncoming bronchial problem. The medical trip was secondary to the one with his insurance agent. Then at some point, he would meet with Elias to finalize his plan.

"You might be too sick to do business, if that's what you have in mind."

"I don't have time for this. Call Mackenzie and have her drive you to the house tomorrow," he groused before pressing the end button.

Catherine looked at the phone. Her son ended the call without so-much-as a goodbye. She was right. Something was very wrong. If she were a betting woman, Catherine would have put money on the bitch he married. Too bad she didn't believe in malocchio. She'd cast a spell causing the woman to drop dead immediately. Although it might have seemed strange to some, Catherine found comfort in that thought. However, those thoughts suddenly changed.

Catherine would have to call her granddaughter tomorrow for a ride. Why couldn't she drive her own car? The answer came quickly. Robert wanted his daughter to visit. If Catherine pretended to be busy, Mackenzie would have to stay longer than she intended.

Catherine began to laugh. Robert was always thinking ahead. For such a smart man how could he have been snookered by his wife? He was too much in love and too blind to see anything bad about her. But Catherine knew. The woman was pure evil.

***

"You poor baby," Raine cooed at Robert lying in bed. "Are you sure I can't sleep with you tonight? I just showered and smell good."

"I can't smell anything," Robert coughed deliberately. "I don't want you catching what I have."

"I'll stay home tomorrow and make a nice soup for you."

"No. I already made appointments with the doctor and my insurance agent." He refused her invitation. "My mother is coming at six to finalize the papers, so I'll have all afternoon to rest."

"Then I'll come home early. Be careful driving. It's snowing outside."

When Raine left the bedroom, her thoughts were not on her husband. She was thinking of the money she would inherit. Her thoughts then shifted to the following evening. Raine would make Robert's last meal enjoyable, a soup to ease his cold. She laughed at the irony of it. When it was over, would she need to buy a new black dress or was the one she had appropriate? Why was there always something to think about? Still, little by little, her problems would be resolved. Mackenzie would have an accident, and she and John could live together comfortably for the rest of their lives. That thought made her smile.

Chapter 39
Accident

The following morning, Robert met with his doctor, the insurance agent and finally with Elias in the park near his weeping bench, although he never acknowledged the slatted confessional.

"You're sure about this?" Elias asked, sitting in Robert's car. He didn't like his friend's plan to have Raine arrested after she tried poisoning him. "What if I'm too late?"

"I'll be dead and you can arrest her for poisoning me. You'll have it all on 'Sweet Pea.' One promise if it happens that way," he said. "I want Mackenzie to know how John and Raine planned to murder me. She should know their plan materialized in Florence. You tell her about John's frequent trysts with Raine when he supposedly pledged his love. Mackenzie should be made aware of the facts."

"If that happens, she will get full disclosure, but don't think that way. I'll be at the house around six."

"That's too early. She'll wait until all the papers are signed. After Mackenzie and my mother leave, Raine will toast "my caring," while wishing me a long life."

"Sounds like my ex," Elias answered laughingly. "I'll be there at half-past. Call me immediately if there's a time change or a different venue for your offing." Elias slid out of Robert's car, entered his and drove away.

Robert watched his friend leave the small lane and hoped his plan would work, not only for his sake, but Mackenzie's as well. The thought of John using her, once he was gone, made him want to kill the man himself. Nevertheless, Robert remained calm. He knew once his plan succeeded, the two would be prosecuted and sent to prison. He doubted Mackenzie would wait for such a lover, knowing she was not his one and only.

It was time to go. Everything had been prepared for the meeting. Robert had the papers necessary for signing and Elias would witness Raine's serving him the lethal wine. Now, it was time to rest. Six o'clock would come soon enough. Long before that, however, he would be watching via 'Sweet Pea.'

***

When Raine returned home that afternoon, she rushed to greet her sick husband who lay under the bedcovers, a box of tissues near his pillow.

"Do you feel any better?" Her fingers pushed a few strands of hair from his face. "Did you see the doctor today?"

"And the insurance agent," he said in a hoarse voice. "I have the papers."

"Don't talk. I know your throat must be sore." She caught his nod. "I think soup would be good for you. I have your mother's recipe for pastina. You can have it later. What you need now is rest."

Robert listened to his "caring wife" take the stairs to the kitchen. Knowing she would phone John, Robert took 'Sweet Pea' from his nightstand and quickly set the device in operation to watch and listen. Raine tossed two large cans of chicken broth into a saucepan, added water and set it on the stove while she engaged in conversation.

"No problem. It's going fine. We're on schedule." Robert heard her say. "No. It's a surprise. I'll give you an update when they come."

Robert watched her end the call. Raine seemed so satisfied, knowing the life insurance money would soon be coming to her. The greedy little bitch counted on Mackenzie's share too, once his daughter was dispatched. But then, Robert had deliberately arranged it that way.

Their previous discussion about life insurance only proved the woman's insatiability for money. And with this in mind, Robert wanted to watch his wife froth and hover over a possible double gain. Raine had been so very agreeable, after learning Mackenzie was named first beneficiary in an estate policy and Raine second, if Mackenzie were no longer alive. Raine thought Robert was being very fair in his thinking of family.

He came out of his reverie to watch Raine cook a pot of pastina in boiling water. After a colander rinsing, she placed the pastina in the heated chicken broth, added salt to the mixture and tasted it. A look of satisfaction crossed her face. Robert waited and watched for more to come. He wanted to prove he was right.

Raine reached into her purse for a pillbox, opened it and spilled the entire contents into the soup mixture. She stirred it carefully with a wooden spoon before turning off the burner. After placing the spoon on a plate she walked away feeling very satisfied.

Robert closed the computer quickly, stashed it in the nightstand drawer and lay on his side, pretending to be asleep. Raine stepped into the room and left quickly, not wanting to awaken him or disturb his sleep. He listened to her take the stairs to the first floor, and before long, heard the news spewing from the television set.

***

At six o'clock Raine greeted Catherine and Mackenzie in a warm and friendly manner. "He's expecting you," she said, knowing they were trailing her upstairs to the bedroom. "I'm worried about him. He's not been well. He saw the doctor before spending the day in bed."

Catherine did not believe one word of her anxiety. Worrying about her husband was never Raine's concern. She was too into herself to fret about someone else. The woman was driven by her own ego.

"Hi," Catherine greeted her son who was sitting on a lounge chair. A dark robe covered his equally dark pajamas adding a dismal aura to his pale face. "You look awful."

"I don't feel well either." He replied, his voice raspy. "Why don't you sit down?" He pointed to the chairs separated by a table. "Mackenzie, I think we should go over your estate papers first. Then your grandmother can notarize them."

"Excuse me," Raine interrupted. "While you're doing Mackenzie's papers I want to run to the drugstore."

"What's wrong?" Catherine asked.

"Just a headache."

"I have aspirin in my purse," Mackenzie offered.

"Aspirin doesn't work for me." She raced downstairs. Moments later, Raine shouted to Mackenzie. "You have to move your car. You parked behind mine."

"Then take Dad's. His keys are on the hall table." Mackenzie eyed her father and shrugged. "Some things never change."

They heard the loud bang of a slamming door and began to giggle.

"Raine's angry," Catherine snickered.

"She'll get over it," Mackenzie countered. "Raine could have moved my car if she didn't want to drive dad's," she said, dismissing the subject. "I think the whole thing's stupid."

Robert knew they missed the whole point. How could they know? The car had nothing to do with her anger. Driving Robert's car was just an added inconvenience. Raine had to call John. He had to know she was going forward with their plan once the papers were signed. It was that simple.

***

When Robert was halfway through the documents with Mackenzie, the doorbell chimes echoed throughout the house.

"Raine must have forgotten her key. Would you go down and let her in?" He directed his question to Mackenzie.

When she ran downstairs Robert told his mother to linger as long as possible. He wanted to talk with his daughter. There were so many matters to discuss.

"Dad." Mackenzie's serious manner drew her father up short. "The police are here." She ushered two men into the bedroom.

Robert recognized detective Ben Wicks immediately but was not familiar with his companion. "What's up?" His raspy voice questioned.

"Your wife had an accident," he offered. "I'm sorry."

"What?" Robert didn't comprehend the man's message.

"Did you take her to the hospital?" Catherine intervened.

"No need." The man's voice fell.

"She's dead, isn't she? Raine's dead." Mackenzie questioned.

"Yes," he nodded and said, "It's the snow, the ice on the escarpment. She lost control. The brakes might have gone out. We don't know."

"I don't understand. Raine was just here. She needed something for a headache." Robert's dazed explanation led them to believe he was in shock.

"Where should we take the body after…?" Ben stopped talking.

Catherine gathered the two policemen into the corner of the room and gave them the name of the funeral home Robert used for Emily. She asked they contact her for arrangements while Mackenzie stood by and listened. After exchanging information, they left Robert sitting in the bedroom while Catherine and Mackenzie escorted the two men out of the house.

"They took her to the morgue, didn't they?" she asked Catherine.

"I don't want to think about it. The funeral home will call us soon enough." She took the stairs, knowing Mackenzie was following her. "Don't upset your father." She admonished her granddaughter before entering the bedroom to revisit her son.

"Upset him? I'm upset," she cried, her thoughts now on an improbable marriage, one she sought so desperately. "He ruins everything for me."

"And just what have I ruined for you now?" Robert snapped as she entered the room. "I'm tired of your constant tirade. It's always some screaming match, whether it's warranted or not." Had he ruined her marriage plans now that Raine was dead? How could that be? The marriage would have taken place if Robert were dead, not Raine. Her invective made no sense.

"You didn't deserve to be married," Mackenzie snarled. "Everything you touch turns to shit. Raine was too good for you, too glamorous. You never gave her the attention she deserved. It's a repeat of what you did with my mother. Only this time, the woman probably went off and killed herself rather than spend another minute with you. It's always the same. The wrong one died again." Mackenzie picked up her sheaf of papers and ran down the stairs with Catherine following her.

"Stop," Catherine shouted. She took her granddaughter's hand and led her to the kitchen. Leaning against the counter, Catherine placed her hand over her heart.

"What's the matter?" Mackenzie asked. "Heart trouble?"

"Shortness of breath. I need some water." While she opened the refrigerator looking for bottled water, Mackenzie stirred the cold soup on the stove. "Your pastina looks good. Is he going to eat it?"

"Right now, I doubt he'll eat anything."

"Then I'll take it home. My friend is stopping by for sandwiches." She gave her grandmother a knowing smile. "I'll return the saucepan later."

"Keep it. Your father has plenty of pots and pans." She walked her granddaughter to the door.

A sudden thought dawned on Mackenzie. "How are you getting home?"

"I may sleep here tonight. We still have Raine's car if I need wheels. Now, go." She gestured Mackenzie to leave.

Catherine watched her granddaughter drive away in the snow and had an eerie feeling of being watched. She locked the door, set the burglar alarm and went upstairs.

***

"That was a stellar performance," Catherine addressed her son. "Who was the target, Mackenzie or the detectives?"

"All three. But of the two men, I only knew Wicks. Had dealings with him. Nice guy." He coughed mucus into a tissue. "The other one might be a new recruit."

"I notice neither of us is crying."

"Hence, the shock." His sarcasm did not escape Catherine's notice.

"What's going on?"

"Nothing really." He shrugged indifferently. "You were right. It wasn't love. She was after my money."

"I knew it," Catherine gloated. "Then why the hell would you buy a life insurance policy naming her beneficiary?"

"Anyone reading it would have known its restrictions. I would have had to die falling out of a plane, off a boat, or get killed in a wayward bus crash. You'd have to read the fine print and garbled legal crap to understand it. I geared it that way. Then there's the kicker. She wouldn't get a lump sum. It would have been paid in installments."

Catherine was puzzled as she listened to him. He must have really hated her to go to all that trouble. "Why? Why would you do that?"

"I was tired of listening to her. All she talked about was money," he lied. There was no point in disclosing the truth now. Her role in his murder was over.

"Is Mackenzie's policy the same? You already have one naming us beneficiaries."

"No. This policy and half of the old one should cover her inheritance tax or a good portion of it. Brat that she is, I wanted to protect her financially after my death. Now I wonder why. She wants no part of me. I am out of her life. She made that clear tonight."

"Robbie, I can't believe that. You'll never convince me of such hatred."

"Suit yourself. I'm tired of beating a dead horse." He threw his robe on a chair and sat on the side of his bed. "You staying here tonight?"

"I thought I'd sleep in the guest room." She took his robe to hang in the closet. "My God!" she cried. "I don't believe it. You still have Emily's old robe, the one she wore…."

"Before she died." He finished her sentence. Robert watched her examine it more closely.

Catherine fingered each pocket. "It was the right one that had a hole in it," she said. "I meant to sew it because she always kept that damn miniature from Italy with her. It kept falling through the hole when I'd walk her to the toilet. I'm sorry, Robbie. It's lost."

With that detailed explanation, Robert lost all vestiges of practiced calm and began to weep. How could he have doubted her, his Emily, the passion of his life…the soul of his existence? She never would have betrayed him. They had so much love for each other, a shared rhapsody of marriage that belonged to them alone. She was his Elise and he, her Mario.

Only then did Robert realize the dual nature of John's cruel hand. He wanted to surround Robert with suspicion and mistrust; the doubts that come with suspected infidelity. He needed to watch the man suffer the pain of betrayal, thriving on the use of an icon, a miniature, a scratched token of forbidden love. John used it to portray assignations with Emily and openly displayed the evidence, knowing it could not be refuted by a dead woman.

His memories of Emily's death became clearer now. For weeks, Robert worked at home, knowing her time was near. Catherine or John would deliver papers for signing and retrieve them the following day. John must have found her dropped miniature on one of those occasions and kept it for a later use.

When did Mackenzie enter the picture? It had to be several years later. Were Raine and John in a relationship at the time? Robert didn't know how or when his daughter met John, but he was certain neither woman knew the full extent of the other. Mackenzie was John's preference, but other than wanting Robert's company, the reason for it seemed hidden. Was he really in love with her? He must have made overtures, ones she considered serious enough to be brainwashed against her father. Why did John want to separate

Mackenzie from him? Why was it so important to tear a family apart? John had Emily's miniature, and now he had Mackenzie's. What was going on in that warped mind of his? Robert took a tissue and blew his nose.

"Are you ok? I'm sorry I brought out the robe," Catherine said, seeing his regained composure. "I put it back but our memories still linger on." She understood how much he loved Emily.

"I'm good. Really," he reassured her.

"I'm going to bed, unless you want me to fix a tray."

"I'm not hungry. The accident or bronchitis affected my appetite."

"Well, it's good you're not hungry. Mackenzie took a pot of pastina with her. She's under the impression I made it, although I did give Raine the recipe. But it will be put to good use." The thought made her smile. "She's having a friend over for sandwiches tonight. I think she has a boyfriend." Catherine kissed his cheek saying, "I'm really tired."

Robert watched his mother leave the room, feeling an unpracticed calm inching through his body. Was this God's way of punishing evil? He could understand with John and Raine, but why Mackenzie?

He climbed into bed and turned off the nightstand lamp. As Robert lay in the darkened room he heard something hit the window. He looked out over the lit driveway but saw nothing. He tip-toed down the stairs, disarmed the alarm and greeted Elias.

***

"How long does it take to get rid of an old lady? I'm freezing my ass off," he groused, walking into the house.

Robert turned on a small living room lamp while Elias went to the bar, poured scotch in two glasses and added an ice cube in each one.

"What did you learn?" Robert took the glass Elias offered and sat down on the couch.

"You're in the clear. She skidded off the icy escarpment into the rocky ravine below. Your brakes were bad but not enough to cause the accident." He sat on a chair facing him.

"What else? What aren't you telling me?"

"You might want a closed casket. Her body's a mess."

"Raine wanted to be cremated."

"Problem solved." He took a long drink of scotch.

"Not really. Raine poisoned a soup that Mackenzie took home. She and John are having dinner tonight."

"Were. I'd use past tense. It's over by now. The stuff would kill a herd."

"How can I live with myself, knowing I'm to blame for my daughter's death? How can I go on? What should I do?" Robert's eyes began to glisten.

"Finish your scotch and go to bed. You have no control over two lovers taking poison, and you can't tell anyone what John's intentions were. Just be a grieving father." Elias studied his friend. "Which is exactly what you are."

"She was my daughter." A tear inched down Robert's face.

"No. She wasn't. Not for a long time. Mackenzie left you the day John met her as a woman. She had the beauty of youth, a trusting mind to mold and a sense of refinement that comes with money. She was no longer the gangly girl he once knew. She had turned into an elegant swan. The picture of them proved that."

"Unfortunately, I have to agree." Robert choked hard.

"But it was much more dangerous than that. When John took control, knowing he could have it all with her inheritance, he brainwashed you out of her life completely. You were diminished by degrees, reduced to a dot on her family tree. All John had to do was wait for your new wife to use her pillbox and he would pick-up the pieces with Mackenzie after your death. And poor Raine would be left twiddling her thumbs. She could never have interfered or stopped John without implicating herself."

Elias paused and took another drink of scotch. He studied the sad expression on the face of his altered friend. There was nothing more he could do for him; no words to comfort the man who had lost the woman he loved three years earlier, and now faced the same prospect with a daughter preceding him in death. His best friend no longer had a family of his own.

Robert sat frozen on the couch and looked up at Elias who now stood near him, preparing for his departure. "I don't know what to do."

Elias placed his hand on Robert's shoulder as a means of support. "Make Raine's funeral arrangements and express shock with the other. But move on. That's my advice." Within seconds Elias left the house with scotch glass in hand.

Robert locked the door, rearmed the alarm and, after turning off the lamp, took the stairs to his bedroom, his thoughts still on the whole situation. Creating suspicion was John's reason for taking Emily's miniature. To believe his wife had been unfaithful would cripple Robert emotionally. In Robert's mind, that was the only possible reason for removing it from his house. Emily had been a faithful wife throughout their marriage: no stolen icon could shake his belief in her.

On the other hand, he disagreed with Elias' theories to some extent. Robert knew the real reason for using Raine to kill him or selecting Mackenzie to brainwash. It wasn't only business and money. No. It was the power John wielded over him through these women, his controlling them like puppets on a string. John must have laughed privately as his plan moved forward. His hatred was so great, the man had to undermine Robert at every turn: make him suffer, become tormented with mistrust and suspicion where it hurt most; first with family, and then declining health and death. These thoughts clouded his mind as he tried to sleep. Now the man was dead.

Maybe his mother's axiom was right after all. *Sometimes, things that are right aren't necessarily legal.*

That sounded like something Martha would say.

***

It never occurred to the grieving father that John loved only one woman. The only way he could only adore her was through a younger image…the miniatures being a constant reminder of past and present.

Chapter 40
Resolution

As Robert lay on the verge of sleep, he heard a pounding on his bedroom door.

"Robbie," his mother shouted. "Someone's ringing the doorbell."

"Just a minute." He turned on the nightstand lamp then grabbed his robe from the closet. "What now?" He greeted her shaking his head.

Within the few minutes that followed, Robert wondered how the police discovered the bodies so soon and mentally armed himself for a shocked response.

With his mother standing behind him, Robert opened the door and expressed surprise at seeing two men who identified themselves as city detectives, Morgan Feerse and Tim Stroud. After ushering both men into the living room Robert stood silently facing them.

"Do you have any idea why we're here?" Morgan asked.

"No clue." Robert coughed into a handkerchief from his robe pocket.

"What's going on?" Catherine addressed her question to the other detective.

But before Morgan could restrain him, detective Stroud blurted, "Mrs. Blake, you are wanted for questioning in the death of John Harris."

Almost instantly, Catherine's legs began to crumble and the men rushed to grab her before she fell to the floor. Her glazed eyes looked up at Robbie who carried her to the couch. "What do they mean?" she groaned before becoming still.

"It'll be alright." He placed a couch pillow beneath her head. "We'll get this sorted out."

Robert intended his answer to be vague, knowing full-well the men were listening to their conversation. He led the detectives away from the living room couch, where his mother lay, to the front hall and confronted them.

"Now, what is this all about? If she has a stroke, I am going to hold you responsible. Why would you say that kind of thing to an old lady and why at this ungodly hour?"

"I would have waited, but Tim is rather new in our precinct." Morgan's disgust was obvious. "I would have handled your mother differently."

"I still don't understand," Robert answered. "How did John Harris die and what's my mother's connection?"

"We don't know," Morgan was quick to reply. "That's why we wanted to question her." He walked toward the front door with his partner following him. "Mr. Blake, I want your mother at our station tomorrow morning, say nine o'clock. I'm trusting you to have her there." He gave Robert his card.

"I will, but I still don't understand her involvement."

"You will soon enough."

Robert watched the men climb into a black sedan and drive away into the snowy night. He retraced his steps back to the living room.

"I'm not the only one who gave a stellar performance tonight." He addressed "Sleeping Beauty."

"Jesus, Holy Christ! Sorry Lord," Catherine looked upward. "I am not being irreverent, but could you bring us a little peace? I'm getting too old for this constant upheaval. And don't keep calling me an old lady," she snapped at her son.

"Mom." Robert wanted her attention. "Talk to me now, pray later. How are you connected with the death of John Harris?"

"I'm not."

"The police think you are."

"And they are never wrong, right? First of all, how did he die? Second, I've been here since six o'clock."

"They never told us how he died."

"Exactly," she mused, "or my connection to it."

"You have to be there at nine."

"I heard." She started climbing the stairs. "I'm going back to bed. You coming?"

"I have to call someone." He watched her climb the rest of the stairs before turning his attention to the house phone. After a brief conversation, Robert heard Elias say, "You are getting to be a pain in the ass."

"Well, ream it a little further. Neither detective mentioned Mackenzie." Robert waited for a response, but none came. Elias had already ended the call.

Robert knew it was going to be a long night. Thoughts haunted him. First, Raine died following a crash off the escarpment; now John was dead. Was it by poison or did he die some other way? He had to think this through. Why wasn't Mackenzie mentioned? Had something happened to her? Were the detectives holding back further bad news? No. That was too illogical. Mackenzie was alive. Robert was sure of it, but knew calling her could implicate himself with the ongoing investigation. Still he wondered how she survived. He was happy that his daughter still lived, regardless of her feeling about him. She was, after all, part him and part Emily. Although uncertain of the circumstances, Robert loved Mackenzie and would do anything for her. Yet, his thoughts turned toward her treatment of him and his reaction upon seeing her again. That prospect would come soon enough. Now, he had to think about his mother's interrogation. Perhaps, it would be best if she had counsel. He ignored the house phone, rushed to the bedroom and scanned the contacts on his cell for the number of his lawyer.

Robert took notice of the time. That it was four o'clock, and not a good time to call a sleeping lawyer, made little difference to him. His mother needed representation and that's all that mattered.

Robert listened to the answering machine, left a message and decided to call again at six. He would not be sleeping much after witnessing the parade of detectives bringing news or asking questions all night long.

The thought of his mother being implicated in John's death did not seem to frighten him. She would be absolved at some point.

She had to be. His mother was not involved, so how could the police say there was a connection? That speculation would evaporate soon enough. His major concern was trying to contain the murder plot. Learning he was the intended victim was one thing; but his knowledge of it was quite another. If discovered, they could begin to question his involvement in Raine's accidental death, John's demise and Mackenzie's connection. Without question, he had to act calmly ignorant of all the facts uncovered.

As Robert thought more about John's death, he suddenly became aware of the vacuum it created within the company. Before taking a morning shower, Robert made a quick phone call to Josh Kwell, an old employee who agreed to cover his absence from the office.

***

At nine o'clock the next morning, Robert and his mother walked into police headquarters where their attorney sat patiently waiting.

"Right on time," Nathan Brand greeted them, before turning to Catherine. "Don't answer any questions unless I say it's ok."

"I'm surprised you brought a lawyer," Morgan greeted Robert. "We're not holding your mother. We just wanted to ask a few questions."

"About what? You weren't very clear, other than scaring her about an employee's death."

"That's what we are trying to clarify." He led Nathan and his client into an interrogation room, leaving Robert sitting on a chair in the hall.

***

"When was the last time you saw John Harris?" the detective asked.

Getting the nod from his attorney, Catherine said, "At the office yesterday."

She watched Morgan Feerse write her statement into a note-book that resembled a sheaf of loose papers. "Where were you last night?"

Again Nathan nodded. "I was at my son's house from six o'clock until now. After the local police visited us, I slept there."

"Local police?" Nathan interrupted, hushing Catherine from saying anything further. "What exactly is going on here? What was the purpose of the first visit?"

Morgan immediately caught his anger and tried to dispel the intention of entrapment. "It was my understanding they came with bad news for Mr. Blake. His wife died of an automobile accident last night. It was quite tragic with the ice and snow. It makes the escarpment a dangerous road in winter."

"Oh, my God!" he cried. "He really loved that woman. You could see it in the way he looked at her." The lawyer recalled their cocktail affair after the wedding. "And now you're after his mother?"

"No. We're trying to piece together a poisoning that occurred in our precinct."

"And you think this old lady did it? How? When did it happen?"

"That's just it. We're not sure." Morgan hesitated. "We were hoping she could help us."

"You tell me what you want to know and I'll determine whether she should answer."

"That's not how we work," Tim, the other detective, interrupted.

"Then you arrest her or we're leaving. That's how I work."

Morgan sighed, ignored his partner and said, "John Harris was poisoned by Mrs. Blake's chicken soup."

Catherine met Nathan's stare and shook her head. "Where did you get that information?"

"We checked the apartment where we found him. There was nothing wrong with the food in the refrigerator. Someone laced the soup with poison. We had it tested."

"And what makes you think my client did it?"

"Because we have a witness." His partner chimed in.

"Did your witness see my client add poison to the soup?"

Before his partner could answer, Morgan restrained him from speaking. "No. She merely gave us a history of last night. I thought Mrs. Blake could clarify a few things for us."

"Who is this witness?"

"Her granddaughter, Mackenzie Blake."

"I want her brought here," Catherine blurted loudly. "Enough of your happy horseshit. I'm not saying another word until you let me talk to her." Catherine crossed her arms in resignation.

"She's in the next room," Morgan said. "She wanted to be here when you came in." Catherine ignored his explanation and marched to the room next door, hoping to scold her granddaughter, totally unaware they were being watched and listened to.

"What is it with you?" Catherine demanded of her granddaughter as she sat down at the table between them. "Have you gone completely insane to think I would put poison in a soup? If you recall, you took it off the stove when we were in the kitchen. I didn't offer it."

"What else was I supposed to think?" Mackenzie snapped back. "You made it."

"It might have been my recipe but I did not make the pastina for your sick father. Raine made it." No sooner had the words escaped her lips when its meaning penetrated her brain. "Oh, my God, the soup was meant for your father!"

Mackenzie studied her grandmother's weakened condition. "Raine wanted to kill my dad. Is that what you're saying? Why would she do that?"

"I don't know." Catherine began to cry. "I thought she loved him." Mackenzie moved to embrace her grandmother and tried to comfort the weeping woman.

As soon as Catherine fell apart, the lawyer and both detectives raced into the room and, with Robert trailing, explained his victimization.

"Mom, it's alright." Robert tried to calm her.

"Why? Why would she do something like that? Try to kill you. Why?" She began to weep all over again. "She had everything."

"I don't have an answer." He continued his practiced calm. "I don't think I ever will."

"Well, I'm glad she's dead. I'll spit on her coffin." Catherine ignored the detectives listening to their ensuing conversations.

"Please, mom. I loved her," he whispered, aware of the audience nearby.

"Then you're stupid!" Her voice echoed all four corners of the room.

"Are you alright?" Robert wanted to change the subject and directed his attention to Mackenzie. "You told your grandmother you were having sandwiches with a friend. Now, I assume that friend was John. Is that why you took the pastina?"

"He was already at the apartment when I came home. We've been seeing each other…" She waited for a reaction that never came. "You didn't mind?"

"I would have said he's a little old for you, but love is a very funny thing. You can't determine whom to love."

"I should have known you'd understand. You've always wanted me to be happy like you and mom were." She approached her father and caressed him.

"Tell me what happened."

"It's totally stupid. I've been constipated lately and had to go. So I told John to take care of the soup. I already had platters of lunch meat and cheese in the refrigerator. My washed lettuce was in a plastic bag. All I had to do was slice a tomato."

"So John was heating the pastina…"

"And kept tasting it, I guess," she interrupted. "I found him on the floor, the spoon too, and bubbled soup all over the stove. That's when I called 911."

"I am so sorry, honey. I really am." Robert helped his mother out of her chair as he spoke, then took her arm and walked down the hall with Mackenzie and Nathan.

"This isn't the end." Nathan informed him. "Anyway you look at it, John Harris was murdered. Granted, it wasn't intentional, but the poison was used with you in mind. They'll dig for a reason. They'll want Raine's motive."

"When they find it, will they tell me? I'd like to know why my wife wanted me dead. I thought we were doing fine."

"With women, you never know. They've got crazy hormones." He left them at the front door and crossed the street to his parked car.

"Can I come to the house?" Mackenzie asked.

Robert dug into his pocket for some bills. "Would you mind terribly going for sweet rolls and coffee? I'm afraid to touch anything in the house that's edible."

Catherine and Robert watched Mackenzie drive away.

"How did I do?" Catherine asked sitting in the passenger seat of Raine's car.

"What do you mean?" Robert acted surprised.

"I didn't know the bitch was trying to poison you. That cuts me to the core. But I meant what I said about Mackenzie and John. I told you I thought she had a boyfriend when she wanted the pastina. I never thought it would be that asshole. It's a good thing I didn't know, or I'd have told her how stupid she was. The man was too old and had nothing to offer."

"You and I know that, but this is a young impressionable girl. We have to be sympathetic with the death of her boyfriend and sound sincere, or we'll lose her again." Robert caught himself, almost calling John, his daughter's lover, instead of boyfriend.

"That I can do. Not to worry."

***

When Mackenzie entered her father's kitchen, she immediately noticed the place settings lining the counter.

"I bought a variety of sweet rolls thinking we could divide the left-overs later." She began placing the boxes on the counter. "I bought everyone a large size coffee. After the stint we just had, I thought we might need it."

Conversation flowed freely, a first for a very long time. Robert seemed happier than he had been in years; Mackenzie felt comforted, knowing the family supported her in her hour of need; and Catherine was satisfied with the knowledge that she now had a cohesive family back again. Raine and John, her two biggest problems, were gone forever.

Later, Robert gave his mother a knowing look, before taking Mackenzie to the living room couch where he sat down beside her. He put his arm around his daughter and grew very serious.

"I have something to tell you," he started. "It means I am breaking a promise I made to your mother when she became ill. But I think it's something you should know…"

Catherine remained in the kitchen, wiping up after breakfast and listened quietly as Robert spoke of a medical trip to New York some three years earlier. She remembered his conversation with Bruce Parks when he recommended a second opinion at Memorial Sloan Kettering for Jenna. The woman listened to her son explain his promise of secrecy, while his wife remained stoic when all hope was lost. Emily wanted life to be as normal as possible during her decline and held him to that promise.

"I am so sorry, Dad." Mackenzie flung her arms around him. "How could I have been so wrong about you with mom? And now to lose John…I knew you would understand. Down deep, I knew it. Now we both lost."

"No. I have wonderful memories of your mother. You must have some with John."

"I do," Mackenzie brightened somewhat. "He really loved me. We talked about getting married."

"Being in love with someone who shares that love is never lost or forgotten. You will always have that."

For the first time in a very long time, Mackenzie listened to her father's meaningful words. From her expression they seemed to hit the right emotional buttons.

"Would you mind if I came by this Sunday for pancakes?" She got up to leave.

"I would love it." He followed her to the kitchen, watched her kiss her grandmother goodbye and sail out the front door.

Catherine's reaction was immediate after Mackenzie's departure. "If I'd have known John's death would have turned her around, I'd have poisoned him myself."

"Easy mom. You have to play the sympathetic grandmother."

"Really? How about a pissed-off mother who wants to spit on her daughter-in-law's grave? To think of poisoning you for money."

"It happens. We knew she was money hungry. We just didn't know how far she'd go to get it. Where are you going?" he asked suddenly.

"Take me home for my car. I'll go to the office. You should stay in bed."

***

A few days later, Robert came home to find Elias sitting on the living room couch swirling an ice cube in his glass of scotch.

"I knew you'd come by sooner or later."

"What's the point if I don't have information?"

"Well?"

"Your buddy down at the local patch got a tip to search Raine's old apartment. They found the remnants of an empty vial of powder, the kind that doctored your soup, and some hidden pictures of her and John in bed. That caused them to dig deeper into John's condo. No pictures, only poison. On the container, John had written Quala."

"What does this mean to me? Where do I stand in all this?"

"Oh, you're free and clear," he said as if an afterthought.

"And Mackenzie?"

"A naïve next victim. Raine does you; John does her. It was all about your money and company…the oldest motive in the world.

"So what's the problem?"

"There isn't any. I'm just curious. Who gave them the tip or hid the pictures in her old apartment? It wasn't me."

"Claude." They said in unison.

"You must have made one hell of an impression on him." Elias got up to leave not wanting to discuss it further.

"You're right." Robert agreed. "Maybe I should visit him in Turtle Creek."

"Check with the woman next door. She takes care of the house and knows his schedule," Elias offered before exiting with his scotch glass.

Although Elias included every detail clearing Robert and his family, he omitted his own theory of Claude's involvement. That was something he would never discuss with anyone. His theory was absolutely insane. Yet, it was the only thing that made sense. In some way, Robert must have reminded the man of his only child, a son named Paul, his namesake known by only a few, who was killed in a plane crash two years earlier. No one knew he even existed prior to his death. That was Claude's way of protecting him. There was no getting to the father through his son. That had to be Claude's thinking with his clandestine lifestyle. Elias looked at his scotch glass and laughed. His shelves were getting crowded.

***

As Robert watched Elias vanish, his thoughts turned to Claude. Only Claude could answer a question burning inside him. Robert could break into the man's house and leave a note on the kitchen counter or he could do the same thing in his own house. He knew Claude continued to spy on him through 'Sweet Pea' and found the latter idea of leaving a note on his counter more agreeable. After thanking Claude for his intervention he wanted permission to see Martha. She was like an itch that needed scratching and he didn't know why the woman affected him that way. He had never met anyone like her.

Although Robert did not need Claude's permission to see Martha, something told him it was the right thing to do. Nevertheless, Robert still had to thank the man for the evidence he uncovered. He owed Claude more than a depth of gratitude. The man saved his life.

As he thought about Claude, he realized something that had eluded him totally. The man had trusted Robert with his innermost secrets, ones that crossed many sections of government, whether it be spying or covert operations. And although Robert had installed 'Sweet Pea' outside of Claude's own surveillance unit, he never asked why he was chosen. But now Robert knew. It was a matter of trust. Claude trusted Robert with his knowledge and his silence. Then too, Robert never questioned the man's motives for spying on his own people. He didn't have to. Claude had his reasons. No doubt, he uncovered something that gave him cause for suspicion. But on that delicate subject Robert continued to remain silent and kept all questions to himself.

In return, the man helped Robert survive the hatched plan to murder him. He brought forth evidence and gave Robert shelter. In trusting Robert, Claude also placed a great deal of faith in Martha. As elusive as the man was, Claude had bonded with only two people. That was the real reason he needed the man's permission to see Martha. If both of them bonded with Claude, was Robert worthy of connecting with Martha?

***

Several days later Robert stopped by his mother's house for the bag of clothes from the surplus store. No break-in was necessary. Robert still had a key. His mother insisted he keep it after he and Emily married. If she became ill, he would have access to her house. This was the reason she gave him.

***

Several weeks later, Robert found a reply to his note. He had no idea when Claude entered his house, but was very grateful that he did. He sat at the kitchen counter and pondered the few words: *Yes, with reservation.*

- 316 -

Robert knew exactly what that meant…casual or for keeps: nothing in between. Yet, Claude knew Robert's moral fiber. Nothing untoward would happen during their friendship.

***

Within a month, dressed in jeans, sweater, jacket and cap, Robert appeared at Martha's door one evening.

"Toby Too," she exclaimed as her German shepherd, smelling something good, edged her outward. "What are you doing here?"

"I was hoping you could take me out to dinner. I brought a bunch of small bills and some salami for Toby." As he extended his arm and slowly opened his hand, Toby lunged for the salami instantly, knocking Martha out-of-his-way and into Robert who caught her immediately. "What do you say?" he asked, steadying her in his arms. Robert looked down at her face and, from the illuminating streetlight, could see a smile forming.

***

Remembering Leonard

My Sturdy Oak

I remember when my tree never lost its leaves
It grew tall and had deep roots and graceful limbs
It stood straight and unbending
Guarding its seedlings until they could grow roots of their own
My tree stood steadfast and strong for eighty-three seasons
Then a sudden gust blew from above
And the unforgiving wind took the leaves from my tree
And damaged its roots, causing it to wither and die
Now the seedlings have grown strong with limbs of their own
And the cycle of life goes on

I wrote this poem shortly after my husband's demise in 2011, but I think the sentiment is universal.

Other Novels by Rachel Gripp

Pursuit of the Frog Prince

Continued Pursuit, a sequel

Made in the USA
San Bernardino, CA
19 September 2016